Wrong Number

(Time Stands Still Book 1)

A novel by Carlie Yates

ISBN: 978-1-7332649-4-5

For my tribe, for always believing in me and giving me the wings to fly. May all of your dreams come true!

CHAPTER 1

If inanimate objects could be murdered, this ringing phone that has jarred me from my sleep would be meeting its untimely demise. I was growling at it as I woke, and now I am laying here glaring at the caller i.d., which shows that whoever is on the other line has blocked their number.

"Fuck. You."

I turn from the phone as my answering machine downstairs kicks on, and I mentally dare them to leave a callback number. You know—paybacks being bitches and all.

They don't.

Instead they hang up, silencing that ancient machine while my generic greeting was mid-sentence. Ah, well. "Good riddance then."

I settle back into my pillows, adjusting them to cradle my head and neck as I think... *Talia Emerson, it's a damn good thing you didn't answer that phone.* I am the first to admit what a bitch I can be when in lack-of-sleep mode. It's 2:35 in the morning, and I have class at eight A.M. sharp, so sleep needs to resume with a quickness. Maybe I can go back to that dream, the one where I'm on the beach and a perfect size zero, or maybe a two. What woman doesn't want to lose a little... bit...

"Fucking *hell*."

My phone is ringing again.

This asshole isn't going to bother with the answering machine, I'm sure, so I do a preemptive strike. I pick up the receiver to my equally ancient bedside phone, then hang up just as quickly.

There.

Hopefully they get the hint.

I close my eyes and begin my backwards count to calm and center myself.

Ten. Nine. Eight. Seven.

"Fuck!"

There's obviously only one way to get this asshole to quit calling, so I pick up the receiver and hope my tone gets my point across.

"Who the hell is this and what do you want?"

"I'm sorry I woke you."

Oh, fuck... that voice... that deep, scratchy male voice with a slight slur in it... I am stunned silent by it.

"I was looking for John."

Huh? Who? "There's no John here." I almost feel guilty for snapping at him, but damn... hello! It's going on three in the morning. He rattles off the number, telling me that's what he'd meant to dial, and I'm almost mesmerized.

Just almost, though.

"Yes, that's the number you dialed. No, there's no John here." Without a second thought I add, "And if you were going to prank me, you could have come up with something better than that."

"Pardon?"

I rub the sleep from my eyes as I answer. "Why not ask for Mr. Pedaso? You know, first name Stu." Why am I even talking to this person? Lack of sleep, that must be it.

"I'm not pranking you, and I don't know a Stu Ped..." His voice trails off and he laughs softly. Did I get butterflies at that? Really, Talia? No... no, I didn't. That would be ridiculous. "That's good. That's very good."

I flop onto my back and stare up at the ceiling, chastising myself for starting even the tiniest bit of a conversation with this stranger to begin with. "Thank you, but really... there's no John here."

"This is the number he gave me, I swear."

"Well, he gave you the wrong number."

And I hang up.

I stare at my phone, a strange sense of... something, I'm not sure what, coming over me. Do I know his voice from somewhere? Impossible. And if I do, I suppose I'll never figure out where I know it from.

Except he's calling me again. Shit, shit, shit.

I'm not even bothering with niceties this time.

"Look, I—"

"Honest, I'm not pranking you. I just wanted to tell you that I'm sorry."

I sigh at his words and shake my head, even though he can't see me. "Okay, so you're not pranking, and you're sorry. Could you have at least waited until a decent hour to call back and apologize?" I watch the moonlight cast an eerie shadow on the wall as I hear him inhale sharply. I don't know why, but I add, "You interrupted a very nice dream."

"Perhaps because I've had a bit too much to drink and would forget at a decent hour." Why this makes me grin, I have no idea. I must be losing my damn mind. "But a nice dream? Really, now? What kind of dream?"

I choose to ignore his question, even though I find myself smiling wider. "Okay, fine, apology accepted. My alarm goes off in a couple of hours and—"

"Good! So, you have time to chat."

I let out one short laugh. "You don't know who I am, I don't know who you are, why would I want to *chat* with you?"

"Well, I know you're not John."

And again, I am laughing.

"So, what is your name?"

No way, pal. "Not telling. Who are you?"

"That's an odd name." He's most definitely a smart ass. "Ello, Not Telling, nice to make your acquaintance." And he also cannot fake a British accent to save his life.

But still, he makes me laugh even more.

"Oh, that was bad. And you are?"

"I'm not John."

Can I blame my fit of giggles on my lack of sleep? Because, really… I don't fucking giggle. At all. "You can't be not John, because I'm not John."

"You can't be Not John because you're Not Telling."

I cover my mouth to stop the near yelp of laughter from escaping. This must be what my best friend Jaden calls being slap-happy tired. "Okay, fine. I'll be Not Telling, and you can be Not John."

"Right."

Are those chill bumps on my arms? Really? It's just a voice, Talia, get a grip.

"So, I'm not John. Except technically I am, or I was but I'm not now, and I'm not that John. You know, the one I'm looking for, because I obviously wouldn't be looking for myself."

"So that's your name?"

"Nope."

Okay, I'm confused. "Then how can you be John but not, and yet Not John if it isn't your name?"

"I used to be, but I'm not that John. Or the kind of John you sit on, either. Or the kind that picks up hookers, because that would be… just no. And you're laughing at me?"

And here I was sure that I'm being quiet. Busted. "Totally not my fault."

"Like *totally*?"

"You ass."

"I prefer Not John, thank you."

I wipe a tear that has formed in the corner of my eye, a side effect of attempting to stifle the laughter. I am obviously failing at this.

"So, we'll just stick to the original. You're Not Telling, and I'm Not John. Except I am, sort of, at least in this conversation. And kind of used to be every day, except... you know..."

"Not," I finish for him.

"See? You're catching on."

Wait a minute... "So, it's your middle name?"

"Ding, ding, ding! It was! We have a winner. Just don't tell anyone. And pretend I didn't tell you. I probably shouldn't have given you that tad bit of information at all, but I did, and you'll just have to deal with it. So there."

"So there?" What is he, five?

"Is there a problem, Not Telling?"

"No, no problem at all."

Except I haven't hung up yet. And I'm sitting here in the middle of the night on the phone. With a stranger, no less.

"And now you know more about me than I do about you, so..." He draws that word out a bit, and the familiarity strikes a chord, disturbing distant memories, stunning me silent once more. "So, yeah. What was I saying? Oh, right. Not Telling and Not John... are you okay there?"

His question brings me back to the present. "I don't know. I'm sitting here in the middle of the night, talking to a stranger who could easily be some freakish stalker, and..." I pause, not knowing if I should say the rest or not.

"And what?"

Fuck it. "And laughing more than I have in ages."

"Right, right, I'm good for a laugh. So, I've been told, anyway." Now he sounds almost sad, and my smile fades. "Look, I'm sorry. I shouldn't be bothering you like this, you're right. It's the middle of the night, and the wrong number—like you said."

I had said that, but now... "Wait... John?"

"Not John." His laugh is soft, maybe with a bit of remorse in it. Why the hell is it causing my chest to ache? "I'll have to remember that one."

"Christine," I say suddenly, with only a moment of regret. "And you don't have to go, really."

"Christine, that's beautiful." The way he breathes my middle name has me shivering involuntarily.

"But not really Christine, and the joke can only go so far because I don't know of anything else called Christine. Except that one car, which I am not."

"Ah, your middle name. Now I know something about you as well." He pauses, the laughter gone from his voice, and I hear him take a drink before a lighter strikes and I hear him inhaling what I assume is a cigarette. "I'm sorry I woke you up, really. G'nite, Not Telling."

I smile wistfully. "Good night, Not John." After I hear the click on the other end of the line, I hang up my phone and settle back down into my pillows.

Wide awake.

There's no way I can sleep now, not with that strange phone call playing over and over in my mind. I feel as if I've talked to this person before or have at least heard his voice somewhere. Maybe my mind isn't playing a trick; maybe it's just someone from school, or at work.

Or maybe it really is some stranger who feels just as alone as I do so often.

And I wonder, even as I'm getting ready for school a few short hours later, if that stranger is thinking of me, too.

CHAPTER 2

Fate.

What a strange word—fate. Even looking up the definition hasn't changed my mind, but I write it down anyway.

Something that unavoidably befalls a person; fortune; lot.

"I think she's referring to the second definition here," Jaden whispers in my direction, quietly enough as to not disturb the professor's current diatribe. Apparently, per the woman lecturing us from below, 'fate' is something merely used as a plot point in some of the novels we will be reading and analyzing and doesn't actually exist. I glance down at the second definition of the word and my mouth draws into a cynical line.

The universal principle or ultimate agency by which the order of things is presumably described; the decreed cause of events; time.

It seems the professor and I are in full agreement on this one.

"Damn, Talia, not you, too."

That's the thing about Jaden Brogotti—as my best friend, she has somehow acquired the superpower of reading my thoughts by my facial expressions. Either that, or I am as transparent as they come. There's no need in arguing with her at this point, though; as per usual, she's correct.

"I have my reasons," is all I whisper in return before I write down that second definition, along with a few doodled question marks around it. Hopefully I can stay awake through this lecture, thank you mysterious, probably drunk, wrong number guy.

I listen to the professor continue about the concept of fate, making mental notes of agreement as I do. Was it fate that had made my father sick when I was young? Was it fate that had stolen him from me long before he'd finally left this world, just when I'd needed him the most? I suppose fate also made my brothers and sisters shun me, and fate had steered me to the wrong crowd of friends. Oh, and let's not forget fate having me steal my oldest sister's medication and any other pill I could get my teenaged hands on to numb the pain. Fate had me running away to avoid the pain only to have my world crash around me. Oh… oh, here's this one—fate had me in over my head and 'in love' with a man who turned out to be married, and also led me to refuse his request of silence when I'd found out. And who was to blame when I told his wife? Me, of course.

"It would also mean we were fated to be friends," Jaden whispers, and I shoot a hardly lethal glance in her direction.

"We will be touching on this… *subject matter* a few times throughout this semester." The professor's voice is laden with disdain, a sentiment I can relate to. "Keep notes; you could be asked to give your own argument for or against the concept."

I look down at my notebook, knowing I will probably be starting on said paper before the night is over. I don't have a rotation at the hospital, I'm not going out with the girls until tomorrow, so what else is there to do? I guess I could clean, or organize more, or…

"Are you coming?"

…or miss that class has been dismissed while I was off in my own little world.

I smile up at Jaden without answering and gather my things into my messenger bag. "What time do I pick you and the girls up tomorrow?"

Her smile is still in place as she contemplates her answer. "You drive all the time," she finally says as we make our way out of the lecture hall. The hot August air hits us when we step outside, its stickiness already wreaking havoc on my curls. I can't imagine what my hair would be like had I attempted to straighten it today.

"And?"

"And you need to have some fun, too." She places her arm around my shoulder and gives me a quick shake without breaking stride. It is I who needs to walk a little faster, as I'm roughly three inches shorter. Her presence alone, though, has a calming effect on my otherwise anxious self, and since she garners far more of the boys' attention with her dark features that her Italian father had blessed her with, I can relax even more.

"I do have fun." My fun simply tends to consist of quietly observing most of the time.

"And I suppose you'll come up with some reason to not drink when we go to Cleveland for the Jase Warner concert, too."

"What?" I'm almost defensive at this point. "That's different. We'll be staying at a hotel, walking to the theater. What if we're all obliterated and one of us gets lost... or... something?" Even I admit, although to myself, that it sounds like I'm making excuses, or grasping at straws, even. "But seriously, there's no reason for me *not* to drive tomorrow. I'll be coming off a shift at the hospital anyway."

I know what she's going to say even before she does.

"We'll discuss it later."

Translation: Jaden will refuse to let me be designated driver again. As a college senior, one would think I would be all about the drinking with someone else to drive me safely home. I suppose I got all my partying out of my system long before I was of legal age, though, because being impaired is hardly high on my priority list.

"Lunch on campus?" I ask as we approach the parking lot. Her raised eyebrow is all the answer I need, so I laugh and agree with a nod that we'll meet at our usual spot at Crystal's Bar and Grill.

Crystal's isn't far from campus and sits just enough off the main drag to not be inundated with tons of students, so we know we can eat in relative peace.

Jaden's SUV is parked a few rows away, so she continues walking while I slide into the front seat of my car. In my haste to leave class, I had failed to properly close my messenger bag, and when I toss it on the seat beside me its contents spills onto the floor.

Of course.

After starting the engine and setting the air conditioning to kill, I lean over to retrieve the contents of my bag. My wallet, still completely closed, is the first thing I toss back in. The second item I pick up is an old, tattered copy of *One Flew Over the Cuckoo's Nest*, its cover bent at an awkward angle to reveal the message written on the front page.

For when you're lonely. ~J

I trace the words with my fingertip, the familiar pain of my long-ago life trying its best to consume me.

"I suppose 'fate' took you from me, too." I say the words out loud, even though 'J' isn't anywhere in my life, let alone my car. With a sigh, I close the cover and stuff the book back into my bag—the same place I've carried it since I'd found it in a box that I'd packed away years before—and headed to Crystal's for lunch.

"So how many tickets should I buy?"

I glance up from my perfectly sauced boneless wings and know that Jaden is referring to the concert again. "I thought we'd agreed on five."

"Right—you, me, Tish, Cass, and..." Her eyes narrow a bit, as if she is trying to remember who the fifth ticket is for.

"Iris."

"Right, Tish's aunt."

"And my boss."

Jaden's eyes light up. "A ha! That's why you don't want to drink in Cleveland."

I shake my head at her incorrect assumption. "Iris has gone out with all of us before."

"And you were DD then, too."

Was I? Fuck. Probably.

"Isn't she going tomorrow, too?"

I nod as I take a drink of my diet cola. "Meeting us there."

"You're drinking."

I don't have to pretend that I don't understand why she's stressing me drinking. Some would scream peer pressure, and in a way, I suppose it is.

It just isn't for the reason that others would assume.

"You need to lighten up, Talia."

I grin at her, but still refuse to give in.

"Seriously, you have got to stop being so uptight."

And my grin fades. "I'm not uptight, Jaden."

Did she just *scoff* at me? Really?

"When was the last time you just…" Her hands are gesturing, but I keep my eyes on her face. "You know, let your hair down? Had a great time, expectations be damned?"

"I don't give a damn about expectations."

"You only say you don't, and before you remind me that you curse like a sailor, that doesn't mean you aren't uptight."

"Yes it fucking does." I'm grinning as I say this, but she isn't biting.

"When was the last time you were in a relationship?"

That would be the time I was involved with the married fuckhead from hell, but that's not a story I'm going to get into. "I don't have time for a relationship. But while you're stating the obvious about my lack of love life, what's up with yours?"

"We aren't talking about me; we're talking about you."

"And drinking isn't going to suddenly increase my social status, nor increase the likelihood of me meeting a man I want to spend time with."

"You might actually, you know… *talk*."

"I'm talking now."

"Ah, so you'll think about it."

There really isn't anything to think about.

"While I remind you that I know Jase Warner personally and can introduce you to him."

Now I'm laughing. I get it, little miss gypsy meets and becomes friendly with nearly everyone out there. This one is legit, though, because I've heard the story about how they'd met before he'd even been signed. However, ... "I'm still not drinking tomorrow, Jaden."

She smiles back at me and bats her eyelashes. "Yes, you are."

I inhale deeply before I take another bite of chicken but say nothing.

I don't have to.

And across the table, Jaden whispers, "Yes, you are."

I throw my wadded-up napkin at her.

My two story, one-bedroom townhome is the best thing that's happened to me in quite some time. I'm still getting settled, rearranging, buying odds and ends that I need, but it's all mine. I used some of the money left to me in a trust that was finally turned over to me for my deposit and some furniture, and my rent is mostly covered by my financial aid. What I can't put a price on, though, is the fact that for the first time I'm completely on my own. If I choose to leave lights on, or clothes not picked up, or a spill on the counter, that's my prerogative. I won't have anyone going through my things the way my sisters had, or invading my space and privacy, or giving me hell about what I choose to do with my time.

So, what do I do the moment I get home?

Eat a quiet dinner, promptly wash and dry the dishes, clean up after myself, change into my pajamas, turn off unnecessary lights, and curl up in my Papasan chair with that tattered book in my hands.

And I sigh.

It's a heavy sigh, one that feels like I've been holding it in for a while. I suppose I have, if I think of how many years I've had this book in my possession. It represents one of the most difficult times in my life. This book was given to me when my father was dying of cancer in the oncology wing of the latest and greatest cancer treatment center that had promised a miracle they couldn't deliver. Okay, maybe they didn't promise, but with the way my mother had hung on to hope far longer than she should have, forcing my father to remain alive long past the time when he could tell us his wishes... I can admit I'm more than a little bitter.

But this book also represents the only light I'd had in my life at the time.

I remember bits and pieces of the boy—J, the only thing I know that is absolutely concrete about him. My memories of this period are sketchy at best, blocked by my refusal to relive the pain. But in that refusal, I also lost this boy. His face is a faded memory that I don't even have a photograph to remind me of. I never knew his last name, and his first name had long since left my thoughts, only to return just last week when I'd unpacked this book. No, wait, I still can't remember his first name. Just 'J'. But the book... I hadn't seen it since I'd packed it away in high school, until my unpacking began.

Again, I'm tracing the words written in slanted teenage boy script, only this time I'm wishing I could remember more. I don't even know why I'm so fixated on this; he hasn't crossed my mind in years, honestly. Maybe it is finding this book, the memories it stirs in me. Or maybe it is all the talk about the nonsense known as fate just a few hours ago.

Maybe it's Jaden's fault for trying to pull me out of my self-imposed shell, the same way this boy had done in a waiting room two states over in Illinois.

I glance around my living room, satisfied I've done all I can for the day, before I make my way upstairs, leaving the book on the coffee table as I pass it.

And the last thought that crosses my mind before sleep claims me is how fate, if it really exists, will bring that boy back into my life.

CHAPTER 3

He hasn't called back. Phone guy, that is.

Of course he hasn't; it had been a wrong number, after all.

That hasn't stopped me from waking up periodically, checking the time, checking to see if I'd somehow slept through my phone ringing. Considering I have a shift at the hospital in the morning, this isn't the smartest thing I could do. I am so tired by the end of it that I barely remember driving home, let alone crashing onto my bed fully clothed.

When the ringing phone wakes me, one glance at the clock tells me that I've been asleep for two hours already. The second thought in my head makes my stomach feel like it has dropped to my feet.

What if it's him?

Mustering up the friendliest voice I can, I answer my phone with the standard, "Hello?"

"Oh, yay! Talli's in a good mood!" Tish sounds happy enough to make me smile, and it doesn't hurt that I can't argue with her, remind her how I haven't gone by 'Talli' since high school. "Cass said she's driving tonight, so we'll be picking you up about seven or so."

Yeah, I don't think so. "Maybe I should drive. I'm really tired."

"All the more reason for you to not drive. And Iris can't make it, so no more excuses." Well, shit. "Now, what's gotten you into such a fabulous mood?"

A guy. A guy who may or may not be a serial killer. A guy who called me up, whose voice gave me chills, who made me laugh and feel completely at ease.

"Can I plead the fifth?" I ask instead.

"Hell no you don't, you'd better spill. What's his name?"

"I don't know. I mean..." Shit.

"What do you mean you don't know?"

Good one, Talia. How are you going to get out of this now?

I hear commotion, the picking up of another extension, and Jaden's voice comes across the line. "You've been holding out on us."

"Not exactly," I try to explain, but it seems I'm not going to get a word in edgewise now.

"She's lying."

That's Tish interrupting me, and Jaden follows directly after.

"I say we pour large amounts of alcohol down her throat."

"Then we'll make you talk," Tish finishes.

"Are you going to sic Cass on me, too?" I ask, trying and failing to stop grinning.

Tish is the one who answers. "She's not here right now. She's taking a nap."

"How's come she gets to take a nap when she's driving, but I take a nap and I'm not allowed to drive?"

"Um, Talli... she's not going to be taking a nap while she's driving," is Tish's smartass reply.

Yeah, yeah. "I asked for that, didn't I?"

"Pretty much. Don't you agree, Jaden?"

"She's losing it, Tish."

"I so am not!" My smile is giving away my lightheartedness, and for a moment I wonder if it's possible to hear a smile through the phone.

"This calls for much vodka," Tish says. "Perhaps with cranberry juice in it. Or maybe some... what the fuck is it that she drinks all the time?"

"White Russians," Jaden answers above my laughter.

"See? I obviously do drink from time to time," I try to interject, to no avail.

"It's not my style," Tish continues, "but if it will get her drunk..."

"...and spilling about this guy..."

"Oh, yeah. I'm all for it. This is happening."

I have to interject. "This is not happening."

"Tish, did you hear something?"

"Not a word," Tish replies, and I'm rolling my eyes at my darling friends.

"Okay, I'm going back to sleep now so the two of you will have to commence your evil planning without me. Just know that it won't work."

"Says who?"

I'm not sure which one of them that was, but I simply laugh and hang up the phone.

Maybe they're right; maybe I need to be the one to loosen up a bit, relax, and just have a good time. I smile again as the phone rings almost immediately, and without hesitation I answer.

"I'm still not drinking tonight."

"I didn't know drinking was a requirement."

Oh... *OH*... Phone guy, Not John... he's calling me again. Well, obviously, since he's on the other line, and I'm just sitting here with my mouth open like some idiot.

"Are you still there, or have you hung up on me?"

I snap out of my stunned silence. How does he always do this to me? "I'm here. Hello, Not John."

"Ah, it is you. Hello, Not Telling. I was concerned I'd gotten the wrong number... or the right one this time... or the incorrect wrong number."

I want to laugh, but I'm afraid I'll offend him. "Are you angry with me?" I ask instead, and immediately regret it. Seriously,

Talia, why would this guy be angry with you? And furthermore, who cares?

Oh, right. For some unfathomable reason, I do.

"No, of course not." And there he goes with that voice, and I relax into my pillows as I let it envelop me. "I was afraid you were angry with me."

Not a chance. "I was wondering why you'd hung up so quickly."

"So you could sleep. You sounded exhausted."

"Liar."

"What?" It's more of a mock exclamation, and I allow myself to laugh.

"You so didn't care that I was tired."

"You hurt me with your words, Not Telling. And how would you know if I was concerned? You don't know me, remember?"

I don't? Because with every passing moment, I could almost swear that I do. "I'm glad you called again," I admit, then bury my face in my hands as if he can see me blush.

"Are you really?" There's no amusement in his voice, only a trace of sadness.

I am quieter when I answer him. "Yes. And just for the record, I didn't get back to sleep."

"So I could have kept you on the phone as long as I wanted then? Damn, so much for chivalry."

"Just until I had to get ready."

What the hell am I doing? What am I saying? Am I seriously inviting some stranger to call me all hours of the day or night?

Well, no shit. Clearly I am.

"Perfect. So, I can call you later?"

"You can't stay on now?" Way to sound desperate. Although how would he know if I'm desperate? Because I'm not. At all.

"Hell no, I need my sleep." He's laughing before he's even done with the sentence, and I am laughing along with him.

And it feels right. Natural.

"I'm sorry... I have somewhere I have to be. I didn't want to call you late if it would make you angry."

"That's sweet. You know, not that you gave a damn the last time."

Oh, his laugh is infectious. Is there a way for me to tape it just to listen to it? Maybe that's it, maybe his laugh is familiar to me somehow.

"Wait, did you find John?" I ask, almost as an afterthought.

"No, no I haven't. I may have just gotten the numbers backwards; I'm horrible with that."

"That's not always a bad thing." Again, I'm hiding my face, which feels like it's on fire. Am I flirting with this guy now?

"No, it isn't." His words are slow, as if he's letting the meaning of them sink in. "Damn, I do have to go now. Are you sure I can call?"

And I'm smiling again. "Positive."

"All right, then. Until later, Not Telling."

Wow, what do you know… you can hear a smile.

CHAPTER 4

I have issues with absentmindedness, or so I'm told. I've only had to have maintenance let me into my apartment, oh... three times? After that, I came up with a brilliant plan: I would have people I trust have spare keys, just in case. Lucky for me, Jaden was more than happy to agree. This also means, though, that when she shows up at my apartment, she *shows up* at my apartment.

"You ready, Talia?"

I can barely hear her above the music I have playing rather loudly. I almost feel sorry for my neighbors, except that this is payback of sorts. Besides, it isn't anything too heavy. Jase Warner's music is rock but is far from 'bang your head go kill your mother' music. And, in my humble opinion, it sounds even more amazing when played, you know... loudly.

Very... *very* loudly.

"Huh?" I say this almost on autopilot; I know exactly what she's yelled up the stairs at me. I'm still putting the finishing touches on something I'm not quite used to putting this much care in—myself. My red curls have brightened a bit over the summer from their usual deep sherry color, and the heat and humidity the Ohio weather has going for it today has made taming them a challenge. I do believe I've managed, though, having it pinned up in the back, and loose curls framing my face. I have applied more makeup than the norm as well. My royal blue shirt is form-fitting, which is unusual for me, and it not only accentuates my curves, but also makes my light blue eyes really 'pop' as Jaden often says. Fitted jeans and heeled boots are on, and I am standing there staring.

Just staring.

Who is this person looking back at me?

"I said, are you…" Jaden's voice trails off as she enters my room. "You're ready. Let's go."

I can only nod, my eyes wide as I turn from the mirror and head for girls' night out.

The four of us—Jaden, Tish, Cass, and myself—have had this Friday night ritual going on since Jaden and I started packing up our dorm the end of our sophomore year at college. Most of the time, like tonight, we end up at Crystal's just to relieve the stress of the week and catch up on anything that hadn't been relayed in one form or another.

"What's your poison of the evening?" Jaden asks me as we enter the sports bar. The music pumping through the speakers is considerably louder than it is during lunch, and the evening clientele is here to get their drink on.

Like I'd said I wasn't going to do.

With a stranger's voice haunting me and a new wave of confidence I haven't felt in quite some time, I smile over at Jaden. "Vodka cran."

Her mouth drops open.

She doesn't question me, though, and lets our waitress know our drink orders, which are brought over to us rather quickly.

As is the second round.

And the third.

"Umm… hello… Talia?" Cass is waving her hand in front of my face.

I've been my usual quiet self this evening, although not exactly paying attention with the roaming thoughts in my head. I giggle through my slightly hazed vision, shaking my head when I think I see two of her. Nope, just one Cass, bright blonde hair and all. Why is that suddenly reminding me of J? No, wait… Crystal's. Friends. Drinking. "I'm here, I'm here. Which boyfriend this time?"

She gasps mockingly. "Hey, I resemble that!"

"Actually, Miss I'm-not-drinking," Jaden cuts in, "we were discussing how Tish is Hungarian, yet I'm the gypsy."

"That word's offensive," Tish adds with a touch of laughter.

"Oops, sorry." Wow, I'm so articulate when buzzed. "Um, so, is our next round here? I'm buying." I pull my wallet out only to almost drop it, but Tish reaches over and takes it from me.

"It's going to be all over you and everyone else if you don't slow down." At least Tish is smiling when she says this to me, or I may have been insulted otherwise. "This is what happens when you have no tolerance."

"You mean like when you're always designated driver?" Jaden is batting her eyelashes when she adds this, and I refrain from throwing a piece of ice at her. I choose to stick my tongue out at her instead, which she ignores. "Anyhow, before someone decided to not pay attention…" She raises her eyebrow at me. "So in spite of my extreme, amazing Italian heritage, I am the gypsy, and our lovable Hungarian princess…"

"Don't call me a princess, bitch."

"Whatever. Our Hungarian princess is the wife, mom, amazing cook…"

"And older than all of you brats." Tish takes a sip of her wine, and I'm taken back to years ago at the house party my oldest sister Lisa threw long before she'd found religion. That was how I'd met Tish, when she'd showed up acting like she owned the place and had pissed me off when she'd told me that my tight clothes and caked-on makeup were hiding my true beauty.

I kind of love her for that now.

"I, for one, am not a brat." Cass sits up taller and smiles across the room at the latest man who's been eyeing her in all of her blue-eyed beauty.

Jaden shakes her head. "That is up for debate. I, however, embrace my bratness and use it to my advantage. You know." She shoots a smile in Tish's direction. "When I'm being a gypsy."

As Tish flips Jaden off, the waitress delivers our next round, and I take a big sip of my fourth vodka cran in less than two hours. "So," I say after sampling my extremely strong drink—had I ordered a double?—"Cass is the brat, Tish is the Hungarian princess, and Jaden's the Italian gypsy. Got it." I nod to myself thinking that I'm officially caught up, although it has me wondering where does that leave me? Who am I, and how exactly do I fit in with all of them?

"And I believe that brings us to Talia's week."

My week... oh, shit. *My* week. Wow, it's suddenly gotten hot in here. Is my face red? If it is, I hope the lights are dim enough to hide it.

"Well?"

And they're all staring at me. Am I that obvious? But nope... I simply smile and say, "Not telling."

Which kind of tells them everything, or at least much more than I was going to say.

Did devil horns magically appear atop Tish's head, or am I drunker than I thought? "Right." She draws the word out, raising her eyebrows as she does so.

"Damn, Talia, you're drinking us all under the table!" Cass's eyes are wide as I finish my drink and flag down the waitress for another.

Time to divert attention. "Why don't you tell us about your latest boy toy, Cass?"

"Same as last week and stop trying to change the subject."

Damn. Busted. "There's nothing to tell, I swear." Which is a blatant lie but gets me off the hook as Tish and Jaden are just as floored as I am that Cass is with the same guy two weeks in a row.

The evening is amazing and flies by quickly. I can hardly believe it when the bartender lets us know it's time for last call. At least I slowed down my drinking to avoid spilling anything about the stranger I want to hear from again. I am checking my cell phone as it creeps closer to 2:30... when was it that he'd called? Oh, right. 2:35. And what is making me think he will again?

"Expecting a call?" Tish teases as we gather our things to leave.

"What? No."

Jaden picks this time to ask, "Why did you forward your home phone to your cell tonight?"

Damn it. I should have known that was obvious, since I never do it. Um... "Because there may be some sort of emergency." I shrug nonchalantly as we step out into the cooler night air.

Cass pulls her keys out as she laughs at me. "Yes, because you're in such great condition to handle an emergency."

"Which is why I should never drink." Ha! Take that one, girls.

"Which is nothing more than an excuse," Tish corrects me.

I'm not quite sure how long we debate excuses, or the lack thereof, but we are interrupted by the ringing of my phone.

Right at 2:35.

Score.

"Ello, ello." I say this with a bit of a slur as I begin to walk away, finding that trying to talk on the phone and walk in a straight line don't go together.

"Either you're making fun of me, or you *have* had something to drink this evening."

Shit, damn it, he would call when I have three pairs of prying ears doing their best to eavesdrop. Okay, so I kind of knew it was going to be him, and hoping, and all that shit, but... damn it!

"I'm so not making fun of you." *Lie.*

"Oh, you have been drinking; this should be fun." He sounds much more upbeat, so I know there's no sarcasm in his statement. Or do I know? Call it intuition.

"Who is it?" Jaden whispers. "Is it him?"

I turn away from them as I call over my shoulder, "Not telling."

"How many times must we go over this?" His voice isn't what's making me shiver. Nope. Not at all. "You're Not Telling, I'm Not John."

"Right, right. Sorry." I turn my head to call over my shoulder. "Not John."

"John? Who's John?" Jaden is obviously confused, but all I can do is shrug my shoulders. I have no fucking clue who John is, either.

"Should I let you go?"

I hear the amusement in his voice, but I still feel a touch of panic at his words. "No, no, don't hang up. I don't have to work tomorrow; I can talk." I have to talk to him. I have to tell him that his voice is amazing, he makes me smile, I haven't smiled like this in I don't know how long. And his number. I want his number, too.

While all of this is running through my brain, I have begun wandering around the parking lot. Feeling someone's hands on my shoulders, I allow whomever it is steer me back in the direction of Cass's car.

"Are you sure?"

About the time I'm about to reply with 'duh,' I hear a commotion in the background, which he muffles after asking me to hold on.

"Okay," I reply, then mouth the words 'I'm on hold' to the girls as we get in the vehicle. Cass starts the car but turns the radio down low so I can hear and they can spy.

"I'm so sorry." I shiver at the way he seems to breathe the words. No... no, it's because it's cold. Near the end of August. That's what it is. "I have a few last-minute things to straighten out. Will you be conscious later?"

"Maybe?"

"I'll try to call later, I promise."

"Well, I can't call you since I don't have your number." Oh, way to go, Talia. Real subtle there. And three pairs of eyebrows have raised at my statement, too.

Not John only laughs. "Don't feel bad; I don't have it, either. My cell bit the dust and I'm on the road."

Hmm. Truth or a bullshit line? Hard to tell. He sounds lonely, that's for damn sure, so being on the road could absolutely be the truth.

"I'll try you back in a bit. If you don't answer, I will call tomorrow."

Like I wouldn't answer. "Okay. Goodbye, Not John."

"No, *until later*, Not Telling."

Chills cover my arms as I hear him hang up the phone.

"Not John?" Tish asks slowly, and I give the girls the most innocent smile I can.

Of course, Jaden won't permit it. "Oh, hell no you don't. Spill. Now."

Right. Like I'm going to 'spill' anything. I mean, why the hell would I spill this when I don't talk about my wild-ass teenage years? Why would I spill this when they can rarely even get me to admit when I'm in a bad mood? Why would I spill this when I don't even know what this is?

Why, indeed?

"Holy shit, it's so unreal." The words tumble out of my mouth. Even covering my face with my hands isn't stopping me from rambling. "I mean, I don't get it, right? And I don't know if I want to. And why am I smiling, for fuck's sake? I don't know this guy, or I think I don't, but holy fuck, you should hear his voice. Oh... hell... his... voice."

His voice resonates somewhere in me, calming me and giving me chills all at the same time. It's as if I know him, and I mean *really* know him, but there's no way that I do.

"Who is he?" I look up at Jaden after she asks this and see the amusement in her eyes. "I know you say you don't know him, but..."

"No, I don't! Or, I don't think I do, except I feel like I do." I sit back, biting on my bottom lip as I attempt to clear my brain. "Seriously, I don't know who he is. And you know what, I don't think I give a shit as long as he keeps calling."

"Unless he's a serial killer," Cass points out, and I nod.

"True. I just don't think he is. He says he's on the road."

"A… traveling serial killer?"

I shrug. "Who knows?" I smile as I watch the passing scenery. "Who knows?"

"His name is John?" That's Cass again.

"Nope." *Not a lie.*

"You don't have his number?"

I smile at Tish's question, even though the answer is obvious since she was listening in. "Nope."

I can feel Jaden's eyes on me before she speaks. "Have you lost your mind?"

I think my cheeks are going to ache from smiling so fucking much. Have I mentioned that I'm smiling? "Yes. Yes, I have."

"So he just called you out of the blue?" Tish asks. My smile widens. My cheeks will hate me in the morning.

"Yep. Sort of. A wrong number."

"That he remembered to keep calling?" I don't know who asked that.

"He wrote it down wrong."

"So he says."

Yep, I'm still smiling. "Yes, Cass, so he says."

Jaden sighs as she pats my leg from her seat beside me. "You know what it sounds like to me?"

I glance over at her, watching how the streetlights we're passing leave shadows that travel across her face. "What's that?"

Oh, that cheeky grin… I can almost guess what she's going to say.

"Fate."

And I was right.

I turn my head back towards the window, this time trying not to smile. Trying, but failing. "Shut up."

"You love me."

She's lucky that I do.

CHAPTER 5

It is close to 4 in the morning when I wander down the stairs to my living room, where the girls are gathering their things to leave. Gone are my night's clothes and makeup, replaced with pajamas and a freshly washed face.

"Giving up before sunrise?" Tish smiles my way as I shrug.

"Says someone who's leaving to do the same."

The hug she gives me has me struggling against my impulse to pull away, to shrink from warmth I haven't felt in years. As she steps back, her head tilted to the side, she says, "It was good to see you tonight."

I cross my arms, my returning smile small. "You, too."

Her eyebrow jumps, but she refrains from explaining what I already know.

She's missed the seemingly free from constraints me.

As if I hadn't been rebelling against those constraints when she'd known me before.

Jaden smiles as another Jase Warner song pops up on my playlist, the colorful swirls of light from my screen dancing shadows in the darkened room. "Just wait until *this* night."

"Too damn bad it's three months away," Cass says as she stands and stretches.

Tish hoists her massive bag up onto her shoulder. "Don't sweat it; Moira has saved everything she can get her hands on. Mark is teaching her how to transfer it to DVD, which she says will be done for us."

I look down at the cordless receiver resting beside my MacBook. Not John still hasn't called back. "Everything? I'm more of a music girl than an interview and fan video girl."

While Tish reminds me that Moira is 13 and therefore has an excuse, Jaden messes with my MacBook for a moment, waking it up where the damning evidence is there—my background picture is of none other than our current subject topic.

"In my defense, he is up on stage. You know, playing music." I walk over and pull up iTunes, changing the playlist to classical music before I pick up the receiver, just in case.

The girls are good naturedly giving me a hard time as they leave, with promises that they'll be careful, and that next weekend will be just as much fun. Jaden pauses at my door and looks back where I'm sitting in my papasan chair, the receiver now beside me and the old, tattered book in my hand. "You don't need alcohol to open up, you know." That's all she says before my door closes, the silence so deafening that it unnerves me.

Most of the time it doesn't bother me. I welcome solitude after I've been surrounded by people all day; they tend to drain me, depending on my mood. Sometimes, though, even when I'm in a crowd, or even when I'm with the girls, I will feel immensely *alone*.

Like now.

I settle back in the papasan chair and grab that book.

For when you're lonely. ~J

Fitting.

I wish I could remember him right now, or more so than I do.

Oh… oh, wait! Blonde… Cass's blonde hair.

J had blonde hair. Not natural, not at all; I'd made mention of his poor bleach job to him, expecting him to be offended.

Instead, he'd laughed.

I pick up the notebook and pen that I keep on the table beside my chair and write it down.

Blonde hair. Bleached. Badly.

Chicago.

Every time I remember something about him, this is where I'll write it down.

Back to the book, I flip to the page my makeshift bookmark is shoved in and begin to read. I'm not sure how many times I've read it over the years. I know that I kept it with me from the moment I took it from him until I packed up my room to leave home. Since getting my shit together, I have kept myself as busy as possible, purposefully blocking out memories of that time. What good could possibly come from dwelling?

Even now as I read line after line, I am still unable to conjure a clear picture of the boy. I remember his hair now, in the complete disarray that it was. Oh, and his eyes... they were a dark brown with a grey circle around them. He was the first person I'd ever seen with eyes that mesmerizing, and now... now I remember how they looked down at me with such hope...

I am startled by the phone ringing on the table beside me, and I blink several times as I stretch and arch my back. I must have fallen asleep in the chair. The book is tucked beside me, its cover bent yet again from the awkward angle it had come to rest in, and...

Oh, shit, the phone!

"Hello?" My voice betrays that I've just woke up, as much as I'd tried to disguise it.

"I'm sorry." He sounds so melancholy, quite a change from the last time we spoke. "I have a bad habit of disturbing you."

"I asked you to call, and you're not disturbing me. Don't hang up, okay? Please." Something in his tone tells me he needs this; he needs to talk right now.

And he's chosen *me* to talk to.

I hear him light a cigarette, and I wonder if he's even been to sleep yet.

"Have you ever been so tired that you can't sleep?"

Well, that answers my question.

"Many nights." I settle back into my chair, feeling comfortable enough with this stranger that I begin to open up as well. "Some nights it isn't even about how tired I am, but more about the million thoughts running through my head."

"Exactly, exactly." I hear him inhale deeply, then exhale with a sigh. "All the questions all the fucking time, and no answers. I thought I'd have the answers by now."

Even with his vagueness, I understand exactly where he's coming from. "Sometimes the answers are right in front of you; others require more soul searching."

"Why is it that things never get easier? Even when you'd think... when you have... well, not everything, but so much more than you thought you would, but still... hell, I don't know. And then... being surrounded by people. Swarms of people, so many you could never possibly remember them all, and just being..."

"Alone," I finish for him when his voice trails off. "Just being alone."

"Exactly."

He sounds so broken, so hurt.

So like me.

"But you're not alone," I say. "Not really. You can talk to me."

"Can I?"

I sit up a little straighter and take a deep breath. "Tell you what, cross your arms."

"My what?"

"Cross your arms in front of you. Got it?"

"Okay." He draws the word out, and I can hear the uncertainty in his voice.

"Now squeeze, as tight as you can." I wait for a moment and add, "Did you do it?"

He lets out a short laugh. "What the fuck is that supposed to do? Is that some new-aged therapy?"

"No, an old fashioned one. It's a hug, from me. You know, since I'm not there to give it to you."

He is silent for the longest time, but I can hear him breathing, slow and a little choppy in places.

I think he's breaking my heart.

"Are you still there, Not John?"

"Yeah, yeah, I'm still here." His voice is lower, more controlled than it was before. "And I needed that. Thank you."

I can only smile.

And I know deep in my soul our anonymous friendship has only just begun.

Mondays are unmerciful, mostly because I have hours scheduled for my internship. These commence after a round of classes structured to sharpen my mind and increase my awareness of the diversity of people in the world, and how to best handle each situation. By noon my head is ready to explode, I have two more papers to write, and four hours await me at the hospital that I desperately need caffeine to deal with.

"So." Jaden falls in step with me, and I'm almost startled. We don't have classes together today; the only class we share is that very last elective I am required to have. "I see a huge caramel macchiato in your future."

"With whipped cream and caramel drizzle?"

She laughs and tugs on the hem of my t-shirt. "I'll buy."

Who am I to say no?

This is no burger and fries day for me. My sandwich is less than filling at the coffee shop, but the ginormous cup of caffeinated heaven that Jaden has purchased for me will more than make up for it. The first sip is always the best, although I don't have much time to savor it, so it's quickly followed by the second and the third.

"Heard from your boy?"

I shake my head, both at her question and... well, at her question. "No, I haven't, and he's not my boy. Wait..." I think for a moment. Did I talk to her the rest of the weekend?

"So, he didn't call back?"

Apparently, I didn't.

"Yes, sorry." I shake my head again. "I haven't heard from him since, though."

"You're different. I mean," she adds before I can voice my confusion, "even since class last week." She shrugs. "It's just an observation."

I nod, but don't let her know that I notice it, too.

Already, I notice it.

"So, this Friday," she begins, and I wait for her to press me about drinking. Instead, she says, "Girls' night in, at Tish's house. Moira has the DVD ready for us. I think Mark will be out of town, too, so it's just the girls. Except, you know, two smaller ones."

At first, I'm confused, then I remember the DVD of Jase Warner that Tish insists we study before we go to the concert. "Sounds like a plan."

"Tish has picked the hotel."

I raise my eyebrow, my silent question to Jaden letting her know I thought we were all going to go in on this decision together.

Jaden sees this and laughs. "You know how she gets."

Meaning she pulled up a list of hotels, got a hunch, and is insisting we stay there.

"Okay, so what's her reasoning this time? Is she convinced it's haunted and it will be cool as hell or something?"

"She's convinced the band will be staying there."

Oh.

Now, under normal circumstances I would be completely skeptical. However, this is Tish, and for whatever reason, her hunches have always been spot-on.

"I didn't want to ask him for passes, or any special treatment," Jaden continues. "Rumor has it that his tour has been brutal, at least behind the scenes." Her grin turns mischievous. "You can always forward your calls to your cell phone."

"And I'm sure this has nothing to do with all of you wanting to spy."

"Oh, it has everything to do with it."

"Brownie points for honesty."

She seems rather pleased with herself over this as well. "So that's a yes?"

Hmmmm…

"C'mon, Talia."

I smile. "I'll think about it."

"Classic TV is officially the best thing since sliced bread."

This is the greeting I get from Not John at 2:35 Friday morning when I answer the phone. He's damn lucky I'm happy to hear his voice. Besides, since it's pretty much my favorite channel as well, I must agree. "I'll give you that one. What's up?"

"Oh hell, you sound so tired." He sounds damn sweet when he says that to me, as if he's genuinely concerned. I, on the other hand, in my own dependency-laden way, have been craving to hear his voice since the last time we spoke.

Which was this time yesterday morning.

And the morning before that.

And… yeah.

"Don't you dare hang up," I say with a stretch and a yawn.

"Or you'll what? Sic the phone police after me? Ooo, I'm so scared."

He is a playful one tonight. I'm starting to guess his moods, and this one is, so far, my favorite.

It's also infectious.

"You're lucky I can't jump through this phone line. You never know; I may be able to beat your ass."

I don't even try to suppress my grin when he breaks out in raucous laughter, the kind that can't be faked. While it tugs at my memory seeming vaguely familiar, it warms my soul more than anything else. This man, this virtual stranger, has somehow wormed his way into my life, into my subconscious, into my…

well, almost into everything. Knowing I have touched him somehow—even if it is just a laugh—makes my entire day.

"Oh, Not Telling, you have no idea how much I needed that."

I smile in satisfaction. "Is that so?"

"Yeah… yeah, it is. So how was your day?"

"Lucky for you, it was rather uneventful. Otherwise I'd have been a real bitch when I picked up the phone."

"When have you ever been a bitch to me?" he asks as I hear the distinct sounds of the channel changing in the background. Really?

"Like now… what the hell, Not John? Am I not entertaining enough for you?" I'm teasing and doing so on purpose just to hear his laugh again.

Instead I'm met with his mock-condescending tone. "Of course you are, sweetheart."

Sweetheart. Ugh. "Asshole." At least I'm laughing when I call him that. "Just for that, I'm not telling you."

"And doesn't that just go with your name?"

"You are such a smartass tonight."

"You eat it up with a spoon, so get over it."

Which is true.

The sounds in the background of the call have settled in on what seems to be the same program that's playing on the television I have accidentally left on. Huh. I rarely watch TV in bed, and this is why. "Today is Friday, yes?"

"Last time I checked."

"Who's being the smartass now?"

"What can I say, Not John? I'm a fast learner."

"Noted."

I almost blush when he says that. Just… almost. "What, have you been so busy that you lose track of days?"

"You have no idea."

"You're off work then for the next couple?" Way to be subtle, Talia. You're not digging for information here at all, are you?

"No… no, I, um… I work the next five, then I'm off. For one."

Okay, so I'm gathering that he doesn't have a traditional nine to five job. I also know he's on the road, or I'm assuming he's still on the road. Do I know what he does for a living? No. Do I tell him what I do, or that I'm in college as well? No. Well, with the exception that he knows it has to do with healthcare, since I'd inadvertently let that slip one night this week. A girl can only be so stealthy when she's this tired.

But that's it.

Neither one of us asks, not quite willing to set that anonymity aside. I do wonder, though, what it is that leaves him feeling so lonely, almost vulnerable. My perception could be way off, but seriously... *I'm* the one he's talking to? *Me?* Does he not have friends? Okay, that's a stupid statement because I have friends, I just...

Well, I don't talk with them. Not really.

Not like I talk to him.

Perhaps it is that future nurse in me, the nurturing side that reaches out and holds him close to me, in a virtual sense.

Or perhaps it is when he does those long groans like he's stretching, easing his aching muscles, and it sounds so fucking sexy that I need a large cup of ice chips to chew on.

Like he's doing now.

"Oh hell." He draws the words out, and I shiver involuntarily. He has got to quit doing that. "Sorry I didn't call earlier. Things just... came up."

It's been three, actually, but instead of pointing that out, I am blushing to the point where I can feel the heat radiating off my face. Because yes, my mind went *there*. "Did you get some rest?" That's all I'm going to ask; the other inappropriate things are best left alone.

"No, not really. I don't rest well when I don't get to... um, hey! Wait, are we watching the same thing?"

There he goes, changing the subject again. "You are watching television and not paying attention to me?" Playful banter is much safer than where my mind was a moment ago. "And if you're watching some bullshit version of what's supposed to be a 'rock and roll' movie on a former music channel, then yes, we are."

"Someone's bitter."

"Hey, I miss music videos."

"They still exist, trust me." Now it's his turn to sound a little bitter.

"Mostly online," I add. "But... oh, lilies."

"What?"

I shake my head as I laugh softly, embarrassed at myself. "There were lilies in the vase on that table. I notice those kinds of things."

"Lilies, huh?"

"I love lilies."

"The love of an inanimate object is a wonderful thing."

See? Smartass. "I was just saying they're beautiful."

"And so they are. Unique, if you will. You don't like roses?"

"I just prefer lilies." I shrug even though he can't see me. "They're... well, you're right. They're unique."

Did he just say 'like you'? If he did, it was super quiet. It's probably just my mind and those fucked up tricks it's playing on me. Besides, if he had said anything, he's covering it up with a cough. And he shouldn't say something like that, anyway, because...

Because I want him to.

I think I need an intervention.

"So, did you miss me?" That damned adorable lift is back in his voice.

"More than you know," I say before I have the common sense to censor myself. Really, Talia? Even though this guy can't see you, he's still...

"Fuck, I missed you, too."

Perfect.

He's fucking perfect.

"You know what I missed the most?"

I am holding my breath, waiting for his reply.

"Your stories."

My *what?*

Here I am getting all flustered over him, his voice doing things to my mind and body that should be completely illegal, and he misses my fucking stories?

"Because you… you just… you know how to live, and you don't… fuck, this sounds stupid… but you don't let anything stop you."

I blink back sudden tears at his comment. He couldn't be further from the truth. "Not exactly."

"No… no, seriously! I mean, like your friend, the… um… the Italian gypsy?"

I am impressed at how he, like me, has picked up and retained so much information from our conversations. "What about her?"

"You talk about how she's so free, but… now, listen to me, okay? What makes you think you're so different from her?"

Doesn't he get it? "Because I am."

He's obviously decided to ignore my comment. "You are just… you're *you*, and you don't let any of your differences stop you from being… *you*, you see what I'm saying? I mean… they give you shit about not drinking all the time, and granted it was a blast listening to you that one night, but you… you stick to your guns."

Apparently not, or I wouldn't have been drinking that night. I blush though, thinking of the other girls' nights that he's called where I've been stone cold sober, designated driver even. "It doesn't bother you that I'm a…" What's the word Cass was teasing me with? Oh, right. "A prude?"

Oh, he's laughing loudly now. "Shit, woman, you are not a prude. Need I remind you we've discussed the fine art and importance of masturbation?"

We have?

Oh, fuck, he's right… we *have.*

"And to top that one, you were sober."

"Yes… yes, I was." I remember the conversation clearly now. I also remember exactly what I'd had to do right after we'd hung up.

"You don't live by everyone else's rules, by everyone else's opinions, by everyone's *expectations* of you," he continues, pausing briefly before adding, "I just... I'd give any... almost anything to be in your shoes."

There it is again, a tiny glimpse into his world, the world I'm not a part of no matter how I wish I was more and more with each passing day, each five-minute to five-hour conversation.

What is happening to me?

No, wait, I know what's happening.

I'm not sure if I'm powerless to stop it, or I simply don't want to.

CHAPTER 6

With September ending and midterms fast approaching, I am not exactly the friendliest person around. My lack of sleep is both a blessing and a curse; on the nights—mornings? —that Not John does call, I have a far better day. When I don't hear from him, my focus is lacking, to say the least. One would think it would be the opposite.

"Still nothing?" Jaden and I are at Crystal's for lunch after finally being assigned that damn paper on that stupid fucking subject known as fate, which I am cursing both literally and figuratively.

"What makes you say that?"

It might be the way I'm attacking my boneless wings with a fork, stabbing them like they're going to come alive and attempt to murder me at any moment. Or maybe it's the way I've shoved a few fries in my mouth, my wish for a thinner body be damned.

"You were quieter at girls' night than you have been in a long while."

True.

"You didn't even pay attention when we were watching the DVD."

I almost smile at this one. I never do pay much attention any time it's on. "I was working on my papers that are due, so no I wasn't paying very close attention at all." Except when they mentioned his brother Michael, who had passed away from cancer... *that* I had paid attention to. It was reminiscent of losing my father. I also paid attention when Jase had answered some question with "Yes. Irrevocably yes," simply because that had to be the most absurd... is that the word I'm looking for? It was silly. There. I think in context it was meant to be, though.

"You're ignoring every phone call that comes in if it isn't a blocked number."

"Not true." I shove a few more fries in my mouth without letting her know I've answered calls from both my mother and my oldest sister, Lisa—the former asking me to visit, the latter telling me what a horrible human being I am for not visiting our mother in so long.

My mood doesn't lighten throughout the day at all, especially not when I receive notice from work that they need me to come in and cover a shift. Luckily, I am already done with my homework, aside from avoiding that stupid fucking paper. Forgetting my wallet, though, means dinner is nonexistent. Pretty much everyone is in a bad mood there as well, so by the time I am settling down with a bowl of popcorn at nine in the evening, today has been one of the worst in a while.

And, of course, the phone is ringing.

"Really?" I say, glaring at the receiver as if it's done something wrong, then pick it up quickly. "What?"

"I... I'm sorry."

I am stunned silent by the pure unadulterated sadness I hear in Not John's voice through the line. A slight sniffle from him indicates he's coming down with a cold, or... or...

"I'll... can I call? Later, I mean?"

I snap out of it, knowing he's had as bad a day as I have. "What's wrong?"

"No, it's nothing... not really." His slight laugh is also tinged with sadness and lets me know that's a lie.

"You may be many things, but a convincing liar is not one of them."

"But an asshole is." His voice is soft, and I can tell whatever, or whomever, has put this in his head is really getting to him.

"Why? What happened?"

"It's... I mean, I can't... ah, fuck, I'm having such a bad day."

Join the club, pal. But apparently, my day isn't as bad as his, so I gently urge, "Just tell me, okay?"

Which, oddly enough, is something Jaden had said to me earlier today.

"I can't."

Understood, anonymity and all. "Then tell me what you can."

"It's just... um... did you... I mean, have you..." His voice trails off and I hear the crack of a bottle opening. "Fuck... I'm not very good at this."

"Well, if it helps there are lots of things that I *did* and *have*." Maybe a little bit of humor will help the situation, make him more comfortable.

"Do you... believe?"

That was unexpected. "Um, I've... I'm not much of a religious person, but—"

"Not religion."

"In what, then?"

He is silent for a moment, and I hear him take a long drink. He lets out a sigh and says one simple, yet insanely complex, word.

"Love."

"Wow." I sit straight up as I contemplate my answer. Warmth envelops me as I remember with fondness for what may be the first time. "You know... yes. Yes, I do. I've seen it."

"Really?"

"My parents." My smile is wistful. "That was love. That was... enduring, patient... not entirely unselfish, but... that was love."

"Was?"

"My father passed away years ago. Mom hasn't remarried, either. She says Dad was her one love, and that's enough to carry her through."

"Wow, that's… that's …" His voice trails off, his sentence left unfinished.

"I'm just going by what I've seen. I, personally, suck in the relationship department. And not in a good way." He laughs softly. "No, seriously, my last real… relationship, if you will, wasn't really a relationship at all. It was…" I try coming up with a better word, fail miserably and end up sounding like a therapist. "It was co-dependent."

Am I really telling him about Keith, aka the married asshole? The one I never talk to *anyone* about?

"Why do you say that?"

"Because it wasn't really him that I needed as much as it was the relationship, if that's what it can even be called. I was never to him what he was to me. Does that make sense?" I hope so, because otherwise we could be blurring the anonymous line.

"So he… was he… faithful?"

Interesting question. My face is burning as I think back to Keith Anderson and his pathetic excuses for lack of time with me. My shame is overwhelming now, knowing exactly what his marital status was.

"I take that as a no."

"No, he wasn't. And… well, not just with me. Or more pointedly, I wasn't technically the one he was unfaithful to."

"Not Telling! You shameless hussy."

I know he means it in a teasing way, but this is a very sensitive, serious subject for me. "Yeah, I know," I reply with a sigh. "And it's not my proudest moment, either. I mean… there was much more going on, but you're right. And there was no excusing my actions."

"I'm just teasing. You know that, right? Please don't be angry with me."

"I'm not, I'm not." And it's true. "So… what about you?"

"What about me?"

"Do you believe?"

"I'm not sure… I… wish? I guess that's the term?"

Interesting. "What makes you so jaded?"

He sighs again, one of those heavily burdened sighs, the ones that he normally does before he tells me that it is either nothing to be concerned with, or nothing period.

"Elizabeth."

"I'm sorry?" I ask quickly, unsure if I heard him correctly.

"Her... name was Elizabeth."

Holy shit, he's seriously telling me something about himself.

"I mean it still is her name, kind of, but she's... um, well, she's not in my life now."

My heart breaks just a fraction for him at the slight waver in his voice. "Middle name?"

"I suppose I'm obvious now."

"Is... I mean, is that why you haven't called? You and... Elizabeth?" Not subtle, but if he's all for sharing, then I am all for listening.

"Oh, fuck no, I'm sorry... no, I was just busy. This happened a long time ago."

My eyebrow shoots up at his reply as I contemplate his words. Maybe he isn't being as forthright as I thought. "Why so upset then? If it was so long ago?"

"Because," he states, without any elaboration.

I laugh despite the situation. "Because is not an answer, didn't your mother teach you better than that?"

"Not really. But it is if I say it is," he says defiantly, and I laugh just a little harder.

I'm not done trying to coax him out of his shell, though, and I find myself repeating words to him that Jaden as said to me. "You don't have to shut me out. Not if you don't want to."

"Thank you," he murmurs. "That... it means a lot."

"Anytime."

With that, I expect him to change the subject as he always does, but no... no, he's not done. "She was it... my first love. And they never last, right? You learn so much about... about others, about yourself when a relationship falls apart. Hell, she wasn't even who I thought she was, and I'm not sure I knew her at all. The lies, the dishonesty, the blame, the guilt, it was all overwhelming. And I was hardly a saint, especially not then. Fuck, not even now. But I want to believe, you know? I really want to believe that what I'm searching for is out there. The kind of relationship that's not poisonous, or tumultuous, or… or co-dependent, I'll throw that one in for you."

"Thank you," I say with a half-laugh, still stunned at his outburst.

"I want… well, I want security."

"Of course."

"No, I mean *real* security, the kind that comes from having complete faith that the person you're with has, you know, complete faith in you. And the kind that comes from knowing they're going to be there when you come home. And… and the kind that comes from knowing that it doesn't matter who's around, they… they are with you, one hundred percent. No matter what."

Wow.

Wow.

That's exactly what I want out of a relationship, too.

I can't exactly say that, though, so I settle for, "Does it exist?"

"I don't know. I mean, I hope it does, but I don't know. But security isn't enough, is it?"

"No, it isn't. I mean, it's wonderful, and it's necessary, don't get me wrong, but I'm a sucker for passion."

"I somehow knew that about you."

Okay, heart, you can slow the fuck down right about now. This guy's still a stranger, remember? "Thank you, sir, if that was a compliment. If not, fuck you."

"Whatever, sweetheart." He says that a lot, mostly since I've told him of my loathing of that particular term of 'endearment'.

"Don't sweetheart me, I'm being serious. Now really… would security be enough for you?"

I hear him take a drink as I wait rather impatiently for his answer, although I have the strangest inkling I know what it will be.

"No."

Am I good at this or what?

"Hell no, because without passion, without the spark, I mean... I don't know, I suppose it's very important to me. We are talking about sex, right?"

"Not John!" I exclaim with a laugh, which he somewhat joins in on. "Okay, so say we are talking about sex. That's not the only thing in this world to be passionate about."

"What else is there?" he asks, and at this point I've spoken with him enough times to tell he is teasing me.

"Life. You know, in general. Life."

"So, security with someone who's passionate about... life."

"Right."

"And sex."

"Of course," I agree, my feeble attempts at stifling my giggles failing miserably.

"What's with your funny bone tonight, Not Telling?"

"Nothing, nerd."

"Ah, so you call me a nerd. Are you sure I don't know you?"

"Fairly certain."

"Sex."

"What?" I ask with a giggle.

"See? You did it again. I say sex, you collapse like a little schoolgirl."

"Hey, fuck you, Not John."

"Oh, is this a proposition I hear?"

Oh, hell. Did he have to say that?

"And what if it is?"

I bury my face in my hands, waiting for his reply, which he fires back a little too quickly for me.

"You're a tease, Not Telling, and you couldn't handle me anyhow."

"What?"

"So back to this... passion thing,"

Oh, hell no he doesn't. "What the fuck makes you think I couldn't handle you?"

"Call it a hunch."

"Your hunch can go fuck itself, because it's wrong."

Talia Christine Emerson, you are so asking for trouble, you need to stop, like... *now.*

"Okay, then, Not Telling, let me..." His voice trails off as I hear someone else speaking in the background, muffled now as he's apparently put his hand over the receiver so I can't hear what is going on.

What am I doing?

I mean... what if he wants to meet up with me? Look at me, for fucks sake! I'm not beautiful or perfect or...

No, wait.

He might be a serial killer.

Or... or maybe he's lying about the whole Elizabeth thing, and he's still with her and they just had an argument, or...

"I'm sorry," he says with a sigh. "Alfred's calling me away."

Which is always what he says when this happens. "Must you go save the day again?" I tease, a mixture of relief and disappointment flooding through my veins.

"Ah yes, madam, I must go secure the city, or some bullshit like that. Hey, listen... um... I'm not going to wait so long to call you next time, okay?"

Which is a good thing, considering the shit mood it's put me in. "Okay," I reply with a smile.

"And if I have to wait, you know... a long time... I'll let you know. If you want me to, that is."

"Yes, I'd like that. Very much."

I wonder if he's smiling as much as I am right now.

"Good. Good, um... fuck, I really do have to go. Are you okay?"

"I'm fine; don't worry about me," I say with a laugh. "What about you?"

"Much better now."

I bite my bottom lip, warmth spreading through my body at not just his words, but the tone in which he says them. Oh, he's good. He's very good.

"So, I shall call you very soon, okay?"

"You better." Fuck! Talia, stop it!

"I shall. Until later."

"Until later," I repeat after him, grinning widely as I set the receiver back on its base. I jump as it rings almost immediately, my hopes sky high only to fall slightly when it's Jaden.

"I got your message," she says as I answer. Oh, right. I had called her, needing to vent... *me*, needing to vent. "Are you okay? How was the rest of your day?"

"It was..." My voice trails off as I think about my day—the crap workload, the bitchy coworkers, a nasty message from one of my sisters...

The phone call.

"Jaden," I say with a smile, "it was absolutely wonderful."

CHAPTER 7

I am lost in a trance as I stare down at the journal in my hand. *All Things J* is at the top of the page, small doodles surrounding it, haphazardly done as I'd pondered over memories lost. I'd come up with little more after the bleached blonde hair, the city, and the name of the hospital where we'd met.

Talli with an i

French fries shared, drowned in ketchup

He loved to play guitar

My lower lip trembles as I add two more words.

New York

I'd tried my hardest to not think of my brief stint in that city, although a message from my sister Lisa has brought it up again. The stolen credit card, the amount of money I'd spent, the fact that I'd run away...

She'd failed to mention how they hadn't noticed, of course. Not for a week.

Nope. Not going to cry. Not tonight.

I can't escape the overwhelming anxiety, not even as I focus on J, writing down any small detail that I can. There's the courtyard at the hospital, where he would smoke. We would look up at the stars, often in silence as the ones we loved were losing their battles.

New York

There were late night drives. Hands held. Fireworks.

New York

Wait...the courtyard... that's where I challenged him to a game of truth or dare. I dared him to kiss me. And oh... that kiss...

New York

My siblings... there was Lisa, telling me what a disappointment I am... was... no, *am* as her perception of me will never change. Shelly was screaming how all I do is lie. Jeff wouldn't speak to me, because I was a waste of space. Eric told me I was acting like a whore, and all of them said I looked like one. And Anna... she said that's all I was worth, since otherwise I was invisible.

Invisible.

New York

Snow, Christmas lights, a borrowed dress, champagne flowing, a phone call, and that kiss... oh... that kiss...

I jump as my phone begins to ring, and I reach for it with a trembling hand while I wipe the cold sweat from my brow with another. My breathing is still heavy, choppy, as I put the receiver to my ear. "Hello?"

"You sound a bit breathless."

"I... had to get up to get the phone." Lie. "I didn't want to miss your call." Not a lie.

"Good save, good save."

Not John's voice has a touch of melancholy to it, and my heart constricts. I know that feeling, especially now, but this isn't something I can share. I hear a noise in the background of the call, a consistent *click, click, click*. "What are you doing?"

"Talking to you, of course. How are you?"

My head is throbbing, screaming at me to get off the phone... or to listen. *Just listen.* "I should be asking that question. What the hell is that clicking sound?"

"Just this pen I've been failing miserably to write with."

Interesting. "You click your pen incessantly when you can't write. Noted. What are you writing, or not writing, anyhow?"

"It's just nerves." Him, too? "And boredom," he adds with a laugh, avoiding my more intrusive question."

I feel the beginnings of a smile. "Well, that's nice to know, since you're talking to me."

"No putting words in my mouth. You know I wouldn't call you if I didn't want to."

I touch my chest gingerly, feeling my heart rate accelerate again.

But this is good... this is wonderful.

"And a good save for you," I say softly. "Now, how was your time off?" He sighs at my question. "What? Most people enjoy it."

"I still had stuff to do, just... um... yeah, so... I'm sorry, it's just been a bad day. And no, before you ask, it's not something I am wanting to talk about, so just tell me how your day was."

I glance over at my answering machine, its blinking light tugging at my anxiety. "Frustrating."

"How so?"

"It seems I have gone into a self-imposed exile from my family, and they're highly pissed off at me."

He is silent for a moment, the tension from his sharp inhale traveling through the line. "Your family."

He doesn't know.

My throat is closing slowly, and each word that manages to escape somehow sounds heartless.

Bitter.

"I have no desire to see or speak to them."

"Are you fucking kidding me?"

His harsh tone grates on my frail nerves, and I close my eyes as his own words of beratement fill my ears.

"Do you have any idea how fucking lucky you are?"

Lucky? No... no, Talia, don't snap at him. He doesn't know.

He doesn't know.

"They're... there for you. *Right there.*"

They never have been.

"And they're your *family*. If you're not hundreds of miles away, there's nothing stopping you but *you*."

"How presumptuous of you." I can't stop myself this time.

"Okay, then what's stopping you?"

"I don't want to see them." Hearing my admission out loud startles me, and I settle back into the chair as he continues speaking.

"Do they know?"

"Obviously." My voice is quieter as I glance across the room. "That blinking red light on my answering machine is probably,"

"I'm sorry, did you say answering machine?" He lets out a short laugh. "Answering machine?"

"Yes, answering machine. That one you kept hanging up on until I answered."

His laughter continues. "What are you doing with that... ancient artifact? Have you never heard of voicemail?"

"It's my father's... *was* my father's." His laughter ceases, but before he can say anything, I add, "Well, his and mom's. She let me take it when I left home." *For good.*

New York

"You still have your mom."

"I know."

"You don't know what could happen day to day. Don't waste this time that you have. Enjoy it, so you can hold it in your heart when the day comes that you need them, and they may be too busy, or just... not there anymore."

Spoken like someone who truly understands this first-hand.

"What about you?" I ask

"I don't want to talk about me, I already told you that. I want an answer from you."

"What answer?"

"Christine, please."

The dip in my stomach at the rollercoaster of emotion that him simply saying my middle name was sudden. Unexpected.

It's the only time since that first phone call that he's said my middle name, and...

No, I'm fine. *I'm fine.* This doesn't affect me.

LIE

I count my rapid heartbeats as he speaks again. "I'm not meaning to be an asshole, okay? Please, just appreciate what you have."

"I will. I mean, I do." I reach for my bottle of water, having the feeling this is going to be a long night.

"I miss them."

"Miss who?"

"Anyhow so I met these people from Australia today, and they were just fascinating, as most Australians are."

Ah. Diversion tactic. I know those well.

Even as our conversation continues, I find myself drawn back to his quiet, haunting admission. I have no idea if he misses friends, family, girlfriend(s), a wife, kids... no, not kids, I already know he doesn't have kids, or so he says. He never does elaborate who he was speaking about, and it bothers me more than it should. I've had this tiny glimpse of the real person behind the anonymity, and it's been taken away. Again. Changing the subject does lighten his mood, so I humor him, and our conversation extends longer than I had anticipated. My alarm clock upstairs is screaming an old eighties tune that should have died with the decade.

"Oh, hell no." Those words tumble from my lips while I take my stairs two at a time, running to turn off the alarm before anyone else can build anymore cities on rock and roll.

"How could you not like that song?"

"Because it's dreadful." I shudder, and he laughs as if he can see me.

"I'm beginning to rub off on you. Dreadful, shesh." He laughs again.

"You're mocking me."

"No, no." He stifles his last bit of laughter. "We both know what you would have said a few weeks ago."

"How would you know?"

"You probably said…" He clears his throat and does his best imitation. "Man, this song sucks." I'm laughing as he asks, "How close was I?"

"You do me so well."

"Ah, you're getting a bit cheeky there, aren't you? And on that note, you need to get ready for work."

"Don't wanna," I protest as I sit on the bed and pull my legs up.

"Too damn bad. Besides, you're going to visit your family."

"Fuck no, I'm not."

"Then just your mother."

"Not John,"

"It would make me happy."

I let out a long sigh. "Fine, but just her."

"And be sure to tell her everything there is to know about your life."

Yeah, right. "Not everything."

"Look at the bright side… at least we're actually speaking to one another and didn't meet in some chatroom online."

As I laugh, I feel heat rising to my cheeks, and am grateful he can't see me. Sometimes he speaks of us as if we are a couple, although it's quite obvious that we aren't. Hell, sometimes I do, too. We joke about it often, but the more that we do, the more he creeps his way underneath my skin. This brings me back to his haunting statement earlier in the call, and curiosity begins to get the best of me.

"Not John,"

"Don't ask," he cuts me off as if he's read my mind. "Please," he adds to soften the harshness. "When I call you tomorrow, I expect a full report."

"Damn, you're bossy."

"So I've been told."

"Fine." I draw the word out as I stretch. "Have a good sleep and an even better day, Not John."

"You have a fabulous day as well, Not Telling."

I have the distinct feeling that I will.

"My goodness, you look tired."

This is the fourth time Mom has verbalized her observation since I'd picked her up for dinner. I smile and insist I'm fine once again before she continues telling me everything there is to know about all of my siblings, aunts, and uncles, and even a few neighbors that I can't remember. She comments how it's difficult to call me Talia when she'd called me Talli for so many years, and this time I refrain from asking her not to. Tish still calls me Talli, but I had left her behind when...

When I walked away from J.

New York

"So," Mom's cheerful voice draws me to the present, "what about you? Do you have anyone special in your life?"

Her eyebrows raise when I sit back, a mischievous smile on my face. "Sort of."

"What's his name?"

Well... here goes nothing.

"I'm not sure what his name is, so I call him Not John. And before you interrupt," I place my hand on top of hers, "no, we didn't meet on the internet, so there are no worries there. We actually haven't met at all; he just accidentally called my number one night, and we've been talking ever since."

"Talli,"

"Mom, he has this unbelievably sexy voice to just die for. I swear to you it is so sexy I feel like telling him to come find me so I can have my way with him, perhaps give you a grandchild or two. And we talk about things like sex, and passion, and self-gratification, and I think he's just the absolute shit. I would probably tie him up and throw him in my closet just to keep him. You know, if I got the chance." I finish my rant, a bit surprised with myself, and lean back into my seat with a satisfied smile.

Mom sits there with one eyebrow up, staring at me for the longest time. Gee, I wonder where I got that look from. Finally, she says, "Riiiiight. Now why don't you tell me what's really going on?"

My smile widens as I realize my strategy has once again worked.

Every time I tell her the truth, she never believes me.

"So, you just told her," Not John is saying later in the evening, after I gave him the water downed version.

"Yep, kinda like when I was a teenager. When she would come back from... well, when she would get back, we'd tell her everything. 'Mom, we had a wild ass party, got drunk, smoked some pot, and had sex with our boyfriends in your bedroom.' She didn't believe us then, either."

His laugh is loud and genuine, one that I haven't heard from him in quite some time. "You had a great day, then. Other than your mother calling you a liar, how are you?"

"Running on no sleep, but I'm good." I touch my cheek, which is beginning to ache from smiling.

"I'm so sorry! Do you want me to let you go?"

Not a chance. "No, no, I'm fine. Don't worry about me. But... thank you."

"For what?"

"I wouldn't have gone to see her."

"What, if I hadn't guilted you into it? I'm good at that, you know."

"I'm being serious. Are you,"

"I'm good, and content to hear about your day."

My smile fades as I think back to our earlier conversation. "That's not what I was going to ask."

"I'll tell you when I'm ready to, I promise," he says to me, his voice soft and low. "But I won't be able to call again until... well, sometime between Friday and Saturday. Is that okay?"

There he goes, sticking to his promise to let me know when he can't call. Can I keep him? "Anytime, Not John."

"You really shouldn't be saying that to me. You never know what I could be interrupting."

With my life? Doubtful. I insist to him that I mean it; he is welcome to call me whenever, whatever the occasion.

And I ignore the nagging feeling telling me some day I may regret it.

CHAPTER 8

It is Thursday afternoon, I have a ton of stuff to do, the girls are expecting me over for dinner at Tish's along with one last run-through of the DVD of Jase Warner that I still haven't gotten around to watching, or at least paying close attention to.

And where am I?

In bed with one hell of a raging migraine.

I have to get rid of it, absolutely have to. I know they happen all the time with me, more so when I'm under stress. But come on! We are leaving tomorrow morning for our road trip to Cleveland, the hotel is booked, and the tickets are still safe with Jaden. And me? I am curled up, covers pulled up around my face, open just enough for me to breathe. I have taken my usual cocktail of this specific over the counter medicine—Tops Migraine, of all things to be called—and a diet cola hoping beyond all hope that this headache won't linger. I haven't called the girls to tell them I won't be coming by for dinner, so when the ringing phone jolts me from my sleep, I am expecting it to be Tish scolding me for making them worry.

I am happily proved wrong.

"Okay, I lied, I'm calling on Thursday instead of Friday, or Saturday, or whenever it was I told you I'd call." You can almost feel the joy in Not John's voice radiate straight through.

"Someone's of the giddy," I comment, trying to not let on how absolutely shitty I feel.

"Today has just been... it's just been... well, it's been one of the best I've had in a long time and I can't really get into details and all that shit, but I wanted to share it... with you."

Wow. Oh...wow.

"Not Telling?"

I smile through my pain. "I'm here, I'm here. I'd ask you to elaborate just to hear you like this."

"I'm just..." His voice trails off and he laughs.

"Are you jumping up and down?" I'm only teasing, of course.

"I was," he admits, still laughing. Guess I can read him fairly well, can't I? I start laughing also then stop abruptly with a groan, grabbing my head. "What's wrong?" His tone immediately changes to one of concern.

Huh uh. No way. "No changing the subject. Not this time."

"I...kinda took my own advice," He sounds a bit sheepish, even. From the noise in the background I can almost see him hop onto a couch, stretch out, that smile I can hear beaming, radiating, all-encompassing. I am racking my brain to try and decipher his semi-cryptic message when he adds, "I called for reinforcements."

"Reinforce..."

"My brother got here a little bit ago, and I'm going to see my friends tonight." He stops short of anything else, as if he's said too much already. Well, huh... I didn't know he had a brother. Guess it's my day to learn a few new things. In the meantime, though, I'm as supportive of him as ever.

"So you're going to go cause all kinds of trouble?" I ask, genuinely happy for him. Even without discussing personal details it is obvious that although he isn't traveling completely alone, he isn't with anyone he considers a confidante, or someone he can truly unwind with. Even with the mention of 'Alfred', whomever this 'Alfred' is, Not John certainly wouldn't need me if...

Wait.

Does he *need* me?

No, wait. Back to the trouble comment...

"Maybe?" The lift in his voice is so damn adorable. Every time I hear it, I just want to reach through the phone and squeeze the holy hell out of him. "What about you?"

"Eh...I'm just trying to get rid of this migraine."

"I'm sorry, here I am bouncing off the walls probably making it worse for you."

"Don't you dare hang up or I'll hunt you down and kick your ass and there goes your night out raising hell with your brother."

"Hell, it might be worth it just to see you try."

He has no idea what it does to me when he makes comments like that. Migraine or not, my stomach does that extreme dip like it does when you're going over one of those hills really fast in your car...the exhilarating kind that make you want to turn around and drive that same path all over again.

Not that I'm about to say that to him.

"Right, ya wimp, you'd never tell me anything that would help me find you."

"Wimp? Right, woman, you'll see. You're gonna eat those words... someday."

What an insufferable tease!

"Anyhow, back to you," he continues. "Did you take anything?"

"The usual," I replied.

"Tops Migraine and diet cola," he rattles off just as easily as he can rattle off my phone number, which he told me offhandedly once that he now knows by heart. "Is it working this time?"

"It better."

"Well, at least it isn't ibuprofen and a sports drink, or I'd know you were out drinking and being a shameless hussy."

I can't help but laugh, which leads to another groan as I hold my aching head.

"Oh wait...that was it, wasn't it?"

"Not yet," I answer. "You're not the only one planning on going out and raising hell."

"Ah, tomorrow's Friday. Girls' Night."

"Damn straight."

"Italian gypsy too?"

"She's driving." Times like these remind me exactly how much Not John and I share without actually sharing anything at all.

"And this time, we can trade stories instead of me just living vicariously through you." He almost sounds as if he is proud of himself for accomplishing such a feat.

"You have adventures of your own," I point out.

"Yeah, but this time..." He stops short again.

I want to ask, 'This time *what*?' just to see if he'll answer, but again I take the coward's way out and allow him to change the subject.

Which he actually doesn't do.

"Does it bother you?" he asks suddenly.

"Does *what* bother me?"

"Not...knowing, not really knowing. Does it bother you?"

I knew exactly what he is referring to.

Me.

Us.

Not knowing.

"Sometimes," I admit. "Sometimes more than you would possibly know." Really? Whatever happened to my inner dialogue staying that way? The more we talk, the more it disappears.

"Interesting." He pauses and I hear him light a cigarette. "You know, I had a dream about you."

I feel heat rising to my face as I think of the explicit dreams I've had of him.

"Did you really?"

"Mmm hmmm, it was rather intriguing." He inhales again, and like the accomplished flirt that he obviously is, he continues. "I think that's another reason why I had to call you."

Interesting, indeed. "Are you going to elaborate, or change the subject on me again?"

"You know how sometimes when you answer the phone, you're kinda breathless? Those times when you say you had to run to get the phone?"

Oh, hell. "Yes," I answer, heat radiating through my body. This man has no idea what he is doing to me.

Or does he?

"You've *got* to stop doing that."

Oh. Dear. Lord.

It isn't so much what he said but how he said it, his voice just a touch lower, a slight rasp to it that makes the hairs on the back of my neck stand up.

Okay, fine, Not John. You want to play that game? I can play.

"And if I don't?"

"Are you forgetting? I have your number. I can find you."

I have to bite my bottom lip to keep from involuntarily sighing, begging, pleading...

"Promises, promises," I tease instead. "I'll believe it when I see it."

"Bet me."

Oh, fuck.

But do I stop there?

Of course not.

"You're a liar and a tease."

"One of these days I'm going to prove you wrong," he says, his voice cutting straight through me officially deeming me in need of a cold shower. I am saved from trying to come up with a coherent reply when I hear someone knocking at his door. "Damn... guess we'll have to continue this some other time. Until later..."

Not so fast there, sir. "Wait a minute, hold up," I cut him off. There is no way in hell he is getting away that easily. "Does it bother you?"

"Does what bother...oh, the not knowing?"

"Right."

He pauses for a moment and I lie here with my eyes closed wondering what his answer will be.

"Yes. Emphatically... yes."

What?

No...

A sudden familiarity floods over me and I sit up with a jolt, ignoring my head. "What did you say?"

"You heard me. Until later, Not Telling."

"Until later, Not John," I say, that creeping déjà vu sensation washing over me as he laughs and hangs up the phone.

But that isn't just a similarity, that is the same as...

No... no, there is no way in *hell*...

But there is a way to find out.

In spite of it being nearly eight o'clock, well past dinnertime, I call Tish's house and inform her that I am on my way over.

"What's going on?" Tish asks, concerned.

"I need that...DVD thingy."

"Oh, that's real specific."

I am practically panicking at this point, praying this is nothing more than my mind playing tricks on me. "That one that Moira made, the one we were going to watch."

That one of a musician who's on the road now, that Jaden has said is having a hard time.

"In preparation? It's on, get your ass over here."

I don't bother with makeup, pin my curls up as best I can, and rush over to Tish's house. It is bustling with excitement as per usual, but perhaps just a bit more this time. My eyes are still straining due to the effects of my migraine, but there is something I just have to know.

Something that I am praying isn't true.

"Aunt Talli!" Tish's youngest daughter, Kiera, greets me with glee as she jumps up into my arms. Lucky for me she is rather small for four years old.

"Hi, Princess, where's everyone congregating?"

"Mommy and them is in the basement with the TV stuff on, and are you really goin away tomorrow?"

I almost wish I could tell her no at this point.

"We'll be back," I reassure her as I put her down and make my way to the basement stairs. I can hear Cass whistling at the TV, and I know they were in the midst of watching Moira's DVD of her favorite Jase Warner moments, interviews and all. It is just about at the spot I am needing to see, and I bound down the steps and turn the corner just as the reporter asks him some crazy question, and he looks straight at the camera.

Straight at me.

"Yes. Emphatically… yes."

And while the other girls begin howling with laughter, I feel my heart drop.

Fuck. Me. Running.

Not John… is Jase Warner.

No… no, no, no, this isn't happening.

I sink down onto the couch, not quite paying attention to the conversation buzzing around me while I stare at the television.

Stunned silent.

This isn't real.

Not John, is that really you?

What was it he had said about Johns? Oh, there it is. His middle name used to be John before he'd had it legally changed. This is apparently a well-known fact for those who consume everything they can about him, which I don't. Not exactly.

The laugh. THE LAUGH! How could I have missed the laugh?

"Mark loves when I watch this DVD," Tish comments with a smirk as she takes a sip of wine. "He always gets the best sex. Oh, but this part kills me."

This was where Moira had added the interview where Jase spoke about his brother, the one he'd lost to cancer, as well as his best friend who had committed suicide. The tears he has in his eyes brings a collective "Awww," from the girls, and another recollection for me... *'You don't know what could happen day to day, don't waste this time you have. And enjoy it, because some day you may need them there and they may be too busy for you, or just.. not there anymore.'*

Oh... oh, God... Not John...Jase... I get it now. I get it.

I choke back tears of my own and Jaden pats me on the back. "It gets me every time, too."

She doesn't know, though.

And I can't tell her.

I can't tell any of them.

But... how could I have *not* known? This whole time, here I was talking to one of my favorite artists, someone whose career I have followed since Jaden played his music in our dorm room, before he was ever signed.

He is one of the only entertainers that reduced if not me, then at least my friends to absolute fan girl status, and *I didn't know.*

Here was one of the world's most eligible, sexy, incredibly talented bachelors, and he has spent the last several weeks talking to me.

Me.

This is bad, this is so, so bad. The timing can't possibly be worse! No time to lose that 20 pounds I keep telling myself I need to get rid of so I can wear a size 4, no time to get that sexy haircut, no time to get a new stunning outfit, nothing to knock this man's proverbial socks off. There is no way in hell I can meet him, no matter how determined the rest of the group is. There is no way I can walk up to him, plain me, surrounded by some of the most beautiful people in this world and say, 'Hey, I know you're way out of my league, but guess who I am.'

Yeah, *that* would go over like a lead balloon.

And the thought of it all, my dreams I have held onto for the most beautiful soul I've ever spoken with, breaks my heart. Why... *why* couldn't he be someone ordinary? Why couldn't he be someone less than perfect? Someone like...

Someone like me?

"Talia...are you ok?" Jaden asks and I nod.

"I'm good, just this stupid migraine." Can she tell I'm lying about that? I hope not.

"Did you take your stuff?"

"Earlier today. I think I may need some more, though."

"Hey," Tish suddenly speaks up, "what did you need this DVD for? I'm sure Moira could make you a quick copy."

Tears fill my eyes as I watch him on that stage again, from an online video some fan had shot at a concert, giving his half smile for his adoring masses. I take a deep breath before I answer.

"Nothing," I lie. "I just wanted to prepare." I plaster on my best fake-but-I-feel-like-shit smile, and although one would think they know me well enough, they all accept my excuse with smiles of their own. I take one last look at the screen before I walk back up the stairs, my heart plummeting through the floor straight to hell.

He'd know, just by the sound of my voice. He would know. He would know something was wrong, he would know I needed comforting... he would know it was me.

I toss and turn all night trying to figure out a way to get out of the mission that the girls have decided we were going on. Said mission is, if Jase isn't able to get us passes, we are going to find him. In the hotel.

This just isn't going to end well for me if it happens.

I finally give up about 6 AM and turn on some music from my laptop, hit the shuffle button, and proceed to go through my bags to make sure I have everything I need. I mean, I've only done this at least five times already, but one last time, just for safe measure, right?

Our hotel is one of the swankiest in Cleveland, something I would never pay for on a normal occasion. Of course, when I had agreed to it, I was in on this mission to meet Jase. Tish had one of those creeping up the spine feelings when she researched this one, so she booked it stating either we'd meet him there or get stalked by a serial killer or something. At the time I had found it amusing, and now here I am scrutinizing every piece of clothing I own, damning the curves I am genetically cursed with.

Why can't I be a size zero, or at least a 2? Why can't I be Hollywood gorgeous? Why can't I...

The phone is ringing, and I rush from my bathroom to get it. I had told Cass I would pick her up on the way to Tish's and thanks to my sudden panic over wardrobe I am running late. I don't even bother checking caller i.d. before I answer. "I'm on my way but I can't find a thing to wear."

"Keep talking that way and you don't have to wear a damn thing."

This time I can see him saying it. I can see his dark brown eyes, see his messy dark hair, see the scruff on his cheeks. I can see the dimple in his left one when he smirks.

I can chastise myself over and over, because there's no mistaking his voice.

I feel my pulse quicken not only at my wandering thoughts, but because it's *him*.

It is still *him*.

Still Not John.

The reality that I am about to lose him is sinking around me, and right at this moment I just can't handle it.

Just once more, let me have this one last conversation with him before this gets shot all to hell.

So instead of coming clean, instead of joking with him, I hold on for just a little longer. "And how many times must I tell you to stop teasing me?"

"How many times must I tell you that I'm not?"

Please don't do that... not now... not now that I know...

I decide to do something he always does and change the subject. "How much hell did you raise?" I couldn't have him saying he'd come see me and risk the chance of it actually happening. Not now.

"Enough to require possible damage control," he says, his laughter easing some of the tension from my shoulders.

Oh hell.

"What did you do?" I can't control the tone of my voice, I know it comes off sounding mom-like, but it makes him laugh even harder.

"Believe it or not you may actually hear about it."

Oh, this should be good. "From you?"

"I wish," he says softly, possibly thinking I can't hear him, and my heart skips a beat. "Nah, you'll just have to suffer. I was just calling to tell you that you have no idea how close to your area code I am right now."

You're three and a half hours away from my house, and I'm on my way up there to see you. "Since I cannot guess, you will tell me."

"Very, and that's all I'm telling you. Migraine gone?"

"Sort of?" My answer is honest. I am under so much stress I still have that nagging tension headache that is hanging on.

"Tell me it's not over not knowing what to wear, Not Telling," he teases me.

Yes, yes it is over not knowing what to wear! And not being beautiful, and not being one of those tiny girls, and not being anything you'd look twice at, and... "No, nerd, it's not over what I don't have to wear." I even manage to laugh a little.

"Liar." Again, I am amazed at how much he knows about me, sight unseen.

"Look...(Fuck, I almost called him Jase!) you have no clue what it's like being a girl."

"You're right, I don't. But I do know that you were in a hurry, so just grab something, say 'fuck it', and go. It will be perfect, trust me."

I can't stop the tear that falls down my cheek. If he only knew, if I would just *tell* him.

"Not Telling... are you still there?" he sing-songs, and I sob again, knowing without a doubt in my mind that if I hadn't already figured out who he is, he so would have just given it away.

Yes... yes, Not John...Jase, I'm here. I'm here and I'm falling apart and I would give anything for the circumstances to be different.

"Heeeyyyyy..." His tone changes immediately. "Wait, don't...Christine, please don't cry."

It's Talia... it's Talia Christine, and I swear I've completely fallen for you, and you would never be seen with me.

"What is wrong?" he asks. "I know...I mean, I'll listen, if you want me to."

"I'm fine; don't worry about me." Again, with the lying. At least it's something I always say, so he's not likely to question it. "It's just an emotional day, that's all. No...nothing to worry about, okay? I just..."

"But I do worry," he cuts me off. "Just...hey, do something for me."

Anything...

"What's that?"

"It's...something that a friend did for me once. Cross your arms."

Oh god.

"They're crossed." My voice is strained from trying to hold back my tears.

"Now squeeze, as hard as you can."

Why, why, why?

But I do as I'm asked, my eyes closed tightly, tears pooling behind my shut lids.

If he only knew.

"There," he finishes, his voice emotional now as well. "A hug from me. You know, since I'm not there to give it to you." He laughs softly at his mimicking of me before continuing. "I know how much I had needed it, and how much it meant to me."

Did it?

Really?

"Thank you." I nearly choke on the words.

Those words don't even begin to convey what I'm feeling.

"When all else fails with me, I just grab something black." He pauses for a moment. "He better be worth all this trouble you're going through."

Damn it, why does he always have to do that? And again... if he only knew.

"What? No, no, no... It's Friday."

"Isn't it a bit early to worry about Girls' Night?"

"Technically no," I say about the time my cell phone starts ringing.

"And that's the person you're late picking up, I'm sure."

"Psychic as ever," I manage to giggle as I wipe the tears from my face.

"I have to go, too."

"Damage control?"

He sighs, and I shiver. "Nah, someone else will handle that. Are you okay?" He sounds genuinely concerned and it tugs at my heart.

"I am," I try to reassure him. The beeping from the cell is notifying me of the voicemail that Cass has probably left in a panic thinking I am still asleep and have my phone off the hook or something crazy like that.

"Are you sure?"

"Positive, now go! You'll be late too, then you'll be all mad and blaming me."

"You're right, I would," he says, and I laugh in spite of myself. "There, now I feel better. So, when I call you later, you'll tell me how you had a fantastic day, and how my wardrobe choice for you was just perfect."

I stare at the black spaghetti strap top in my hand that hugs my curves and captures the attention of at least one or two drunken patrons of any bar I wear it to.

Here goes nothing.

"Not Telling..."

"Okay, okay, you win."

"Of course I do." The tone he uses with me brings another smile to my lips. "Until later?"

Please… please let there be a later. Please don't take this away from me.

"Until later," I agree, and hang up the phone only to have it ring right away. I answer it with, "What now?"

"Um, you're LATE!" Cass says in her cute little panic.

"I was looking for something to wear." And talking one last time with Not John.

"Just hurry, hurry, hurry! Come on, it's Jase Day!"

Jase Day… I just… I can't tell her; I can't tell them what I've found out. They'll never understand, not in a million years.

"Um, about that…"

"You're not backing out of the mission, so just get your ass over here."

Since I figure there is no sense arguing with her at this time, I simply agree and promise I will be leaving my house in less than ten minutes. As I walk over to my laptop to turn it off, I hear that familiar voice sending shivers down my spine. I stand there by the speakers, hanging on every word about love and loss and time standing still.

If only it could.

CHAPTER 9

"Dancing… on the bar." How many times have I said this now? I'm guessing I'm up to a thousand, still with the same incredulous tone. Jaden, Tish, and Moira are still in tears from laughing so much as Cass and I stand here gaping at them. While Cass begins to tease them, all I keep thinking is how much shit I can so give to Not John over this…

Only I can't.

Today is going to be so fucking difficult.

"Seriously! It's on Celeb Gossip!" Jaden is finally able to speak, and she's pulling it up on Tish's computer to show Cass and me exactly what she's talking about.

"So, Jase and his brother…" My voice trails off as I remember the laughter in his voice this morning, and a wistful smile crosses my face. I know from all of our talks how much he'd wanted to let loose, just have a night *out*, as he put it. Emphasis on the 'out', even.

Looks like he got his wish.

I move slowly towards the computer, having to see it with my own eyes.

Sure enough, there are Jase and Pete, and they are having the time of their lives dancing on top of the bar. This is much to the delight of the patrons and the lone cell phone video recorder, who was probably paid a pretty penny for the evidence.

"Oh hell, to be *that* girl!" Cass giggles as we see a beautiful blonde reach up and stuff money into both Jase and Pete's waistlines of their jeans. I cover my mouth with my hand to stifle the laughter, but it just doesn't work. Soon I am howling with laughter right along with the two brothers on the tape that are toasting each other's success as the video ends. I mean, I know the girls find this tape hilarious, but... I've had discussions about masturbation, and strippers, and... oh, the hell I wish I could give that man right now! Except only one thing keeps crossing my mind.

Not John, you so needed that.

"Okay, since you two were late, we really need to get going." This is coming from Tish, but I'm a bit busy wiping tears from the corner of my eyes. Probably hear about it... that's what he'd said, right? "C'mon, Late Girl, we need to get your bags in the back of Jaden's car."

"It's a shame we missed it," I hear Jaden say as I try to gather my senses. "I had gathered from the few emails that this tour was kind of rough on him, but he'd seemed to be doing better."

And I freeze.

Oh shit... oh shit, oh shit, oh shit that's right.

Jaden knows him.

Kind of, so she says.

I look down at the carpet, trying to hide anything that might give away that I kind of know him, too. Okay, and I'm also wondering if he's said anything about... no, she would have told me.

Right?

"Nah, actually this works to our advantage," Tish disagrees with Jaden.

I tilt my head slightly to the side as I watch her expression. "How so?"

She almost looks exasperated. "Helloooo ladies, what's gonna happen tonight?"

"Uh, the concert Mom," Moira pipes up in true thirteen-year-old fashion.

"Yes, and since this is now all over the place, management is gonna wanna do damage control, meaning the boys are gonna be..." The rest of us stand silent, waiting for her to finish. "Work with me here, girls."

Moira's eyebrow raises slightly. "Grounded?"

"In a sense yes," Tish replies, her eyebrow also raised.

Oh shit, there goes her mind into overdrive. Whenever that happens it normally results in us either achieving even more than we have set out to do or getting into massive amounts of trouble.

I am guessing both.

"Who's gonna lay bets?" Jaden asks with a smile. Of course she would be smiling; she has no idea.

"On what?" Moira asks excitedly, not quite grasping what is bound to happen this evening.

Fuck... fuck, fuck....

My voice is barely audible when I answer. "On Jase being in the same hotel."

I don't sleep on the way to Cleveland, as I'd planned. Amid everyone's laughter and recollections of things they'd seen on the DVD that Moira had made—the same one that would have alerted me far sooner had I bothered to watch it—I stare at the passing scenery wishing for a miracle of some sort. I feel like I'm in mourning and I haven't even lost Not John yet.

But I will.

The hotel lobby isn't too entirely busy, probably because Tish had ensured we had an early check-in time. She wanted us settled, well rested, with time to sightsee if we so choose to. After we are properly checked in, we enter our huge double king-size bed suite on the 34th floor with the oversized couch that Moira puts first dibs on. We agree since she'll probably be asleep long before the rest of us, who no doubt will be in the bedroom rehashing every detail of the evening we can conjure up.

Talk about the lap of luxury, though... it's beautiful. I would have eaten it up with a spoon the same way that Tish and Cass are—Jaden, being her normal self, is not fazed in the least—but I have walked in here with my hand on the side of my head, praying it won't split open. Stupid fucking migraine that just won't go away... damn it. The pain is so unreal, and I truly feel it is karma. This is what I get for having such impure thoughts about someone I don't even know, right? This is what I get for not telling him the moment I picked up the phone this morning. This is what I get for wishing I could continue the charade.

Although it really hasn't been a charade.

I've been more open with him, even with our anonymity, than I have with every other person in this suite.

I check my appearance in the mirror and grimace as I note my obvious lack of sleep. My hair is up in a messy bun with curls falling haphazardly around my face, I am wearing minimal makeup, and have my sunglasses on still as any light feels like it is piercing my head. I have on my comfy travel pants that cling to my hips and accentuate my assets, for lack of better word, a shirt that clings a little tighter in the chest area than I am comfortable with, and my slip-on tennis shoes. Do I look like I belong in a five-star hotel? Hell no. Do I care? As if. Who will possibly see me that I know?

I am going through my travel bag searching futilely for the bottle of Tops Migraine that I know is on my nightstand by my bed at home. Damn it, of course it would be. I'd taken some just before I left and had not bothered to put the bottle back. Good one, Talia. Good one. I remember a shop along the back wall of the lobby, and fuck, I hope it has what I need.

"Hey, I need to run down to the little shop downstairs," I say, grabbing my purse and a keycard to the room. "Do you need anything?" I say this to everyone in general, expecting requests for candy or pop of some kind.

This is not what I get this time.

"Jase Warner with nothing but a red bow on his head and a smile?" Cass suggests, and the rest of the older girls quickly agree.

Oh, they're so hilarious.

After everyone insists they don't need anything—short of Jase, that is—I make my way down to the first floor to their little convenience store. I am perusing their row of overpriced medications praying that they carry the only over the counter pain reliever that can touch my migraines, unconsciously rubbing my temple. I know I look like shit. Hell, I feel like shit, so why not match it? What will possibly happen to me... plain, looks and feels like shit me... in this tiny convenience store on the first floor of a large hotel in an even larger city?

I sense his presence before I see or hear him. It is one of those moments that Tish always describes but I have never quite experienced; the hairs on the back of my neck stand straight up and I feel the tell-tale tingle run down my spine just before I see one of the most perfectly shaped male hands reach around me and pull a bottle of Tops Migraine off the counter. He holds it out to me and speaks softly, nearly directly in my ear, as if to keep others from hearing.

"A friend told me this stuff works wonders."

Fuck. Me.

Damned if my body doesn't betray me as goose bumps cover my arms. How many nights have I dreamed of feeling his words on my skin? How many different scenarios have played in my mind every time he'd teased me that he was going to find me?

And here he is.

Say something, Talia! Anything!

"Are you cold?" he asks.

"No," I admit, keeping my voice just as low. My breathing is shallow as I shyly take the bottle from him and turn slightly.

He is so beautiful, standing directly beside me holding about four 20-ounce bottles of cherry cola. So gorgeous with his dark hair sticking out from under his baseball cap, the one that isn't quite hiding those piercing eyes, the ones that are so dark right now. He's so... so... *perfect*.

So out of my league.

"Oh, this?" he asks, slightly raising his arms, nodding down at the bottles in them. "An addiction. Stay away from it, it's hell to try to break."

There is that damn grin! That wicked sexy make me shiver lopsided grin that holds the public captive. *Oh hell, why did I have to wear a shirt this tight?* I cross my arms in front of me self-consciously, praying that he won't notice.

Why is his smile so infectious?

I find myself smiling back at him, all of our conversations replaying in my mind as I try to dig up the nerve to tell him the truth.

"You know, she... my friend, she swears by diet cola," he continues, still leaning in, his nose crinkled up adorably. It takes everything in my power to keep from reaching up and touching the side of his face, a gesture he wouldn't expect from someone who should be a stranger. "She says that those pills alone won't work, you have to add that crap, if you can stomach it. Which, as you can see, I can't."

I bite the inside of my lip remembering the exact conversation that has to be replaying in his mind... the cherry/diet cola debate that he swears he won. Which he did, because he kept going on and on until I told him to just shut it.

It's me... it's me! I... I know I'm not the kind of girl you would be seen with, but... it's me, Not John.

"But seriously... she's dealt with this for years, right? So... those and that crap she drinks. You know, unless you want one of mine."

"No thank you," I say with a soft laugh, trying to keep my voice unrecognizable, damning myself, my timing, my... everything.

"Yeah, my friend would say that too," he replies, again with that sexy grin.

His friend.

Me.

My heart warms as the realization washes over me; he is talking to someone who he thinks of as a stranger about... me.

As his friend.

I talk to people about you, too...I wish I could tell you...

Just as quickly as that thought crosses my mind, I am reminded why I can't tell him who I am. A group of three well dressed, perfectly groomed and manicured Barbie dolls come up to him and ask him for autographs. He graciously agrees to sign and take pictures and I take it as my cue to make my purchase and retreat to my room where I can decide whether to glow or cry.

"Hey," he calls out to me as I walk up to the counter, and I turn to him. "Are you okay?"

Without even thinking about it, I smile and answer as I always do.

"I'm fine, don't worry about me."

Oh, shit.

Oh... oh, shit, I can see it in his eyes...

He blinks a couple of times as I realize the error of my ways, and through my peripheral vision I can see him trying to get my attention. Luckily, he is busy with the growing group of fans, a group he's far too gracious and humble to walk away from for someone like me.

I'm sorry, Not John... I'm so, so sorry...I just... can't.

As quickly as I can, I pay for my provisions and escape up to the safety of my room.

"How's the shop downstairs?"

"I hate you, you know that?" I say offhandedly to Tish as I walk in, damning my eyes, damning that migraine, wishing I could at least be dressed nice or something.

"Was that directed at me or yourself?" she asks with a laugh. My sunglasses hide the tears in my eyes as I turn to her.

"Congratulations, you picked the right hotel," I reply, then bite the inside of my lower lip to keep it from trembling. As the rest of the girls begin celebrating, I take my medicine. I glance down at my phone to see if he's called, and instead I see a text from Iris.

Checked your home phone like you asked, and no you didn't forward it. Still have the key. Want me to forward your calls?

Can't I do anything right?

I shoot her a quick text back, damning everything about me, my absentmindedness, my... everything, and ask her if she would.

Just in case he calls.

Hell, will I answer if he does?

"Hey, Talli," Jaden says as she pokes her head into the room, "are you gonna get some rest? We were gonna do sight-seeing first before the show."

"I just need some sleep," I answer honestly. Sleep and time to reflect and make some decisions.

CHAPTER 10

Who exactly is it that is playing such a cruel trick on me?

I mean, I *can't* tell him who I am. I *can't* let him know that I'm the one he's been talking to, I mean... look at me!

But the problem with that statement is that this girl... this girl staring back at me in the mirror, all showered, primped, and headache-free, just can't be me. The jeans fit just right and when I turn to the side... damn! Is that my ass? I mean, it doesn't look like it's been plucked off someone else's body and stuck there, it *almost* looks... good. And the tank top is clinging in just the right places, and yep, there they are. My boobs. For the world to see. But I don't look like a whore, or... or like... I don't...

I don't look *fat* tonight.

Or do I?

And my hair! Fuckshitpiss it's the golden rule, it's never a perfect night when the hair looks good! Why did it have to cooperate tonight then, huh? Why can't it be frizzy or kinky or *something?* But no, the curls are perfect. I have pinned most of the hair up, and I'll be damned if all of a sudden, my neck doesn't look longer, more elegant, and...

Oh, I just need to stay back here at the hotel. And... and hide.

"Hey Talia, are you about...whoa." Cass stops short as she looks at me. "Wow."

Wow? Really?

"I don't get it," I say softly.

"You look perfect!" she exclaims, causing me to blush as I hear Jase's words come back to me: *"...just grab something, say 'fuck it,' and go. It will be perfect, trust me."*

No... no everything can't be falling into place, because that can only mean they'll fall apart later. And my hair! "But, but... our rule! I never have a great night unless my hair looks like shit!" I say in a panic. I'm no stranger to superstition, and I've seen quite a few of them come true. I just... I can't deal with the possibilities.

Or can I?

But the girls would never understand why I'm so nervous, not about this.

Not unless I tell them.

And I *can't.*

Cass laughs at my comment and drags me out to the living-area of the suite. "She says we can't go unless her hair looks like shit."

"Oh, it's horrible." Jaden's voice is dripping with sarcasm.

"Disgusting," Tish agrees. I have to at least give her points for briefly keeping a straight face.

"No, it doesn't, it's... oh!" Moira finally catches on when Tish nudges her. "It's so gross, why don't you try to fix it?"

Damn it. Overruled again.

But you know what? I... I think I *can* do this! I can waltz into that hall like it's no one's business, I can have attitude for days, and what are the odds of him seeing me anyhow?

Tish stands up and reaches for her leather jacket. "Wow, something is in the air, isn't it?"

I actually had to agree with her.

Everything about this night is just the way I would picture it to be, in a perfect world. The air is crisp and cool, so we don't have to worry about wilting hair or makeup that has disappeared from sweat during our short walk to the concert hall. There is a certain vibe that we all collectively feel, the general hum of the city adding to the ambience. This is a night where all the planets have aligned, everything is buzzing with energy, and I am ready to throw caution to the wind.

Almost.

I lose my nerve about the time my phone starts buzzing, and without even checking caller i.d., I answer with a very cheerful, "Ello, ello!"

"So your migraine's gone, then?" Jase's voice warms me from head to toe, also letting me know that Iris has succeeded in forwarding my calls from my home phone.

Damn it, why does his voice still have to turn me to goo?

"Oh yeah, cocktail works every time." Does he suspect, or possibly know? I automatically start biting my lip from nervousness and Jaden gives me a puzzled look.

"Since when have you been nervous talking to Not John?" she asks, loud enough for Jase to hear.

"Ah... I see," I hear him say.

"Girls Night," I cover with a grin. "What can I say?"

"Well, I have a few questions for you to start with." His voice has a sweet lift to it, the one where he has something to share and...

Oh... oh, fuck, here we go.

"Like what?" I try to cover with a nervous laugh. As he begins to speak, our very dear, sweet Moira, at her mother's urging, grabs the phone from my hands and puts it up to her ear. "Hey!" I exclaim as I grab the phone away from her, her stunned face showing me she caught on so much quicker than I did. "Sorry about that, what were you saying?"

We have come to a stop since Moira is just standing there, staring at me like I am from outer space. Tish is trying to pry information from her as Jase asks very sweetly, "Have you checked your messages?"

Messages?

Oh... oh he *had* called... he had called before Iris had made it to my apartment, and...

He left a message? He's never done that before... ever.

Fuck... fuck, he *knows*.

"No, no I haven't. They must be on my home phone. I just had a friend go over and forward them..."

After I'd seen you in the shoppette at the hotel.

After I'd slipped up without thinking and ruined everything.

Or have I?

"Can you check them?"

Can I? Wait, yes, I have a code to check that ancient answering machine from anywhere. "Yes, but not while I'm on the phone with you."

"Okay, smartass. Just do it; I'll talk to you later." He hangs up the phone as if to try to cover that sound check is starting in the background. *Dude, I already know who you are, no point in you trying to cover it up...* Not that he can hear my thoughts, and not that I can say them out loud.

As I put the phone back into my pocket, I turn to find four pairs of stunned eyes looking at me.

"Aunt Talli, there's something I think you need to know," Moira says slowly. I open my mouth to ask her what it is when she continues in a rush. "He... his voice... and he asked if that was you in the convenience store, and you'd said that Jase was down there, and I'd know that voice anywhere, and..."

"I know, I know," I say with a resigned sigh, "it's Jase Warner, but don't *any* of you say *anything*, not even to him, got it?" I am looking at Jaden specifically when I say this.

And...yeah. This is gonna go over *real* well.

I am still arguing with them when we find our seats, third row a little left of center to the stage. I knew we were close, but I suppose I never actually realized just how close we were going to be, which causes me to go into sheer panic mode.

"So does he know?" Jaden is asking for about the millionth time in the past five minutes. I don't shoot back with a smartassed 'you email back and forth with him, ask.' I can be a bitch, sure, but I'm a bit busy at the moment.

"I'm not sure," I answer honestly as I try in vain to retrieve my messages from my home phone. "I can't get to my messages! It says my code is incorrect, I know it's not. There's no way I'd forget my code."

"Like there's no way you'd forget your keys," Tish pipes up.

"Or your purse," Cass adds. "Or to forward your calls to begin with."

"Or to tell all of us you were talking to Jase Warner," Moira has to add, still glaring at me. "Geez, if I coulda had some kind of warning..."

"So, you honestly didn't know, all that time?" Tish asks again as we sit down, with me motioning Moira not to say that information quite so loud.

"Not until yesterday. Damn! What the hell could that code be?" I put my cell phone down in my lap and bite my bottom lip, trying my best to recollect exactly what four numbers I had put together so I would never forget them.

"Why didn't you tell us, though?" Jaden asks, and I sigh.

Because you'd all take turns talking me into something that I'm not ready for, and I'd end up annoyed because unsolicited advice always puts me in a pissy mood, and I don't need to hear from others how they think I'm being ridiculous when it's my damn life anyhow, and...

"Because... because he's Jase Warner, that's why."

"Oh, that makes a whole lot of sense that's... not." Jaden never strays from speaking her mind.

Damn it... "Don't you guys get it?"

"Excuse me, ma'am," a young man with a yellow vest on interrupts our conversation.

I have no idea why, but this term has always grated on my nerves. "Ma'am? Oh great, now my night's shot to hell," I mutter, which makes him laugh nervously.

"I was asked to find out if your headache had gone away."

Oh, well, that is simple enough. "Yes," I reply, then turned back to the girls who are gaping at me, their mouths hung open. "Anyhow, as I was saying…"

"He so knows!" Jaden exclaims.

"He can't know it was me, he just knows that I was in the shop and had a headache, that's all. And, as I was saying, he can't know…"

"Ma'am?"

The kid is back. I keep from shuddering at what is supposed to be a sign of respect and turn back to him.

"Can I help you?"

"I was asked to find out what…area code you're from?"

"937," I respond without thinking, and as he quickly walks back around the curtain I turn back to the girls.

Tish speaks in a hushed voice. "He's so behind that curtain telling this kid what to say, he knows who you are, and you would be an absolute freakin' idiot to not tell him!"

"But you don't get it!" I implore them to listen to my reasoning. "He's Jase Warner! *Jase Warner!* He can have any woman he wants, he… he dates famous people… he goes out with models and singers and…he's not going to want me, and pardon me for being selfish but I would like to at least keep talking to him so that…"

"Ma'am, I'm truly sorry."

"Is he grounded or something?" Moira asks, stepping closer to the young man who clearly is a bit rattled already.

"Pardon me ma'am… er, miss,"

I throw my hands in the air. "Oh, she's a 'miss' and I'm a 'ma'am'. Great."

"No disrespect meant, ma'am."

"Of course not," I reply with a forced smile, and Moira taps him on his shoulder to regain his attention.

"Is he *grounded*?" she repeats.

"I… don't think so, miss, I'm fairly certain he's too old to be. But…I was asked," he turns back to me, "what's your name?"

"Talia," I reply, and he scrambles back around the curtain. Simple enough, now maybe he'll get the hint and drop it.

Cass reaches over and nudges me. "He wants to know; you should tell him!"

No, no I can't do that, not right now. "I'm not ready for him to know."

"Well like it or not, Ms. Not Telling, I guarantee he's going to find out tonight," Jaden states matter-of-factly.

"How?" I asked, using my hands for emphasis. "Are you going to tell him?" I know she can, but she stays silent as I feel a tap on my shoulder. There's the young man with the yellow vest again. "Oh, what now? I'm... sorry, can I help you?"

"Yes, um... no, he's not grounded," he says to Moira, "and... I was asked to clarify... what's your *middle* name?"

"Elizabeth," I lie quickly and loudly to drown out everyone else's answers, wincing slightly at my choice of name. Stupid, stupid move Talia! Oh, well. At least he won't think twice about it now. Each of the girls, however, glare at me as the young man scrambles back to the backstage area quickly as to avoid other girls screaming their requests and shouts of messages at him, the loudest being from Moira.

"He is too grounded!"

Jaden, who probably knows the whole Elizabeth story, is seething at me. "How could you say that?"

"Because...would you guys keep your voices down? Because I don't want him to know, I'm not ready for him to know."

"When he finds out,"

"No, he's not going to!" I stop Jaden from continuing. "Guys, *please*."

"When he finds out," she ignores my ramblings, "it's not going to be from us, it's going to be from you. Right, girls?" I relax slightly as everyone agrees, although somewhat begrudgingly, when suddenly the air is filled with ear-splitting screams.

Jase is peeking his head around the curtain.

You bastard, do you have to be so fucking beautiful?

"I'm so not grounded!" he yells in our general direction.

"Then prove it! Come out and play!" Tish yelled back. There is a double entendre to her words that Jase seems to pick up on. He smiles that cocky little half smile of his before he replies.

"All right then, you're on!"

Is that so, Mr. Not John Jase Warner?

His eyes find mine, and his smile widens.

He's definitely into the plan.

Well, all right then indeed.

CHAPTER 11

From the moment Jase Warner steps on the stage, all rational thought flies out of my head. He lights up the hall with his unbridled energy, playing songs off both his major label albums as well as some of his songs on his independent ones, from the era when Jaden had discovered his music. He doesn't play my favorite, a poignant ballad about love and loss called *Time Stands Still*—one he won't discuss the origins of, but I am now guessing is all about Elizabeth. I'd known not to expect it, though, since he never plays it live. Shortly before the concert is over, Jaden passes me a scribbled note about meeting up with Jase in the convenience store of the hotel after the concert, and I swear it is some kind of well-timed ploy as I'd quickly agree.

Without thinking.

And then… then, the concert is over.

And reality begins to sink in.

I can't really do this, can I? I mean, I've talked to him for several weeks… I even had several long, drawn out conversations about masturbation for fucks' sake! No pun intended, of course.

On the other hand, I do want to see him. Again, I mean. Come face to face with him, wrap my arms around him even if I can't tell him who I am and just say thank you. Can I do it, though? I mean, the only way in hell I can meet up with Jase, meet up with my Not John was...

"I have no voice," I am attempting to say as I grab a diet cola from the convenience store shoppette thing in the lobby. Wow, someone up there must really like me tonight!

"I'm sorry, what was that?" Tish teases, then smiles at me when I shoot her a mean look. Or an attempted mean look, I should say. I'm in far too good of a mood right now.

Cass sighs. "Guess you got your out."

"Oh, hell no!" My voice is barely above a whisper and it gave a kind of squeak when I say it. It is an absolutely perfect way to end an absolutely perfect night.

Jase thinks my middle name is Elizabeth.

I have no voice whatsoever for him to truly listen to.

Yes, the scenario is perfect.

I am turning to tell them that I have no qualms, no reservations, no worries whatsoever; however, my thoughts fly straight out the window as Jase and Pete saunter in, baseball caps pulled down low. The brothers, even while attempting to be inconspicuous, are bound to draw attention with their mere presence.

And Jase...

I take a deep breath as I attempt to conceal the animalistic gaze I must be throwing his way as I look him up and down. So the baseball cap doesn't really go with the white button-down shirt. So what? The jeans are enough to make me not give a damn. Perfectly worn, perfectly tailored to show off toned legs, and not so tight his voice would go up an octave. There is something about the way he moves, too, with a grace and precision that so few people are blessed with.

I avert my eyes when he looks at me and try to calm my racing heart. It's just Not John, Talia...

Oh hell...

It's Not John...

"What's up with Squeaky over here?" Jase motions my way, which lets me know he's heard my attempt to speak. My heart skips a tiny beat, but without anything to give me away I feel more empowered than I had earlier.

He noticed me.

"It's all your fault," I say, although it is nearly inaudible.

He puts a hand up to his ear. "What was that?" he teases, and even though I laugh barely any sound is coming out. He reaches over and playfully tugs on one of my curls as if we've known each other forever, sending chills straight down my spine.

Moira places her hands on her hips. "Ok, Mr. Hot Stuff, where are we going?" She is a feisty one, even for thirteen.

"Ooohhh, about that," Pete starts, then laughs slightly. He messes with the back of his dark hair—so similar to the way his brother does it—and squints is dark green eyes before he adds, "Funny thing..."

"Yeah, I was told I need to lay low after last night," Jase says after Pete's voice trails off, and he adds a quick, muttered, "Thanks Pete."

Pete scoffs at him. "Hey, you called me!"

Moira looks back and forth between them and nods. "So, you're grounded."

"Noooooo," Pete disagrees. "No, we're... we're too old for that."

"Right, no, we have to... *lay low,*" Jase reiterates.

Moira points back and forth between the two of them. "You're... grounded."

"We're just..." Jase is attempting to use his hands to gesture something, but it seems no words are coming to him. Considering all of the hours I've talked to him, I know how rare this occasion is.

But still...

"*Grounded,*" all of us girls say at once.

"Oh, shut up," Jase replies jokingly. "Come on, damn it. Penthouse suite." He motions with his arm for all of us to follow. "You too, Squeaky."

He places his arm around me and drags me towards the front of the store, and I find myself in an almost instant need of... well, something. A drink? I swear that man is a walking aphrodisiac. My breath catches in my throat as he removes the diet cola out of my hand and places it on a shelf. "I have plenty of stuff up there."

I smirk up at him... even with my heeled boots, he stands almost a head taller than me. "Is that so?"

"I meant drinks, woman. Damn!" And there goes that sideways grin that he just has to flash at me.

I have no idea how I keep my face from flaming bright red at the thoughts that run through my mind at his offhanded comment, even with his attempt to cover it up. Then again, I have no idea how the five of us girls manage to act as if we've known the boys our whole lives as we walk past the many hotel patrons towards the private elevators.

The music is playing softly in the background while over two dozen people mill about the penthouse suite. Huddled in the corner along the table by the large sectional sofa are the seven of us, with the final two opponents in the midst of a candy-or-death battle.

Jase is sitting to my right staring intently at the cards in his hand, occasionally glancing over them to size up the competition. Looking back down at his cards again, he lowers them slightly, and then leans forward.

"Do you have any threes?"

Moira grins smugly. "Go fish."

"Damn it." Jase picks up another card from the table. I notice that he draws the three, but he winks at me as he shakes his head and sticks it in with the cards in his hand. "I'm going to be beaten by a thirteen-year-old!"

"Thirteen and a *half*," she corrects him, and I stifle a giggle. Not that said giggle would have been heard, of course.

Tish rolls her eyes. "Because the half is so important. Don't you agree, Talli? Or should I say, Squeaky?"

Jase's head snaps over rather quickly, his expression puzzled as he looks at me. I honestly pay no attention to it as I am used to odd looks on the occasion when people hear it, at least for the first time. I've been getting those looks since elementary school.

"You're so funny," I attempt to say, but it comes out little more than a wheeze and with a tiny squeak at the end, and when she laughs, I promptly flip her off.

"Talli?" Jase says, and I look over at him, my eyebrows waiting for his question. "Um... that's..."

"Odd, I know."

"No, no... it's... unique."

Unique.

He's used that word for me before.

On more than one occasion, even.

He's still looking at me, even more closely now. "Do I... know you from somewhere?"

Tell him... tell him, stupid!

"No," I say instead, with a shake of my head just in case he can't hear me.

To avoid the disapproving glares from my friends, I glance around the penthouse, noting that most of the other people in the suite are merely schmoozing or doing business, completely ignoring us. Occasionally someone will come by to make sure our glasses are never more than half empty, but they don't even seem to acknowledge our presence.

I steal a sideways glance at Jase and wonder briefly just how lonely it must be to have to live this way. As if on cue, he glances over and our eyes meet. I could look away, maybe I should, but instead I smile softly. The corner of his mouth lifts in his famous half smile as we seem to get lost in the message we are conveying to one another. "Are you sure?" he asks, and like the fool I am I nod. "You remind me of someone," he says softly, leaning into me, and without even thinking I reach out and kiss the scruff on his cheek. If I had expected him to become angry or uncomfortable by my actions, I would have been disappointed. Even in my alcohol-induced haze I am saying to myself that I am being stupid, though. An idiot. A fool. I need to tell him, just... blurt it out, because the more I deny it, the deeper the hole I am burying myself in.

But he is just... staring at me. His eyes, so very kind, are taking in my features, focusing on my lips...

And he accidentally lets his hand tip back, showing Moira the row of threes.

"You've got to be kidding me!" she exclaims, shaking her head in disbelief.

Just like that, the spell is broken.

"Oh, come *on*, you chicken!" The laughter is infectious as Moira quickly gathers up all of the candy. "All of you can eat my dust. You really wanna play cards? Let's play some poker, I'll so beat every last one of you!"

"It's almost one in the morning," Tish says to her daughter. "I think it's about time to wrap this up and get you home, or to the hotel suite, or wherever."

Pete stands up and rubs his eyes. "Ah shit, I gotta get going. Dude, I'm sorry."

Jase stands for them to say their goodbyes. "Ah, don't sweat it."

I sit on the big comfortable couch, sinking back into the cushions, not wanting to leave just yet. I know by glancing at the clock exactly what time is coming; everyone will take his or her leave and Jase will be in this big suite, alone. I know this because that's when he calls me, pouring his heart out without truly saying what is going on.

Jase walks back over as the rest of the girls... minus Jaden, I have no clue where she's disappeared to... are cleaning up their collective mess of cups and bottles. "Nah, don't worry about it. There's...well, someone will get it."

I know that tone, that masks how he truly feels tone that he uses so often on the phone with me.

"Hey, Squeaky, what about you?" he asks, his head tilted slightly to the side as he stands beside me. "How are you doing?"

I hope he can hear me over the dwindling visitors. "I'm good."

"Do you need any tea?" I scrunch up my nose at the thought since I find tea one of the most repulsive things on the face of this Earth. "Nah, nonsense, I'll get you some apple cinnamon tea, put some honey in it."

"Can you actually leave to do that?" I tease, my voice slightly back but not even close to what he would recognize. The sweet mischievous smile he gives me answers without him saying a word.

But he answers anyway.

"See, if they won't let me out, then they have to go get it." The way he shoves his hands down in his pockets and bounces lightly is so damn adorable that I can't resist.

"Okay, you win." I return his smile, the sense of familiarity washing over me. He falters for just a moment, a smile tugging at the corners of his mouth. I wonder if he feels it too, if that is what the smile is for. How many times have I said exactly the same thing to him, anyhow?

He holds out his hand to me and I take it, feeling lighter than air as I walk with him hand-in-hand towards the kitchen area of his suite.

"Jackie, my friend needs some tea," he is saying.

Again, I'm scrunching up my nose. "But not real tea, that's…"

"Cruel?" Jackie, the burly man who I'm sure is actually named Jack, pipes up.

"No." I attempt to giggle, but it doesn't really work. "It's gross."

Jackie smiles at me. "But apparently needed."

"Apple cinnamon with honey," Jase requests. "Pretty please." He stands behind me, wrapping me in his arms, and places his chin on my shoulder as we both give Jackie our cheesiest grins.

"What a picture this makes," Jackie comments. "How could I say no? Give me a few minutes."

"Thanks, Jackie, you know how much you rock." Jase's voice directly in my ear is pure heaven, although in my nearly inebriated state I could have chosen a few other phrases for him to mutter against my skin. The thought brings the goose bumps back up on my arms, which he rubs lightly as if trying to warm me up.

Oh, hell, don't do that... please...

"Are you okay? A little cold?"

"Not in the slightest," I admit, slightly breathless, then stop myself from saying anything more as I try to control my quickened breathing. I hear him inhale sharply as he turns and brushes his lips against the nape of my neck.

"Please...stop doing that to me," he whispers gently in my ear before he lets me go and turns away.

What the hell?

At least that is my first thought, and then reality comes crashing through to my lightly intoxicated brain. I turn to find him saying his obligatory goodbyes to the people who haven't bothered to even say hello to him all evening, and when he looks up at me he smiles—not the cocky 'you know you want me' smile; this one is genuine, warm, inviting. I have to believe that deep down in his soul he knows exactly who I am.

Even with all of the alcohol we've both consumed.

Even with as much as I have lied to him.

Now I have to find a way to correct the wrong I have made.

"We have to get going," Tish finally speaks up. It is almost two in the morning at this point, Moira is dragging. In spite of our resilience and experience in staying up until dawn the other girls (where the hell is Jaden?) look tired as well.

I, on the other hand, am still benefiting from having a nap in the afternoon and, in spite of my lack of voice, I am not quite ready to go. It doesn't help that every time Jase passes by, he will reach out and gently touch me—not in a sexual way, either. Sometimes it is just a slight touch on the arm or shoulder or placing his hand on my back when he leans around to say goodbye to someone. He has to know what he is doing to me, especially when he will lean in and quietly ask if I am okay or if I need anything. I am already so wound up by the time the girls are saying they need to leave that if he asks me what I need I will simply tell him to take off his pants.

Not such a good idea, right?

As the girls are getting ready to leave, Jase is standing beside me, his head tilted slightly to the side, as if he is trying to read my thoughts, trying to gauge what to do or say next. He takes his time hugging each of the girls goodbye, thanking them over and over for how much joy they have brought him this evening. When he hugs Moira, he lifts her small frame into the air and squeezes so tight she giggles and says she is being deprived of oxygen.

And then, he came to me.

I'm not ready for the look in his eyes as he takes my hands into his. The mixture of hunger and longing causes my pulse to quicken as his eyes seem to absorb the memory of me into his soul. His thumbs are brushing the backs of my hands, each stroke sending a shockwave through my body, lighting me on fire, making me want his hands everywhere.

But I shouldn't...

Should I?

Besides, he wouldn't...

Would he?

I lightly run my fingertips up his arms before I wrap my arms around his neck to hold him tighter than I've ever dreamed I would be permitted to. Oh, it feels so good... just like heaven, just like we are right where we should be. I never want to let him go, never want to say goodbye to him. He has made a permanent impact on my life, on my soul, on everything there is about me.

He has to know.

But... what... *what* is going through his mind? Is this just a figment of my overactive, wishful imagination, or does he feel it, too?

I don't ask him, though.

I don't need to.

He leans into the embrace, wrapping his arms around me, and whispers one sweet word into my ear.

"Stay."

CHAPTER 12

"We're going to play a game."

My eyebrow raises as Jase pulls up a stool to the makeshift bar, motioning for me to sit on it. "A game?" I ask, and I know he can hear me since all of the radios and televisions have been turned off.

"Must I repeat myself? I'm fairly certain that I can be heard, unlike some people." He laughs as I flip him off. "Anyhow, the object is to guess the names of the drinks. You know, as I make them."

"Sounds simple enough."

"So you think." His smile is a bit wicked, and I feel my temperature rise. "But there's a catch."

"Oh, this should be good."

"Hey, fuck you." His smile tells me he's teasing, although I'm not sure if there's a double entendre in there somewhere. "But, um... yeah, if you don't guess correctly, you have to remove one article of clothing."

Really, now?

Also, he must not think that I'm Not Telling. Because seriously? He knows my vast knowledge of drinks. Or... or... he knows it's me and he's not wanting to get into my pants, he just wants confirmation, and…

"Here's the first."

The drink he hands me has a milky white color to it, and the taste… oh, it is divine! A bit of pineapple, some coconut, and…

Got it.

"Screaming Orgasm."

"Very good, very good. You're safe on that round." He glances up at me, that half grin back on his face while he makes the next drink for me to guess.

"Yay me." I lean in, smiling and batting my eyelashes.

"Oh, don't even go there, woman. I'll win. I always do."

"Keep telling yourself that."

"You sure I don't know you?"

He asks that so quickly that I blink back my surprise, a slight blush touching my cheeks.

Just as quickly, he's shaking his head. "No… no, I'm sorry. I'm sure you wouldn't lie to me about something like that."

My heart plummets to my stomach as his words sink in. He's… he's right. He really believes that Not Telling would be honest with him, and… and I should be, and…

"Jase…"

"Try this one." Jase pushes a glass towards me, then he begins to work on his next concoction. I take a sip, then a larger drink of it.

"Red Headed Slut." It's my turn to grin. "I'd know this one anywhere."

"Really?" There is a sparkle in his eye as he asks.

"Yes…see?" I lift a curl and give it a little shake. "Many a bar patron finds it amusing to send me one."

"So I'm not being original?" he asks, and I shake my head 'no.' "Okay, well… you guessed that one, too, so you don't have to remove anything."

"What? That's not fair!" I squeak. I know I didn't want him to hear me, but this is bordering on embarrassing here.

"What's not fair?"

"I don't know the first thing about mixing drinks!"

"And I do?" Good point. "If it's not fair then you would have to take off an article of clothing regardless, now wouldn't you? Besides, you've done pretty damn good for someone who can't mix drinks."

"And what if I guess them all?" I ask, one eyebrow raised.

"Then," he says as he hands me the next sample, this one in a small shot glass, "Then you retrieve all of the candy from Moira. Or you choose, whichever is up to you."

Oh, the myriad of thoughts that come up in my head. I could tell him that it's him I want. Easily. Instead, I say, "Wait... if I guess these, then you have to take an article of clothing off."

"Fair enough." He slips one shoe off. "Go ahead, try it."

"One shoe?" Instead of answering, he points at the shot glass in my hand. "No, no... I've guessed two." He rolls his eyes and slips the other shoe off, pointing to the shot glass again. "Oh, fine." I take a sip, absolutely love it, and toss back the rest of the shot.

"Okay, lush, name it."

"Lush? You're the one that's feeding the alcohol to me," I point out the obvious. "And... I have no idea."

"One article," he says, and I sigh. I kick off one of my boots, just as he had done, and grin at him.

"Are you gonna tell me?"

"That was a One Night Stand," he teases, and adds "Hey!" when I swat at him.

"Who's being cheeky now?" I ask with a laugh, and he looks at me curiously.

"Who said anything about being cheeky?"

Oh, shit...see? I should never, ever drink. It was something he had said to me all right, he just doesn't know it.

Or does he?

"Jase..."

"Wait a minute," he cuts me off and hands me another beautifully colorful drink. "Try that one."

"Jase, this..."

His green eyes lock with mine, rendering me speechless. "Please?"

How can I resist? I take a sip, letting the liquid glide down the back of my throat.

"Mmmmm, this... this is heaven."

His smile could have lit up that entire hotel. "That's mine. I concocted it the beginning of this tour, and Al... Jackie's been my only guinea pig. I call it The Cookie."

I notice how he almost called Jackie 'Alfred' just as he does when he talks to me. I don't question it, though, partially because... well, completely because I'm afraid of his answer. Instead, I take another sip of the drink. "It tastes like a cookie!"

He leans down placing his elbows on his makeshift bar and rests his chin in his hands. "Hence the name. Talia..."

"What?" I ask, the tone of his voice causing a blush to rise to my cheeks.

"One article... give it up."

Does he have to wiggle his eyebrows that way, the sexy fucker?

I kick my second boot off, and wiggle my toes, which seem grateful to be free. Jase is walking around the makeshift bar towards me, tousling his hair, setting my heart off at a galloping pace. "Are you happy now?" I ask him, and he shakes his head.

"Not entirely...there's something I need to know." His voice is lower, a rasp to it that hadn't been there before. Now is the time...I have to tell him, I have to...

"Jase,"

"Shut up," he whispers as he cups my face in his hands. For just a brief moment I think I should stop him, then all thoughts are chased from my mind as he softly teases my lips with his. His kisses are feather-soft, sweet, searching for intent as he lightly tangles his fingers in my loose curls. I sigh against his mouth, and as if he senses an invitation, he parts my lips with his tongue, taking his time exploring me, touching me as if I am so fragile I may shatter in his hands. The feel of him brings about a sense of familiarity, as if we'd shared many kisses together.

But we couldn't have.

I would remember this, remember him.

Because his kiss...

Oh, hell, his kiss...

And wasn't I just thinking he'd never see me this way?

The room is full of the sounds of our breathing, our sighs, the soft moans from each of us as each kiss begins to build in intensity. He shivers and sighs against my lips as my fingertips brush the back of his neck, tangling themselves in his hair. Oh, it is soft... so very soft in my hands, so unlike other parts of his body that I can feel pressing into me.

A whimper escapes from me as he gently nips at my bottom lip before kissing a trail to my neck, lightly biting in all the right spots.

"Did I hurt you?" he murmurs, and I gasp at the feeling of those words against my skin as I shake my head no.

"Talia..."

I rock my hips against his at the sound of him moaning my name.

"You... you wouldn't lie to me, would you?"

I find myself unable to speak, merely shaking my head just before he captures my lips once more, this kiss much more demanding than the last.

No... no I wouldn't lie to you, just... I need to tell you, I'm just...

"Oh..."

That is about all I can cohesively put together as his hands begin to roam, cupping my breasts, sliding over my hips as he pulls me closer to him. I am clinging to him as his hands move beneath the hem of my shirt, brushing up against my skin, lighting every nerve ending on fire as he does. Without thinking, without hesitation even, I begin fumbling with the buttons on the front of his shirt, craving that skin to skin contact, each of us breathing in heavy gasps between kisses.

"Is... is this what... you want?" he asks between kisses. "Are... *fuck*, are you sure... this is... what you want?"

I've wanted this longer than he could possibly know.

His lips are once again on my neck, latched on as he slowly pushes my top up, his hands caressing my back, my sides, my entire torso.

"Yes," I breathe, unable to say anything more.

And then...

Nothing.

He pulls back slightly, his eyes troubled as he studies my face, drinking in every detail. He's gasping as he struggles to get his breathing slowed, and it hits me then—a bit slowly—that he must be regretting this already.

What the hell?

"I... I'm so sorry." His voice is soft, emotional as he removes his hands slowly—so slowly I could almost swear he is reluctant to. "I... I can't. There's..." He closes his eyes tight and rubs his temple before he continues, without looking back at me. "There's..."

"Someone else?" I ask, trying the best I can to stop my heart from slamming into my ribcage as I wait.

Just tell me, Not John. Just say it.

"It's... complicated," he finally says. "And I shouldn't have done this to you, or... or *with* you, and it's not... it's not like she'd give a damn, but..."

Elizabeth.

Of course.

Who else could it possibly be? How many conversations have we had about her; how many times has he told me he'd lost all faith in real relationships over her? I bite the inside of my lip, trying to keep the stinging tears from surfacing as I look at him. I feel the heat creep up to my face as I fight with myself, debating to know why he's called me repeatedly for the past few weeks, why he's been so flirty... but, no. No, why bother?

What the hell difference will it make now?

"Don't beat yourself up over it." I give him the best smile I can conjure up. "It must be hell being on the road so much."

"You have no idea," he says softly, still looking at the ground, messing with the back of his hair.

Bet me!

I know what hell he's gone through on an almost nightly basis, because he's told me. Not always in complete terms, but why else call a complete stranger? And I have obviously deluded myself into thinking that maybe he felt the same about me, but no... no, here he is telling me all about his precious Elizabeth, and how she wouldn't care, but he can't be with me because of her.

Really?

I should just walk away. Right now.

I reach out and take his hand in mine instead, and when he looks up at me, I can see the telltale reddening in the corners of his eyes.

He's as close to tears as I feel.

I... I can't do it.

All traces of anger leave my body and I pull him into a warm, comforting embrace, softly playing with the hair at the nape of his neck. I feel his arms envelop me and his hands are trembling ever so slightly as he holds me, rubbing my back with a softness I will remember forever. My heart is splintering as he inhales sharply and squeezes just a little harder before he steps back.

"A little awkward?" he asks.

"You know...I dunno," I admit. I mean, sure I was ready to pounce on a man who is so obviously in love with someone else, even though he'd asked me to stay. He looks a little sheepish, his shirt half undone, the most adorable grin on his face as he gazes down at me.

"Are you sure we don't know each other?" he asked with a soft laugh.

Had he not admitted to me he can't be with me because of someone else, I probably would tell him. No, I *know* I would tell him. I would tell him in a heartbeat and share a laugh with him and...

And I'm just too hurt, and maybe too angry to.

"I'm positive."

"I wish..." He sighs, his smile fading as he watches me pull the hem of my shirt down. "Something black, it will be perfect," he murmurs softly, reaching out to help me.

Why else would he say that if he doesn't know? He has to know. Okay, so the words weren't exactly the same, but...

He *has* to... right?

The girls were right. I have to tell him.

I grab his hands to stop him, his fingers inadvertently brushing against my skin, and again the chills spread all over. My breath catches in my throat at the contact, my body once again aching at his touch.

He doesn't look up at my face, but instead keeps his eyes there, where his hands are, his own breathing catching slightly. Instead of pulling away as perhaps he should, he releases the hem of my shirt, his hands opening wide as he caresses my skin, sliding his fingertips along the small of my back. His eyes fill with hunger as he watches his hands until they disappear behind me, then slowly...so slow it seems to last an eternity... his eyes travel upwards. His breathing becomes shallower as his gaze watches my chest rise and fall with each breath I take. I suppress a moan as he licks his lips, his eyes darting back and forth where the fabric stretches across my breasts. Up... up, so very slowly, his eyes are now level with my neck, his expression one of pure desire. He seems fixated on a spot at the base of my neck where I'm sure my pulse is visible...it has to be, with as hard as my heart is pounding.

This isn't happening...

Not John, what are you doing to me?

Is this your way of saying goodbye?

I close my eyes briefly, wanting to cherish this moment forever. I know in my heart I will never be the same having known him, having shared so much with him not just this evening in person, but over the weeks. He has brought so much light, so much happiness into my life. If this is it, if this is all I am going to have, if he is going to disappear, I at least have to tell him what he has done for me.

It's time.

When I open my eyes, there he is...his intense stare shooting straight through me just as he has done all evening. I open my mouth to try to say something, to tell him the absolute truth, but the words fail to come as I gaze into those unimaginably hypnotic eyes. Unable to hold his gaze any longer, I look slightly lower... oh, bad move, Talia. His mouth- his perfect, full, soft lips...the skill he uses them with...

I swear we move at the same time, no pretenses as he pulls me in, my hands holding onto his shirt as our lips meet, hearts pounding, tension building to a near-fever pitch when his hands grip my hips. His kiss is full, lush, punctuated with moans and sighs, our tongues dancing together as our bodies move. His fingertips dig in as our hips touch, grinding together leaving no suggestions behind, the friction as I rub up against him drawing a low growl from the back of his throat.

And that sound... oh, that sound should be illegal.

I'm not the only one who is ready, willing, and able—he seems to grow even harder as our tongues dance and tease together. One of his hands grasps the back of my head, holding me closer as he continues his assault on my senses. I whimper softly, my hands losing themselves in his soft hair, and he responds by pulling me closer... and closer... and closer...

Then his damn phone rings.

He growls his frustration, that low sound in his throat that has already caused my pulse to quicken, as he ends our kiss and glares in the direction of his cell. Talk about timing that absolutely sucks.

"*Fuck*, I better get this," he says, still breathing heavily. I laugh nervously as I unwrap myself from his embrace. He holds up one finger as if to say 'hold that thought' before he jogs quickly across the room to answer his phone.

Does he even have to look sexy doing *that?*

I'm not at all surprised to find that my legs are a little shaky as I walk over to the couch, sinking down into the comfortable cushions. Jase's brow was furrowed in concentration, and he tells the person on the other end, "Hold on, just a sec, ok?" He covers the mouthpiece and looks at me. "I have to take this, I'll be right back."

"Okay," I say with a smile. Jase turns from me and walks quickly back to the bedroom area of the suite, closing the door to give him some privacy. At the sound of that click, I lay back, a lazy smile touching my lips, then it fades just as quickly.

What the hell am I doing?

Okay, obviously I know what I am doing, but how the holy hell did this happen? Especially when I had been so, so sure that he wouldn't want anything to do with me. And he had said there was someone else! What...the hell... am I doing?

How many times has he asked me if we know each other?

How many times have I insisted that we do not?

My phone vibrating in my pocket interrupts my thoughts. I laugh softly thinking to myself what that would have been like if Jase was still out here, pressed up against me when it happened. *That* would have gone over wonderfully.

I glance at the unrecognizable number but seeing that it isn't a blocked call and not knowing if it is one of the newly transplanted doctors at the hospital where I work, I answer. Hell, I never know when it is an emergency.

"Hello?"

The other end of the phone is completely silent.

"Helloooooooo?" I hear a 'click' as the person on the other end of the phone hangs up and I shrug. 'Wrong number,' I think, then giggle at the thought.

I hear the door to the bedroom open as Jase walks out slowly. He places his phone on a random table as he walks towards me where I lay on the couch, his face unreadable. I sit up, taking in his change of demeanor, watching the way he approaches me. He moves slowly, meticulously, every step causing my pulse to quicken. He reaches down, removing my cell phone from my hand, not even glancing at it as he lightly tosses it to the other end of the couch. My breath catches in my throat as I look up at him, the light illuminating from behind him casting his face in shadows.

He looks like an angel...just like an angel...with the devil in his eyes...

He stops beside me, his expression taut, his eyes shimmering. I notice a muscle in his jaw twitching, and I wonder how long it will take him to tell me it is time for me to leave.

That had to have been her, the someone else.

Right now, I wish with everything in me that I had left after he'd told me about her the first time. He watches silently as I stand and raise my eyes to his face. He looks so troubled, almost heartbroken. Part of me wants to comfort him, take him in my arms, tell him it will be okay.

The other part of me is thinking selfishly that he should suffer for leading me on.

You picked the wrong person to play your game with, Jase.

"I should go," I say, holding my chin up defiantly. His eyes slide shut as I speak, and when he opens them, I can almost swear they are filling with tears.

"Why?" His voice is barely above a whisper, causing my anger to rise. The fucking *nerve* of this guy!

"Is that a rhetorical question, or do you really want an answer?"

I know it is harsh, but damn it does he expect anything less?

But the look on his face, the one that looks like I've just kicked him in his gut with my words, hurts down to my soul. *Don't do it, Talia... don't... don't fall...*

"Oh...all right..."

What the hell? How can he act as if I am wounding him when here he was trying to get into my pants, when there was someone else? How can he turn this around on *me* when the one he wished he was with had stopped him, stopped us?

My eyes blaze with anger, but I decide against having a full-blown argument. He wants his Elizabeth so badly? He can fucking have her.

I move to walk past him to get my shoes and phone, but he gently touches my arm, his fingers like five small suns burning into me. I glare back up at him, doing my best, holding onto my resolve with all I have.

I can't fall… I should have known better…

"Talia, I just…" He shrugs, looking so forlorn. "Are you gonna say goodbye?"

That hits me like a sucker punch, and I feel as if all the air has escaped the room.

Jase *never* says goodbye to me.

It is always good night, or until later…never goodbye. He will chastise me, remind me to never say those words to him, and now…

Damn you… damn you straight to hell…

I can't do it.

I open my mouth, willing the words to come, screaming them from my brain, but…silence.

Silence and two large tears that spill over my lashes.

He reaches up as if instinctively, cupping my face with his palms, brushing the tears away with his thumbs. I try willing the tears to stop, but the effort is futile as I look into his eyes, so full of emotion I can't place my finger on. I don't want to walk away, I don't want to lose my confidante, I haven't wanted to admit how much I have come to depend on him.

"Why the tears, then?" His question, spoken so softly, seems out of place, but I don't have time to answer as he leans in to gently kiss my lips. This is meant to be his goodbye; it has to be…

"Oh…god…" I breathe against his lips, my brain registering that no matter how much I care, no matter how much I want him at this moment, this is it, the end of the line…

Our bodies decide otherwise as all friendliness flees from our touches, and piece by piece our clothing is discarded across the floor. He throws that black tank top that has worked so well for me across the room and makes short work of my bra as we fall back into the couch. His hands, his lips find their way down to my breasts where he kisses every inch, nipping, sucking, responding to every moan and sigh from me. His hands are spread wide, his calloused fingers trailing down my side, reaching between us, settling between my legs, and he moans as he feels the heat that seems to be radiating from me.

How long have I wanted this?

How many nights have I dreamt of his hands on me, moving, seeking, gripping...

I push him up to try and gain control, and he shrugs out of his shirt that I have finally managed to unbutton. We turn and I end on top of him, straddling him precariously as I nip at his neck while unbuttoning his jeans.

"Fuuuuuck." He draws out, his hips surging up towards my hand as I reach down into the fabric, touching him intimately for the first time. I wrap my fingers around him, moving my hand in time with our bodies, my thumb circling the tip with each squeeze as I pull my hand up.

Have I ever wanted someone this much?

No... no, I know I haven't.

And here we are, just as I'd imagined us to be.

Turning as one, cushions coming with us, we are on the floor as he finishes kicking off the remainder of his clothing and urgently begins to undo my jeans. I gasp as he yanks them down, tossing them to the side, and stares at me like a predator studying his prey. He is completely naked, his skin glistening with sweat as he kneels beside me, his eyes drinking me in.

And I'm not afraid.

I'm not ashamed.

I've never felt so alive, so desirable as I do in this moment.

I watch through heavy lids as he moves, roughly pushing my legs apart before continuing his sensual assault, starting with my thighs. His open-mouthed wet kisses on the inside of my thighs have me moaning, sighing, begging for mercy. And then... then, I watch him take that lace thong of mine in his teeth and slowly, meticulously pull it down my body.

Fuck...me...

I can honestly say this is the first time any man has dared to tease me in such a way, biting, nibbling, sucking on my inner thighs. The harder he bites, the better it feels, and the wetter I get. I can't take it, can't handle the teasing anymore. I bury my hands in his hair, pulling him up further, my hips surging upwards as he finally reaches exactly where my body is screaming for him to be.

His tongue is swirling, stroking, teasing me, leaving no mistake he intends to have me screaming before tonight is over, lack of voice be damned. Somehow, we've ended up on the other end of the couch, though still on the floor, as he brings me closer and closer to that edge. As my whimpers and cries grow, he pins my hips down on that floor, holding me still and refusing to let me move until the last moan and sigh.

Holy hell, that man... oh, he's so... so very good.

I whimper softly afterwards as he kisses his way up my body, to the base of my neck, latching onto that sensitive spot where my pulse is still throbbing.

I feel alive, invigorated, insatiable as his mouth meets mine once more, the taste of me on him driving my desire to an unmatched peak. What the hell is he doing to me? I feel the pressure building again, knowing there is no way we are done. I wouldn't be done with him until he was inside of me, spent, satiated.

We are moving again as he drags me off that floor, the hard, bruising kisses making me ache even more for a bigger release. There are no gentle touches, no caresses, no sweet nothings whispered in my ear. What is before me is a man possessed, a man driven by passion, a man intent on finding release. The sheer heat, the blinding desire, holds me captive, my body screaming for more... more lips, more teeth, more tongue, more...

A gasp leaves my lips as I am slammed against the wall, a table next to us toppling over. A large vase crashes against the wall, the glass scattering in the carpet as he pushes me roughly towards the bedroom, pausing his kisses only briefly as he pushes me back on the bed. I hit with a bounce and he is instantly on top of me, parting my legs with his knee.

"Please... please..." I am begging, pleading with him as he pushes first one, and then a second finger inside of me.

"Please what?" he murmurs in my ear, his fingers pumping in and out, making me writhe beneath him.

"Fuuuuck, *please...* oh, please."

He buries his face in my neck, a long moan escaping him as I am breathlessly pleading. Just when I can't take it anymore, he presses up against me, our legs entwined, a thin sheen of sweat covering us both when I hear his voice, his words spoken up against my lips.

"Open your eyes."

It is an effort, they feel so heavy...but I do as he asks, wondering if mine are as bright as his at this moment. This is it, what I have wanted for so many weeks, to be skin to skin with the man who has captured my heart.

He reaches up and holds my hand, never losing eye contact, and with one swift movement I am in pure ecstasy. He shudders and moans, his breath coming in ragged gasps from merely the first thrust inside of me. And oh... oh my, it feels... so very good. He fills me completely, leaving my body little time to adjust to him before I feel my muscles already begin to quiver.

For one brief moment, we lay there, our eyes and bodies locked together in the most intimate embrace. He slowly releases my hand, his expression softening for a fraction of a second before his eyes grow dark once more.

My eyelids slide shut as he begins to move against me, each thrust harder, pushing... punishing, it seems. His eyes never leave my face as he holds me captive, body and soul. Even when I gasp, cry out as best I can, moan, plead, ask for more, faster, harder, his eyes stay focused on my face, on my expression. Every time I opened my eyes, there is his gaze.

I cry out, arching my back as the first wave passes over me, our bodies touching nearly head to toe. His name is torn from the back of my throat, somehow my voice finding its way back for that one moment when I feel I've nearly died and gone to heaven.

Is... is that a sob... from him?

I have no time to think, to question as he roughly turns me on my side, my back to him, and pulls flush up against his body. "This... isn't over..." he moans, pushing himself inside of me once more.

"Jase..."

"Is this what you wanted?" He grabs my hips roughly, pulling me back towards him as he thrusts forward.

"Yes... yes..." I am lost once more as he continues, driving against me as hard as he can.

"Then you got it, babe," he growls into my ear, sending me spiraling into another orgasm that he rides straight through into the next one.

Time has no meaning for either of us; phones have been discarded, couches in disarray, tables are toppled over...all that matters is each other, the pleasure being given and received, the intimacy that it seems we both crave. As the early morning rays of sunrise begin to peak through the heavy curtains, we lay there breathing heavily next to each other, the sheets and blankets all pushed off the bed. I damn that man for the look in his eyes as he reaches over, brushing a sweat-slicked curl off my forehead-- the first gentle, sweet gesture in hours-- as I drift off to sleep.

And I damn my heart for falling in love with him.

CHAPTER 13

I'm not sure when Jase had quietly slipped from the room, but I wake alone in the large bed with the comforter pulled up around my shoulders. It is almost a startle-wake, one where you are having what you think is a strange dream and you realize you're in a strange place, and... bam! My eyes open to just a sliver of light in the room, and my arm is thrown to the opposite side of the bed.

He is gone.

I remember quite distinctly that all covers had ended up on the floor and we hadn't bothered to pick them up, and a smile touches my lips as I realize he had to have covered me when he got up. The optimistic part of me, the part that remembers the look on his face as I drifted to sleep, believes he did it to show a little kindness. That has to be it, right?

I stretch with a soft sigh, and then wince as my muscles begin screaming at me. Holy hell, it hurts to move. My poor, poor thighs...

So, so worth it.

Out of the corner of my eye I glimpse what looks like my overnight bag. I blink, rubbing the sleep from my eyes as they adjust to the lack of lighting, then I fumble for the switch to the lamp. Sure enough, there are my things. Not just my overnight bag, either. There is another small bag beside it with the clothing I'd worn the night before, along with my cell phone perched on top of it. Next to that sits my boots, neatly placed as if he's taken his time to arrange it. Well, huh. A small note in slanted writing is placed in the opening of my right boot, sticking out enough so that I will be certain to see it.

Had some stuff to do. Be back soon.

The slanted writing is familiar, but all I can think of is how it seems a little impersonal after the night we just shared.

Then again, there is someone else in his life.

I guess this is what I asked for, sleeping with an up and coming rock star, someone who has the world in front of him and a hefty amount of sales of his albums to prove it. I will never be someone special, just… next. And yet, I did it anyway, and here I sit alone, my heart taking intermittent turns between soaring and splintering. I never thought Not John would be so cold, so cruel. He hadn't left me with that impression, no matter what conversation we were having, no matter his mood.

Apparently, I was wrong.

I take a long hot shower, trying to wash all reminders of the evening from me, although I am sure it will take a while for those bite marks between my thighs to fade. Just another reminder to take with me, I suppose.

I towel dry my hair, letting the curls fall around my face, and barely put on any makeup. What is the point, right? No one to impress. I figure now is the best time to make my exit while he is away; if he wants to be the kind of guy who screws around on this "someone else", or if he is the kind to use someone to forget about his precious Elizabeth, he won't get the satisfaction of even watching my backside as I walk out of his life. A little vindictive, yes…and in the next moment I have to stop the tears from flowing.

Walking out on Jase is walking out on Not John.

He deserves better than that.

Even though I have my things gathered together, I have no intentions of leaving this suite without telling him everything. And I mean everything... down to when I'd known and why I hadn't said anything. I only hope he will listen. So, I decide that while he is gone, I'll go make myself comfortable on his couch and go over every minute detail of every little thing I have to say.

This has the potential of being very, very bad, I know this. It should have been said the night before; I know this as well.

I could easily walk out the door to the suite and never look back, still have the possibility of having Not John in my life.

I just don't think I can live with myself if I say nothing.

I throw my duffle bag on my shoulder and walk out of the bedroom, turning to shut the door, ready to get this started, to come up with everything I need to say.

"You found everything okay?"

Jase's voice causes me to jump and screech, holding my heart as I turn around.

Fucking hell, I was not expecting him here.

"Yes, thank you." My voice has nearly returned to normal, but he shows no sign of surprise as he sits there on the couch, its cushions firmly back in place. He looks as if he's barely slept at all, the dark circles under his eyes adding to the morose expression on his face. He tries to hide his grimace as he moves to set his guitar aside, but he doesn't stand; it was as if he is afraid to, or perhaps it hurts him as much as it hurts me. Even the last thought can't bring a smile to my face, knowing what I have to do. "Who brought my things?" I ask, trying to cut through the blanket of tension in the room.

"If I'm not mistaken, I believe it was the Italian gypsy."

Wait, we hadn't brought that up last night...

Oh, fuck.

There goes my bravado. I silently walk over and sink down on the couch across from him, keeping eye contact the entire time.

Where do I go from here?

What do I say?

114

"Nothing to say? I think that's a first." Oh, his words are biting. Cold. "You couldn't even come up with a better bullshit middle name? Elizabeth? Fucking...*Elizabeth*? *Really*? That was harsh, even for you."

Even for me?

My eyes close briefly as I remember all the stories of a lost love who had broken his heart, unable to count the number of times he and I have spoken about her.

"Then again," he continues, his tone icy, "it really fits you."

While I know I deserve his anger, it doesn't alleviate the pain it causes. I know I was wrong—there was no question about it—but does he have to be so cruel?

"Are you done?" I ask, keeping my tone steady as best I can.

"When did you know?" Wait, are his eyes red? It has to be from exhaustion. I mean, he wouldn't be that upset over something... someone... like me. "How long have you been playing me for a fucking fool, Talia?"

What? "I wasn't—"

"When!" he demands, cutting off my feeble attempts at telling him I haven't played him.

This isn't a game to me.

"Thursday." Lying is futile at this point, the damage is already done. I can't tell if it is a laugh or a sob from him as he covers his eyes for an instant before he regains what little of his composure he is holding onto.

"Thursday," he repeats softly, his eyes still cast downward.

When he brings he gaze back up to me, the anger and hurt etched in his features, I want to cry. But his words...

"And you said nothing. Not on the phone, not in the store, not at the concert, not back here..."

Every syllable from him adds to the inconceivable guilt I already feel, but I keep my chin held high. "The reasons seem rather moot at this point."

"No...no, they're not. You had every chance in the world... I even... hell, I even practically asked you to your damn face, and *nothing!* Why? Damn it, Talia... *why?*" There is no hiding the hurt in his features, in his voice when he asks, sounding almost like a lost child. "What...what did I do? What did I do that was *so wrong*? We... we *both* had that anonymity, and it was okay, but then..." His voice trails off once more as he takes several deep breaths, once again regaining some semblance of control. "Why wasn't... why wasn't I worth the truth?"

That *hurts*.

"Don't think that," I say quickly. "That's not what happened, Jase."

"No, no... I asked you last night," he leans forward, and it almost looks as if he's fighting back tears. "I asked you *why*, and you said, 'Is that a rhetorical question'. This time, I want to know."

No, no... "You asked why I was leaving,"

"No, I didn't, Talli, and you *know* better." He pauses, clenching his jaw with his eyes closed tight. When he opens his eyes again, they're harder, darker than they were before. "You said you could get your messages, you had the number, you knew it was me calling."

What? Oh...no, no, no...

"Jase, I couldn't get to my messages."

"Oh, bullshit." He stands then, turning away from me and running a shaking hand through his hair.

"I couldn't remember my code."

"Stop."

"I was coming out here to tell you."

"Stop!" He turns to me, hastily wiping his eyes. "No more lies...please. I can't take... Just tell me why."

"I'm not lying to you. Not now." I can't stop my own tears from forming at this, and not only from shame. I know I was wrong, but I have to explain it to him. "It was because..." My face turns pink at the thought of what has happened on the very couch where I sit. "Because of..."

"Because of what I do, because of who I am..."

"No, but..." I stop suddenly, realizing that regardless of the consequences, regardless of obvious error of my ways, he needs to know my exact reasoning. "Okay, *yes*...but not the way you are thinking right now."

"How very presumptuous of you; you obviously don't know me at all."

"You asked for a reason, I'm trying to tell you." His glare could bring me to my knees, but I continue. "I...thought that if you knew this was me...this..." I emphasize the word by pointing at my less-than-perfect body, "was me, the person you'd been talking to that you wouldn't..." The blush creeps over my entire body as I see a small mark on the side of his neck as he turns slightly away, proving I had been wrong. He looks back at me, his eyes narrow, full of hurt.

"Nice opinion you have of me; remind me to return the compliment someday."

"Does it make you feel better, Jase? To talk to me this way?"

"Don't turn this around on me."

"No, let's hear it from you, Jase, when did *you* know?" I stand up, walking over to him.

"The message was very fucking clear, Talia."

Oh, the way he says my name is cold. "I didn't get the message, how many times do I have to tell you?" I wince as he backs away from me. "Okay, now your reasons. Why?"

"Why what?" he snaps.

"Why did you sleep...no, you haven't slept yet..." He steps back again as I reach to brush a strand of hair out of his eyes. "Why did you have sex with me?" The muscle in his jaw twitches again. "Couldn't very well call it making love, could you? So come on, let's hear it."

"Did you come up here expecting to be treated like an object?" he asks, his voice breaking slightly. "That's what you came up here for?" It is still worded as a question, and I shake my head no.

"But you slept with me knowing...that there was someone else," I continue.

"Someone else," he repeats, then lets out a short laugh. "Wow, that's... nice."

"You said it, damn it, not me!" I can't help my voice from rising, and my finger is pointed directly at him. "You said..."

"I was talking about *you*!"

His admission leaves me speechless, a trembling mess wanting so badly to reach out to him. Me? He is... he feels...or felt...

"Stop playing the innocent victim who had no fucking clue how I felt, Talia."

Past tense. Felt. But for such a biting tone, his expression just doesn't match.

"I wouldn't know; I told you..."

"Why did you, Talli?" He pauses again as he uses that nickname again. "Why did you...have sex with me?" His voice is soft now, his eyes searching for answers in my face.

"I wanted to." It sounds so trite now, but I can't lie to him anymore.

"Jase the rock star." The bitterness is still there, but it is as if he can't put forth the effort to try to hurt me anymore.

"No...no, that's not true,"

"It's ok, Talia, I'm used to it now," he says, a thin smile on his face, his eyes a little glassy. Tears? I don't know; I can't ask. "I just thought you were different, and that if you knew me...knew...*me* first, then you could accept the rest. And I thought you would, but...I was wrong." He shrugs sadly, brushing off my hand as I place it on his arm.

"You weren't..."

"You," he interrupts me again. "You were the one crazy thing in this whole fucked up ride that...made some sort of sense, and I looked forward to sharing everything with you, and I thought maybe it was that way for you, too," he ends, his voice trailing off as he finally brings his gaze back to me.

"It is," I try to say, but he shuts his eyes and shakes his head slowly.

"You don't have to pretend anymore, I promise," he says, trying to smile at me. He reaches out and catches one of my tears with his fingertips. "Talia...Christine. You are so... so very wrong, you know that? Can you... can you remember that? Please? You... you are absolutely beautiful."

I can't hold back the tiny sob that escapes me when he steps forward and takes me into his arms. He isn't warm or inviting as he had been, and even wrapped in his embrace I can feel him holding himself back.

I feel his words resonating in his chest, shooting straight through me. "I guess this is it."

My heart seems to stop dead in its tracks. No, no, no, no...

"It doesn't have to..."

"I can't go back," he states as I feel a tear fall. He shrugs again as he steps back, both of us visibly shaken by these turns of events. I look up at him as he seems to struggle with his next words.

I ask myself over and over *"What have I done"*, but the answer is as obvious as the disappointment etched in his features.

"I can't say it," he admits, stepping even further away... he is trying to tell me goodbye; I know it. "I can't fucking say it." He inhales sharply, closing his eyes.

"Then don't," I beg him, my voice thick with emotion. "Please..."

"Talli... this has to be..."

I reach up and cover his full, perfect mouth with my fingertips.

"Until later," I say, my eyes pleading with him to say the same.

We stand there for a moment, each of us broken, hurting. A strange sensation floods over me as I almost swear he lightly kisses my fingertips before he places his hand on my wrist and gently moves them away. He stands there silent for one last brief moment before turning away and walking back towards the couch, away from me, away from everything I have completely fucked up.

Without another word, I grab my duffle bag and walk out the door.

CHAPTER 14

I sleep most of the way home or attempt to at least. I still can't wrap my head around everything that has happened. I replay bits and pieces of the entire night over in my head, wondering how the hell he knew. I stare at the phone number in my call log, the one just before Jase had walked out of the bedroom.

Oh…

Oh, fuck.

That… that was him.

"You had the number; you knew it was me calling…"

How could I be so fucking stupid?

I lightly trace the number with my fingertips, committing it to memory, arguing with that devil on my shoulder.

I can't call him. I… I can't.

I'd tried apologizing to him, and he wouldn't listen. I'd tried explaining myself, and I'd only made it worse. If I called that number, what would I say?

I didn't mean to fall in love with you…

I listen to Tish and Cass ribbing Jaden over her night with Pete, which I'd only heard a tiny bit about when I'd returned to the room that morning, and a tear runs down my cheek.

There will be no teasing me.

There will be no fun-filled night of gossip and gasping, no withholding only certain small details.

There will be no laughing denials the way Jaden is right now.

No. No, with me there will be shame. And guilt. And hurt. And anger.

And a man too beautiful for words... an angel, with the devil in his eyes.

"Talia, we're back." Cass is shaking my shoulder slightly. I hadn't even noticed we had stopped moving.

I wipe the sleep from my eyes and attempt to stretch before wincing in pain. "Thanks."

Tish pipes up as she grabs her bag. "Um, Ms. Thang, you realize we haven't had a full report from you?"

And they never will.

"Oh... um... can we do it later?" I ask instead.

"Awww, please? Jaden won't spill her deets with Pete, and we want to hear *something*."

"There's nothing to spill with me and Pete," Jaden adds.

"Whatever." Cass's tone indicates she doesn't believe Jaden for a second.

"I have much ice cream in the freezer," Tish tries to entice me.

"I have a bed in my room calling my name saying I don't need to hear it," Moira pipes up from her seat in between Cass and me, and I laugh softly.

They'll never let me out of this if I don't say at least something to them. "I... um, I promise I'll give a full update later, okay?" It's a lie, one that I am hoping no one catches onto.

I think Jaden is pouting. "Damn, I was hoping I'd be off the hook."

Tish's eyes are on me, I can feel it even as I shimmy out of the seat. "As long as you promise."

"Of course." Another lie, but I paste on my best grin. "Um... Cass, you need me to drive you home?"

"We're doing pizza here, remember?"

Oh, right. Pizza, the DVD, and going over every detail of the concert that we can remember.

I just can't.

"I… I'm sorry, you guys. I'm in desperate need of sleep. I need to get home."

I can already feel a fresh batch of tears forming, and I'm not ready to deal with it, not publicly, not when I still can't grasp everything that has happened myself.

Tish gives me a one-armed hug. "I think you get a free pass on this one. But soon, yes? If not before, then this Friday?"

Cass's smile is beaming. "How perfect will that girls' night be?"

How perfect?

It won't be.

Because I fucked everything up.

If they only knew.

Escaping to the solitude of my apartment somehow doesn't have the same appeal to me. It seems cold, uninviting compared to how it had felt, how I had felt, before.

Even without Jase having physically been here, memories of him are everywhere, clinging to my skin the way he had with his own hands mere hours before. I walk over towards my papasan chair, stopping short as I remember the morning I'd sent a hug to him over the phone. No, I can't sit there, not yet. I turn to my couch, a tear threatening as I remember stretching out there as we had a long-involved conversation about a person traveling with him. "He's Alfred to my Batman," he had said with the sweetest laugh.

"Jackie," I say out loud to the empty, echoing room, and I smile. I had once imagined this person old, graying, proper, stuffy… having now met Jackie, I have to laugh.

But I have no one to laugh with this time.

I never knew how much it could hurt to truly be alone.

Next to the couch is my answering machine, the ancient one I'd brought with me when I'd moved away from home, the one I use to screen calls, the one I can retrieve the messages to from anywhere so long as I know the code. Lucky for me, here I can just push the button. A large number "4" is blinking at me, taunting me of what is on the other end.

Do I listen to his messages?

Do I hear his voice that a few short hours before had been in my ear, moaning, telling me exactly what he was going to do? Do I hear his voice that just this morning had chastised me, yelled at me, tried to... to say goodbye to me?

Too weary to deal with any more heartache, I curl up on the couch beside that answering machine and try to cry the 'what-ifs' away.

For the next four days, I stay in denial land, not answering the phone, not checking messages. Essentially, I go back to being the old Talia: the prude one, the aloof one, the loner, the outsider. I go to school, or work, or my internship, come home, and spend most of my time here curled up watching TV or sleeping my lack-of-life away. I don't tell anyone what had happened, I don't enlighten even Iris when she asks me during one of my shifts. I can't tell her, even though I know she has seen the change in me.

I see the change in me.

And a couple days during that lovely stint of self-loathing, I even skip class, just to avoid running into Jaden, or any reminders of that night, or that class we'd taken, or that stupid paper on fate. It wasn't 'fate' that my anonymous phone friend turned out to be none other than Jase Warner, the same Jase that Jaden knows, the same Jase that is the brother of the guy that Jaden may or may not be seeing. Every instinct in me is screaming to go to her, talk to her, ask her if everyone hates me, but it doesn't matter much now.

I can't even read my book, focus on anything of the boy named J.

Here on night four of my self-imposed solitude, I am flipping through the channels cursing the lack of decent programming. Should I pull out a movie? While I'm contemplating this, my phone rings for about the millionth time. I glance at the caller i.d., hoping for a miracle; instead, I see the hospital's number and again damn my romantic heart.

Jase won't call.

When I answer, I expect it to be someone calling me in or asking about a chart. Instead it is my oldest sister, Lisa.

This can't be good.

"Talia, we've been trying to reach you," she is saying, sounding exasperated. "We're at the hospital with mother."

I sit up abruptly, fear and alarm coursing through my veins. "What happened?"

"It's her heart."

No... no, not Mom. *Not my Mom*. With everything I've already lost, I can't lose her, too. I mean, I know she has a heart condition—I know, because I'd been born with nearly the same thing—but it hasn't bothered her in years. She hasn't had any episodes of even the slightest arrhythmia since about a year after Dad passed away.

I think I break all speeding laws driving to the hospital and give the night nurse a look that could kill when she attempts to inform me that visitors' hours are over. Don't lecture me on the rules of the hospital I work my ass off at, especially not in the section I've been interning in.

When I walk into my mom's room, she is sleeping peacefully. The machines...so many machines, and I know what each of them are for. Without any staff speaking to me, I know how serious the situation is. I sit beside her and lean against her bed rail before I reach in and take her soft hand in mine.

"Talli?" She asks this without opening her eyes.

I sniffle slightly. "How'd you know it was me?"

"Your hands are always so soft...so soft and so warm."

They are? What is that wives' tale... oh, right. I squeeze her hand just a little. "Guess that means I have a cold heart?"

"No, don't be silly." She barely opens her eyes and smiles that warm, loving smile. I need that. It is the first warmth I've felt in days. "You're the one exception to that rule that I know of."

I wish, Mom... I really wish that were true.

"I can actually disagree with you on that one," I say as one tear escapes from me and falls to her pillow.

"Nonsense." She looks exhausted, her skin too pale, the circles around her eyes too dark. "Just ask that Not John of yours; I'm sure any lonely soul reaching out knows when a heart is warm."

I blink a couple of times, not quite knowing what to say. I mean... she didn't believe me, right?

"Did you really think I was that naïve?" She attempts to smile up at me, and in that one sweet moment I know.

I know.

She knows everything there is about me, the good and the bad. She has her rose colored glasses on most of the time, I'm sure, but... no judgment. No criticism. No wishing I were different, no being any less proud that I didn't follow an easier path.

And I love her even more for it.

"Enough of that now, we'll talk more tomorrow. Then you can apologize profusely for everything you did in my bedroom as a teenager." She pats my hand as I laugh for the first time in days. Oh, that is going to be an awkward conversation.

"I love you, Mom," is all I can say. I lean in to kiss her cheek softly. "I'll be back in the morning, first thing, okay?"

"Just come in with your normal shift, baby. You have school, too."

"No... no, I... I'm setting my alarm, and I'll be here. Bright and early. With... with bells on, except..."

"...you don't have any bells," she finishes for me. "I love you too, Talli. You... you do a lot of good, you bring a lot of light to this world."

If only I could believe her.

I am reluctant to leave, standing outside her door watching the monitors through the small glass window. I remember back to my childhood, running to her in tears, begging for her to take all my troubles away, and I curse myself for growing so distant.

Why have I done that?

Why have I done that with everyone in my life? Why have I pushed them all away? Is it anyone else's fault that I've made the mistakes I have? No. Is anyone else responsible for my actions? No.

"Talia?" Dr. Craig, the new hotshot cardiologist, walks up to me. He holds out his hand and I shake it, not really giving a damn if he is trying to impress me as he has the reputation for doing with most of the nurses. He flashes his dimples before continuing. "I'm taking the best possible care of your mother. She's stable, resting comfortably. You should probably…"

"…go home, get some rest, and let us do our jobs. Oh, and I can come see her in the morning, right Dr. Craig?" I pause then, my eyebrow raised. "Did you forget for a moment that I know what's going on?" I jot down my home phone number on a notepad I always keep with me. "This is my number, I don't care how insignificant the change, you call me."

He glances down at it briefly, his eyebrows raising beneath his bangs. "Damn, our numbers are only a couple digits apart."

I roll my eyes at him, my hand resting on my hip as I wait for him to acknowledge my demands, and I don't really care how difficult this could potentially make it for me if I work with him.

"I promise, Ms. Emerson, that I will call you the moment there is any change. If I can't do it personally, one of these nurses at this desk will," he adds, winking in their direction, smiling smugly as they giggle.

He is the least of my worries, though. One last glance at my mom, so sure of herself when she'd said those words about Not John, and I know what I need to do.

That doesn't mean I go straight for the answering machine as soon as I get home.

No, first, I need ice cream. A pint of it. Mint chocolate chip, because Jase told me I should try it some time.

And a pillow.

And my jammies.

Then, I curl up beside the machine, my finger lingering above the button for a moment before I quickly press it and settle back into the couch to listen. My heart is pounding before message one ever plays, and when the voice of some computer telemarketing device comes through the small speaker I mutter, "Oh, shut up," and hit the skip button.

"Hi...um...Not Telling...Christine. I know this is your voicemail or answering machine or whatever because I recognized your voice and even though you didn't give your name, I know the phone number you recited, and wow." He was speaking so fast, he sounded so happy...my heart longs to hear that lift in his voice just one last time. "You know, I really wish you'd answered your phone because...well, because...I think I just saw you."

This must have been after the store. I smile through my tears as I take a bite of mint chocolate chip ice cream. I should have told him then.

"Just...now, here at this hotel that I'm at, I swear it was you. I just..." he pauses, and now having met him face to face I can almost see him doing hand gestures trying to relay his message. "I just...felt like it was you. And, um...if it was, I...well, I'm the...I'm the asshole that handed the Tops Migraine to you and didn't run after you to ask if I had honestly been that lucky. Oh, fuck, that was cheesy, but damn it...that's what you do to me. I swear..." He paused again, giving me a moment to wipe another tear away and reach for a tissue. "But, if it wasn't you, then there's something you need to know.

"See, I'm on the road right now, but you knew that... I'm on tour. This is me, Not John...and my real name is Jase. Jase Warner. And I swear I'm not lying, and...and, please tell me you're not the type of person that would matter to." I sob at his words as the message continues. "I just...feel like you know me, we know each other, and it wouldn't matter, and I guess I'm trying to find out if I was wrong."

I set the ice cream aside, sick to my stomach, wishing I could turn the clock back.

"So...this is my number..." I mouth the numbers as I'd memorized them on the way back from Cleveland, staring at it in my call history. "And this is just me asking you to call. No more pretending." My heart feels as if it is going to come out of my chest, remembering some of his last words to me, *"You don't have to pretend anymore, I promise."*

"I'd ask if you wanted to do something after the show, but...if you've seen any of the gossip shows or whatever, you kinda know what me and Pete did...you know, I think I'm kinda grounded for the next few days." I laugh through my tears at that one, then pause reflectively, remembering Moira's question for him. Was this another reason he believed I'd heard the message? "Not that I would tell Pete, because he'll never let me live it down. But I can tell you..."

The beep shows where my answering machine had decided to cut him off, leaving me sobbing quietly on the couch as the next message starts to play.

"Damn, I hate it when that happens!" I laugh as Jase's voice fills my empty heart once more. "Stupid machines, that's why you should answer your phone! Except either you're sleeping, or busy, or it wasn't you in the store...or it was and you're avoiding me." Even though he said it with a laugh, it still brings another onslaught of tears. "But, yeah...I have so much to do before tonight's show. I hope you're there."

"I was," I say out loud to that stupid machine that I can't remember the stupid code to.

"And...if not, I'm in Cleveland Saturday and Sunday too, before I leave. Pete has to leave after the show; we'll have time, just you and me...if you want. And then you can tell me that I'm absolutely crazy, and I can say that no...I'm just crazy about you. So, there. There you go, Ms. Not Telling Christine. Until later." Then with the click of the phone, he is gone.

I hit the stop button to gather my senses, letting everything sink in.

Wow.

Wow...he ...he felt it, too. He felt the same way I had, and... and...

I deserve every cruel, hateful word he had sent my way, but I need to explain it to him, somehow. I just feel clueless how to fix it.

Brushing my tears away with sheer determination in my brain, I know it is time for reinforcements, although I'm not so sure how they feel about me at this point. I know Tish and Jaden have tried to call several times, and I'm sure some of the accumulating messages that I have yet to listen to are from them. If Pete had called anyone on that list of phone numbers they'd talked about giving to him, I am also sure they know exactly what I had done to his brother and how I deserve anything Jase threw at me and then some.

There is only one way to find out.

I hit play again for the rest of the messages, the next one being some kind of mumbled failed attempt at me trying to get to my messages since I couldn't remember my code. I laugh bitterly at how fate—there's that damn word—had decided to screw me once more before reminding myself that no, I did this.

Me.

I walk to my kitchen, the answering machine still going. The next one is from Tish asking if I am okay, because something seemed a little off to her.

Then there is Jaden, and I can tell from her voice that she was more than a little concerned. I guess she may have talked to Pete at this point, and I contemplate what he could have said to her while I wipe up a mess on my counter. At least she doesn't sound like she hates me, or she didn't at the time.

There are at least two more from each of them along with various so-important-a-computer-has-to-make-the-call messages, which instead of forwarding I let play just so I won't have to walk back out to the living room. As the messages are winding down, I am gaining the courage to call Jaden, which I should have done days ago. I walk towards the table where that damn machine sits and have almost reached it when I stop in my tracks.

One familiar voice, two simple words.

"I'm sorry."

CHAPTER 15

I lose count of how many times I hit the replay button, just to hear those two words from him. Each time, I find myself analyzing, over-analyzing, re-analyzing exactly what it is he could have meant.

Other than the obvious.

He's sorry. I get that.

But what is he sorry for?

I check the time and date stamp, my heart pounding in my chest feeling as if it will come out of my ribcage at any moment. Oh hell...*yesterday*. Why couldn't I have checked my messages sooner? Why did I stop forwarding my calls to my cell? Why...

I stop pacing back and forth for a moment, collecting my thoughts.

Do I call?

Do I not call?

And what is he sorry for—the way he reacted, how we left it, or the fact that he slept with me? And if he's sorry for that... do I really want to know?

I continue agonizing my over-analyzation of his short message while glancing at the clock, worrying about my mom and waiting for regular visitors' hours to commence. Sleep? What the hell is sleep? It certainly isn't coming tonight. I mean, how am I supposed to sleep when my mom's in the hospital, my friends probably want to kill me, and Jase... is... sorry?

What's a girl to do?

"I called in reinforcements."

I remember Jase saying once, referring to his brother whom he contacted when he was feeling so low. He isn't like me, though; when the chips are down, I draw inward, shutting out those I care about the most. It has always been a weakness of mine, and will probably continue to be, unless...

Unless I do something about it.

I jump as the phone rings, and I answer it immediately. "Hello?" I try not to sound too anxious, fearing it will be the worst of news.

"So you are alive."

Jaden.

Jaden, who apparently is getting, or has gotten, rather friendly with Jase's 19-year-old brother Pete. Jaden, who knows above all the other girls that sometimes alone time is what the doctor ordered. "Were you thinking I was someone else?"

No. Just wishing you were. "No...no... I didn't know who it would be."

"Listen, Talia, I think—"

"My mom's in the hospital," I blurt out, holding back tears. With that first tiny sliver of information, the dam seems to burst. "And...and I feel helpless, and so, so guilty...no, ashamed...I feel *ashamed* for what I've done. I don't know if you hate me, I wouldn't blame you if you did. I wouldn't... I can't blame anyone if they do, because I was wrong, and I know that, and I can't deal right now but I'm trying to, and..." I cover my mouth with my hand, choking back a sob. "I don't think I can do this alone."

Did that just come from me?

"I'm on my way," she says without hesitation, and hangs up the phone.

She wisely decides against waking the rest of the girls and shows up, a pint of ice cream of her own, ready to listen to me, listen to everything I have to say, and is met with…well, silence.

"I don't know where to start, I don't know if I should say anything." I sit down tentatively in my papasan chair for the first time since returning from our trip. "I mean… not… well, I don't know how much I can say without betraying him even more than I have."

"If it helps, there isn't much that I know," Jaden says, then takes a bite of her cookies and cream ice cream. "Pete's trying to pry info from me. I guess Jase's not talking either. With the exception that at least Pete says Jase's still *answering his phone*."

I can't help but grin. "I told you I'm sorry, damn! Way to kick a girl when she's down."

"You're right, you don't need kicked," she agrees, and then quickly adds, "You need bitch-slapped, right upside your head."

My eyes widen. "Thanks!"

She continues on, saying all the things I have been avoiding listening to, all of the things that need said.

"Look, you're the T to my J, so I'm just going to spell it out for you. To hell with all the hindsight, Talia! Who cares what who did or said, or what should have been done? He said he's sorry, for whatever reason, and it's about damn time you did the same."

"At…" I glance at the clock, "two in the morning."

"You'd be returning the favor," she comments with a grin. "Oh, oh, oh! Wait! Don't call him yet. Two thirty! Isn't that when he called?"

"Two thirty-five," I correct her, a wistful smile touching my lips. Oh, to return to the simpler times.

"So that gives you…thirty-four minutes roughly to tell me everything that happened because either Jase didn't spill to Pete, or Pete isn't spilling to me."

I wonder briefly if I should. I mean, here it is, my shot at getting everything off my chest. I can tell her the specifics without being specific, though… although she'll see right through that since I am never one to shy away from talk of sex.

What a contradiction.

I'm just... full of them.

I am still taking glances between the clock and the phone, sick with worry over my mother, contemplating what I should say when she speaks again. "Hey..." Jaden's voice is very soft now and I look over at her. "Your mom is in the best hands possible, okay? I'm just trying to help you here, if you don't want to talk about it,"

"He's... amazing," I finally say, sinking back into the chair, still smiling wistfully. "He's so funny, witty... thoughtful..."

"Holy fucknuts, he sounds so romantic."

I pause for a moment, reflecting.

Romantic?

"I don't...well, he wasn't, not with me."

Not even close.

"I don't understand."

"When...when we..."

I can't tell her about the sheer determination in his eyes, the way we greedily stole every ounce of passion from one another. It is about as far from romantic as one can get, it was...

"He...hates me," I say softly, fresh tears filling my eyes.

"What? No...no, you've got to be mistaken."

"I'm not, Jaden, he...he was so, so angry."

"I'm not asking that, I'm asking if you had sex with him!" She emphasizes with her hands and I sigh softly.

"And that's what I'm telling you."

"Angry sex? Like... get even, all hot and bothered..."

"Destroy the room and try to destroy each other...sex," I end for her. "Yes."

She sits there, spoon in her hand, its melting contents dripping into her bowl, her mouth wide open. She blinks a couple of times, mouth still open, not moving a muscle.

Now I'm even more self-conscious. "What?"

"Hot.... damn," is all she says, and she drops her spoon into her bowl and sets it aside. "Wow, that had to have been...well, aside from what millions of other women dream of..."

And therein lies the problem. He lumps me in with them.

"But he hates me, you don't get it." I take a trembling breath before I continue. "I didn't even know what was going on until the next morning."

"How so?"

"Because I went out to tell him, and that's when he blindsided me."

"Not to sound insensitive, but don't you think he was a tad bit blindsided himself?"

I lower my head at her words, knowing it is true. Of course he was blindsided. I'd been so dishonest with him; how could he even consider apologizing to me?

"You should have seen how ecstatic Pete was when he found out who you were! He couldn't wait to call Jase and give him hell over it. And you," I glance up and she points at me for emphasis, "You had said you were going to tell him yourself. And you should have, just like we told you to."

"Jaden,"

"No, listen to me, because I'm your friend and I'm going to be the first one to call you on your bullshit, got it?"

I nod slightly, wiping a single tear that has fallen.

"You have got this...this chip on your shoulder that I just don't get, other than understanding we're all our own worst critics. You are beautiful, one of the most beautiful things about you is you don't know it."

Isn't that what he'd said? Or...something similar...

"And pull your head out of your ass for one minute and look around you. You have this whole perception of yourself where you're convinced you need to lose weight, but I'm telling you that you don't. And what is this bullshit about you not thinking you're intelligent or witty enough to carry on a conversation? Do you think that I, or any of the rest of the girls, would consider you such a good friend if you were some airhead?"

"Jaden..."

I'm not even close to the same caliber as any of you.

"And you second guess yourself all the damn time!" She stands up then, pacing, arms gesturing to try to get her point across. "And then...along came this...knight of sorts, not in shining armor, but on a blocked call, a... a wrong number, and boom! There you were, there was the Talia that only a good twelve pack could bring out, and all he had to do was say hello and you would just..." She stops then and looks at me. "Did you know that Jase said your smile could light up that whole concert hall? He said that back at the hotel, when he was watching you deal out a few cards from that stupid deck, and at that time he didn't know it was *you*."

"That was for me?" I ask, briefly remembering the comment, thinking it was for Moira who was the life of our small party.

"Who'd you think it was for? How many times have we told you that you have the most beautiful smile known? But, no, you don't listen...but you know what? You're going to listen now. You're going to listen not just to me, but to what your heart is telling you to do right...now."

She reaches back and grabs the receiver to my cordless phone and sets it in front of me.

I can only shake my head. "No... *no.*"

"Don't even think about saying 'no' to me, not now," Jaden continues. "To hell with two thirty-five, you pick up that phone and you call him now. You said that last message was from him, you said he was apologizing... call him."

"I...can't."

"Don't even try to tell me you don't know his number, because Pete said he gave it to you in the message, which means now that you're home you have it. Hell, I sat there and argued for almost an hour about how you couldn't get your messages when we were in Cleveland!"

I sink back into the chair, remembering how Jase had accused me of lying about that as well. Who could blame him? And... and Pete knows about me? Pete knows about Jase leaving me a message with his number?

"When it finally sunk in, he thanked me and said he had to call his brother right away." She sits back on the couch, crossing her legs.

"When was that?" I ask, my voice small.

"Yesterday," she replies, and I stifle another sob.

"So it took that for him to apologize."

"Pardon me for stating the obvious, but technically it is *you* that needs to apologize to *him*."

"I did! I tried, and he just wouldn't listen! So what the hell am I supposed to say to him now?"

"You really want to know?" she asks incredulously. She messes with my answering machine for a moment, then Jase's voice fills the room.

"I'm sorry."

As his voice reverberates around me, Jaden's words finally sink in.

I have so much to say, so much to apologize for.

Hoping he can forgive me not only for what I have done, but also for waiting so long, I reach for the phone. Jaden giggles with delight, then whispers "Sorry," when I glare at her.

I take a deep breath, and…

The phone begins ringing, causing both of us to shriek and jump slightly.

"Is it him?" she asks excitedly, and I shake my head no as I answer, my heart up in my throat.

"Talia, this is Dr. Craig. We need you to return to the hospital immediately."

CHAPTER 16

The numbness is consuming me.

I'm staring blankly ahead as Jaden holds my hand while the words are spoken. I hear them, I register them.

I just can't believe them.

How can my mom be gone?

She... she and I are going to talk, about... about *everything*. And she is the only one in my fucked-up family that actually accepts me.

What will I do without her?

"I'm so sorry,"

"I want to see her," I interrupt the condolence speech. "Tell them...all of them... to get out. I want to see her."

"Of course, ma'am," the nurse that walked in with Dr. Craig says quietly.

Again with the ma'am... Why are they calling me ma'am?

I am trembling uncontrollably, clinging to Jaden for all it is worth. Have I cut off circulation in her hand? I'm not sure.

"Talia, you can save it for," Lisa, my dutiful older sister, is saying, but Jaden cuts her off.

"She wants to see her mom; she's going to go see her." Jaden seems unable to hide the biting anger in her voice.

"She could have seen her alive if she,"

Jaden isn't having any of this, and luckily, unlike me, she can speak. "She was here earlier, don't start your shit Lisa! And don't you open your mouth about that damned DNR, either. You knew it was what your mother wanted."

"My mother deserved better than to have people just... let her die," Lisa retorts.

But I know... I know what Mom's wishes had been.

I know because she'd told me, because I'd helped her. With Iris, with Tish I'd helped her.

"I hope you're fucking happy, Talia," Lisa practically spits out.

Happy?

My mom's... my mom's... and I'm supposed to be... happy?

"Talli," Jaden says softly, "you can go. I'll take care of this."

It seems so natural to be called 'Talli' now, as I had been back when I lost Dad.

But...

Take care of what?

Not that it matters... not that anything matters as I make my way back to Mom's room.

I walk in slowly, the silence enveloping me, suffocating me. Gone are the tubes and the wires, no more beeping machines to annoy or worry me. There is just...Mom.

Alone.

She is still, peaceful, with a serene look, perhaps just a hint of a smile on her face.

I brush a strand of hair back from her face. "You must've seen Dad." I lower myself onto the chair beside the bed, holding her hand one last time.

She is cold...so, so very cold.

"You know," I keep going, perhaps to stay sane, "you were supposed to wait for me to talk to you. See, you said we'd talk tomorrow, and I know it's tomorrow and all, but..." My voice trails off as I give her hand a squeeze she'll never feel.

"I have so much to tell you." I inhale a shaky breath and let out a short laugh. "I know how much you missed Daddy, though.

But... I just...I can't think of the last time I really, really needed to talk to you because I screwed up and..."

I bite my bottom lip, remembering our conversation just a few short hours earlier. How enlightening that had been...

"You knew, huh? Well... I mean... you... you couldn't know everything, right? I always wondered why you just seemed to fall for it, every time. Maybe... maybe you kept it up just... so you could know what was really going on. Was that it, Mom? That... that's clever. So... Mom, you're freezing."

I reach in, adjusting the cover over her before it registers in my brain she doesn't need that.

She won't need that anymore.

"You... I know you knew about Keith, Mom. I know because even when you played that game, I kept insisting it was true. And you... you would say no child you raised would do that, and... oh... god, I'm so sorry, all the things I put you through. You... you even acted like that—Keith—was worse than... than the drinking, worse than the drugs, and I know... I *know*. Maybe I was just searching for the elusive... *it*, you know? What you and Daddy had, and I know I wouldn't find it in him, in Keith. And even... even though you knew, about Keith, about the drinking, about everything... you still loved me. You still accepted me. And..."

I lean up against the rail, willing her to open her eyes, knowing it will never happen again. "How did you know that you were in love with Dad?" I pause briefly, remembering how happy they always seemed. We never knew if they had any problems, although I'm sure with them being human they did. That is where my perception of love comes from, that's what I hold so close to my heart.

The acceptance.

The complete unconditional aspects of it all.

And I'd never questioned it before, see. I figured I'd just... know, and I am sure I do, but I'd never talked to her about it, and we were going to talk about it today, and...

"Was it just a hunch, or something that you feel right here, deep inside, when you saw him, or heard his voice? Because... well..." I fight back the tears that I just don't have the time for and keep going. "Mom, I really think that I love him...Jase. Well, you know him as Not John, but he has a name, a real one, and you were right, I wasn't lying. Again. Go figure, right?" Nearly oblivious to Dr. Craig entering the room, I continue. "See, he had this number written down, but it was wrong. And I found out a little while later that it was Jase Warner...remember me telling you how much I really liked his music? Yeah, Mom, it was that Jase, can you believe it?

"But this is where I need you to... to...tell me what to do, I screwed up so bad." Again, I take in a breath, keep myself from crying. "I met him. Yep, I did, and I was so afraid that he would take one look at me and never call me again, so... I know you taught me better, Mom, I know you did... I lied to him." My voice is barely above a whisper now. "And it was horrible when he found out the truth, and I know he says he's sorry, but I don't know what for, and I don't know what to say to make this right, and this..." I look over my shoulder as Dr. Craig leaves the room, then turn back to my mom. "This is what I needed to talk to you about, because I don't know how to fix it, and I'm so, so scared of screwing this up, and I'm even more scared knowing you're not going to be there to listen to the truth, and... and to tell me you think I'm lying to you even though I'm not, and... and... to pick up the pieces."

I sit there in silence, staring at her peaceful frame. "I complained on more than one occasion how I thought you meddled in my life," I admit. But she knows that now too, doesn't she? "I'm so... so very sorry for that, you know? And when I saw you last, when we went out to dinner... it was Jase that talked me into going, and I'm sorry that I was so reluctant, so secretive all the time." I shrug as if she can see me. "That's a part of me I don't like, and I don't know how to change it. Mom... who's..." I squeeze her hand again, as if I can draw strength from her. "Who's gonna pry into my life now?"

Jaden walks in the room and comes up behind me, giving me a slight hug. "I called the girls. I called Iris, too. They wanna know if you want them to come here or meet us at your place."

Meet? No, see... meet means... I'd have to go away, and I can't.

I can't.

"She was alone, I can't... I can't leave her..."

"Talli, she's not alone anymore."

No, no tears. Not now.

"But she...she's just..."

She's so cold. Nothing... *nothing* I can do is going to make her warm again, or make her smile again, or make her laugh, or...

"Let's have them meet us at your place, okay?" Jaden says. "When you're ready." I turn to ask her how I can ever be ready when Dr. Craig enters the room.

I'm not quite sure I can read his expression.

"There's a phone call for you," he says, looking straight at me. "You can take it in my office, if you like."

Who the hell would call me here of all places? And why tonight?

"C'mon, Talli," Jaden says softly. I merely nod, still completely numb, and follow Dr. Craig down the hall to the elevators while Jaden goes out to the lobby to make the obligatory calls. As Dr. Craig and I ride to the next floor up where the offices were, he turns to me.

"She passed very suddenly, in her sleep," he says to me, his eyes troubled. He is a doctor; he sees this every day, why does it bother him? "I wanted you to know, and I'm sorry, we did what we could."

"She had that DNR for a reason," I am finally able to say, although I think it was to convince myself. He nods without saying anything else as we walk down the nearly deserted hall to his office.

"Is it Iris?" I ask, suddenly thinking she would be the only one with a more private hospital number.

"No," he replies. "I'll let your friend know you'll be down shortly."

I sit down and answer the phone, still numb, still shaking, just needing some warmth around me. I feel as cold as my mom lying lifeless just one floor below.

I am met with the softest, kindest voice I've heard in far too long.

"I'd ask if you were okay, but I already know the answer."

As if Mom is smiling down on me, Jase is there, on the line, comforting me when I need him the most.

Suddenly it is just a little easier to breathe.

"I'm sorry—"

"Stop, stop, now's not the time for that, I'm asking about you." His voice is soft and gentle. "Who's with you?"

"Jaden's downstairs." Why he would ask? She had to have been the one to let him know, even if it was through Pete.

"Good, I didn't want you to be alone."

"Thank you," I begin, but again he interrupts, perhaps not knowing what I really mean to say.

"What are friends for?"

Friends.

With me.

There isn't much of anything else that could warm my heart more.

But I need to tell him this, it is far too important. "Jase, I mean...thank you, for talking me into going to dinner with my mom that day."

"Guilting you is more like it."

"Yes, but...I wouldn't have gone, and we had the best time, and...hey! She did believe me."

"Did she, now?" he asks, his voice still soft. I've missed his voice, the way it touches my heart.

"And...we were going to talk about it tomorrow...today...Jase, do you ever sleep?"

"What?"

"It's... it's four? I think? Or is it three? Do you ever sleep?"

"Not much lately, but this isn't about me, Talia, it's about you."

"I'm fine, don't worry about me."

It's automatic.

And a lie.

I'm not fine... how can I be?

"Don't do that, please." There is something different about his tone. "I do worry about you. I can't help it."

I bite my lip to keep the tears away, his words only partly registering, but it is getting more and more difficult to hold on to my composure.

"Talia, you need to deal with this."

"Not now, please not now," I beg, not necessarily to him, but in general. My heart is already in pieces, bleeding, feeling beyond repair. If I let myself feel this too, I will explode.

"I know I'm not there right now,"

"I wish you were," I breathe into the phone. There's no point in denying it; I'd denied too much for too long. I hear him inhale sharply and wonder if I have gone too far. "Jase..."

"How many times must I tell you not to do that to me?" He's joking, but his voice tells another story, sounding nearly as emotional as I am.

"It's not like I'll listen." My voice also doesn't match my words.

I hear commotion in the background with him and he swears under his breath. "I have to go," he says wearily. "I don't want to...you know that, right?"

"I'm so, so..."

"Not now, ok? Go, find your reinforcements."

But I have to tell him. "Jase... about Elizabeth..."

"No... we'll talk about it later."

He needs to know. He needs to understand.

"That's my mom's name," I say quickly, and he pauses, as if waiting for more. "When I was too scared to tell you, I gave you her name. She... was the first person I thought of, the first name I came up with. I didn't mean it to offend you."

"Your mom's name...then I'm honored." I close my eyes, that one small sentence bringing a hint of relief. "Have Jaden drive you home, okay?"

"I will," I agree, then pause before asking, "Until later?"

Please...

"Until later."

I hold those words in my heart as I rise from the chair to go face my reality that seems to be crashing all around me.

CHAPTER 17

"Hey, baby girl." Tish puts her arms around me after entering my home, and I hug her tightly. "We've got you, you know that?"

"I'm not running away, I promise," I whisper back.

New York

"Physically isn't the only way to run." She steps back and places her hand on my cheek. "You're okay. You're going to be okay. Stop running."

But I'm not running.

I haven't.

Cass arrives shortly after with a huge box of donut holes and four caramel macchiatos. "I love it when they're open all night," she comments as she sets everything down. "Oh, my goodness, Iris! I didn't know you were going to be here."

"It's okay, baby, I don't need more caffeine right now," Iris replies before I watch her reach for the box of donut holes. "But I do need sugar, so you got me good."

They're all here—Jaden, Tish, Cass, Iris. They've all come to comfort me, to rally around.

To reinforce.

"Lisa best not be a bitch to me," Tish comments, handing her macchiato to Iris. "I'm the one who shouldn't."

"Thank you, sweetheart, but I shouldn't, either."

"Extra for Talia." Cass smiles at me.

I can't smile back.

How can this be happening?

"Okay, so," Cass is still grinning, "let's play 20 questions to help everyone's mood."

"You're fishing for information," Jaden teases. "And I've already heard some of it, so."

"No fair!"

"Totally fair," Jaden said confidently.

I ease down into my papasan chair, watching them, and Tish walks closer to me. She's known me the longest, spent time with my mom over morning coffee when they talked me into rehab, together.

New York

"I can't tell her I'm sorry," I say aloud, and Tish takes my hand.

"She knows, Talli. She knows."

She's holding my hand.

I still feel so wrong.

So alone.

"You're not alone."

"I know," I lie.

"Stop that."

"Stop what?" I feign innocence.

Tish kneels beside me. "I've seen that look, Talli. I know it. Jaden knows it. Cass and Iris know it." She squeezes my hand. "Lean on us, okay? We've got you."

I nod as I pull my hand away, and my eyes settle on my phone.

The morning is cold and gray as I say my final goodbyes to my mother. It hasn't snowed in a while, leaving the ground unfrozen. The last conversation I'd ever dreamed I'd be having is one about the quality of the ground and whether or not...

Whether or not Mom could be buried beside Dad.

But she can.

I am still numb, unable to process much information, have yet to shed a single tear since I'd stepped foot in the hospital that night. I am grateful for the girls, though. They've been here as much as they can, helping field phone calls, helping set up a small gathering of some sort, hell I don't even know what they're called, but they've helped me. Tish worked with Iris to let the hospital staff know the funeral arrangements, where donations can be sent in lieu of flowers, the best way to contact me. The girls practically handle everything minus going to the bathroom for me.

"What is this black dress that your sisters were bitching about?" Jaden asks, and I glance over at her. She's driving me to the graveside, where the service will be concluded.

"Black dress?"

"Tight, sparkly, hooker dress is what they called it."

"I didn't see anyone in... oh."

My family had been talking about me.

Not from today, of course, but from years ago, the night we'd lost Dad.

New York.

I'd been in New York.

I'd been at a table in a swanky restaurant.

With J.

With his girlfriend.

New York

I close my eyes, remembering the restaurant, remembering the phone call.

Remembering the kiss.

"Come with me."

Could I have sounded more desperate?

"I... I can't."

Because he chose her, just as he had the night she'd caught us making out in the orderly room, the night he'd claimed she was just a friend.

"You're not going to tell me, are you?"

I almost smile at Jaden. "Maybe someday," I say as I pull out my notebook and jot down the latest bits of memory of J, the only other thing keeping me sane now aside from my best friends.

Stepping out of the car to walk up to Mom's gravesite, right beside Dad, I reach for Jaden's hand. I just don't think I can make it up there without it, without her support, without that physical contact. With each step we take the sky seems to brighten until we were there, under the canopy. The rain has stopped, and tiny rays of sun begin to peak through. Just beyond the hill beside us, I can see the most beautiful rainbow, so close, so perfect.

I allow myself one small smile.

Dad is welcoming Mom home.

"Who needs to go over to your stuffy sister's house anyhow?" Moira is saying later at my apartment that is overflowing with guests. She is in the kitchen with Iris and me rearranging the counters with the abundance of food that is being brought in.

"Not us, that's for damn sure," Iris chimes in. "You okay, baby girl?" I don't answer, thinking she was speaking to Moira.

"Aunt Talli?" Moira asks, breaking into my thoughts.

"What?"

"Are you okay?" Iris repeats.

"That was for me?" I ask, and she nods. "I'm fine, don't worry about me."

That last statement brings another wave of recollection.

In spite of his words, I haven't heard from Jase since the night my mother passed away. Perhaps he is letting me have my space, although I'm not so sure. I haven't slept well in days, and I'm not allowing myself the time, space, or luxury of grieving. Who knows what I would say if he called me? It is for the best that he keeps his distance.

Right?

I make my way out to my living room area where at least twenty people are milling about, which is plenty for my apartment and makes it seem much smaller. I am hugged intermittently by different people, mumble many I'm okays to concerned faces, and squeeze my friends just a little tighter than I normally would.

"You look beat," Tish is saying to me.

No kidding. "I am. And what's with you? No wine?"

"Well... I kinda can't right now." She grins sheepishly.

I squeeze her again, knowing yet another spawn of Tish and Mark is on the way. "Congratulations! Why didn't you tell me?"

She shrugs. "I just didn't think the timing was right."

"Oh, don't hand me that shit, we could all use some good news."

I hear the words come from my mouth, the truth of them washing over me.

I know what I have to do.

She starts saying something to me, but I speak quickly. "Listen, I'll be right back. I need something from upstairs." It's a lie, I know. I just have to get the hell out of here, regain a little more semblance of normalcy. She smiles and nods, but I don't catch what she is about to say as I grab the receiver to my phone and turn for the stairs. People are still arriving as I make my way up to that second floor as quickly as I can, my heart racing a million miles a minute.

I walk quickly to my bedroom, pushing the door almost closed behind me, my breathing coming in short gasps.

Calm down, calm down... call in reinforcements, call in reinforcements...

For the first time, I dial a number I have memorized. After two rings, his voice comes through, instantly calming me.

"Well, look who knows how to dial a phone." It sounds like he is in a crowded room, several people talking over each other.

"Don't hang up," I plead, not able to say anything else at the moment.

"Why would I do that?" I can hear him moving away from the noise, and I walk further into my room, away from the door that barely muffles the sounds from downstairs.

"I...I don't know, I just needed to talk to you, I'm sorry."

"Where are you?"

"Home," I say, confused by his question. "Why?"

"No, *where* are you?"

"What are you doing?" I ask, noticing the noise in the background of his phone has faded greatly. I hear his phone click about the same time my bedroom door slides open.

"Following your voice."

Oh... that didn't come from my phone.

I turn slowly and see Jase standing there, silhouetted from the light behind him. My phone slips from my fingers as I take my first tentative step towards him, his smile inviting. He holds out one hand to me, but instead I walk straight into his arms.

There is such gentleness in his embrace as he wraps his arms around me, his hands lightly rubbing my back, trying to ease the tension from my aching shoulders. I simply cling to him, bury my face in his chest, inhaling the all-so-familiar smell of him, and do something I haven't been able to do in days.

I cry.

CHAPTER 18

The apartment has cleared of my co-workers, Iris being the last of them to go. "You take care, baby girl," she says to me as she hugs me goodbye. "And Mr. Rock Star," she says to Jase, who is standing by the stereo looking at my rows of CDs with Moira. He turns towards her, an inquisitive look on his face. "What the hell took you so long?"

"I got lost?" It sounds like a question, and his cheeky grin causes Iris to laugh.

"Well, don't let it happen again," she warns, then with another big hug for me, she is out the door. This leaves just Jaden, Cass, Tish, Moira, Jase, and me.

I let out a sigh, my shoulders slumping. "Love you all, but I've got to get out of these clothes," I announce, heading to the stairs. I am tired, emotionally drained, my nerve endings raw over the events of the past couple of weeks, and the last thing I need are the confinements of dress clothes.

"Are you blushing?" I hear Cass ask someone as I am almost to the top of the stairs.

"No." That was Jase, and I stop for a moment, a smile touching my lips, the feel of it almost foreign.

Wow... I haven't truly smiled this much in a while.

They continue teasing him as I walk to my room. After changing into my comfy sassy pants and an oversized sweatshirt, I pull my hair into a loose bun. Standing at the vanity in the master bathroom, I splash some cold water on my face. Oh, I am far from a graceful crier, but remembering the way Jase had just held me makes me not give a damn anymore. So the tip of my nose is red. And... great, so are my cheeks.

But... but he is here.

"Hey, listen," Tish is saying as I walk down the stairs, "I need to be getting back, I'm beat."

"Sure thing, pregzilla," I reply, and Jase turns to her, a genuine smile on his face.

"Hey, congratulations!" he says, giving her a one-armed squeeze.

She's absolutely glowing. "Thank you, thank you. But don't shake me, you may regret it."

"Sorry, sorry." He steps back, still smiling.

"It's kinda full circle," I comment, a slight smile on my face as well. I give her a hug, without the squeezing, tears back in my eyes when I step away. The circle of life is ever continuous, and as sad as it is to say goodbye to Mom, this tiny glimmer of happiness is a reminder that life does indeed go on, and sometimes brings absolute joy.

Jaden is saying goodbye to Tish and Moira when I feel Jase softly place his hand in the small of my back, and all thoughts seemed to fade. I need this. I had needed him—the real Jase, the Jase that I have grown so fond of during all those anonymous conversations on the phone. I turn to him with a smile.

"Thank you." I take his hands in mine. "I can't...find the right words..."

"Don't sweat it," he says with a shrug, lightly caressing my hands with his.

Oh, Talia. Now is not the time to get that feeling in the pit of your stomach.

"Although I was a bit late, I'm just happy I could be here... for you."

"Me too." My voice is almost a whisper. "So..." I continue, my voice louder, my grip on his hands tightening slightly, "how long do I have you for?"

"We have about... 36 hours, I think?" He squints at a clock, then looks back at me. "I have a room downtown."

"Can you stay just a little bit?" I have to talk with him, without the prying ears and eyes of everyone around. Fate—is it fate? — has intervened rather rudely to bring him back into my life, and it is an opportunity I can't afford to waste. There are far too many issues still hanging in the air between us. "Tonight, after everyone leaves. I just... think we should..."

He kisses my forehead sweetly, causing my heart to skip the tiniest of beats. "We don't have to tonight, if you're not up to it. But I'll stay, regardless."

There are no sensual overtones between us at this time, simply two people who need to right everything that has gone so horribly wrong. Two friends who have admitted to one another that they care, the admissions possibly coming too late.

Tish and Moira leave shortly after, taking Cass with them, and the atmosphere becomes that much more casual, much more home-like. Jaden and Jase are in the living room, Jaden in my papasan chair that on any other occasion no one would dare sit in. Jase is kicked back on my couch looking relaxed as they discuss how Pete is far too busy to get away.

After putting the rest of my leftovers in the refrigerator, I carry my glass of wine with me and sit beside Jase on the couch, leaving plenty of space between us. "Are you two good, or do you need anything?"

"You ask after you've already sat down," Jase teases, nudging me with his foot.

"Hey!" I nudge him back. "Just for that you can get it your damn self!" He holds up his bottle of beer and raises an eyebrow. "Yeah, whatever. What about you?"

"Oh sure, you say 'whatever' to me, but,"

"She may be so busy robbing cradles that she forgot about the alcohol," I say, to which Jase mouths 'oh, right.'

"Fuck you both." Jaden's smile shows she isn't truly offended.

Jase is grinning. "Aren't you a harsh one this evening?"

"Was that for her or me?" I ask, and he points at me as he takes a drink of his beer. "Well, fuck you too." He winks at my last comment before turning to Jaden, causing the heat to creep up into my face.

That teasing little fucker.

"And you," he says pointing at Jaden, "thanks." I assume he is thanking her for calling and letting him know what was happening.

"Don't mention it," is her reply.

"I just… I don't get it." Jase turns back to me, his eyes intense. "I mean…I know you said you weren't close with your brothers and sisters… you'd told me that on numerous occasions… but this is just unfathomable."

I shrug at his comment. It's nothing I'm not used to. "It's actually always been this way, unfortunately. I suppose I'm the black sheep for now, mostly because I just don't play the game."

Jaden shakes her head. I'm surprised she hasn't said more, since she's seen so much of the bullshit I go through with them. "I'm at a loss here, being an only child. You, Cass, and Tish are the closest thing to sisters I've ever had."

"Thank you," I say, smiling. "It's an honor." I mock-bow to her, and she raises her glass of wine that I was unaware she had.

Jase is still perplexed by my situation. "While my family's far from perfect, though, we've always been…family. We have always been there as a source of strength for one another, and we wouldn't have it any other way."

Wow, that must be nice. I remember how close he and Pete seemed in the short time I had watched them interact. "You've been blessed."

"Yes," he agrees, looking me in the eyes. "I have, and I'm grateful for it." He reaches over and takes my hand in his, his smile warm.

Does he have to look at me that way? Like I have been a blessing, too?

Jaden stands up slowly and walks towards the kitchen, her wine glass in her hand. "Hey, it's getting late, I have to go."

"Are you okay to drive?" I call after her as Jase releases my hand, motioning me to get up and say my goodbyes to her. I walk into the kitchen behind her as she is rinsing her glass and placing it on the counter.

"I'm good to drive, and if I wasn't, I'd get a cab." She smiles back at me over her shoulder, then turns towards me, drying her hands on a towel I have by the sink. I hear the TV turn on in the living room and have to smile also. "He's just making himself at home, isn't he?"

"Fine by me," I say with a shrug, then I pull her close, hugging her as tight as I can. "I can't thank you enough, Jaden. You..." I begin to choke up, unable to tell her everything in my heart.

She wiggles my arms after we let go. "Seeing you with spaghetti arms is thanks enough. How long is he here?"

I glance at the clock on my microwave. "About 35 more hours or so?"

"Go, enjoy, do what you gotta do." She smiles at me and kisses my cheek, a gesture I don't shy away from this time. "Trust that it will be enough, okay?"

I can only hope so. I just can't have him walk out of my life again. Even if we are only friends, even if that's all I can have from him.

After our goodbyes, Jaden waves at Jase, who is still on the couch. "I'd get up to give you a hug, but this couch has me sucked in."

"It kinda does that to you," I comment as Jaden walks over and hugs him.

"I'll see you," he says, adding "I'm sure," with a laugh, another jab at her and Pete's non-relationship-thing they apparently have going on.

"Behave," Jaden scolds both of us as she walks out the door, leaving us truly alone for the first time since I had walked out of his hotel room in tears. We share a shy smile, as if each of us is wondering where to start, if we should start at all.

What do I do? What do I say? Hell... where do I sit? I can't just go curl up next to him and...

"C'mere," he says, his voice more than a little sleepy.

Thank you, sir, for answering my question.

So, instead of my usual perch in the papasan chair that Jaden had recently vacated, I sit beside him on the couch. I'm still a little distant, not wanting to give in to that urge to throw my arms around him.

"Oh, for fuck's sake, Talli, I don't bite."

Why does that name on his lips sound so familiar?

I don't have time to contemplate it, since he tugs on my sweatshirt and I scoot up next to him, resting my head comfortably on his chest. He wraps his arm securely around me before I have the chance to remind him that yes, he does in fact bite. I open my mouth to reply, but he stops me with a laugh saying, "Yeah, that was a lie, sorry."

"I'm not," I mumble back, relaxing into him as the beating of his heart calms me beyond all comprehension. He laughs softly and I feel a brief sensation, as if he is placing a kiss on the top of my head. "I missed you," I breathe into his chest.

I hear his heart beat just a little faster as he inhales slowly, deeply. "I missed you, too." I hold him slightly tighter for a moment, a brief hug from me as he softly plays with my hair. We say nothing else as we continue watching something neither one of us is really paying attention to on Classic TV, the same channel this television is on any time I think of him. There is no awkwardness to it as we sit here, curled up together as if we've done this a million times before. There is only comfort, soothing, warmth. He continues playing with my curls softly, the motions of his fingers slowing as the show wears on, before they come to a complete stop. His breathing has slowed to a steady rhythm, relaxing me all the more.

"Jase?" When he doesn't answer, I steal a glance upwards. His head is resting comfortably on the back of the couch, his eyes closed, a serene look in his features. I have to smile. I guess he does sleep, at least sometimes. Laying my head back on his chest, I drift into the most peaceful sleep I've had in days.

CHAPTER 19

I normally don't sleep in a sweatshirt, or with a bra on for that matter. For some strange reason, any time I attempt to sleep with either, I tend to wake up with them in a heap on the floor as if they have been thrown haphazardly across the room. Do I ever remember how it happened? Of course not. Do I think about this when some time in the middle of the night Jase had woke and suggested we not sleep on the couch as his neck was hurting? No. That would have been the smart thing. I simply followed blindly as we walked up the stairs and crawled into my bed together, both so obviously exhausted that we drifted straight back into sleep.

And yet, here it is... 10 a.m., sun peeking through my not-so-light-reducing curtains. We are lying in bed, his arm draped over my bare torso. My sweatshirt and bra are thrown over towards the dresser, completely out of arms reach.

Well...fuck.

How the hell am I going to get out of this one?

I try wiggling slightly out from under his arm, only to have him sigh softly and pull me in closer.

Oh... this feels... nice.

I don't remember being in his arms after our one wild night. Wait, that's right... I hadn't been. I'd drifted off to sleep with his eyes on me, his chest rising and falling with each gasp of breath he took. I'd later woken up alone, only a small, impersonal note left tucked into my boot.

But now...

Now his arm is securely tucked around me, my back up against his chest, the heat from the skin to skin contact radiating through my entire body.

Part of me never wants this to end.

As he shifts, his hand travels north and my body begins to betray me. I feel chills on my arms and a tightening in my stomach as his hand opens wide, pulling me even closer to him. He settles in, holding me firm up against his body, as I lay here helpless. Oh, sure, I could throw his arm off me, push him away, walk across the room, and get dressed; this would also most likely wake him, and for some reason unknown to me I just don't want him to see me...well, vulnerable?

Is that the word I'm looking for?

Hell, who knows what is going through my mind, because it flies out the window when I feel him turn his head slightly, breathing in the scent of my hair.

Oh... my...

In the recesses of my mind I wonder if he can still smell my jasmine shampoo. He answers with another sleepy sigh.

"I thought you used vanilla."

Vanilla? When have I ever used vanilla?

"I've never used that," I reply warily, and he jumps as if I startled him awake, his arm still holding me so close I can't move away.

"Hmmm?" That seems to be all he can manage, and I turn slightly, or as much as I can, to look at him. He smiles softly and lays his head back on the pillow. "Morning. Missing something?"

My face must be turning about five different shades of red as he just lays there grinning at me. That fucker is lucky he's so damn adorable. I pull the covers up to nearly my chin as Jase turns on his side and rests his head on his arm. His other arm is still draped across me, his fingers lightly tracing some unseen outline on my skin.

"You know," he continues, that impish grin firmly planted on his face, "it was quite the vision watching you wrestling with that thing, struggling to get it over your head."

Over my...ah, hell, my hair! I gingerly put a hand up to my hair, wincing as I feel the hot mess it must look like. Groaning, I pull the covers over my head as he laughs.

Peeking his head under to look at me he adds, "The bra was one hell of an added bonus."

"Well...shit!" is all I can say as I scramble to get out of bed. I hurry to my discarded shirt, holding it up in front of me.

"Must I remind you I've seen you in much, much less?"

Does he have to sound so damn sexy, even when tired? Unable to form a coherent answer, I walk to the washroom to survey the damage, his easy laughter following me.

"Oh... god." I wipe a smudge out from under one eye and try to pull the curls out of their mess to at least pin it up so I can retrieve clothes and other provisions for my shower.

"Well, I can't take credit for that statement...today."

Jase is obviously standing right outside the door. I stand there thinking momentarily about what he said before I blush even more.

Wow, does he really think about that night?

And how many times had I said that phrase anyhow? I lost count somewhere around ten? Twelve? When he kissed me before the clothes went flying, on the couch, on the floor, up against the wall, in several positions on the bed...

What a fucker. He wants to tease me? I'll teach him.

I open the door so quickly it catches him off guard and he stumbles a bit into the washroom with me. He looks perfect, absolutely perfect with that hair sticking up in all the right places...absolutely perfect, grinning down at me before he pulls me into a warm embrace, my shirt caught between our bare chests. His hands caress my back, his fingertips on my skin sending shivers through me. "Talli?" His voice is soft, soothing, inviting. I don't correct him, tell him I don't really go by that name anymore. At this point, he could ask me to jump off the Empire State Building and I would say yes. Hell, he probably knows it.

I bury my face in his chest, smiling despite it all. "Hmmm?" I mumble my response, keeping my eyes averted.

He is quiet for a moment before I hear him take a breath as if he wants to speak but doesn't. It is about then that I remember we are standing in front of a mirror. When I peer towards it, I meet his eyes in the reflection as he is looking at me, his gaze softening.

"You have such a beautiful smile." His expression is sweet and relaxed. Although I think it impossible, my heart melts even more as we stand there, studying each other's faces in the reflection. I wish I could read his mind, but I'm not so sure if I want him reading mine at this moment. It isn't that I am thinking about the hot, steamy, multiple-orgasm sex... no, it is the sweet moments, the conversations, all the laughter we've shared over the weeks.

How did I get so lucky?

Standing up against the length of him, I can feel his phone begin to vibrate in his pocket, breaking the spell he seems to have me under. He sighs as he reaches for it, stepping back from me as he pulls it out slightly to check the number. His eyes widen then, a look of surprise and perhaps delight filling them. "I have to take this," he says, and I smile at him as he steps from the room. I suppose his work is never done... no, I know it isn't. How many times have our conversations been interrupted, sometimes in the middle of the night?

I head back towards my bedroom to find my clothes for the day as I hear him say with absolute joy in his voice, "Evans! Holy shit, I've been trying for, like... *weeks* to find you again! You got my messages then?" I smile softly to myself as his laughter fills the entire apartment from his perch downstairs, and when I peek down, I can see him once again kicked back on the couch. I don't think I could ever tire of hearing his sweet laughter. I remember many days how I would think about it at work, and suddenly everything would be okay.

I still hold my shirt in front of me although Jase is downstairs and can't see what I am doing. As I lean into the hall closet to get fresh towels, I notice just how well his voice carries throughout the entire apartment. Damn, it's a good thing we were in that hotel in Cleveland when we'd gone at each other with such abandon.

I'm not eavesdropping, not in the least. But there's no mistaking the change in his voice when he speaks again.

"You're... kidding. Really? You? And... wow, um...congratulations." He sounds more shocked than happy to me, and I don't even know what is going on in this private world of his. As I walk back to the washroom, I hear him add, "I guess I won't be able to call you Evans after that, huh? Married...wow. Yeah, of course I'll be there, why wouldn't I be? Besides the obvious, but we'll plan around it."

Wow, what a difference in his tone. And why would he not be happy?

There is just something in the change of his voice that sends a warning signal through me that I try to ignore during my preparation for the rest of the day. Despite that, I still feel as if I am intruding into something I shouldn't be witnessing, even if I am only hearing his side of the conversation. We only have a few hours left, and I have so much to tell him that I don't want to waste any time on something that so clearly doesn't concern me.

After I am ready, I take the stairs two at a time. Is it sick that I am excited to get to spend more time with him, with my Not John, with no pretenses, no questions, no secrets? But it is as if he doesn't hear me, he is so lost in his own thoughts, staring at the television, where a movie I don't even recognize is playing. He is absentmindedly turning his phone over and over in his hand, a slight scowl keeping his eyebrows closer together. "Hey," my voice seems to break through, and he looks up at me and smiles.

Jase stands and stretches. "Sorry, it's one of my favorite movies." Yeah, that's a real reason to look at the television as if it has cost you your best friend. "I need to head back to the hotel and get cleaned up."

Damn, so much for spending the day together. "Oh, okay."

He tilts his head slightly to the side and grins at me. "You could be a doll and drive me there. I'll even be nice and not take as long as some people to get ready."

"Hey!"

"Just kidding, just kidding." He pulls me into another soft hug that I couldn't help but return, then steps back. "Thanks, Talli...I needed that."

Wow... what happened? Is it something I said? Is he going to the hotel to avoid talking to me?

"Feeling's mutual," is all I can say.

We are silent for the most part on the drive all the way to his hotel, with Jase staring out his window at the passing scenery. When one of his songs comes on the radio, I am surprised that he reaches up and switches the station. "Why'd you do that?"

"Just didn't feel like listening to it today."

Wow has his mood ever changed. Gone is the joking, smiling, teasing man I woke up with, and here sits a sullen shell of him instead. He turns towards me suddenly, his face serious. "I know you've been through a lot these past few days, we don't have to..." He looks down, not finishing his sentence.

Wow. He's avoiding talking to me.

"Don't you think we should?" I ask. He nods slightly, still not looking at me. We pull up to a red light, and I reach out and touch his arm. "I have so much to say, and it isn't going to be easy." He still isn't looking at me, his eyes now staring over to the right to where I'm not even sure he can see my face. A car horn behind me signals that we need to start moving again. When I put both hands on the wheel he reaches over, lightly touching where my hand had once been.

It is all the subtle, or perhaps not so subtle, body language coming from him that is ripping my heart to shreds. What have I done between last night... between this morning, when I got into the shower, until now? No... no way in hell am I going to let him get out of this.

I pull into the parking garage of the hotel and reach out to stop him from exiting the car once we come to a stop. I need to approach this delicately, not scream at him over how Jekyll and Hyde he has become. "I...don't know what's wrong, and I'm not sure how to ask whether or not it has anything to do with me."

"I could talk to you," he says softly, then looks over at me. His eyes are stormy as he studies my face, perhaps gauging my reaction. "And...that meant something to me, and I don't think..."

Of course.

"I understand." I pull back, not waiting for him to finish.

"No, stop." He grabs my hand, and a chill passes through me. "I don't think I'm ready to let go of that, I don't want to let go, and all of this 'we need to talk' and all of these damn...these...questions, or whatever the hell they are, I don't know if I can handle the answers to them right now." He shakes his head as if to clear it. "Right now, I just need to... be. Can we just... be? Right now? You know... like we used to, all the time."

I don't realize I have stopped breathing until I let out a long sigh. What do you know? He wants the same thing I do.

"Yes. Irrevocably... yes."

He squeezes my hand at my miserable attempt to copy his famous words, a half smirk on his face. "Confession time later, then." It is more of a statement than a question, and when I nod in agreement, he smiles. "Well, okay, so come on up with me while I get ready."

I had fully expected to have him call me when he was ready to be picked up, but I smile and follow his lead.

It seems I'm not the only one in need of comforting.

CHAPTER 20

"Wait...wait," Jase is saying as we are raiding my refrigerator a couple hours later, "weren't we gonna sit on the phone and...kinda...watch this together?"

I smile up at him, the memory of that conversation warming me from the tips of my toes. He remembers... what do you know? We would have ended up spending the afternoon together anyhow, even though it would have only been through the phone line. I wonder briefly how different it is going to be, watching something with him sitting beside me instead of us doing commentary for each other through the phone.

"It kind of baffles me, though," I say, "how you would want to sit through a marathon of Tour Life. I know you are about your privacy." This is presently one of my favorite shows, featuring James Slade and his 'band of brothers' as he calls them.

"But, see, he's... thank you," he says politely as I hand him a beer. "He's a friend." How quickly I forget what world Jase resides in. "And besides, he's welcomed them into his life, per se. It isn't as if this is done by paparazzi."

True. "Okay, point made. How much time do we have?"

He glances around me at the clock on the microwave. "Fifteen minutes, maybe?"

"Have I told you how happy I am that you're here?"

I just throw it out there, in this moment where I feel so alive just 24 hours after saying goodbye to my mother. He seems genuinely touched by my sentiment and reaches out, gently tousling my curls.

"It's nice to know," he replies as he helps me stand. Damn it, my stomach really needs to quit doing flips when he touches me. "Do we have everything?"

I grin at him. "For now. Remember we were waiting until hour three—"

"For popcorn, right!" His smile widens at my recollection. "Wow, I'm impressed." We settle into our seats on the couch and I pull the coffee table a little closer, clearing its contents so we can prop our feet up. "One last thing," he says, reaching in his pocket for his cell phone. As he powers it off, he adds, "No interruptions."

"Okay," I agree, unplugging the phone line from the base. This means even though I am off on convalescent leave, no hospital. This also means no family, not that they will bother to call. Oh, and no friends. Those I *do* have. I shut off my cell phone also, placing it beside the couch on the end table. We won't be able to hear the upstairs phone if it rings, so we are good to go.

No interruptions.

Just... us.

He holds up his beer and we clink our bottles together and each take a drink. Before I have the chance to wonder which side of Jase I am going to get this evening, he speaks up.

"You really shouldn't drink too much tonight, though; you know, since you can't handle your alcohol." He isn't even looking at me but has that damn impish grin on his face.

This is bound to get interesting.

"I can't... what do you mean I can't handle my alcohol? I handle my alcohol just fine, thank you."

"Suuuuuuuuure." He draws the word out then takes another drink of his beer. "Uh huh, see this?" He tilts his head to the side, the remnants of our evening just barely visible.

My heart skips a tiny beat, the heat radiating through me as the memories of the night replay in my mind. Mmm hmmm, all right. Two can play that game. "And?" I ask this as if it is no big deal despite my temperature steadily rising. "I'd show you what you did, but I'd have to drop my pants to do it."

Take that.

He looks over at me then, still grinning, eyebrows disappearing under the shock of bangs that have fallen across his forehead. Damn, does he have to look at me that way?

I raise my eyebrow. "No way, pal. You wanna see that, you have to take them off yourself."

The look on his face absolutely generates heat, but he says nothing and turns back towards the television as if all these commercials before our marathon are the most interesting things on the planet. Damn it, damn it, damn it... I am going to need to ditch the beer and chew on ice cubes at this rate.

As we sit in silence, I wonder, yet again, if I have stepped over the line. He answers my silent question by leaning over and gently kissing my cheek. Perhaps someone else would be insulted over such a sweet, chaste gesture, but I find it far too endearing and can only blush and smile in response.

Yeah. He knows.

We enjoy the silence, picking at our plates of leftovers, stealing short, almost shy, glances at one another. Okay, so occasionally I am remembering him hovered over me, his hair damp with sweat, his skin glistening as he moved...

Stop it, Talia!

Not tonight. We need to talk, we need to lay all of our cards on the table.

But where do we start?

During a commercial break he suddenly says, "Time's not exactly on our side today, is it?" The hours are dwindling down to when he has to be back on that plane, under very strict orders from his management, and here we sit, saying nothing.

I swallow once before answering. "No...no, it's not."

Here we go.

His sigh sends chills through me. "I don't know where to start."

I lick my lips out of nervousness and decide to give it a shot. The worst he can say is no. "You could start with... what changed your mood this morning."

He is looking straight ahead, but I doubt if he is seeing anything. He sighs heavily then and places everything on the table, then sits up straighter and runs his fingers through is hair. "She was my best friend. No, more than my best friend. She was my first...my first... everything."

"Elizabeth?"

He still isn't looking at me when he speaks. "Kaitlyn Elizabeth Evans was my first crush, my first love, my first...no, not broken, *shattered* heart, and sometimes I think I still haven't found all the pieces."

I've never heard that name mentioned and believe me during my self-imposed exile I scoured over the internet a time or two gathering information on him. This name isn't mentioned anywhere.

"I don't talk about her, see? Because I can't, because that's just...well, it's no one's business and it's something I have to shoulder the blame for. But she was still my best friend, and I loved...I love her." *Oh... oh, fuck.* "And I always will, in that part of my heart that only she resides in. Does that make sense?" He finally looks at me, and I half expect to see tears with as much of his heart as he is laying on the line, but there are none.

"It makes perfect sense." Right now, this is the best I can do, but at least it's honest. I do understand, even if I've never felt anything remotely close. Perhaps this is his way of telling me that there is no hope for us because he will spend the rest of his life pining away for her. I give him a soft smile, urging him silently to continue. This, his baring of his soul, is for his benefit, not mine.

"I want her to be happy, with everything that's inside of me. When it was...when that part of our journey was over, I couldn't even stay there. I moved out of the fucking state, away from New York when it felt like home, and I begged her to just...be happy.

And she is." I cringe at the mention of New York, my memories of my time there less than pleasant, but he misses that. He smiles and shrugs, glancing briefly over at me. "I suppose I just never believed she'd be happy with anyone but me."

"So...you don't want her to get married." He starts to say something, his face registering confusion, so I add, "Sound carries rather well throughout this apartment. I overheard your end of the conversation."

He looks down for a moment, and then his eyes are back on me. "I don't know what I feel about it." Other than uncomfortable, which I am gathering from his demeanor. "Kate and I haven't been together for years. Fuck." He breathes in, leaning back into the cushions and stares at me. "I've not talked about this with anyone, not in...this position." He gestures between the two of us as if to clarify what he means. "This is foreign territory to me. Well, kinda...because I feel I can talk to you. I've always been able to talk with you."

I reach out and hold his hand. "So...that's what's been bothering you today. I suppose I'd be fairly upset myself."

"I'd be lying if I said that was all of it." He gently squeezes my hand before continuing. "There's... also... you."

Me? Oh... fuck...

He wants to say goodbye, I can feel it.

"I'm just not ready to hear that you don't want me in your life. I know it's coming," he adds quickly, placing two fingers over my lips. He has no idea... none. "I know it's a lot of bullshit to deal with, and I'm sure you wouldn't believe me if I told you I didn't fall into bed with every beautiful woman I met, and...how is it that we seemed to trust each other so implicitly until we,"

"I'm the one that messed that up." It is my turn to interrupt him, and since we both know that statement is the truth, he has no witty retort. "And I'm asking that you hear me out without jumping to conclusions, please."

He nods, his voice soft when he does speak. "Okay."

My heart is hammering, and I wonder if he can hear it over the television. I take a deep breath, smiling softly when he gently squeezes my hand. "I didn't know for a long time. I realize that might be hard for you to believe, but it's true. I mean, I look back now and there are so many clues I should have picked up on. Your... your laugh, your accent,"

His slight scowl is so fucking adorable. "I don't have an accent."

"Yes, you do, and quit interrupting me. I never stopped to think about who you were, because it... it didn't matter." He closes his eyes briefly at my last words, and when he opens them, he is now focused on our hands, still joined together. "All I knew was how you made me feel, how happy I was whenever I got to talk with you, about anything and everything. It meant the world to me to have someone listen without judgment. It still does."

"But it *did* matter to you, who I am." His voice is so melancholy when he says those words. "When you found out... it mattered."

"Not in the way that you have in your head," I correct him. "It mattered because of... me." His eyebrows furrow together in confusion. "I'm not...perfect, I'm not arm candy, I'm not a model, or an actress, or... stop shaking your head at me! I'm serious!"

"And to me, that's insulting."

"It's hard to explain my insecurities, what can I say? I mean, the list of all the women you dated,"

"I didn't date *all* of them."

Oh, that helps. "I'm just trying to be honest with you, Jase, because I felt...*then* what you're feeling now, like you would just disappear, and I'm not ready for that to happen. I don't want it to."

"So, you think I'm hung up on the superficial, that I wouldn't find you attractive, and that because you felt this way about yourself, I wouldn't want anything else to do with you. That suddenly I wouldn't want to speak with you or have, or... or *be* anything else with you."

In hindsight, I can see I was wrong, at least about part of it. "Strike that first part and you have it in a nutshell." I can tell by the twitch in his jaw that his perception of my opinion truly bothers him, but there is a lingering question in my mind that I really want an answer to. "Tell me why you thought I would want nothing to do with you."

"Because of what I do." His voice is small, barely audible above the show we are now ignoring. "Because I...shouldn't have... I don't want you to take this the wrong way, but it shouldn't have happened...us, like that."

Oh wow, so he does regret it. I back away slightly, my chest heavy as I struggle to take in a breath, my heart beating so loudly in my ears that I can barely make a cohesive thought.

"I only meant to say..."

"Goodbye," I finish for him. "You were going to say goodbye."

"I was hurt, Talia." He is finally looking back up at me, back into my eyes, and I find myself unable to look away. "I thought I could trust you... you, Not Telling... and when Pete called and told me that this beautiful woman in my room, the one I had tried to convince myself wasn't the one I was falling desperately for, the one who'd insisted we didn't know each other, was... when I found out who you were, I refused to believe him so I called your number, and...there you were. And with the message I had left,"

"I didn't get the message..."

"I know that now, but you understand why I didn't believe it at the time?" I nod 'yes,' my heart breaking a little more. "You had plenty of chances, though, after you knew your theory was wrong. Why not tell me then?"

"I was... upset."

"Over what?" His eyes are so troubled, so familiar. "God, Talli, what did I do wrong?"

My breath catches in my throat as my memory attempts to draw me back, but I shake it off. "Someone else," I murmur, looking away for a moment before I take a deep breath and turn back to him. "You said there was someone else, and I didn't understand why you would be with me, and then when was I supposed to say something? When you were telling me to be quiet, or when..."

"When I was kissing you." His fingers are lightly touching my lips like they are fragile. An involuntary shiver passes through me and he quickly draws his hand away.

"But then…" I keep going, my breathing slightly labored with the memory of what happened after that phone call. "Then you knew, and… why, Jase? Why did you kiss me then? Why did you…" My voice trails off, unable to finish my sentence as my eyes unwisely travel to his lips.

"I wanted to."

That is simple, direct, and to the point.

Why had I been so blind?

"Talia, please don't think I was using you. I swear to you I wasn't. I thought you would know that, but," He shrugs, unable to form any other words either. We sit in silence, both of us looking at our hands that are joined together, his thumb lightly caressing the back of my hand.

"I think…I wasn't thinking," I finally say. "I wasn't wanting to think, I just wanted…to be… with you."

"That's what I wanted, too." His voice is barely above a whisper. We continue staring at our hands, his squeezing mine as I begin to tremble.

"But now…" I can hardly believe I've said those two words. Do I really want to know the 'but now'?

We can't move forward, if there is a forward, without it.

"Now I… I have to know if you're wanting Jase the man, or Jase the rock star."

"If you don't know the answer to that, then you never knew me at all." We look into each other's eyes then, my heart constricting when I see the sadness etched in his features. "You… really thought that's what I came up there for?" He shrugs one shoulder, then nods slightly. There is no point in him denying it now. "It wasn't, Jase, I… I swear it wasn't. I was there because I wanted… you. Not John, you. I… I watched everyone leaving, and I knew what time it was, and I knew how you felt so alone. I know because you told me, and I didn't want you to feel that way. I didn't want you to see me that way. Jase, I have to know that you believe me, and … and that you forgive me for being so wrong."

Jase releases my hand and tenderly tucks a curl behind my ear, his fingertips lightly brushing against my face, before he returns his hand to mine once more. "Fair enough."

I'm not going to say it doesn't hurt me that he can't say the words, but I'm not quite through yet. "I also have to know," I continue, my eyes locked with his, "that it really is me you want to be with right now, not the version you had put together before we met... and not..." my mind travels to this morning, when he had sleepily asked why I stopped using vanilla shampoo. "...not someone else entirely."

"And for now?"

Don't cry, don't cry, don't cry.

My calm exterior contradicts my racing heart. "Do you want to say goodbye?"

"I already told you that I don't, pay attention." He is trying to lighten the mood, and even if he hasn't meant for it to be amusing, I can't help but smile. "What about you?"

"Say goodbye? Not a chance." I manage a smile even though my heart feels like it could splinter and shatter at any given moment. "You're stuck with me."

His smile is radiating. "Good, now go make some popcorn woman. This stuff isn't cutting it, and we're missing our marathon." I nudge him playfully before I walk towards the kitchen. "Who needs Jackie when I have you?" I hear him joke as I retrieve a bowl and start the popcorn in the microwave.

I glance at him in the living room, re-stretched out with his feet resting on my coffee table, and I sigh. For as relaxed as he attempts to portray his body language to be, I can't help but feel that in his heart he wishes he was somewhere else.

CHAPTER 21

Jase is quiet, maybe a little more withdrawn, after our talk. Hell, I'm not kidding myself; I know there is a lot more that needs said, but at least we'd begun. There aren't any more shy glances at each other, no more cheeky comments, but at the same time it isn't uncomfortable.

Not in the least.

It is... nice.

And then, smart ass Jase returns.

We are in our seats, settled in and watching that marathon, the bowl of popcorn between us. Jase eats a few kernels, crinkles up his nose, and sets the bowl on my lap.

"Not enough salt," he says, pointing towards the kitchen as if I should get up and take care of it. I look over at him incredulously and set the bowl on his lap.

"Get off your lazy ass and get it yourself."

"You wound me with your words, Not Telling." He places the bowl back on my lap. "Am I not a guest in your home?"

"Who has taken over my couch, my car radio, my remote control..." I place the bowl back on his lap, taking a few kernels out and eating them as he continues.

"You weren't just being hospitable?"

"Hell no, and I'm not Alfred, or Jackie, or whatever you're calling him these days. Go get your own damn salt."

"Jeez, all you had to do was say so." His pout, while cute, is fake as he walks into the kitchen, holding the bowl of popcorn in one hand and the remote control in the other. I can't help but giggle as he stuffs the remote in his back pocket and grabs the saltshaker, vigorously pouring it over our popcorn. Really?

"Um...you mind not putting so much on there?"

He looks at me out of the corner of his eye and continues shaking the salt over the popcorn. I roll my eyes and look back at the screen where James is being...well, *James*, while planning a bachelor party for one of his best friends. Is that Jase's name he just mentioned? It's hard telling, since my mind is firmly elsewhere.

A few more shakes of salt, and Jase is back on his way over to the couch. He sits down placing the bowl back between us, proud of his accomplishment as he takes a large handful and begins eating it. He doesn't seem fazed in the least by the overabundance of salt that he must have put on the popcorn, so I shrug and grab some. I am confident that he has pretended to put so much salt on.

I am wrong.

"God, this is awful!" I cough a few times and grab my drink to wash what I have eaten down.

"Is there a problem?"

Is there a fucking problem? "You ruined my popcorn!"

"Oh, it's *your* popcorn now?" he asks, raising an eyebrow.

I point towards the kitchen. "Go make some more!"

"Oh no, no, no..." He can't keep the smile off his face. "Get off your lazy ass and get it yourself." I merely stare at him with my mouth open, my own words being thrown back at me. Without taking his eyes off the television he reaches over with a single finger and pushes my chin up to close my mouth.

"Oh, for fuck's sake," I mutter, turning before he can see my grin.

"There you go, that redheaded temper coming through," he calls out to me as I make my way towards the kitchen. "You know, I always pictured you with red hair. I don't know why. But it was ever since that day when you were just hating on that Starship song."

"That song sucks," I reply, garnering a large, genuine laugh from him, which causes me to peer through the cut out at him, where he is doubled over. "What?"

"That's...that's exactly what... I said..."

"...I would normally say," I remember out loud. "Except for the fact that I was trying to sound like your nerd ass."

"Nerd ass?" He is still trying to control his laughter. "So much for your extended vocabulary."

"Bite me," I call back to him, and his laughter suddenly ceases.

"Talia...Christine...you know better than to say that to me."

Damn it.

Of course I know better.

My neck knows better, my breasts know better... hell, my poor thighs with all of their war wounds know better. I feel the heat course through my body and am thankful for the distance between us as our eyes meet from across the room.

Fuck me, does he have to be so gorgeous?

You know, that couch is really comfortable... I could always just... push him back and...

"Saved by the bell," he says as the microwave beeps, which, apparently, I miss thanks to my mind being in a much different place. I shake my head as I walk over to the counter, getting a new bowl and pouring the contents of untainted popcorn. I make it a point to only shake a small amount of salt on it, then walk back over to the couch, taking my usual seat. This time there is no bowl between us as Jase has it on his lap. I can barely concentrate enough to eat a piece or two. Somehow his presence has taken hold of my brain. I am merely a shell...not a stuttering fan girl, but a woman with intimate memories of an extremely passionate man who looks like a god when he hovers close, hair and skin damp with sweat, and...

...and his hand is in the popcorn bowl on my lap.

"What the hell are you doing?"

"Eating popcorn," he says slowly. "And.." he lifts his bottle, "drinking beer. Oh, and there's this show I'm trying to watch that you keep interrupting."

"You have your own damn popcorn!"

He scrunches up his nose. "Too salty."

I reply by taking a few kernels and throwing them at him.

"What?" he asks, turning towards me. "You're gonna...hey! Quit throwing shit at me!"

"Oooo where'd your extensive..." I throw another piece at him, "vocabulary go to?"

"Is this necessary?" He puts his hand over his heart as if wounded, and I laugh as I throw another piece at him. "Mmmm hmmm, okay."

He sits up straight, feet on the floor, placing his bowl on the coffee table before he turns to me. I am giggling at his expression, then let out a small squeak as he reaches, and ends up wrestling with me for, the bowl on my lap.

"Mine!" I yell, trying to pry it from his hands, popcorn spilling everywhere as we continue our tug of war. I struggle beside him, laughing as he pushes me over, still reaching for the bowl that I somehow still hang onto. He finally knocks it out of my hands, its contents showering over couch, the floor, coffee table, and us, which has us both laughing uncontrollably...

Until our positions break into our consciousness.

I am pinned beneath him, his face mere inches from mine. Our breathing is in unison, causing our bodies to move together adding to the friction building between us. With each breath we take, my breasts lightly touch his chest, the sensations making me squirm just a little beneath him. When he shifts ever so slightly, now resting between my legs that have somehow become parted, our hips are together, his erection pressed right between my legs.

This isn't good...this isn't good at all.

Or... or it is *too* good.

He lets go of my hands that he has pinned above my head but doesn't move. His eyes are studying me, my features, committing me to memory. My breath catches in my throat as his gaze skim over my lips, the pure hunger making me weak.

Don't let him do it, Talia. He doesn't want to be here. He doesn't want to be with you. Don't do it...

"You have the most beautiful eyes." His voice shoots through me as his eyes lock with mine. "I've never seen eyes this bright, this blue...not like this."

I will myself silent to keep from screaming at him, demanding to know why he would do this, why he wants to hurt me. One soft kiss, his lips feather light against mine, and all my best intentions are in danger of flying out the window.

But I want that kiss; hell, I want more than that kiss. I want clothes off, bodies wrapped together intimately. I want to feel him inside of me, thrusting harder, faster, making me scream in ecstasy. As he gently teases my lips with his, coaxing a sigh from me that sends a shiver I can feel through him, and as his hips grind against mine, there is no doubt it is what he wants, too.

But does he want it with me?

I'm not able to ask, not that I think for one second I could as our kisses begin building in passion, our tongues battling for control. Each moan from him causes me to push myself a little closer, my nerve endings tingling as I become increasingly aroused. He is far, far too good at this—I should have remembered that.

He has one hand on my hip, guiding me as our bodies move together just as perfectly as they had before, only this time the barrier of clothes is in the way.

This just... it isn't good for us...

He kisses a trail down my neck, causing me to gasp with pleasure.

Now is the time to tell him to stop...

I can only whimper against his lips as he is kissing me again, his hands everywhere, caressing, seeking...

And then he stops.

He stops abruptly, leaning down, burying his face in my hair, taking in long, shuddering breaths. I try to move but he holds me still, his hands so strong against my wrists it is almost an aphrodisiac. "Ssssh, please, don't move...I'm so, so sorry." His voice is strained, his words hushed against my skin, and I stop the gasp from leaving my lips at the sensation. "I didn't mean to start this."

I feel a tear escape my eyes that are shut so tight it hurts. It is nothing compared to my heart that this man seems to have a habit of breaking. The lone tear slides down past him and I hear him inhale sharply. "Fuck, you must hate me."

No, you asshole, I can't hate you... I can't hate you because I love you, even though you wish I were someone else.

"Talli..." Oh, he needs to move, not hold me so close, not let me feel his words right up against my skin. He seems to read my mind and pushes himself slightly up, studying my face, his eyes clouded over. "I'm sorry."

Those two words, from his lips, that had at one time made my heart soar now send it crashing to the ground.

"This just... it just happens, when I'm with you, and... and I don't know why, I don't know how to explain it, I don't... I don't know if I want to explain it..." He leans down, his lips softly touching mine once more before he groans, pushing himself back up. "I'm sorry, I... I know this isn't what you wanted."

What?

"Don't turn this around on me, Jase." The words don't sound harsh, which is a good thing as I don't mean them to, but he still draws back further, standing up and running a shaking hand through his hair. He tugs slightly at his jeans, and when I realize it is to readjust, my body begins to betray me once more.

This time, though, my heart is going to prevail.

Why had he started, why had he kissed me, after everything he'd just told me? He hasn't even said that he believes me, and he is upset over his ex-girlfriend. Oh, that... that has to be it.

I just need to hear it from him.

Silently he bends down by the couch and begins scooping up the mess of popcorn, putting it back in the bowl it has spilled from. I watch him move, his face masked over with an unreadable expression, and I can't take it anymore. Reaching out to him, I touch his arm and he stops, looking up at me.

"I'm not sorry I'm here." His eyes are determined, intense as he tries to explain. "I'm here because I want to be, and I don't want you to think differently."

I can feel my body relax at his words, my expression soften. I open my mouth to speak, but again he has taken my bravado, so I merely nod and drop my head to hide the new tears springing up. I try to hide them, I really do, but I'm certain he notices. I feel his hand gently touch my leg before his other is underneath my chin, his fingertips slowly lifting my face.

"Hey…" His voice is soft, the tone of it touching me, making me fall just a little harder.

"You know, the popcorn can wait," I cut him off, just wanting him back up here beside me. "We have a marathon to keep watching."

"Yeah, well, you're gonna kill me since I just spilled my beer on your couch," he says as he moves quickly to grab the overturned bottle. I move my legs to keep them from getting wet as the foamy liquid seeps down into the cushion. I look at that large wet spot, the mess in my living room, then back at Jase….and we can't help ourselves.

We laugh.

CHAPTER 22

The television in my bedroom is smaller than my living room set, but it is positioned on my dresser so that I can comfortably watch while propped up in bed. Jase and I have gathered all the available pillows during commercial breaks, and they are positioned just so before we stretch out to continue with the marathon. It beats the alternative of sitting on a soaked couch, which I swear is my only reason for having him up here. Honest, I wouldn't have suggested it otherwise.

His confession of sorts, where he'd told me he wanted to be there, has eased much of the tension I had been feeling. I suppose there is truth in moods being contagious as Jase is also more notably relaxed. I notice during the next episode that Jase really is, for lack of better terms, a very physical person. I'm not saying his hands are all over me or that he is overly sexual in any way—it is the little things. When he knows something hilarious is about to happen, he'll reach over and gently touch me before pointing at the TV and saying, "Oh, watch this." It is as if the invisible barrier that has been up keeping us both guarded has disappeared, freeing us to be ourselves.

Unfortunately for me, it also means seeing face to face the same man I've fallen so hard for.

He smirks at me when another commercial comes on. "You know, I poured my heart out about my ex... someone I've never really talked about before."

I return his smirk with one of my own. "And?"

"And, what about you?"

"What about me? I already told you about me."

"Just the one boyfriend, like, ever?"

I roll my eyes. "You did not just use the word *like* in that context."

"So what if I did? Come on..."

"I said he was my only... relationship type deal thing. And I wasn't lying."

"Relationship type deal thing. Damn, no wonder you and Jaden are friends," he quips, then yelps a tiny bit when I elbow him. Wuss. "What the hell was that for?"

"For being... you."

"Thanks, babe," he mumbles, still grinning at me.

Babe?

I swallow over the lump in my throat, suddenly nervous. I shouldn't be, but I haven't told anyone what I'm about to tell him. And how the hell do I explain this anyway? "There was this other guy... a long time ago. And he wasn't really a boyfriend, just someone I talked to. But he was... special."

"Define special."

"He... I could talk with him." My voice is softer now as I remember the boy with the beautiful eyes and elusive name.

"Like you can talk with me?"

Oh, the look on his face... if I could just capture it, the hope there, and bottle it up, I'd be a very rich woman. But he's asked me a question, and I need to answer it.

"Kind of," I reply, tilting my head slightly to the side. "I am more honest with you."

He opens his mouth to make what is sure to be a cheeky reply, but he stops instead and turns back to the television. Wow, me and my big mouth. Here I am reminding him of how I had been completely dishonest with him.

"I don't have anything witty to say," he admits, then shakes his head slightly. "Will you at least tell me his name?"

"Why, so you won't feel so guilty about... Kate...put that pillow down this instant!" I say quickly, ready to shield myself in case he hits me with it.

"Do you want me to feel guilty that I can talk with you?" he asks, catching me off guard. "I mean... I can... *not* tell you."

"No, no. That's not what I mean at all," I say, placing my hand on his arm, my defenses down just enough to where he catches me with that pillow right upside my head. "Fucker."

"Nope, just walked her home."

"Oh, ha ha." I roll my eyes at him and settle back into the pillows. The show isn't back on yet, but I'm not sure if this is why Jase has continued with the conversation or not.

"You mad at me now?"

"His name was Jack," I say, then scowl slightly and add, "I think." Maybe. Hell, I don't know.

"Jack?"

Now that I hear him say it, I doubt it even more. Or is it? Fuck, I don't know. "I think, and what's so bad about that name?"

"Jack?" he asks again, this time with a mock southern twang, prompting me to hit him with a pillow.

"He was really sweet."

"Sweet. Ugh. Kiss of death."

"Mmmmm, he could kiss though," I say as almost an afterthought, my face turning slightly red at my admission. I may not remember much about him, but that I do recall.

"Hmph." Jase apparently doesn't like this.

"Are you pouting?" I ask.

"No."

"Sulking?"

"No."

"What the hell are you doing?"

"Have you lived anywhere else?" he asks, his expression rather serious as he looks at me.

"I'm sorry?"

"Like, any other state. Or… or has it always been Ohio?"

I lower my gaze as I remember the numerous trips to various cancer centers looking for the latest miracle cure. "I've always lived in Ohio. I mean, I've visited a lot of places, several states. But I've… I've only lived in Ohio. Why?"

When I look back up at him, he seems to be studying me intently. He shakes his head briefly and shrugs. "Just a question. Are you sure we've never met before?"

I shoot him an incredulous look. "We talked for several weeks on the phone before Cleveland. There. Are you happy?"

"I'm sorry, no… that wasn't what I was talking about, and it was stupid anyhow. C'mere." He pulls me slightly closer and places a soft kiss on my temple. "Oh… oh, sorry. Was that reserved for Jack?"

"You're pushing it, Warner."

"Whatever, woman."

We are quiet during the next entire portion of the show, or at least quiet as far as conversation goes. We both laugh and cringe at the appropriate moments, and it hits me with a sudden clarity that even with what we've just discussed, nothing has changed.

This is still… *nice.*

Like we are meant to be here.

I smile, wondering if Mom has put in a bit of divine intervention for me. Maybe now that she's reunited with Dad, they are going to see that I got another chance.

Can you see me here, Mom? This is him… this is the boy I was telling you about.

"You think she would've liked me?" Jase asks suddenly, and I wonder if he could hear the thoughts that were going through my head just a moment before.

"Who, my mom?" I ask and he nods as he turns on his side to face me. I smile as I turn towards him, leaving us nearly face to face. Hmmmmmm… yep, it's a no-brainer. "She would have loved you."

It is his turn to smile. "Really?"

"She's a sucker for all that charm you bullshit people with."

184

He pushes my shoulder slightly. "It's not bullshit; I am charming."

"And not cocky in the least." I push him back as I say it.

"You're so damn mean to me!"

"You know what she would have loved? Besides the obvious...you know, the whole drool factor."

"Oh, of course," he says with a roll of his eyes.

"Your intelligence, and the fact that you actually put it to use," I continue, ignoring his interruption. "She always said how an articulate man was the most incredible turn on ever, which I must admit, I agree with."

"Oh, really?" he asks slyly, raising an eyebrow. He looks so adorable doing that, the fucker. Before I know it, I am continuing on.

"It's sexy." I emphasize the word as much as I can, even using my hands a bit. He begins laughing in earnest, causing me to add before I think, "How do you think I fell so hard for you when we'd only spoke on the phone?"

Damn it, Talia! Think, then speak!

He stops laughing, his gaze thoughtful as he looks into my eyes.

Have I gone too far?

"I didn't know that," he says softly.

My laugh shows a bit of my nervousness. "Oh, come on, yes you did." I shake my head when his eyebrow raises. "How could you not know?"

"You never told me." His expression is one of wonder, making my heart flutter.

"I didn't? Are you sure?" I had to have mentioned it.

"Positive," he replies, then adds quickly before I can argue, "You said you found out, and didn't want me to know because you thought I would never speak with you again. That's it, that's all you said."

My brow is furrowed in concentration and he gently caresses it with his fingertips. Such a sweet gesture, so simple, so kind. Does he know what the simplest of touches from him does to me?

My voice is soft when I finally speak, and it almost falters. "Even if I didn't say anything, you had to know. It was obvious."

"How so?"

My eyes widen in shock at his question. Really?

"Talli, please…in my position… how could I know?"

"The man, or the rock star," I repeat his words, and his eyes show I've hit the point spot on. "Why else would I be so upset, if you… Jase, you…" I touch his chest softly. "If you didn't mean so much to me?"

His smile is sweet, genuine, as he tugs on my shirt and pulls me into a kiss. I am surprised when it happens, but I'm not about to protest as the kiss deepens ever so slightly, his tongue gently playing with mine. With a soft moan, he pulls back slowly, that smile still there.

"Anything else you've forgotten to tell me?" he asks, raising his eyebrows.

"Yeah, I'm really a very horrible person, a serial killer, married with kids that I keep in a completely different location… um… Oh, I use you for your body, all that stuff about caring, eh… it's a load of bullshit."

He continues grinning at me, as if he's found some sort of treasure.

"What?" I ask, batting my eyelashes at him.

He kisses the tip of my nose and goes back to his original position, on his back, propped up against the pillows, watching the television. When I begin to turn also, he stops me by scooping me up into his arms to lay against his chest.

Oh… oh, this is…

Perfect.

It's perfect.

I never want this to end.

"Comfy?" he asks, his fingertips lightly caressing my back as he speaks.

"Mmmm, you may not want to do that." My body is relaxing into him, the rhythm of his heart sounding in my ear. I can feel the tension of the past few days slowly leaving with each passing moment, each stroke of his fingertips.

"Is it gonna make you all hot and bothered?" he teases, and I laugh softly but I don't answer him. "You don't have some ice pick hidden under anything here a la 'Basic Instinct' do you?"

"They're all over the house, didn't you know?"

"Great, that's comforting. What are you doing?"

"Listening to your heart." I inhale deeply and snuggle in.

"You say that like it's special," he remarks just before I feel him kiss the top of my head once more.

"It is," I say, and his arms tighten slightly. "I'm happy you're here."

He is quiet for a moment, then I hear him whisper, "I am too."

"Don't you have a plane to catch?"

"In the morning. Why, you want me to go now?"

"Huh uh," I say before I attempt to stifle a yawn.

"Are you going to sleep?" he asks.

I don't know whether or not I answer.

CHAPTER 23

I hate nightmares, with a burning fiery passion. There's nothing more disturbing than dreaming that something has happened to someone you care about, let alone dreaming that you're being chased by some deranged lunatic who's trying to kill you. And why is it that nightmares somehow resemble every single horror movie you've ever seen? The long corridors, the creepy shadows, swearing Jack Nicholson is going to come after you with an ax? Yeah, been there, dreamt that. And let's not discuss shower dreams; they bring on a whole new meaning of panic. This night, however, it is some creepy fucker chasing me in the woods, and when he catches me from behind, I struggle as best I can, feeling as if I am being strangled and smothered all at the same time.

Gentle hands on my skin jolt me out of my terror as they help me with tangled mess that is my shirt. I wonder in a brief moment of panic if this is what causes me to throw my shirt every time, but I am still shaking terribly, grabbing at the arms that are either friend or foe, far too groggy to be able to differentiate between reality and dream.

Soft lips touch mine while those arms wrap themselves around me. It comforts me, calms me as I sigh against him. It is sweet, gentle, heartwarming, and I can feel the tension ease from my body. As the kiss ends, I lean into the strong arms of the man who is trying to keep my heart from bursting in fright.

That is when I become fully awake.

I am safe, secure in Jase's arms, emotions overwhelming, body on fire. Even with his clothing still on, I can feel the heat radiating from his body, bringing about that familiar tingling throughout me. His rapid heartbeat mirrors my own, though mine is now less from fright.

I want him.

No matter how I try to keep this as platonic as possible, no matter how I try to deny it, no matter how much I tell myself now is not the time...

I want him.

I turn my face into his neck and inhale that familiar scent of his skin, all the while fighting the overwhelming urge to kiss that sensitive spot that I had taken advantage of not so long ago. The memory of that low moan in the back of his throat comes crashing around me, and I need to hear it again. I need to *cause* it again.

I remember the taste of his skin, as intoxicating as any aphrodisiac known. In that one moment of weakness, my vulnerability tangible, I feel a desperate need for some sort of reassurance not just in myself, but in life; I have to feel alive, and here I am in the arms of the man who made me feel in that one long night that his very existence depended on me.

Shy, almost timid in my touch, I give into temptation, that devil on my shoulder rejoicing as I begin leaving light kisses on his neck. I start first with just my lips, then tease softly with my teeth and tongue. His hands grip my shoulders as he begins to pull back, then as if I've found that right spot—I know I have—his grip tightens, changes, pulls me closer to him. As we sit there close to my edge of the bed holding one another, I receive instant gratification from his labored breathing, his attempt of restraining himself. His skin tastes just slightly salty from the light sweat he is breaking into, and I want to devour him on the spot, taste every inch of him.

"Oh...god..."

With that strained whisper from him, I waste no more time. There are no doubts how much he wants this as I move to straddle him, finally kissing those perfect lips while I press myself up against him. His lips part, granting me access, and I capture every sigh from him while I rock my hips against his. Beneath the barriers of clothing, I feel him grow harder as I continue to move, the friction equal parts exhilarating and frustrating.

But it isn't enough.

I should know it wouldn't be.

The slight stubble on his jaw is the perfect canvas for my fingers to trace unseen patterns as our kisses gain passion. He is moaning against my lips, his responses as I move my hips ever so slightly, just a hint of what is to come, fueling my overwhelming desire. My hands move of their own volition to his shirtfront, my fingers surprisingly steady as I continue my quest, craving to feel skin on skin. Somehow I have become the queen of multitasking this night as our mouths don't lose contact until I push him back slightly to pull his shirt off his shoulders. He doesn't stop me, his eyes searching mine for intent, his arms moving slightly as I pull the shirt completely off and drop it beside the bed.

"Talli...I... I want..."

I know, Jase... I know.

He licks his lips, his breath still coming in small gasps. "But I don't know..."

But I do.

His voice trails off as my hands go behind my back, unhooking and discarding my bra swiftly. His eyes widen slightly as they drink me in, reminding me of his response in Cleveland.

I feel every bit as empowered, as desired as I did then.

It's as intoxicating as feeling him pressed between my legs.

"What was that?" I ask, a slight smirk on my lips.

An audible sigh comes from both of us as I press myself against him once more, the sensation of skin on skin inducing another onslaught of kisses, given and taken with pure abandon. His hands grip my hips roughly, pulling me closer, as he growls deep in his throat, that sound I've wanted to hear, the one he made repeatedly that long night as he would take control of the situation, do whatever he wished with me.

But not this time.

This time, I am in control.

I grab his hands, pulling them off of me, and he abruptly sits back. Watching him visibly attempt to regain control of his breathing, his chest rising and falling rapidly, I wonder for a brief moment if this is wise. Won't this make things more complicated?

Then, he looks at me...

Straight through me.

His stormy eyes capture the glow from the hall light that has been left on, his lips are slightly parted, almost begging to be kissed. His hair is perfectly tousled, as it always is, his broad shoulders, those biceps... everything about him reminds me of his exquisite control, his expertise, the way he moves, the way he feels inside of me...

I have to feel that again.

His expression is unreadable, as he possibly thinks I am stopping what I have begun.

He couldn't be more wrong.

Placing my hands on his shoulders I nudge slightly, silently telling him to lie back. As he lays there, looking up at me curiously, another sly smile touches my lips. I grab his wrists then, pinning them above his head as I lean in to continue my mission that I have embarked upon. His soft laugh reminds me we both know my holding onto his wrists is merely symbolic; he can easily flip me over and do exactly as he pleases.

He's already proven so.

I silence his laughter with a trail of kisses, releasing his wrists as I move slowly, meticulously down his body the way he had done before with me. I take my time, using his reactions—his breaths, his shudders, his sighs—as my guide. Growing bolder as I make my way down his abdomen, I recall our night together, the way he had left no place of my torso untouched, unkissed. One of his hands is softly playing with my hair, urging me forward as I move all along the waistline of his jeans, sometimes kissing, sometimes lightly biting, sometimes just a touch of my tongue.

I pause briefly to undo his jeans, kneeling beside the bed as I slowly pull the rest of his clothes off him, and return to my quest. I nibble and kiss my way up his thighs, just as he had done to me, taking my pleasure from every gasp and moan that comes from him. He is going to know, as I had learned from him, what it is like to lose all control if it is the last thing on this earth that I accomplish. Just one slight movement, and I am there...

"Oh... fuck..."

Those words fall from his lips as I tease the length of him with my tongue and just a feather-light touch from my fingertips, my own breathing labored at his uninhibited responses.

"Mmmm... Talli..."

The way he moans my name as my mouth closes around him nearly makes me want to tear my jeans off and climb on top of him, but I am determined to be the one who maintains control. I take my time, applying pressure, and slowly take him all in.

"Fuuuuuuck."

His hips surge forward as I moan with him in my mouth, and he tangles his hand in my hair, moving up and down with me. When I glance up at him, his eyes are heavy laden with desire holding me captive as I continue teasing him, licking and sucking, stroking him with my hand. Glancing over, I happen to see his fist clenched in the covers, veins prominent in his arm as if trying to stop what I am doing my best to make inevitable. *Just the reaction I am going for.* He is close, so close to losing control.

Just... a little... bit more...

Seemingly on cue, his hands tangle themselves in my hair and he is pulling me up, back on top of him as his mouth is working its magic on the most sensitive places of my neck. I smile in triumph as he roughly pushes me onto my back, his hands trembling as he urgently pulls at the button of my jeans. Without pulling the zipper completely down, his hand is reaching between my legs, his fingers searching—and finding.

"Fuck, baby," he moans in my ear. I whimper as he roughly moves his hand against me, pushing a finger inside.

The building pressure within me is already screaming for release. Just his voice, his moans, his hushed whispers have me ready to explode, my body craving to have him inside of me.

"I... I can't help myself with you."

His voice is strained as he murmurs those words in my ear, his fingers moving in and out. I gasp, arching my back, and he moans against my skin.

"I... I don't know why I thought... I could..."

His hand leaves me, and my eyes flutter open just in time to see him expertly grab my remaining clothing. He pulls them completely off and leaves them on the floor as he crawls back up the bed to me. Damn, that image will forever be engraved in my mind, to taunt me, remind me.

But I'm not done.

Still wanting to be in control, I begin to sit up only to be pushed back as he grabs my hips and pulls me to him. I can't contain my soft cry as he forces me back into the mattress, his weight fully on me, and fills me completely.

Finally.

All restraint is gone as we move together, already close to the edge before either of us had started. The force of his thrusts pushes me further and further up the bed, each one drawing a gasp or a soft cry from me, the pain and pleasure a heady mix that I can't get enough of.

"Baby?"

I am already close to falling over that edge. "Oh... harder..."

"I... don't..."

It feels amazing, complete, like I would die if he stops, or if he slows down, or if he...

"Harder," I repeat breathlessly, pleading with him to give me the immense release that only he has ever brought me to.

"Fuck, Talli..."

Oh... yes... yes that is it...

He holds onto my hips, breaking into a sweat as he thrusts forward, his eyes sliding shut, chills spreading across his skin. One hand moves, grasping mine, pinning it to the bed, the features on his face showing the bliss, the ecstasy.

And I...

I am so... so close...

I hear the headboard crack and splinter as it crashes against the wall behind it, followed quickly by the moans of pleasure when we both lose all semblance of control, going over the edge together with our hands grasped so tightly it is going to hurt to let go. I am shaking... no...not just shaking... shivering, moaning, gasping for breath as my muscles clench around him. He holds me close, our bodies still tangled, our chests pressed together while he drops soft, sweet kisses on my face.

There it is...

That look.

The same look he had in his eyes in Cleveland.

No, this isn't like Cleveland.

This... *this* is different.

He smiles as he slowly pulls out, biting his bottom lip slightly when I gently gasp at the sensation. He even knows my favorite sleeping position, and he nudges my shoulder, urging me onto my side. Curling up behind me, he pulls me against him, his arm securely around me, our fingers intertwined. Our breathing is returning to normal slowly while we drift back into peaceful sleep, and I can feel myself smiling softly despite his impending departure. He kisses my shoulder with a sigh, and I almost swear I hear him whisper, "Please don't be sorry."

Sorry?

I sigh contentedly, snuggling back into him, too exhausted to dream, too satisfied to care.

Jase is looking through a small notebook while I drive him back to the hotel the next morning. We had grabbed breakfast sandwiches through a drive thru, and his sits beside him untouched as he flips through page after page. He stops only to switch the radio station, which once again is playing his latest hit.

He closes his eyes and lays his head back. "Thank fuck this tour is almost over. I need a break."

I welcome the conversation to the uneasy silence. "Will you actually get one?"

"Kind of. I've been jotting down ideas, and I do want to get back into the studio. I just need time to breathe, so much has happened." He looks over at me, studying my face as I drive. "You've kept me sane through this, you know. I really appreciate that." I smile at him, still troubled by his tone. "Can... can I still call you?"

We are at a red light now, and I look over at him, unable to mask the hurt in my eyes. "Jase...why..." I take a deep breath, afraid of the answer, but I ask anyway. "Why the hell would you ask that? And why are you..."

He smiles then and leans over to kiss me on the lips lightly. "Just checking." His cheeky grin is firmly on his face, comforting me. Still, I roll my eyes and continue driving. The car in front of us abruptly stops, and I slam on my breaks to avoid a collision, causing not only my bag, but Jase's sandwich and notebook to tumble to the floorboard. I'd forgotten to properly close my bag after the drive thru, so its contents spill out as well, and I wince at the mess.

"Sorry."

"Not your fault." He grins at me as he picks up the notebook and his still-wrapped sandwich. "See? No harm."

We've reached his hotel, and I pull into the parking garage and find the spot closest to the private elevators. Before I am able to shut the car off, he reaches over and touches my arm gently.

"Please...don't hate me, Talia." Oh, it's back to 'Talia' now. "I have to go to the airport alone, you know, with all the damn... paparazzi and shit, I just can't..."

"Stop, stop, I understand," I cut him off, smiling at him. His explanation makes perfect sense, again easing my anxiety. "I do need to get going; I actually have to get a few things done before I go back to work tomorrow." And school, though I don't make mention of it.

He smiles at my understanding and leans in to kiss me sweetly, the briefest touch of tongues before he sits back. "So I can't call you tonight?"

"Of course you can."

With a grin and one more kiss, he gets out of the car and walks over to the elevator. He turns back to give a slight wave before the doors close.

And suddenly... suddenly my heart constricts in my chest.

The distance between us is tangible, closing in around my heart, constricting my throat, making it difficult for me to breathe. Maybe it's all in my mind, though, residual of how we'd last parted ways. With a sigh, I shove scattered contents back into my bag before I head home.

CHAPTER 24

My cell phone ringing jars me from my sleep and I reach towards my nightstand, fumbling for it with my eyes closed against the first rays of sunlight peeking into my room.

Wait… sunlight?

One glance at my phone screen lets me know it's Jaden calling, I've slept until just before my alarm, and that I have no missed calls. I shake it off, knowing I need to check the ringer on my phone upstairs as well as my answering machine. Jase had said he would call; he probably left a message on the machine, not calling my cell phone when I didn't answer so that I would sleep.

I mumble my hellos as I answer, stretching slightly as I do so.

"How are you?"

I smile at Jaden's concerned tone. "I'm fine, don't worry about me."

"Talia,"

"I know, it's my first day back to everything since I lost Mom." I sit up and roll my shoulders back, mentally preparing myself to re-enter the world. "But really, I'm okay. Are we still doing lunch today?"

She's silent for a moment, so brief that it should have been missed, but I immediately notice something is off. "Yeah. Same time, same place. I'll meet you there. I have some stuff to do this morning before I go."

"Go?"

"Illinois."

I blink several times as I try to remember if she's told me anything about this before.

"I'm going to see Pete. You know, just... hang out. And stuff."

My anxiety begins to ease, and the beginnings of a smile touch my lips. "And stuff? Cradle robber."

"Shut up. I'll see you at lunch. Are you sure—"

"I'm fine," I cut her off. "I promise. I need to get ready and all that other shit, so I'll see you at Crystal's."

"Okay, and Talli?"

I pause, frowning slightly. Did Jaden ever call me that? "Yeah?"

"Bring the notebook."

I don't get a chance to question her before the call is disconnected. That doesn't stop the myriad of questions racing around my brain, though. Notebook? I hadn't said anything to her, or anyone, about the notebook I'd been carrying around, writing down every speck of recollection, no matter how small or seemingly innocuous, in attempts to jog my memory, shake loose the parts of the past I'd buried so well that even I couldn't find them.

Needing coffee in the worst way, I head down the stairs, pausing in the living room to check my answering machine.

No messages.

I pick up my receiver, thinking maybe he just decided not to leave one, and the lack of missed calls has an uneasy feeling settling over me. Maybe he was tired, or maybe his flight was delayed.

Or maybe he got exactly what he wanted and had nothing left to say.

While my coffee is brewing, so is my mind, all of the 'why's interrupting any productive thinking I could be having this morning. With my hair in a messy bun, minimal makeup on, comfortable clothing, and my messenger bag packed, I sit down at my computer. The sigh I let out has been building all morning, I take a sip of my coffee, contemplating the one 'why' that baffles me the most.

The notebook.

I reach into my bag, fishing around blindly until I feel the metal spiral, and I lift it out, ready to go over the contents of my fragmented thoughts of J. I set it on the desk, not even looking down at it, until I notice the feel of the pages that I'm flipping is different.

Worn.

And my heart speeds up slightly as I look down, Jase's slanted writing staring up at me from the slightly yellowed pages. I flip through them slowly, not quite reading, not quite ignoring. There are poems, lyrics that I recognize, notes, drawings, declarations of love.

All for Kate.

This entire notebook is about—is *for*—his first love, his first everything.

And with a sickening lurch, I realize that *this* is the notebook Jaden was referring to. Either she'd talked to Jase, or Jase had talked to Pete, asking for her assistance in retrieving this.

He had chosen to not contact me.

I can no longer ignore the crushing sensation of rejection threatening to envelop me. How could I have been so stupid to think that we were fine? And why had I? Because we had sex? Yeah, *that* had turned out so well for us before. No, it was his words, his declarations that he didn't want to lose me…

As a friend.

I know what's waiting for me before I even type his name into the search engine. I know the pictures are coming, the ones of him at an airport—not just *any* airport; the one in *my* town—embracing a beautiful brunette, gazing longingly into her eyes, holding her hand as they walked along the corridor, boarding a plane together to whatever destination they'd gone to.

And I know, even before I read the captions, that the girl in his arms is Kate.

It's at least four hours later before my phone finally shows Jase's number. I'm torn on whether or not to pick it up. I mean... he'd lied to me. Flat out lied. He'd known he was about to see his first love, his first everything, so he'd ushered me off with a promise to call when he got home last night.

And now I've seen the damning evidence with my own eyes.

Along with a notebook dedicated to her, while he had my ramblings of a boy I'm trying so desperately to remember.

With a heavy heart, I decide it's best to answer anyway.

"Good... morning?" he says with a slight lift making it sound like a question.

"Hi," is about all I can manage.

"Hey, um,"

"Yes, I have the notebook. The one that you had Jaden call me for." I don't mean to sound harsh, but damn.

He'd lied to me.

"And I have yours."

"Obviously."

"Okay, what gives?"

What gives? "People like to take your picture, don't they?"

"Um, yeah," he draws out slowly.

"And they like to post them."

"Ah, fuck." I hear him typing on what I assume is a laptop, and then he lets out a heavy sigh. "Yeah, I should have warned you about paparazzi. Or did I already? We talked about so much, and,"

"That's her, isn't it?" I cut him off. "Your first love, your first everything."

And I'm met with silence.

"And you had her fly here, to my home, to spend time with her," I add.

"Look, Kate and I are friends, okay?"

"But you lied to me."

Again, silence.

"You know," I say, "that's all I needed to hear."

"Last night doesn't give you the right to question... no, stop, I didn't mean it like that."

"Yes, you did." I can't stop the tears at this point. "You did, and I can't do this right now."

"Then when can you?"

I stare around my empty townhouse, the one I'd just spent the past four hours deep cleaning. "My place is a mess," I lie. "I need to go."

"I've been there, Talli," he says, the emphasis on my name. "Is there anything you need to tell me?"

Fuck, this again? "We've been over everything already."

"No, we haven't."

"We had one hell of a discussion about honesty, and now I'm feeling like it's rather hypocritical of you to ask me if I have something to tell you," I snap.

"Wait just a damn minute," he replies. "We never said we were going to divulge every minute of our lives to one another, nor did we say either of us have a right to demand it."

"Got it. Point made." Damn these tears and damn my voice for wavering.

"I don't think you do. You know I have questions in my life that I'm seeking answers to, and the answers aren't always in front of me. That's a conversation we did have."

He's being so short, so defensive, and my bullshit radar—this is what Tish must be talking about—goes on high alert.

He's still not being honest with me.

"And just that night," he continues, "you told me you weren't going anywhere, that I was stuck with you. Was that another lie?"

"Stop turning this around on me, right now," I demand, my anger overriding my hurt. When he pauses, I add, "Your omission of what you were doing is the same as lying, so don't you dare get high and mighty with me."

"I'm sorry," he says quickly. "Shit, Talli, I just... are you walking away from me now?"

Didn't he just walk away from me to go spend time with his first love?

My tears are freely falling now, and I hear him inhale sharply.

"Please don't cry."

I can't help it.

"God, I hate this," he adds. "It shouldn't be like this, okay? It shouldn't."

"What shouldn't be?"

"Just... I need to know if you'll answer when I call again. I'm so... I'm so fucked up, so confused right now, and... will you talk to me? Later? Please?"

I should say no.

But then I'd be a hypocrite, wouldn't I?

"I'm going to take your silence as a yes, so I'm going to let you go now. Until later, do you hear me Talli? Until later."

I place the phone back in its base for it to charge as I sigh and glance over at the notebook. I've only thumbed through it, not really read enough other than to know it was all for Kate.

Do I read it now?

Do I go over every declaration of love, every note in the margins, every song that he'd written for her? This time, the angel on my shoulder tells the devil to piss off, and the notebook sits untouched for the next week.

CHAPTER 25

Where did that dress come from?" Moira is asking. I am cleaning out my closet for the clothing drive that her middle school is sponsoring. "That's, like... my size!"

Ah. The dress. The dress I borrowed in New York.

New York

I have no idea why it is still in my closet, other than for some unfathomable reason I can't let it go.

"No, Tinkerbell, this is *not* your size," I correct her. "This...well, I wore this when I was a teenager."

"Your butt would hang out of it!"

I shake my head, laughing softly. "It so did not hang out of it. Not that it didn't try to. I couldn't bend over much, see." I hold it up to me, giving her an idea of how short that little black number is.

"Or look down because it probably pushed your boobs up to your chin."

"No, it actually fit...very nicely. See the fabric? It hugs, it doesn't push." I run my hand along the edge of it, showing the give of the fabric, the texture of it.

I had loved that dress. Believe it or not, back in high school I actually really enjoyed wearing tight clothes, playing the curls up, wearing the dark makeup. I'd liked the attention, mostly because it took my mind off of everything else. I was wearing it to meet Keith, who never showed.

But J had.

With someone else.

And my, oh my, how the curse words flew that night from my darling older sisters when I finally made it back to the city, back to the hospital. Lucky for me I had also gotten into Lisa's stash of anti-anxiety meds and taken my fair share of them. I was too numb to care.

"Um...Aunt Talli... can I take this or not?"

Ha! As if.

"Your mother would kill me. You know, since I'm not dumb enough to think you'd put this in the donation box," I have to add before she interrupts me.

"But...it's not like I have your boobs. Or your butt, either."

"Ouch, thanks," I say, crinkling my nose up as I place that little black dress back in my closet, towards the very back of it to hopefully be forgotten all over again.

"That was a compliment, you know," she counters, throwing a wadded-up piece of paper at me.

Wow.

Really?

I blush and smile at Tish's daughter, unable to form a simple thank you since I am so stunned over her statement. That tiny little girl said *that*? About *me*?

"Hey, I think we found just about all of the clothes you were looking for," Tish says as she walks into the bedroom. She peers into my closet, where I stand towards the back, placing the once-treasured garment back on the rack. "Ohhhh, the dress. You still have that?"

"It holds fond memories." There's just a hint of sarcasm in my voice. I've told the girls about the dress, but none have ever seen me in it.

"That's the epitome of a fuck me dress, though...no repeating that, Moira."

"Lips are sealed," Moira singsongs, and I have to laugh.

"I have you know," I say to Tish, "I never once got laid while wearing that dress...and don't even say it, you know what I mean." I point at her, raising my eyebrow in a mock veiled threat. "That dress never made me...well, lucky."

"I say keep it, take it with you when you have to go to your seminar," Tish suggests. I give her the 'you've got to be kidding me' look, and she continues. "Hey, what happens in Vegas, right? Besides, Jaden will be out there doing the tattoo convention, and you have that hot Cardiac doctor going with you guys too."

"He's not going with us per se," I corrected her. "He's speaking at the seminar. I don't even know how I got added."

I was somehow put on the list for this trip, even though I'm still a student. I'm close to graduating, of course, and I'm pretty sure I've found my niche in the cardiac wing.

"So, when you all go out, you wear the black dress, and get lucky," Moira pipes up.

"Ugh." I mock-pout as I make my way out of the walk-in closet, partially from Moira's comment, and partially because, of all things, Jase's latest single is playing.

Damn it.

"Oh, that's right... you've already done that," Tish whispers in my ear, and laughs when I elbow her.

"You're so not funny."

"Of course I am," she disagrees.

"Okay, fine, how's this? Me taking that dress? Not on your life," I say, closing my closet door.

"Hellooooo is anyone in here?" I hear Jaden call out as she is letting herself in. Ah, the joys of friends with keys.

"No, not a soul," I reply loudly as she takes the stairs and comes into the bedroom. "You're leaving tonight, right?"

"Yeah, I'm heading out to Chicago for a couple of days, see the sights, you know," Jaden says with a shrug.

"Yeah, like you and Pete are gonna do sightseeing," Tish jokes, and Jaden merely shrugs again.

"You're doing an awful lot of shrugging," Moira points out. "Is it because I'm in the room? I can leave, you know… although I totally get the adult humor."

"I'm all about the adventure," Jaden says, ignoring Moira's comment. "Speaking of adventure, I know you have a room elsewhere in Vegas that the hospital pays for, but you're so staying with me at the Hard Rock," she says, pointing at me.

"Oh, my heart's broken," I quip, handing her Jase's notebook, still unread. "There. Now he can quit going gray with worry over it."

She immediately begins flipping through the pages, which is the last thing in the world that Jase had wanted, not that I am overly concerned with his wants at this moment.

"Hey, what are you doing?" I ask, trying not to pay to close attention to the expression on her face, which is one of pure disgust.

"Who the hell is Kate? And this stuff is…look at the dates, it's old," she comments, and I try in vain to get the notebook from her. "What, like you haven't read this?"

"No, I haven't, and you shouldn't either," I say sternly, trying to get it from her.

"God, this guy was a little man-whore," Jaden continues, ignoring me as I throw my hands up in frustration.

"Let's all forget that he didn't want anyone to read it," I comment, but she continues on.

"Niiiice, all of this… 'I was thinking about you the whole time,' Oh, make me gag."

"He seriously wrote that?" Moira asks.

"Yeah… it's… look at this! He's writing about his exploits with other girls and writing notes to this Kate about how he wished it was *her*!"

I just…don't need to hear that.

"Moira, if you ever date anyone like that, I'll… lock you in a convent or something," Tish says, reading over Jaden's shoulder.

"Look at this!" Jaden exclaims again. "It's lyrics and shit…I recognize this one from his first album, the first indie one."

"This guy wrote all this stuff about exes to some chick?" Moira asks, perplexed. "Why would he do that?"

"Stay out of it, please." I snatch the book away from them then.

I am heartsick hearing about all of his proclamations of love to Kate... I certainly don't need to see or hear any more, not after the pictures.

Tish's eyebrow is raised as she looks at me. "Very overprotective of someone who's just a friend."

That is the story I told all of them, and I am sticking to it. I can't bring myself to admit that I'd slept with him when he was wishing I was someone else... I mean, how humiliating, right?

"Anyhoooo, is it pizza time yet?" Moira asks. Bless her for the subject change.

"Cass should be here any time now with it," Jaden answers, and as they busy themselves in their world of gossip I walk downstairs, holding onto the elusive notebook.

"Pizza was fantastic, as per usual," Moira says, licking her fingers.

"I suppose this is in lieu of girls' night this week?" Cass asks. This is a rarity, and hopefully not a sign of things to come, not when I need them the most.

"I'm sorry, I'm just not up to it," Tish admits.

"I'll be..."

"Busy," we finish for Jaden, who grins sheepishly.

"What about you, Talia?" Cass looks at me, her smile genuine.

What about me?

I am going to be here in this apartment all by myself wishing I hadn't fallen in love with a man who is so obviously still in love with someone else.

"I need to get some rest before my double on Saturday," I lie. "And... I think I have a paper due." Not a lie.

Truth be told, though, I'm not ready to go out and paint the town.

"Yes, but in two weeks, Vegas baby!" Jaden exclaims, and we clink our glasses together.

"I will be there for a seminar, though, so…"

"Afterwards we get your ass drunk and let you sleep on the company-paid trip home," she cuts me off.

"Okay, arm twisted," I say, although my heart wasn't quite behind the words.

"She's taking her little black dress," Moira speaks up.

"I'm so not taking that!"

"And the hot Cardiac doc is gonna be there," Tish adds.

"Dr. Craig?" Cass asks, and I nod.

"He's not *that* hot."

Okay, that is a lie, he is completely hot, with his dark hair and eyes, and those damn dimples…but I'm not into him.

"Are you blind? Or just blinded by the Sex Voice still?" Cass asks, her eyes wide as she looks at me.

Ah. So, the subject has been brought up.

"I haven't heard from Jase in a…week," I reply, my head held high. *Remember, Talli, they believe you left it as friends…*

"A week? Has he been that busy?" Tish asks, looking between Jaden and me for an answer. Jaden throws up her hands.

"Paint me red and white and call me Switzerland, I know nothing."

"Translation: she loves me, but really enjoys screwing his brother." I am actually able to semi-joke, which makes the older girls laugh and Moira stick her fingers in her ears and singsong "La la la la la". The phone ringing interrupts our much-needed laughter, and I answer without really looking at the number. "Hello?" I say between giggles.

"What the hell is so funny?"

Perhaps Jase is taking advantage of my supposed good mood by trying to keep the conversation light, but that overwhelming rollercoaster feeling in my stomach makes me stop laughing. If he only knew what his voice… what *he* does to me…

"Oh…um…I'm sorry, is this a bad time?"

I do my best to recover. "No, no, we were just talking about Jaden...and your brother." I stress the last word, throwing a piece of pepperoni at her.

"Hi, Jase," the girls all say, and he laughs softly.

"It's not Friday, is this an early girls' night?"

"That is on hiatus this week." I feel odd having idle chitchat with him. I motion to the girls that I will be back and head upstairs for some privacy.

"Is everything all right? Are...you, are you all right?" He sounds so sincere I can't bring myself to give a hateful reply. I opt instead for the usual.

"I'm fine, don't worry about me."

"I...haven't heard from you."

"I haven't heard from you either, Jase."

"Touché," he replies, and lets out a small laugh. "I guess I've tortured myself long enough and needed my fix."

Damn him for making me grin in spite of my heart breaking. "Nice one. I'm a fix now?"

"What can I say? You're addictive."

I laugh at that. "The shit's getting deep in here."

"But you laughed...laughing is good."

Laughing eases the tension.

Laughing also reminds me of the simpler times, back when we were merely Not John and Not Telling, back when we could divulge whatever we wanted to, no worries about hurt feelings.

"Jaden has your notebook," I say, trying to steer the conversation from anything too personal. I just can't handle it right now. "She's taking it with her when she visits Pete."

"All right." I can tell he's forcing himself to keep his tone light. "Did you read it?"

There he goes again.

"Did you expect me to?"

"I don't know what to expect from you anymore."

Is he doing this on purpose? Okay, that is a stupid question, but damn, does it have to hurt so much?

"Is that a bad thing?" I ask.

"No, not always. Sometimes I'm pleasantly surprised."

I blush in spite of myself, remembering how I had turned to him the last night he was here. Is that one of his pleasant surprises?

No... now is not the time.

"And other times you want to pull your hair out," I add for him, and he laughs.

"I'm not going to say no, but..." He draws in a deep breath, just like he always seems to do when he contemplates whether or not it is wise to continue the conversation.

"But what, Jase?"

"I don't want to fight with you tonight, I... don't like fighting with you. And..." He pauses, which doesn't help my heart that is pounding madly. "And I don't like the fact that it bothers me."

My eyes slide shut at his admission, knowing exactly what he means. A part of me wants to scream that I feel the same way; the same part of me wants to beg him to come back so we can talk about this face to face. Knowing I can't do either, I try to remain rational and calm. "Hence the confusion?"

"Funny how I knew you'd understand," he says. "At least I think you do."

"I'm trying."

"That's all I'm asking from you."

"I think that's about all you've asked from me," I comment. "Ever."

"Then...it's settled." His voice is still calm, controlled. "I'll let you get back to the girls now. Give me a call, when you're ready."

When I'm... ready.

When I can talk with him.

When we can be... just... *be.*

"Okay," I say softly.

"Until later?"

I shiver before I answer him. "Of course."

One small click, and the line is clear.

I sit here for a moment, remembering our last night together. I remember him holding me as I fell asleep. I remember how tender, how gentle he'd been when he tried to calm me from my frightening dream.

And then after...

I remember his arms around me, that soft sweet kiss on my shoulder. And then... then I remember those words he whispered as we were drifting off to sleep.

My brain, my whole conscience is screaming at me as my fingers make quick work of a memorized number.

"What took you so long?" is how he answers the phone.

"I'm not sorry."

He knows exactly what I mean.

CHAPTER 26

Two hours before I am supposed to leave for the airport, Jaden is in my apartment helping me pack. "This just isn't you to procrastinate this way," she says, watching me as I run around.

No kidding.

Me... the way I had been... would have been ready days ago, had an actual list of everything I was going to take, had the list on the refrigerator along with a very important document that I am scrambling to find. But have I? No. No, because my mind will wander to a certain rock star and all of his hotness that he just should be shot for, and everything that has happened in this apartment when he was here.

"There's a lot that just isn't me anymore," I mumble as softly as I can in my lovely state of a near panic. "Where is my itinerary?" I ask loudly, as if that will make it reappear. "Dr. Craig said I had to have it because it has all the confirmation numbers on it."

"You know, I've heard the expression of screwing someone's brains out, but I had no idea that Jase had actually done that to you. Hey! Ow!"

I hit her rather hard with a throw pillow that I am still holding in my hand, ready to strike again. "I need to focus."

"Shall we put on the Karate Kid so you can remember the way of Mr. Miagi?" she asks. I pull the pillow back to hit her once more and she screeches, "I'm kidding!" She reaches over, prying the pillow from my fingers, the look on her face one of pure amusement. "Easy, crusher. Let's just think here; where do you remember having it last?"

I have to roll my eyes at what is right up there as one of the most asinine questions on the face of this planet. "If I knew that it wouldn't be lost, would it?"

She stands there for a moment, contemplating. "Okay, point made. So...let's just go through and make sure you are packed completely, then we'll worry about the itinerary."

I take in a deep breath and nod. She is right. She is always right.

"I should have been ready days ago," I mutter under my breath. I have lost so much motivation, not even looking forward to this trip to Vegas as I should. Sure, it means I have two long days of lectures, or classes. I don't need continuing education credits yet, but if I turn in my papers to the college it is supposed to count for... something. I'm sure they've told me what. I get out of classes, out of work, out of my externship. Okay, it also means that one of my travel partners is none other than the hottest doctor in the entire state of Ohio (who, of course, knows he is hot, much to my chagrin) with the most famous dimples in this city at least. Most importantly for my sanity it means the gypsy of the group is all up for a Vegas vacation, which has something to do with a tattoo convention that she wants to attend, and she's promised me she'll make sure we paint the town black, red, purple, and every other color under the sun, to which I immediately protested but I'm not entirely sure that will work.

Ah, yes. Uptight Talia is back; the Talia who watches those 'What Happens in Vegas' commercials and swears she'll never go. I can't risk putting myself out like that, having my co-workers look at me in a different light, minus my penchant for swearing that this time I am going to conquer, and...

"I thought you were packing that dress!" Jaden comments, looking through my bags.

"I thought you had more sense than that," I reply, looking through my makeup bag, thinking maybe I have put the itinerary in there. Why not? I could swear I've looked everywhere else.

"Bring this, and those hot black pumps," she tries convincing me, but I am saved from yet another retort by the phone. I walk quickly across the room to get the receiver, thinking it may be Dr. Craig who is arranging for us to be picked up.

"Hello?" I ask a bit breathlessly as I pick up the phone. I hear a soft sigh on the other end, and the hairs on the back of my neck stand straight up.

Oh, I know that sigh.

"Damn it, Talia, quit doing that to me."

Fuck. Me.

No... no, not now, he can't call *now*. Not when the itinerary's missing and I have to have it before that stupid car or taxi or whatever comes to pick us up.

"Well...you call, I'm in a rush and a panic, that's your fault, not mine." I say it so quickly I am surprised he picks up on everything, but his easy laughter lets me know he did.

"Rush and panic? Oh, this is great. What did you lose now?"

"Hey! I... resemble that." I am moving everything around on my dresser, cradling the phone between my ear and shoulder.

"You're hilarious. Breathe, Talia. Just breathe. What did you lose?"

"You're hundreds of miles away, I hardly think you can help me find it." Thankfully he understands me when I get this frazzled and never takes it personally.

"Can I try?"

Oh, that is too damn cute for words. The fucker.

"Sure," I play along. "I cannot find my itinerary."

"Itinerary?"

"See? Told you that you couldn't help me. It has all of my confirmation numbers and the passes for the seminars with it."

"Oh, that? Weren't you making fun of it last time you were on the phone with me?"

Well, huh. Fucking smarty-pants a few hundred miles away can remember that but can't remember to tell me his ex is coming to meet him here. If he was in striking distance, I would take my best shot.

"Talia?"

"Well yes, I was. But, so? What good does that do me now?"

"Weren't you in your walk-in closet, going through that little chest in there? Speaking of which, damn woman you have more clothes than most Hollyrock bitches I know."

"Bitches, charming...walk-in closet?" I am walking, listening to him try to be his witty self and make me laugh. Jaden is stuffing something into my bag as I pass her, and I am completely trusting that she is grabbing an item off my list that I have *just* written this evening. I walk to the back of the closet, pulling some clothes forward on the rack as I keep moving.

Well, I'll be damned.

"Is there some kind of hidden camera that you put in here?" I interrupt Mr. I'm-Too-Sexy-For-Words as he continues poking fun at my insane amount of clothing that I never wear.

"Well... no, but thanks for the suggestion. Next time I'm out, we can arrange that."

"Very funny, you insufferable tease."

"Insufferable tease... is this your way of getting around telling me that I was right?"

Like I'll tell him.

"Right about what?" I ask, grabbing the itinerary and passes, handing them to Jaden before I lose them again.

"Where did you find these?" she asks, and I wince inwardly, knowing what is coming from that cocky boy on the other end of the line.

"I was, and you weren't going to tell me!"

"Why should I tell you, so you can throw it in my face?"

He laughs then...one of his real laughs, one that shows me we are making some sort of progress. "I could throw something in your face, Talia Christine, but it would be ungentlemanly of me to do so."

"Easy, Warner," I say, garnering another laugh from him.

"So...um..." He is getting his laughter under control. "This seminar, when is it?"

"I'm leaving in less than two hours."

"Ah," is all he says to that. "Well, damn, I was gonna see if you were busy, but I guess that answers my question."

My heart flutters for just a brief moment, until he continues.

"I mean, I know you're busy and all, I just know that...well, this weekend, this whole weekend, I... have a lot riding on it, and I don't want to impose with any...phone calls and such if you're busy."

Sure, pal. Back to needing Not Telling...

No... no, that's okay, because I want that so badly, too.

"I'll have my cell." I could kick myself for telling him that. Way to look desperate, there. "What's happening this weekend? I thought your next show was Wednesday."

"It is...and I can't... I mean, I..."

"...can't talk about it," I finish for him. Of course. I am walking downstairs now, giving the rest of the apartment the once-over while still on the phone with him.

"Forgive me?"

"Someday," I answer honestly. "Listen, I have to go." I could stay on the phone just a little while longer, but some wounds are still too fresh.

"Okay." He sounds disappointed, but I can't give in. I have to protect my heart somehow. "When will you be back?"

"Monday afternoon, but I told you I'll have my cell."

"I'll remember that...you know, just in case."

"If you need reinforcements," I said softly.

That is the way our conversations the past two weeks have gone; he'll make a few off-handed comments, and then proceed to tell me how much our friendship means to him, in some way or other. Part of me is genuinely happy to have him in my life, another part of me longs for him to feel the same way I do.

Avoiding the issue instead, we skirt around it as he tries to figure out exactly what it is that his heart wants. And, like the fool I've become for him, I wait.

An hour and a half has passed since we hung up when the taxi pulls up. Jaden is chiding me because I've insisted that we be outside waiting for it. "This way, we know we have everything," I explain.

"You know, I can't wait to get your ass to Vegas, get you drunk, and make you forget all about the insanity that has consumed your brain."

She has the best of intentions, she really does.

But we all know what they say about the best of intentions, don't we?

"Explain to me again why it's so important that we're flying in at night," I say over my shoulder as I look out the window.

All drinks have been discarded, trays folded down, and seats are in their upright positions. Jaden has sweet-talked a fellow nurse of mine on her way to the same seminar into switching seats so that she can sit beside me. She even has the nerve to force me to take the window seat, which I hate.

"Just...trust me."

That phrase is getting old.

"Dr. Craig was an absolute doll to work it out this way, you know? Mmmm, he's actually a doll regardless."

"I see nothing, Jaden," I reply, ignoring her last comment. Do I need to say anything about the adorableness or sexiness of Mr. Dimples? No. Besides, that is the last thing my mind is on. "That's all I see... nothing."

"No, seriously, keep watching. It's going to look like...like...well, like Disney World threw up in the middle of the desert."

Before I can even shoot her the incredulous look that she knows has to be coming, right before my eyes...there it is. A mass of colorful lights strings out below, one large beam shooting straight up to the sky. It is absolutely breathtaking, and I can't stop the chills that spread all over my body at just the sight of it. I suppose my eyes widen a bit because Jaden lets out a short laugh.

"Can you just feel it?" she asks.

"I think that's turbulence," I reply without thinking. She leans over and whispers in my ear.

"That's your life about to change."

McCarren Airport itself is impressive. The first thing that hits me once I've adjusted to being on the ground is the sound of bells—over and over, ringing and chiming. The lights are blinding, the air humming with excitement as all around me people are losing themselves in the great art of indulgence.

I certainly am not going to be one of them.

Nope, no way. Las Vegas is not the kind of city for Talia Christine Emerson, Ms. Stay-at-home-and-watch-Classic-TV girl. Las Vegas is a city where too many things can go wrong.

And probably would.

"Hello, ladies, did you enjoy your flight?" Dr. Craig in all his tall dark and handsomeness stands before us, an easy grin on his face. Damn, there go those dimples again.

"Not as much as your first-class self did, but yes," Jaden replies, and he laughs.

Wow, he has a nice laugh too.

"I am told I need to thank you for having us fly over at nighttime, Dr. Craig," I say to him, my formal self as is the norm those days. Besides, formal Talia doesn't get into trouble.

"Talia, we're in Vegas. Unless I'm behind that podium, the name is John, got it?"

"Sure," I mutter, not paying much attention as I am staring all around me. I swear I feel like I've stepped onto the planet Mars or something. It is absolutely unreal. I mean, who *dresses* like these people? Who *acts* like these people? Well, minus the frat boys that are yelling and laughing rather loudly about all the babes they were going to score—my first thoughts about them are they must be from Ohio. Actually, come to think of it, they may even live in my apartment complex.

"You know what she needs, Dr. Crai...er, *John*," Jaden speaks up, a big cheese-eating grin on her face.

"I'll be right back," he says to her before going off in his own direction.

"Don't we need to wait?" I ask her, and she shakes her head, half-dragging me to the luggage section. Apparently, someone else is already there gathering all of our luggage for us, the other nurses chatting the poor fellow up. "Why aren't we waiting for him?"

"He knows what he's doing," she says to me before turning to the employee and telling him, "Dr. Craig's things should be on that rack as well."

"And yours?" the young man asks.

"Nah, I'm at a different hotel." She puts her bag on her shoulder and grins at me, winking.

"Well, for everyone here for the Cardiac Seminar, your shuttle is waiting outside. I will take your luggage out there."

"Do you have your cell on?" Jaden asks me, and I nod right about the time Dr. Craig returns, two *very* large drinks in his hands.

"No dice," he says to Jaden. "But..." He hands me one of the large sweet-smelling concoctions. My first guess is margarita, but I am uneasy to take a drink. "That will do for now."

"What will do? And for now what?" I ask, confused.

"Drink up, I'll be by to get you in about an hour," Jaden says, not answering my question.

"I can't take this on the shuttle," I protest. "Or drink this outside on the street, or..."

I stop mid-sentence, noticing several people milling about with the same exact drink in their hand.

What the fuck?

"Welcome to Vegas," Dr. Craig says with his devil may care smile.

It is probably not the wisest thing for me to drink that entire margarita in an hour, but for some unfathomable reason I am an absolute bundle of nerves. In all actuality, the drink is gone in less than an hour because I also shower and change into a comfortable pair of jeans and a curve-hugging t-shirt. Pulling my curls into a big mess that somehow works in the back, I survey myself in the mirror, scrutinizing everything I see. I add some light makeup just to feel a little better, reminding myself the whole time there is no one here I am trying to impress.

The seminar doesn't kick off until 10 AM each day, and since it is only 9 in the evening, I figure it will be just fine to go see the sights with Jaden. I am finishing up the last of that far too delicious margarita when my cell rings, probably signaling to me that she is on her way.

"Ello, ello," I answer, finally relaxed enough to sit down at the desk.

"Is murder always a crime?" Jase asks, and damned if my heart doesn't begin to race. How does he always do that to me? Composure, Talia. Composure.

"Sometimes?" I say, giggling slightly. "Who's frazzled now?"

"I don't get frazzled, you do. I get...frustrated."

"Potato, potahto," I counter, then giggle again. Stupid fucking alcohol.

"Aren't you, like...on a work seminar or something?"

"You just talked to me a little bit ago, so you already knew that, duh."

"Duh? Oh, this should be fun—Talli's drinking." I swear I can hear his smile.

If only I could reach out and touch it.

Damn it, Talia. Focus!

"What does that have to do with you being frazzled?"

"Frustrated," he corrects me.

"Whatever. 'Sup?"

He growls out loud. "People, damn people are what's up! I have somewhere I have to be, but am I there? Nooooo. And why not?"

"Um...people?"

"You're mocking me."

I smile, even though he can't see me. "Yes, I am. What people are you mad at and why is it their fault you're not where you're supposed to be?"

"When your entire life is planned by several different people, and none of them are talking to each other, things get...so...fucked up." Those last two words seem to be said through clenched teeth, and for some reason it is oddly...hot.

"Define fucked up, and use that growl for me, could ya?" Damn it! See? Alcohol.

He is silent for a minute as I collapse with laughter, then deadpans, "You had to go there, didn't you Emerson?"

"Last name even! You really must be having a bad day."

"I've seen better. I just..."

"What do you want?" I ask, and he sighs.

"Everything fixed," he says softly.

Oh god...

I want that, too...

Snap out of it, Talia! That's not what he's talking about!

"Can it be fixed?" My eyes are clenched shut as I await his answer, even though I know that he and I are talking about two different things.

"I hope so." His voice is soft, sending a shiver straight through me.

If only.

I hear commotion in the background, and he sighs again. "Fuck, fuck, *fuck*."

"That doesn't sound good."

"No...it's not. Hey, sorry...I didn't mean to unload on you or anything,"

"Yes, you did," I cut him off. "And if it helped you any, then I'm happy."

"I'll s...I'll call you later, okay?"

"Okay," I reply, then we hung up simultaneously.

I close my eyes once more, making a tiny wish to some unseen force that won't hear me anyhow that he will get his wish.

Even if it isn't with me.

Only fifteen minutes have passed since I hung up the phone when Jaden is at my door. "You up to seeing this?"

No matter how ready I say I am, actually living it, experiencing it is... indescribable. I know I look like the wide-eyed tourist as she drags me down the streets, new rounds of margaritas in our hands. Every few feet I am handed a flyer for a strip club or the newest up and coming band playing in the various clubs dotted all along as far as my eyes can see. Pyramids, tall grandiose buildings, people dancing down the sidewalk, street performers everywhere...

"Isn't this like...Mardi Gras?" Jaden asks.

"I never went to Mardi Gras," I remind her, stepping around about the fourth person in the past five minutes to be walking around with a drink in their hand. "And what if we want to go over there?" I ask, pointing across the street.

"Nah, we're going up this way...just a little off the strip, John said there was a fantastic hole-in-the-wall bar that we can just relax in without all..." She waves her arms around, "this."

"I thought that this," I wave my free hand around imitating her, "was what we were shooting for."

"Oh, you'll get this tomorrow, I promise. And Saturday, and Sunday, before we send you home on Monday."

My eyes are wide as I look ahead at a replica of the Eiffel Tower, and I shake my head.

"You'll have time…maybe," she says, and I am unable to ask her the exact gist of her words due to all the commotion surrounding us. She leads me by the hand down a side street, stopping directly in front of a small wooden door. She gives me a once-over, fluffing my hair and smiling.

"What the hell was that for?" I ask, but instead of answering she drags me into the small bar. Inside is a thin layer of smoke hanging, a jukebox playing an old Guns n Roses tune, and a few patrons who seem to be locals. Oh, and Dr. Craig…er, John, sitting at the bar, alone, signaling to the bartender that he is buying our round. I note curiously that he seems to shrug when he looks at Jaden. What the hell is up with that?

"Good call to bring us here," Jaden is saying, although her expression is unreadable. "I don't think we want our Vegas Virgin going into shock her first night."

"Too late," I speak up. "You've really gone out of your way for this trip, Dr…um…John, and I appreciate it."

"Don't mention it," he says, his grin dazzling especially in my somewhat tipsy frame of mind. "You know, I was just trying to handle a crisis, a friend of mine called, and it was a good thing I was in here so I could semi-hear what was going on."

"Ahhh," Jaden says, accepting her beer from the bartender who hands one to me also.

"Is your friend okay?" I ask.

"He's working it out," Dr. Craig replies. "So… let us salute our long weekend in Vegas, seminar and all. Not everything is about work, right?"

Right.

We salute the weekend and take sips just as Dr. Craig's cell phone begins to ring.

"I thought it wasn't all about work," I joke, and he flashes me a grin as he answers his phone. I turn to speak to Jaden, with bits and pieces of Dr. Craig's side of the conversation trickling into my brain.

"So tomorrow night you're coming to my hotel. I guess you have to sign in tomorrow for your thing or I'd have you come back with me tonight," Jaden is saying. I open my mouth to agree when something about Dr. Craig's voice stops me.

"You've got to be kidding me! This weekend? Why this weekend? And why... you know, we can do this, we can work around this. What do you mean I have to be there, too? Yeah, I know, it's just so last minute."

I shake my head to clear it, and say to Jaden, "Apparently his friend isn't out of his crisis yet, or it has gotten worse. But your hotel, tomorrow, I'm in."

"We'll hit the bar, do some gambling... they have different clubs and restaurants right in there, and since your lecture or whatever doesn't start until 10 each day you should be fine."

"I'm not a teenager anymore, Jaden," I remind her with a laugh, and Dr. Craig's voice drowns out her answer.

"Fuck, how could she... ok, so it wasn't her fault, it was his, but yeah you're right; it does throw a wrench in there, a big one. We will...dude, shut up for two seconds! We'll work it out."

"Dude? That's extensive vocabulary for a cardiologist," I remark with a grin, which he returned.

"Yes...yes. And no." Dr. Craig is obviously talking to his friend as he is turning slightly away, perhaps to hear better.

"And I didn't hear what you were saying." I point at Jaden, who is studying Dr. Craig's face. "Helllooooo, Earth to Jaden! Oh, wait..."

No.

Hell no she isn't.

I pull her close to whisper in her ear. "What's up with you and Dr. Craig?"

"Nothing," she replies with a sheepish grin, making me raise my eyebrow. I pull her close again.

"Are you trying to set me up?"

"With him? No."

"With who, then?"

"No one, and you are paranoid," Jaden answers. "Now drink your beer." I promptly stick my tongue out at her but do what I am told.

"Okay, ladies, now, where were we?" Dr. Craig asks, turning back towards us and putting his phone in his pocket.

"In a small bar in a really big city," I reply, and he laughs.

"You got me there. So, round one tonight is here. But we're on...for tomorrow."

Jaden smiles at his comment. "At that one bar?"

"I...believe so." There is so something going on but being in my inebriated state I can't quite place it. Before I can ask them what the hell is up, my phone is buzzing in my pocket. This time it is my turn to try to hear through the noise that is filtering in every time the door opens.

"Hello?"

"Behave yourself."

Damn, damn, DAMN!

Jase fucking Warner when I'm buzzed and a bit wound up is *not* a good thing. I mean it *could* be, but not when he isn't in front of me, and besides we aren't *that* way now, not that we were when we *did* but...

Fuck.

"What is 'have' and how am I supposed to 'be' it?" I ask Jase, who still seems a bit riled up.

"Christine..."

"Mmm, I love it when you call me that," I say breathlessly, again without thinking.

"Really, now?" he asks. "I'll remember that one."

I just may have to hold him to that.

CHAPTER 27

Ibuprofen and my favorite sports drink are my best friends this morning. Damn Jaden and John, I was fed so much alcohol I must have just passed out in my clothes the moment I'd gotten back, after taking said concoction.

Concoction.

I'm a nursing student and still can't say or think of the word without giggling.

But I digress, I'm still unsure how I've managed to ward off the hangover, thinking surely I had drank too much for the magic concoction (ha!) to work...but it does, and I am infinitely grateful. I wake up still in my clothing, hair an absolute hot mess, a little makeup smearing my face, but hangover free.

And late.

I am in dire need of a shower no matter what the clock says, so I take a quick one, hoping it will wake me up just a little bit more. Being sleepy is bad to begin with. Being sleepy with a million things on my mind that tends to wander to begin with? Recipe for disaster.

Hell, I don't even have my clothes unpacked.

After the shower, I am finally pulling my clothing out of my bag and suitcase as I had been in no shape to do so the night before. Wrapped in a pair of jeans on the bottom of my bag are my four-inch, elegantly simple, insanely flattering, black leather pumps.

You've got to be kidding me.

These were the shoes I wore when on the prowl back in my wild days, never anything I would pack for a seminar even if it was in Vegas.

I know exactly who was responsible for this.

"Jaden," I say with a giggle, knowing that somewhere in one of my pieces of luggage is…yep, there it is.

The dress.

The dress.

The curve hugging, man-eating, fuck me dress that I'd borrowed in New York.

New York

A knock on the door signals that I don't have time to find out.

I still haven't gotten dressed after my shower, so I throw on my robe and run to the door. Dr. Craig, all business-suited up for the occasion, stands there grinning down at me.

Dude… put the dimples away. Please.

Jase, Jase, Jase.

No… not Jase, we aren't a *we*…

Pompous, arrogant asshole? Yeah, that will work. All the nurses adore him, and he knows it. Arrogance is *not* a virtue.

"How are we feeling this morning?" he asks as I step aside to let him in. Ah, it worked. Zero butterflies.

"I don't know about you," I say, rushing to get ready, knowing exactly how late I am now, "but I feel just peachy. Late, but peachy. Have a seat, or whatever…I'll be just a few minutes." I stop briefly, frowning as I ask, "Do I have a few minutes?"

"Yes," he replies, grinning once more, sitting at the desk while I grab my provisions and take them to the washroom.

Dimples don't work, John. It's all good.

I am notorious for getting ready quickly if I have to, when I am unconcerned with impressing anyone. I loosely pin my curls up, apply minimal makeup, and slip into a pair of khaki pants and a lightweight, short-sleeved black sweater. Simple, business casual, to be comfortable as I endure a few hours of lecture...

After lecture...

After lecture...

After lecture...

Oh, fuck.

"I need coffee," I announce as I walk out of the washroom. Dr. Craig is eyeballing my heels that are still on my bed. "Should I be frightened?"

"I was about to ask the same question, but I see you've decided against wearing these," he jokes. He sets them aside and flashes those damn dimples at me again. "And coffee...I agree. We'll grab some on the way."

Dr. Craig is a rather engaging individual, very witty and articulate. Who knew he was more than just good looks? Oh, right, probably his professors in medical school. He also has the routine down pat where he can make whomever he is with feel as if there is nothing and no one else more important than what they have to say. Oh yes, there is a reason he is so popular with the ladies; however, my heart is wrapped up in a pair of dark eyes with a grey circle around them.

Wait a minute...

Nah. Impossible.

It also goes without saying that Dr. Craig and I have a somewhat complex relationship of sorts. In addition to me still being a student rather than a fully licensed nurse, I have lost count of how many times he has apologized, as if personally responsible that my mother had not survived. Depending on my mood I either find it endearing or annoying. Occasionally it is both.

As we ordered our Starbucks, he attempts to apologize again.

"Dr. Craig,"

"It's John, Talia," he reminds me, his voice soft as he touches my arm, guiding me around to the end of the counter.

"Ok, John. I've told you repeatedly that I do not, in any way, shape or form, blame you for what happened with my mother. She suffered two major heart attacks in a short span of time; I saw the report of the damage that was done. Even if she had survived, she would never have lived a productive life afterwards. So, for the final time..." I raise my eyebrow as I look at him, daring him to apologize yet again.

He holds his hands up in defeat. "Okay, fair enough. I have to say, though, that I'm pleasantly surprised that you agreed to come to this seminar."

Like I'd pass up the chance, especially if the hospital puts me in a nursing position after I graduate. It's nice already being employed as an aide, but it's not my end goal. "I've always been fascinated with cardiology," I admit. "I understand that your lecture today is about the physiological differences in the heart of a man versus a woman."

"One would think that there wouldn't be too much of a difference..." He is interrupted when our drinks are placed on the counter, and he thanks the lady behind the counter.

"So it isn't just the symptoms that are different?" I ask.

"Not according to the research that I've been a part of." We are walking towards the conference room where the lectures are being held; lucky for the both of us, the Starbucks is located right around the corner. "I promise, though, if you nod off, I'll give you my notes." He winks playfully at me and I smile.

"Okay, deal. You know, since you're part of the reason I ended up drinking so much last night. "

"John!" I hear a somewhat familiar female voice calling out. We turn together, and walking briskly up towards us, looking absolutely stunning... strikingly beautiful... immaculate...

"Kaitlyn Evans, what brings you to Vegas?" John asks, flashing the infamous dimples in her direction.

What the hell?

I watch them hug, a horrible sinking feeling in my stomach as I remember seeing this woman in Jase's arms in photo after photo not too long ago. I walk away quickly and quietly, into the room where the lecture is about to take place and sit in the back row, only a few people to my left.

What is happening? Why the hell is Kaitlyn here... *here* of all places?

Why? Why of all weekends... *why* does she have to be here when I am trying so desperately to feel just a little bit better about myself? And why the hell does she bring out that damned inferiority complex in me in the first fucking place?

Oh, right.

The reason for that would be Jase.

Damn that man to hell.

My pulse is hammering, my throat dry in spite of the sips of my caramel macchiato. I try in vain to listen as our first speaker is making her presentation, but my mind is going in a million different directions.

Dr. Craig knows Kaitlyn. Did this mean he knows Jase, too? And with Kaitlyn here... oh, god, is this what Jase's plans are? Is that why he's been so curious about the details of my trip?

My hands are shaking, and I accidentally spill a tiny drop of coffee down the front of my sweater. I swear silently, thankful I've worn a dark color but sure now that regardless it will show. Apparently, that is going to be my luck.

Here I am, across the country, and the one person who makes me feel smaller than the norm is outside that door.

It's okay, I'm just here on business. And besides...even if this is where Jase was planning on being, he is having problems getting away. That green-eyed monster lurking beneath my surface holds some sense of gratification knowing that even if he does make it, he is going through hell to try to be here.

For her.

I wipe a stray tear and chide myself for automatically thinking the worst, making a mental note to ask Dr. Craig a few pointed questions at the next possible chance I get.

We break for lunch about 1 PM, and to say I am starving is an understatement. They provide lunch for us in a dining area they have set up around the corner in another conference room, and although I try to find Dr. Craig, he has been conspicuously absent. I turn on my cell to contact Jaden, just needing a friendly voice.

"Hello?"

Oh, she sounds bad. I have to stifle a giggle, noting it seems like she's just woke up. "Feeling a bit...hungover?"

"Nah, not exactly. Just resting for tonight."

"Yeah, I saw what you packed in my bag."

She laughs softly. "Are you mad?"

"Nah, not mad. I'm not wearing it, though." I sigh softly and pick at my food.

"Are you okay?" she asks. "You just don't sound...well, you sound like something's on your mind."

I haven't told her about Kaitlyn, or about Jase and Kaitlyn. I know she's read the journal, or parts of it, but I just don't know what to say. Really, what *would* I say? *Hey, Jaden, Kate is here in Vegas, and Jase's been complaining that he had plans this weekend, so I'm being my usual dumbass self and automatically thinking the worst.* Nah, that doesn't sound so great after all. So, I stay silent, fumbling over what excuse I can possibly come up with for being so melancholy.

"Talli?"

"I'm fine," I lie. "I'm just tired, that's all. So, the seminar is over at four today. Only three more hours to go."

"We'll grab some eats, get ready, and hit the Center Bar and such here," she says, as chipper as she can sound after just waking up. "You will get over whatever it is that's ailing you when I'm done."

Sure, sweetheart. Whatever you say.

The last lecture of the day is Dr. Craig, and this is one that I want to pay close attention to. Stress the *want to*. It is a conscious effort to not let my mind wander to all of the questions I have for him, as well as how to approach him to begin with. At the end of our day, I wait by the door until Dr. Craig is walking out of the conference room. He is shaking hands with a gentleman standing just inside the door when I feel my phone buzz in my hand.

Jase.

I honestly can't believe that I hesitate before answering, but since my mind is my own worst enemy, I try to come up with a reason to let it go to voicemail. It is my heart rather than my curiosity that makes me decide against that.

"How was the seminar?" he asks.

"Parts of it were very interesting," I admit, without adding that the most interesting is how Dr. Craig knows Kaitlyn and that I have seen her.

"Tired?" he asks, but his tone shows he is still aggravated.

"Yes," I reply, somewhat short but I don't want Dr. Craig to walk by me without getting to talk to him. "Still stuck?"

"Damn it, yes," he says. I'm sorry to admit I actually smile at that. *Ha! So much for your plans with Kate.* "What's the game plan tonight?"

"Just me and Jaden at the Center Bar, so I'm told…maybe, you know, Dr. Craig too."

Oh yes, two can play this game.

"Huh," is all he says.

Huh. That is it.

Fucker.

So, in the midst of my failed attempt at making Jase jealous, I completely miss Dr. Craig walking the opposite direction and end up taking the shuttle back to my hotel, questions unasked. What a great trip *this* is turning out to be. I am admittedly sulking in my room, wondering what the hell is going on, and why no one will bother to tell me.

I looked at the dress that now hangs on the supplied clothing rack. For a brief moment I consider donning that dress, walking into that hotel, raising absolute hell and leaving with anyone I choose, Jase and everyone else be damned.

The memory of the last time I'd worn it stops me.

New York.

The restaurant.

The failed date with Keith Anderson, who'd never showed.

The anxiety meds I'd stolen from my sister.

The phone call, telling me my Daddy had passed away. And where was I... who was I with? Oh... *Oh...*

The girl with the flowing dark hair, and Him.

The boy...*that* boy with the beautiful eyes.

My fragile shell breaks, and I begin to cry.

CHAPTER 28

"Um, Talia," Jaden is saying as we are eating a light dinner, "I realize you didn't want to wear the black dress, but... we're in Vegas."

"What's wrong with what I'm wearing?" I ask, a tad bit defensive. Okay, maybe more than a tad.

"It's screaming that something's bothering you."

I look down at my comfortable jeans, sneakers, and casual T-shirt. My hair is pinned up, I have merely touched up my make up, and have traveled the short, but a rather long time to get here, distance to the hotel where Jaden is staying. Sitting next to Jaden, who is dressed in black pants that hug her and a white sleeveless button-down top, along with her black boots...yeah, I look like I am ready to curl up for a nap.

Maybe that's all I am ready for, all I am in the mood for. If she knew what I do... but no. No, I don't want to bore or burden her with the details.

"I...didn't want to wear that dress," I say quietly. And that is the absolute truth.

She lets out an exaggerated sigh. "Well...lady...hate to break it to ya, but we're going shopping."

"I don't feel the need for retail therapy right now." No new clothes, no dolled-up hair, nothing. I don't want any attention at this time; I honestly just want to go back to the hotel room and crawl under the covers.

No such luck for me.

Less than an hour later I am dressed all in black, Jaden joking that I must be in mourning still, but the soft, flowing material of the shirt makes me feel very...girly, feminine, like I'm not lacking in that department, no matter how inadequate I feel. Just to prove her point, Jaden proceeds to pull the material back just a little, tying the strings in the back that I didn't know were there. Voila, there are the curves I hate so, *so* badly. The pants hug my hips and are boot cut, my absolute favorite style, so that they aren't too tight, or too loose, down at the bottom. I have to admit, though, I adore the shoes—feminine, elegant, high-heeled lace up boots that set off the outfit, making me just a little taller. If nothing else, I get a nice pair of boots out of it, right?

After changing up in Jaden's suite, she pulls out her makeup bag and says, "Either you do it, or I'm going to."

"That's a scary thought," I mutter, snatching the bag from her. I don't darken my makeup too much and keep it fairly natural but accent my eyes. I hesitate for a moment, wondering if I should, but decide against doing the full smoky-eye effect that I used to combine with glossy lips...ah, the attention that would garner way back then. I'm not after attention, though.

Tonight, I need to forget.

"Ok, I'm ready," I announce. "And I have my separate gambling money, so I won't kill my budget, thank you for the tip."

"Don't mention it. Now...to de-virginize you."

"At least you didn't say you were gonna pop my cherry," I quip as we walked out the door. "That just would have been disturbing."

"Thank you for the visual." Dr. Craig startles me; I hadn't realized he was so close. He is making his way down the hall, presumably towards Jaden's door. Oh, doesn't he look so smug? And put away the dimples, mister. Just put them the hell away.

"Well, lookit there...How goes it with you, Dr. Cr...John?" Jaden asks, a twinkle in her eye.

"Better than you could possibly imagine," he conveys his private message. What, is Jaden in on this whole hide-Jase-and-Kate-from me? Nah, can't be, because her face lights up like a damn Christmas tree.

Oh, this whole mess is giving me a fucking headache.

I need a drink.

"So...we were headed down to the Center Bar," Jaden is saying.

Perfect. "Yes, bar! Bar is good, I need a drink." I hold my temple for just a moment as I walk vigorously towards the elevators. I need to drink just a little bit of courage before I corner Dr. Craig with my suspicions. Believe me, I am going to, and that man will answer to me.

"What the hell have we done to her?" he is joking with Jaden behind me.

"Turned me into a lush," I call back over my shoulder. "Guess you two shouldn't have been feeding me alcohol yesterday."

Of course, they find that amusing.

They are joking and laughing on the elevator ride down, but I make it a point to just listen, not join in. If they are going to give any hints as to what is going on, tonight is the night I will catch them and call them on it. Well...call them on it once I am just a little more numb. I am holding my cell, so I set it on vibrate and slide the thin device in my front pocket. I have my sincere doubts that Mr. Warner is going to even consider calling me this evening. He is probably still all pissed off because people keep fucking with his schedule even though he promised his precious fucking Kate he'd be here.

Please don't let that last part be true... please...

My nerves are slightly frayed as we walk into the casino. I can't remember the last time I've seen so many people packed into one place, and the lights and sounds would have been overwhelming if I wasn't beginning to become immune to it. I am about to pull a complete Talia and ask Jaden where the Center Bar is...um, hello, it's in the center. Yeah, I am frazzled.

No, I'm not frazzled, I am...

Who am I kidding?

I am frazzled.

"Beer or liquor? Beer or liquor?" I ask myself, tapping my foot slightly.

"I'd opt for something light," Dr. Craig suggests, his dark brown eyes full of mischief. "And not to worry, you can take it out to gamble, too."

"Right, with my luck all my gambling money's gonna be gone in five minutes," I mutter, choosing beer. Yes, it means that my courage will be built up slower, but hell...I have all night, right?

Jaden turns to me. "Okay, do you want to hit the slots first, or try your luck at...um...something else?"

"You're the seasoned pro at this, even for an Italian gypsy." Dr. Craig's laugh at that comment makes me smile. Wow, he has a nice laugh.

No, wait.

Possible traitor alert, Talia. On guard. Now.

"Yeah, I heard about that one," he says.

I eyeball him curiously. "I never told you.

"Yeah, about that..."

He seems on the verge of telling me something, but Jaden grabs my hand and says, "Slots!" loud enough for me to hear her as she drags me over towards the machines. "We'll go back to the bar in...an hour?"

"An hour's good," Dr. Craig agrees. "Hey...listen, I'll catch up with you then. I have something to do real quick."

Before I can protest and tell him I want him to finish what he was saying, Jaden has me perched in front of a nickel machine...I think?...I'm not quite paying attention to what I am doing as I am busy downing my beer. Something is up, most definitely.

"Hey Jaden," I finally say above the noise, "are you going to tell me what the hell is going on?"

"I have no idea what you're talking about."

Right. "I'm sure. Hey, I'm off to the washroom, I'll be back. And no, I don't need an escort."

"You sure?" she asks, and I nod.

In all honesty, I am a girl on a mission. I have that nagging voice in the back of my head that tells me it is time to go exploring and try to find where the hell Dr. Craig has disappeared to. I seriously doubt I will say anything to him if and when I find him, but for once I am going to follow my gut instinct that is telling me to make my way out of the casino area.

The hallways, lobby…every place is bustling with the excitement that is Vegas. Several people are headed to the nightclub Body English, and I secretly hope that Dr. Craig is not on his way there; that is one place that I have vowed I won't enter.

I am walking towards a small group of people that are huddled by another hallway, and noticing Dr. Craig standing there, his back to me, I make my not-so-stealthy way around the corner. As long as he doesn't see me, I'm not worried as none of the others know me, or at least would recognize me. Not even that beautiful, glowing girl who happens to be the center of this bit of attention.

"So, when's Jason coming in?" Dr. Craig was asking.

I fucking knew it.

"Not until tomorrow, can you believe it?" Kaitlyn's voice carries quite well, almost as if she wants the world to hear. "Leave it to him to get all of this started and have me come in to make sure the arrangements are all in place."

"I didn't think the bride made her own arrangements," someone else jokes, and my heart jumps into my throat.

Settle down, Talia. You knew she was getting married, perhaps Jase was just doing something nice for her.

"Not normally, I don't suppose," Kaitlyn replies with a laugh. "But for him I'll make an exception."

Does she have to be so fucking perfect?

I absentmindedly touch my hand to my hair, thinking I need a touch up, so I use that as my excuse to go find the washroom I'd originally lied about. Once I am safely inside, I brace myself on the sink for a moment, my heart racing.

Jase is coming here, he will be here tomorrow.

For her.

I am wandering a bit aimlessly around the casino, not quite looking for Jaden or Dr. Craig, and ignoring the buzzing of my phone in my pocket. Above everything else, I need to speak to Jase. I know this, with all my heart. I know his number; I have every intentions of calling. But first...yes, first, I need more courage, so I make my way back to that center bar.

I am waiting for my drink—a much stronger drink this time, opting for a Long Island Iced Tea. My hands are shaking ever so slightly as I accept the drink, leaving a hefty tip for the bartender to ensure that if needed I will be refilled quickly. I jump as I feel a hand placed on the small of my back, and I turn quickly to give a piece of my mind to the touchy-feely stranger.

"Do you mi..."

The last word trails off as I stare up into those beautiful eyes and that smirk on his beautiful freshly shaven face...

Oh...my...

No.

No. Fucking. Way.

It's J

He's... he's here, right in front of me...

"Of course I do, Christine."

Fuck. Me.

It's Jase. And he's J. And...

His voice is low as he leans close to me so I can hear him. Damn it, damn it, *damn* it! I feel him give me a brief kiss on the cheek, not daring to do more in such a public place. Did I really let out a sigh? No, no I most certainly did not. I'm not sure if the look on my face is one of shock or anger as he smiles down at me, visibly restraining from tucking a stray curl behind my ear. I see him put his hand down quickly, and he turns to the bar to order a beer.

Voice, Talia. Find your voice.

"It's you... it's... it's *you.*" I'm sure my tone can't be registered above all the noise. He merely smiles in return, leaving money for the bartender as he retrieves his beer. He turns to walk away from the bar and motions for me to follow him.

Really?

The mean, hateful part of me wants to stay put, let him wander off on his own, go find his perfect, precious Kate the way he planned to.

The other part of me is freaking the fuck out and is drinking the Long Island as we walk together, far enough apart as to not attract attention, a million things running through my mind that I am going to give him a piece of just as soon as I can.

I need to talk to him, tell him, ask him if he remembers me.

As we reach the front of the casino, I am already finished with my drink and I hand my empty glass to a passing waitress. I see Jase flash me a quick grin as he walks out of there, still carrying his bottle of beer, no one daring to stop Mr. Rock Star from doing precisely what he wants to do. He looks back at me and motions with a tilt of his head for me to catch up with him, and while part of me finds it endearing the other part of me wants to slap the shit out of him. No one has the right to be that fucking sexy. No one.

There are a handful of people on the private elevators that I follow him onto. I stand on the opposite wall, stealing a quick glance at him...he is absolutely gorgeous. His hair is just a little shorter than he had been wearing it, his skin smooth as porcelain, defining his lips all that much more. Oh...and there he stands, all in black, his leather jacket open. The way he leans against the opposite wall, glancing sideways at me as three of the five people depart before it continues up to the next level makes me wish we were in this elevator alone. One floor up the other two patrons make their exit, leaving us alone for the first time since I had dropped him off at his hotel.

The hotel... remember, Talia, you're pissed at him...

"You could at least act happy to see me," he says, his voice soft. He takes a drink of beer as I turn to answer him.

"Would you have preferred that I pounce on you in front of everyone?" I ask coyly, and one side of his mouth turns up in a smirk.

"Is that a rhetorical question, or do you really want an answer?"

Oh, you fucker. Way to throw my words back in my face.

But the look on his face... oh, yeah. I am going to be in trouble if I don't watch it.

Damn hormones.

The elevator doors open before I can reply, and I follow him down the hall to one of the larger suites. I keep quiet in the hall, not knowing if anyone is around, all of the questions and accusations flowing through my head, ready for me to scream them as soon as I have the chance to.

You are absolutely livid with him, Talli. Fucking livid.

Damn it, does he have to look so fucking sexy using a keycard to get in a stupid room? Really? What is it about his hands, his wrists, his arms as he shrugs out of his leather jacket the moment we step into his room...

Oh, holy hell, what is it that I am going to say to him?

I jump slightly as the door clicks shut, every thought racing from my mind as he smiles. "Come on in...I'll only bite if you ask really, really nicely."

Okay, drinking...not such a good idea now.

Is he really here, right in front of me?

"I need to talk to you," I say quickly. "I need to ask if... if you,"

"Remember you?"

My mouth drops open.

The notebook.

"You fucker! You couldn't say anything to me on the phone?"

He shrugs. "I had to tell you in person, so... here I am." He grins, that fucker, and holds out his hand.

I shouldn't.

But I should.

I take a couple steps forward, tentatively. He sighs then, looking down and tousling the back of his hair. "Are you really that uncomfortable around me now?" His voice is soft, his eyes searching as he looks back at me. I feel the tears threaten as I shake my head 'no'. "Do you hate me?" he asks, taking slow steps towards me, and again I shake my head. "Are you sorry?" My eyes slide shut for a brief moment, one tear escaping, and I jump when I feel his fingertips brush it away.

"I...already told you that I'm not," I am finally able to say, my breathing becoming more difficult in his presence. "What are you doing, Jase? What are you thinking?"

"I was thinking how nice it would be to just... kiss you," he replies, his voice still so very soft, his eyes drinking me in. "To just...kiss you...do you think it's a bad idea?"

"Is it?" I ask, my voice barely above a whisper.

New York

Every word, every question, every accusation fly from my mind as his strong hands caress my face, tilting it up slightly as his lips brush against mine.

Oh... god...

For one fleeting moment I resist, my hands resting on his, and then... I can't help myself. My fingertips trace up his arms, my body reacting as goose bumps rise on them, and I wrap my hands around his shoulders. I pull him closer to me, the kiss deepening when I sigh against him, his tongue caressing mine. He tastes of Budweiser and mint gum, and somehow the combination is all the more intoxicating. It feels so wonderful... so... so right to be here, in his arms, his mouth drawing the most exquisite emotions from me.

I feel his hands in my hair, pulling the pins out as the kisses grow more and more urgent. One by one the pins hit the floor by my feet, making small thuds in the carpet, the sound barely audible over our breathing, our kisses, the soft moans and sighs. Once he is sure my hair is free, he steps back, his breathing labored, his eyes glazed over as he runs his fingers through my hair, the curls now framing my face and hanging loosely in what has to be an absolute mess.

But not to him.

"This is you, Talia Christine. *This*…is you. I… I can't believe… it's *you*. It's… it's really *you*."

Did I say I have questions for him? Because they certainly aren't there as I wrap my hands in his shirtfront and pull him close to me again, kissing him as if I can erase tomorrow, make him stay with me. And he is kissing me back, the urgency in his touch, in his lips making me weak. I moan in protest when I feel his phone vibrating in his pocket, and he laughs softly.

"Mmmm… I just meant to kiss you, Talli, that's all," he says, his trail of kisses leading down my neck now, his phone still signaling that someone is trying to get a hold of him. I tangle my hands in his hair, holding him as close as I can as he continues his assault on my senses. *Fuuuuck*, it feels so good when he lightly bites my neck, sucking ever so slightly before doing it again… and again… and again…

Damn it, damn it, damn it! What is it I am going to say to him?

A loud pounding on the door causes us both to jump and Jase stands upright, his arms still around me. For just a brief moment I think there is a look of panic in his eyes until we hear Dr. Craig's voice.

"Jase, this is your conscience talking, open the door."

What the hell?

Jase smiles sheepishly at me and steps back, reaching for the door handle. I barely have enough time to straighten up my blouse before he opens that door, and when he does, there stands Dr. Craig and Jaden, who immediately pulls me into a bear hug.

"Are you insane?" she asks quickly. "You wander off, don't come back to the table, don't answer your phone…"

"I think I can take care of myself," I say with a smile, my hand self-consciously going up to my hair that she is looking at curiously.

"This isn't Ohio; you've got to be more careful," she scolds. Before I can open my mouth to protest, Jase speaks up.

243

"She's right, Talli, you really shouldn't do that; you need to have some sort of buddy system here."

Thanks for sticking up for me, pal. I feel my eyebrow creep up, unable to stop it.

"What, am I supposed to call you, then?" I ask, shooting him a look of defiance, but he doesn't have time to acknowledge it.

"You were gone more than an hour!" Jaden practically squeaks, running a hand through her hair as she speaks. "Do you know how panicked I was?"

"We can all see she's just fine," Dr. Craig stops their inquisition of me, and I smile in thanks. "And you," he pointed at Jase.

"I'm behaving myself," Jase says, putting his hands up, his eyebrows raised. Hmph. Liar. "How you holding up there, John?"

You're...kidding...

"Oh, for fucks sake," I mutter, covering my face with my hands.

"What?" Jase and Dr. Craig ask simultaneously.

"John?" I ask incredulously. "You're...*John*? As in John, John... not Not John." Jase laughs then, patting me gently on the shoulder.

"Yep, that's him," Jase is saying as I continue hiding my face.

How could I miss something *that* obvious?

"Talli, even I knew that," Jaden says, and I glare at her.

"Oh, shut up," is all I can mutter as a laugh is shared at my expense.

I should have known, though.

There were many things I should have caught onto.

Like now, when I look at Jase's smiling face—yes, it has matured, it has filled out from the scrawny boy I'd known all those years ago.

But I see him now.

And that smile... that one that's softening as his fingers lace with mine...

That tells me he sees it, too.

CHAPTER 29

Precious.

That is the only word going through my mind as I sit curled up on the floor next to the couch in Jase's suite going through the pictures he is showing me of his nieces and nephews. Absolutely, without a doubt...precious.

And that is just the pictures.

How am I feeling?

Adored.

Jase is kicked back on the couch, his feet resting on the coffee table in front of him, his legs close enough to me where if I want, I can rest my head on them. He is absentmindedly playing with my curls, twirling them around his fingers softly and letting them fall, as he is catching up with Dr. Craig...er, John. Ugh, it is going to be difficult to let go of the formalities. But there is something so soothing, so sweet about the gesture, about how I may not have been the center of his attention, but it seems to mean something to him that I am here.

Take *that*, Kaitlyn fucking Evans.

Oh, right. Pictures.

I smile as I continue looking through them. "They are adorable. Jaden, did you take some of these?"

"Yeah, but only the last..." her voice trails off as she reaches over from her seat on the floor close to me, "three. Just these." Two of them have Jase in them being tackled by all of the children, and I can't help but laugh.

"What's so funny? I could have been hurt," Jase interrupts his conversation just to say to me.

"Wimp," I tease back.

He actually rolls his eyes at me. I am half tempted to push him off the couch for being so damn cheeky. "Whatever," is all he says as he turns back to John

"When did you take these?" I asked Jaden.

"When I went out there." Her cheeks turn pink, possibly because she remembers she hasn't mentioned seeing Jase to me at all. But of course, she had... she'd taken his notebook to him.

Wait a minute..."Is that when this scheme was concocted?"

"Talia!" She places her hand over her heart. "I'm hurt! You think we'd... of course we did." Her smile is a bit mischievous. She's lucky I adore her

I look up to Jase and John, who are still talking away on the couch. "You're evil, you know?"

Jase is still playing with my curls. I don't think I ever want him to stop. "How so?"

"Because! You couldn't tell me? Any of you?"

John just has to flash his dimples in my direction. "And ruin the surprise? Wouldn't dream of it." It is still odd seeing him out of the workplace, a beer in his hand. I shake my head that I have to admit is a little fuzzy.

"So...this... this whole wrong number thing... is all your fault, right?" I ask John, and he bows his head slightly.

"He swears it wasn't on purpose," Jase says, his eyebrow up as he looks over at his friend. "He still thinks he gave me the right one, and I just wrote it down incorrectly. What do you think?"

John leans back as he laughs. "If I did, it was an honest mistake. Had I known her number, do you think I'd just pass it off to you?"

"Ha ha, very funny," I say as I give in and leaning against Jase's legs.

"Who's kidding?" *There you go, mister arrogant doctor, thinking you're all that.*

"It's getting deep in here," I mutter as I turn my head slightly to look over at Jaden. "Hey, is Pete coming out?"

"He wasn't going to, but—"

"He changed his mind," Jase speaks up quickly. I can't see his face, but I catch the look Jaden is giving him.

Like a kick in the stomach, I remember why Jase is really here, and my mood sours.

Jaden flashes a wicked grin at the thought of Pete, though. "Um...he'll be out tomorrow. But...I think that...he'll be busy for just a little bit? So um... that club, Body English, we're gonna go."

"We as in we *who*?" I ask. "'Cause I'm not going in there."

She shoves me slightly. "Yes you are."

"Why should I?"

"Because you'll have fun?" Jase sounds as if he is asking a question, being his usual cheeky self. *Like he would know.*

"Eh, likely story, you're just trying to keep me occupied." I am only half-joking, the serious side of me knowing he has plans with Kaitlyn, even though I don't know what. Yet.

Jaden honestly looks excited, though. "How long has it been since we went dancing?"

Um... how long has it been? Shit. "I don't know."

"Settled, then." She sits back as she places the photos back in their envelope.

Great, one more thing I am getting roped into.

"I'm sorry we're going to miss it," John comments, grinning slyly as he looks at Jase. *Men.*

"Only part of it," Jase counters. I look up at him then, trying to read his expression, and when he glances down I feel my heart flutter just a tiny bit.

"I can't imagine you in a dance club," Jaden says to him, mirroring my own thoughts.

"Why...nah, I know why not, but hey!" Jase places his hand over his heart. "I can mingle...I'm a people person."

John starts laughing in earnest. "Which is why we actually reserved a table for your ass to sit at and watch."

One corner of Jase's mouth turns upwards in a smirk. "Watching is not always bad."

"Yes, but..." John stands and stretches. "...watching will have to commence tomorrow. The hour is late, Warner."

"Yes, that it is," Jase says with a sigh. I am again a bundle of nerves as I sit straight up so he can stand. Damn it, what do I do? Do I stay? Do I go?

Does he *want* me to stay?

Do I beg for the truth?

I look at Jaden for guidance, wondering exactly how much she knows, but she merely grins at me. "It was hard to keep the secret from you. I hope you're not mad."

"So...*this* was the secret? That he was coming here?" I don't add that I'd been spying on Dr. Craig when he was talking to Kaitlyn, or that I know she is here. I want the truth without provocation.

Jaden smiles so sweetly, so genuinely. "Surprise?"

Perhaps she doesn't know.

"Hey," Jase is saying to me, offering me his hand to help me up. I accept, wondering what the rest of the night is going to bring. As Jaden is saying goodbye to John, I look slightly up as I stand in front of Jase. He looks so damn good, although a bit tired. I feel him take my hands in his so softly, caressing them as he smiles wistfully at me setting off a string of butterflies. Is he remembering our last night together, the way that I am? He releases one of my hands and gently runs his fingers through my curls once more. "Please don't be angry with me."

Well. Either he wasn't, or he was and not in a good way.

"You want me to go." I feel the disappointment as well as suspicion creep in.

"No...well, yes...but no. God, Talli, I just..." He sighs, raking his hand through his tousled hair. "I want to...*talk* with you, and I don't want it to be when either of us has been drinking."

I pull away from him, my defenses in high gear. "So you kissed me because you've been drinking?" Wow, thanks for the reality check there.

"No...no, see? Don't think that, the worst of me, please." He inhales deeply before continuing. "I kissed you because I wanted to. And if you stayed, I'd... want more than that, and I just can't."

My eyes narrow slightly as I let the words sink in.

Oh, I'd been spoken to before that way, almost those exact words.

In a restaurant in New York, back when we were teenagers...when I'd interrupted his lovely anniversary dinner with Kate, and the call... the phone call that had me running away in tears, and he'd followed me.

He'd stopped me, turned me towards him.

I remembered his thumbs brushing my tears away.

I... I don't know who kissed who first—I'm so sure it had to have been me—but he'd kissed me back. Boy, had he ever kissed me back... but he'd pulled back, and I'd begged him to come with me. Just... leave.

Run away.

Disappear.

"*Talli... I... I have to go. I want to stay... please... please don't look at me like that, please don't cry. Talli, if I stay... I... I'm going to want to be more than... than just a friend... just a confidante... and right now, I can't.*"

How could I have forgotten?

Kaitlyn Evans wins again.

"So...I know you have more lectures tomorrow." He takes my hands in his, as if that will make everything okay. "You're staying with Jaden tonight, right?" I nod, unable to speak, equal parts angry and hurt. "So you'll be coming back here, and I'll see you before I..." His voice trails off and he looks down at his feet, then back up at me. "We'll talk tomorrow?" His voice is soft, his eyes silently pleading with me.

Tomorrow.

After you've met up with the girl you made the plans with.

I force a smile of my own. "Of course." His eyes seem to cloud over, as if he is struggling with what he wants to say to me, and for a brief moment he closes them.

"I'm sorry," he whispers before kissing me softly, our bodies responding almost immediately as if starved for each other. So often it is that way with us... one soft kiss will explode, our bodies admitting what we are avoiding confronting out loud.

"Hey, hey, *hey*! Romeo!" John's voice reverberates through the suite. "Come on, Juliet's gotta go."

Jase steps back first, watching me intently as I back away from him. I can feel the tears forming, and I don't want to give him that satisfaction. Without another word, I turn and walk with Jaden out into the hall.

The next morning, I am running around trying not to let my emotions get the best of me. Even with lectures not starting until 10 AM, I am running slightly late. I have taken my shower, put just enough makeup on to hide any dark circles, and am rushing down in tan pants and a white top, hoping I'm not nearly the klutz I was the day before when I stopped to get my coffee. The last thing I need is a nice coffee stain adorning my clothing today.

I am finally at my destination, in line for coffee even, when I feel a hand softly touch my shoulder. I turn around and have to think quickly to hide my expression.

Kaitlyn Evans.

Smiling at me.

"Hi," she says, extending her hand that I shake slightly. "I'm Kate; I'm a friend of John's. I remember seeing you speaking with him yesterday."

Do you now? Hey… remember me sitting rather close to you, say, a few years ago? When you were giving Jase dirty looks for having the nerve to invite me to your table?

New York

Not that she needs to know that. No, not in all of her perfectness and me… looking… drab. Homely. Like nobody Jase Warner would ever waste his time on.

"Hello," I say shyly. I'm not about to tell her my name, if she is only claiming to remember me from yesterday.

Her smile widens. "Will you be coming with him this evening?"

Does she have to look so happy…so nice…so…perfect?

"This evening?" I repeat, trying to retrieve information if I can.

"The engagement party." She's absolutely beaming right now… oh, right, she's getting married. *See? Married. Relax, Talia.* "I know you two were here on business, but this came up, Jason just insisted it was this weekend, and here in Las Vegas." She laughs softly, pushing her hair back, the light catching that beautiful ring on her hand. "John said he'd talk to you about it; I think he's rather smitten with you."

"Is that so," I say, unable to stop my eyebrow from raising, and she laughs.

"And I'm sure Jason won't mind," she continues.

"Jason," I repeated, hoping my face doesn't register the shock that she would bring him up in that context.

Does she really know who I am?

"Jason," she replies, then shakes her head slightly with a laugh. "My fiancé."

It feels as if all the air leaves the room, as if the floor drops away from under my feet.

As if my world has crashed all around me.

Jase.

Her fiancé.

"Oh," I am able to somehow say as I turn towards the counter since it is my turn.

"I didn't catch your name," she says, again placing her hand on my shoulder.

There is no way in hell I am giving it to her now.

"Ma'am, I need your order," the young man at the counter interrupts us, saving me from further interrogation. As I place my order, another of Kaitlyn's friends came up to her, and I am forced to listen to her talk so happily of her upcoming party and wedding.

"It's about damn time you and Jason married," the mystery girl is saying, and I am unable to stop the tears as I take my coffee and hurry around the corner, furiously dialing my cell.

Why... why had I been so foolish to have let one fleeting sliver of hope stay with me? I mean... he'd only kissed me last night, right? That is it. That is all he'd wanted, all we'd done.

Just like all those years ago.

And he wants to *talk* with me?

"Hello?" I finally hear Jaden's tired voice on the other end.

"I need a favor," I say through my tears.

It is wrong, it is so very wrong.

"What's that?"

"I left my keycard to my hotel on the desk there, by the computer jack."

"Why do you need your keycard? You're staying with me tonight, right? Talia...God, what happened, are you crying?"

"Just...do this for me, please," I choke, stopping to rest along a wall. I pause briefly, wondering if it is wise, if it is worth my time or effort when he so clearly has made his choice.

And then I catch another glimpse of that beautiful perfect girl gushing about her upcoming wedding.

I take in a shaky breath, tears ceasing, numbness setting in.

"There are a couple things I need you to get for me."

CHAPTER 30

Talia Christine Emerson wasn't always an uptight prudish snob. Talia Christine Emerson, once upon a time, could have any man eating out of the palm of her hand.

Talia Christine Emerson needs to pull it off again.

Do I always talk about myself in the third person? No. But do I always have this much at stake? Hell no.

This has to be done.

Sometimes it isn't even necessary for me to be dolled up get to a man. I'd learned everything about that years ago, and when the situation was warranted, no one could work a man quite like me. So, when I spot Dr. Craig...or John, I have to remind myself that's what he wants to be called...at lunch, I know the time has come.

Show time.

I pick up my tray of food that once again is provided and make my way towards the table where he sits. I walk slowly, my hips swaying lightly. He is in deep conversation with another doctor, but when he looks up at me, I raise an eyebrow and smile...just the right smile, inviting, perhaps a little coy...and motion him to follow me to a less crowded table.

I have taken the time during one of the breaks to do a touch-up on my face thanks to one of the other nurses and have pulled a few stray tendrils of curls down so that they hang loosely around my face. Also, knowing where this man's eyes tend to wander, I strategically unbutton my blouse to just the right place knowing that even if I can't get him to keep eye contact, his eyes will still be on me at all times.

When it comes to being bad, I am truly one of the best.

But John isn't about to fall for any girly-type games; he is a very smart man. Well-schooled in the classroom as well as the field; I know this from all of the locker room talk at work. I have to play this just right.

"So, you're coming to the club tonight, right?" I ask, tilting my head just a little and smiling as if I don't have a care in the world.

"Yeah, I have a few things to attend to first though," he replies. There is no need for me to inquire what those few things were, and if they involve being someone's conscience then more power to me.

"I don't think it opens until after 10 tonight anyways," I say, keeping conversation light, my eyes on him rather than the food I am merely picking at. "So, you dance?"

"Occasionally. And you?"

"When the mood strikes me. Or I'm forced to, whichever comes first." Again, with the smiling, which he seems to enjoy. "Jaden will probably be first out on the floor."

"And you'll follow?"

"Depends." I lean forward just a little. I raise my eyebrows playfully, biting my bottom lip. "I will if you will."

"Is that so?" His sly grin gives his thoughts away. *Dr. Craig, you may be a womanizer, but you are not the only player in the game.* With that one smile, there is no question. I don't have to bat my eyelashes or make lewd comments.

All I have to do is set the bait.

"Will you dance with me?"

"Ms. Emerson, why would you ask me?"

"Well...Dr. Craig, I thought you might be interested." I smile again, sweetly. "I prefer to not dance alone."

"I wasn't aware that you were alone."

Hmm, is that so? Okay, I can play along with that one too.

"I'm far above the high school games." I had learned every trick in the book while I was there, and they are all coming into play. He sits back in his chair and takes a drink of his coffee, eyeing me up and down.

And, as predicted, his eyes linger right at my chest, at the swell of my breasts, the cleavage showing through my opened buttons.

"Okay," he finally says. "You're on."

After the last lecture, I make my way towards the doors to get the taxi that I have called for, since I'm not taking the shuttle back to the hotel with the others. I remain aloof about my plans with the other nurses, simply stating that I have friends here in town that are taking me out. Even though Dr. Craig and I work in the same hospital, even with his reputation as a womanizer, he also knows how to keep his mouth shut. It is the women he's chosen to keep company with who have done the talking, but I am definitely not one to do so. No one will be the wiser.

"Ms. Emerson."

Speak of the devil.

I turn and smile at him as he flashes those dimples at me.

"Are you not taking the shuttle?" he asks.

"No, sir, I have other places to go." I pull out a keycard to Jaden's room.

"A quick bite to eat beforehand?" he suggests, and I have to smile.

I'm good.

"Sure," I agree, and we walk side-by-side to the awaiting taxi.

Dinner is pleasant, even a bit subdued as I know from experience that John is trying to see exactly what my intentions are. I know that he and Jase are friends and that they've known each other for many years, although I'm not clear on exactly how close they are. That being said, I also remember the comment he had made to Jase regarding the wrong number issue.

"So," I finally say to him during our after-dinner drinks when I have ignored approximately the third call from Jase 'I have to tell you I'm marrying my first love' Warner, "I have a question for you. I really need you to answer this honestly." I reach over and touch his hand for effect. "Did you mean it when you said you wouldn't have given him the number, even inadvertently, if you knew it was mine?"

He pauses before answering, looking down at my hand before resuming eye contact. Believe me, I can work the earnest eyes when I have to. He studies me for just a fraction of a second more before answering.

"Yes."

Hook.

Line.

Sinker.

I'm in.

What are you doing, Talia?

That is the question that keeps swarming through my head as I am showering, preparing for the evening. I ignore it, remembering with that sickening feeling in my stomach how it felt to see Kaitlyn in Jase's arms in those pictures; remembering the look of longing on his face as he sat in my living room... *my* living room, knowing he was wishing he was with her no matter what line of bullshit he'd fed me; remembering that damn journal, how every girl he was with was a replacement for her, and now how I had been so insignificant that I wasn't even mentioned.

"Talli!" Jaden's voice registers as she is entering the room. "Are you about done in there?"

"I'm out of the shower, if that's what you mean," I reply, stepping out of the washroom with only a towel wrapped around me. I jump slightly when I see who was with her.

I am so not ready to see him.

"Where have you been?" Jase's voice is low, even-toned as he looks at me, his eyes dark, unreadable.

"I went to dinner," I reply as if it is the most natural thing in the world. "Sorry, I couldn't find my phone." How easy it is to use that excuse when I am known for losing everything.

Composure, Talia. Don't break now.

"Hey, I have to go get ready," Jaden says quickly, giving me a kiss on the cheek before grabbing her things and heading to the washroom. Jase and I stand there alone, his eyes drinking the sight of me in.

Yeah, I recognize that look.

The hunger.

The longing.

The pure unadulterated lust.

"Why are you here?" I ask coolly, walking past him to grab a diet cola out of the small fridge, knowing the jasmine scent of my shampoo will linger behind me.

"I wanted to talk with you," he says, standing still, watching me.

"Ahhh, 'The Talk.' I see. I think I've heard it before but lay it on me." I sit on the couch, still in only a towel, as aloof as I can muster up the courage to be.

He isn't supposed to see me yet; I'm not ready for him to see me yet.

But I can handle this. I have to.

"What the hell," he mutters, pinching the bridge of his nose as if trying to ward off a headache. He glances over my way and threw his hands up in the air. "Okay, I give. What did I do now?"

You lied to me.

You came out here for Kate.

You know… your fiancée?

"I'm not following you, Jase," I say sweetly. A flash in his eyes, perhaps a flicker of memory at my words, is the only emotion I get from him before his phone starts ringing. "And you're saved by the bell."

He glances at his caller i.d. and hits the button on his phone to stop the ringing. "I'm not going to stand here and try to pry out of you exactly what it is that I've fucked up. I have a few things to say to you, Talli, and they're things you need to hear."

"Really? This should be good then."

Those words I *do* say out loud.

The look on his face registers the hurt, the confusion over my abrupt change. If I was in any different state of mind, then perhaps I would care whether or not I hurt him. Unfortunately for him, I've reached the breaking point of him hurting me.

"Talia, I..." We are interrupted again by his phone. He takes a deep breath, glancing down at the caller i.d. again, the look of frustration giving me just a tiny feel of happiness, justice if you will.

I don't even have to guess who it is.

I'm sure his fiancée would be thrilled to know what he's doing right at this moment, too.

"Well, looks like you're out of time," I say smoothly as I stand up and walk past him. "You don't want to keep... whomever that is waiting." Meaning his precious Kaitlyn, but if he won't admit it to me, then...

Well, then, I guess I have to go through with it.

"What the hell happened?"

I am happy my back is to him when he asks that question, just the sound of hurt in his voice wavering my demeanor.

"Talia?"

I still refuse to turn around, taking a drink of diet cola and flipping through a tourist guide on the counter instead.

"Christine, please, look at me."

I turn around then, my defiant stare daring him to say my name that way again, with him knowing what it does to me. I see the muscle along his jaw line twitch slightly, and he looks away, defeated. He walks swiftly to the door, swings it open, and then turns to face me again.

"I'll see you later," he says softly. "Promise me...Talia promise me you won't do anything you're going to regret."

Regret? Not a chance. "Of course," I reply icily. As he leaves, I turned up the volume on the cd player and lose myself in the loud angry music that so matches my mood.

"Exactly how long is it going to take you to get ready?"

Jaden has been asking that question for about 15 minutes or so. Perhaps under normal circumstances it would grate my nerves, but I am far too numb to let it get to me. Besides, I know what I am doing. I know exactly the look I am going for, though, and feel no need to rush it.

"You can go ahead, if you'd like." The door to the washroom is still closed as I put on the finishing touches. The smoky eyeshadow has to be just so, not so dark that I look like I am stepping out of a goth magazine. The cheeks have blush applied lightly in just the right places, accenting my cheekbones. The lips...those are my pride and joy of this look; a soft wine color, with a clear sheen of gloss on them. Any man looking at my lips will have one thing only on his mind.

And the one man's reaction I wish for already knows what I can do with them. I have shown him, and he has moaned his approval rather loudly, thank you.

Such a shame he is busy.

I have applied gel to my curls so that they will keep their shape, reminiscent of all those years ago. It is too long to simply hang to my shoulders the way it had that fateful night, so I pin it up and let several tendrils fall around my face. The effect is a more mature, more sensual version of my wild teenage self, the curve of my neck exposed and adding to the whole package. This look... it isn't just for attention tonight.

The only thing missing is...

The dress.

What can be said about the dress? Black, hugging, sparkling when the light hits it just right. It fits like a short, tight glove showing every curve that Jase has spent hours exploring. That first night in his hotel room, when we had overturned furniture, pulled the cushions off the couch, the covers off the bed...

I shake my head to clear it, my curls falling right back into place. Tonight is not the night for *that*.

Slipping on my heels, I am suddenly much taller. Thinking that I can possibly look him in the eye when I make it very clear what my intentions are causes my heart to begin beating faster, but I do my best to quickly put it out of my mind.

Numb. I cannot let him get to me. The more I think about him the more I just... I just don't know. I need to be numb.

In the absence of any anti-anxiety meds, which I wouldn't touch anyhow, I opt for a beer. I am expecting Jaden to be gone when I emerge like a butterfly from a cocoon, attitude galore as I waltz past her to the mini fridge for a cold beer. I honestly can't tell who is more surprised, her or me.

"Who the hell are you and what have you done with Talia?" she asks, her eyes wide.

Oh... that's right...

"Ah, you missed this part of me," I comment. "You were still in New England in high school, weren't you?"

"Yeah...are you feeling okay?" Her gaze shows a bit of concern, which I really don't need. I am just fine.

I cock my eyebrow and look at her. "Does it look like I am?"

"That's not what I'm asking." She takes a couple steps towards me, her eyes narrowed slightly. "What the hell is going on?"

Oh, no. Not the twenty questions now. Time to divert.

"You know," I begin as I pick up my clutch purse and head towards the door, beer still in hand, "I'm not quite sure. I'm about to find out, though."

She seems to buy it or is at least playing along because she stuffs the hotel key in her pocket and follows me. As we walk towards the elevators, I hear my phone begin to ring in my purse. I signal to Jaden to hold on a moment and stop, handing my beer to her as I answer.

"Hello?"

Wow. Even my voice sounds different.

260

"Ms. Emerson." It is John, just as I suspected it would be. Score one of many for Talia. Lucky for him I am on a mission or I would quickly tell him how much it irritates the holy living hell out of me to be called Ms. Emerson, opting instead to coyly pry for information.

"Hello, sir, I am guessing your evening has been a smashing success so far."

Jaden smiles, incorrectly assuming I am speaking with Jase. Score another one for me; I am just as good at keeping secrets.

"Rather boring, to be honest with you."

Jase and Kaitlyn's engagement party boring? Oh, boo hoo for them.

"Then you need some action to liven your evening up," I say, trading Jaden my purse for my beer and downing half of it.

"Right now, I'm almost beginning to believe you."

"So is that an invitation?" I ask, smiling and winking at Jaden. John is quiet for a brief moment and I hear Jase in the background making some off-handed joke about him being on the phone in the middle of a party. Apparently, this is the wrong thing to do.

"Yes, it is," is John's reply to me.

Thank you, Mr. Warner, for pissing off Mr. Dimples.

"Perfect. Tell me where to meet you." I wink again at Jaden as I finish my beer while John is telling me where he will be coming to meet me. "Mmm. I'll see you there."

"Holy shit, Jase doesn't even know what's going to hit him!" she exclaims with a girlish giggle, and I smile slyly in return.

"No, he has no idea," I say, walking arm-in-arm with her the rest of the way to the elevators.

I talk Jaden into going to the club first and tell her that I'll only be an hour at the most. She jokes that I am probably gone for the night, but I assure her I have every intention of going to the club this evening.

I have no doubts that an hour is more time than I actually need.

I stand alone by the private elevators, waiting for John to come for me just as he said he would. When he steps off, I am slightly amused at his expression as he scans the crowd, looking for me even though I am a mere ten feet away from him. The look on his face is priceless as I approach him, taking pride in the slight flush of color in his exquisitely tanned cheeks. He is dressed in a black suit with a blue shirt, no tie and top button undone. Damn, that man is handsome. But... tie gone? Top button undone? Apparently, this party has been going on for quite some time.

Mmm hmm, I see the way you're checking me out, Mr. Dimples. What's the matter? Cat got your tongue?

Playing the game to the hilt, I take his hand in mine and gently kiss his cheek, smiling as I wipe the smudge of gloss from his clean-shaven face with one finger. He looks just slightly down at me and flashes his million-dollar smile.

"Ms. Emerson..."

"Tonight, it's Talia," I purr into his ear. "Just...Talia."

His eyes narrow as they rake over me, one side of his mouth coming up in a smirk. "Well... Talia... shall we?"

I take his arm, walking the few short steps to the elevator that has since departed. As we wait for it to arrive again, I steal several glances his way, none of which are the least bit shy.

Damn, Mr. Dimples... where were you before?

We step onto the elevator, surprisingly ending up alone for the first few floors. He turns to me, placing one hand on my hip, being his suave self and trying to assert his place as the alpha male in my life. "I'll never understand why he strung you along."

Is that so?

"His loss, your gain."

So much for insecurities this night.

He laughs low in his throat. "I know when he called you, he was trying to reach me. He was looking for Kate then too, you know. She'd moved, he knew I'd have her number."

Keep talking John. Keep telling me everything I need to hear to prove I'm doing the right thing.

"And instead he got me." I shrug nonchalantly as if I have meaningless affairs all the time, forgetting John had been in the room when I was with my mother after she'd passed away. I am quickly reminded, though, when he speaks again.

"Does this mean you're upset with me?"

"About?" I ask, confused.

"About phoning him when your mother passed away."

I feel my heart flutter, and my bravado falters for a brief moment.

"You called him?" I ask, regaining my composure. I have always assumed Jaden had.

"Yeah, he seemed concerned enough at the time."

So concerned he had flown across the country as soon as he could, thank you very fucking much.

Jase had held me in his arms while I cried, soothing me as I poured my heart out to him, helping me laugh when I needed him the most...

"You look absolutely stunning this evening, Talia." John's voice is low as he breathes those words into my ear. I close my eyes and stop the shudder from flowing through me.

What am I doing?

"I still can't believe he was fool enough to brush you aside," John murmurs, still by my ear.

Thanks for the reminder.

A few more people join us in the elevator, so I move slightly away from him, looking over my shoulder to catch his eye. Perhaps in some way he is just as eager as I am for some sort of retribution for some wrong he felt he's been dealt. Either way, it is not my concern as we step off the elevator and walked down the hall, his hand on the small of my back. As we reach the door of our destination, I feel as if my heart will explode in my chest. I close my eyes briefly. *I know it's wrong, I know it's wrong. Damn it, I've been wronged, too.*

"After you," John says.

It is now or never.

I opt for now as I step into the suite full of people celebrating the engagement, the banner swinging slightly as we step inside.

Congratulations Kate and Jason

It's time to offer my congratulations as well.

CHAPTER 31

Even in the sea of people I spot them; Jase has Kaitlyn wrapped up in his arms, slow dancing to a rather fast song. He is whispering in her ear and she throws her head back in laughter, as my heart is shattering into a million pieces.

Jase... how... how could you?

Jase has changed clothes since he left Jaden's hotel room. He is now in black pants and a sharp, button down white shirt, the top button undone. His hair is perfectly tousled, he is once again freshly shaven, his slight dimples flashing as he is smiling...that amazing, heart stopping smile...

At *her*.

Kaitlyn's long, dark brown hair is flowing as he spins her around. Her makeup on her beautiful flawless face is subtle and soft, her brown eyes sparkling as she laughs at yet another sweet-nothing being whispered in her ear. Her peach slip dress fits her perfectly, twirling around her long, lightly tanned legs as she sways to the music, her body fitted up against the man who had been kissing me less than 24 hours before.

I needed to know, I needed to see it with my own two eyes. And I have.

Fuck, it hurts.

No, hurt… hurt is such an understatement. I am crushed, my heart ripped from my chest, shattered into tiny shards of what it once had been, lying on the floor being danced upon by the couple before me.

I… I am broken.

But I'll never let him know.

John is beside me, his hand still on the small of my back, when a true slow song starts playing. It seems nearly out of place to hear an eighties tune, *Hands to Heaven*, but listening to the haunting tune and the words that follow it is fitting as I watch him hold her in his arms, the familiarity between them that only lovers can have.

No one can fake that kind of body language.

Unless…

Unless they are like me.

"Shall we?" I hear John's voice in my ear, and I turn into his arms easily, as if I've danced with him a million times before. I can feel several pairs of eyes on me, men eyeing the candy on Dr. John Craig's arm. Knowing that I am becoming a bit of a distraction to those around me is all the empowerment I need.

You think you can put on a show, Mr. Warner?

I twirl my fingers in John's short hair and snuggle up closer, placing a sweet, soft kiss on his neck. Lowering my lashes slightly, I glance up at him, throwing the shy, timid, cautious girl aside for the wanton vixen intent on getting her man.

And the universe shifts right before my eyes.

There are certain moments in life when time stands still, and you know the memory, whether good or bad, will stay with you forever. When it happens, whether or not you're ready for it, those moments change the path your life is headed on. And it happens right then, in front of this crowd, as I sway seductively in John's arms and Jase's eyes meet mine.

At first, I see the confusion in those beautiful eyes that are a sparkling this evening, then shock as recognition sets in, and finally…unreadable as they harden, his jaw set as he stands completely still now, our eyes locked. His breathing quickens as his gaze rakes over me, his eyes narrow, a muscle in his jaw twitching slightly as John pulls me closer.

Ah, you remember now... don't you, Jase? What? You dislike me being in someone else's arms? How very hypocritical of you.

Kate turns towards us to see what has suddenly taken Jase's attention away from her. I'll be damned if she doesn't hold on to him just a little bit tighter, a little more possessively as it registers with her exactly who I am. A flush creeps into her cheeks, anger flashing in her chocolate brown eyes. I merely smile at the two of them, the sadist buried deep within me relishing every moment of their suffering.

Ah yes, memories can be a real bitch.

And I can be an even bigger one.

Jase's eyes are darting between me and John, who has also turned in their direction. He stands behind me, his hands sitting possessively on my hips as other couples dance all around us, oblivious to the scenario unfolding before them. Jase's arms are sliding slowly to his own sides in spite of Kaitlyn's arm around him, her hand clutching his shirt as if using it as support.

Don't bother, sweetheart. You know you're busted.

I lean back into John easily, pulling his arms around my waist, holding onto his hands, my eyes burning into Jase as I do so. I note the twitch in his jaw as I do this, and his eyes...tears?

Really?

Does he have the fucking *nerve* to stand there in his own fucking engagement party and have tears when he sees John's arms around me? Is this guy fucking real? I can't stop the smirk that is forming on my face at this. This boy should win a fucking award for his acting skills. Bravo, Warner. Bravo.

"Talli."

It is Kaitlyn who speaks finally as she glares at me.

"And your memory finally returns," I say, my tone biting. "How about yours?" I am looking at Jase then, whose eyes narrow at my words.

"What are you doing?"

Oh, you know exactly what I'm doing, you asshole!

"Whatever do you mean?" I ask sweetly. "What am I doing here? Why, Miss Kaitlyn herself invited me, didn't you?" I look at her for a fleeting moment, smiling the best faux smile at her that I have before returning my eyes to Jase's. "She said you wouldn't mind."

Kate opens her mouth to say something, but we are interrupted by an incredibly handsome, and incredibly drunk, man in a suit who is passing out flutes of champagne to everyone he can, dragging a server behind him that is carrying a tray full of them. "Come on, everyone, a toast! We need a toast!"

"Absolutely!" John agrees, taking two of the glasses, handing one to me.

"Dude," the drunken man is saying as he is shoving a glass in Jase's direction. "Man, you have to take one of these. You, too," he says to Kaitlyn who murmurs a polite thank you to him.

What a sight it must make, the four of us standing there, Kaitlyn's eyes glistening with tears; Jase seething at every touch between John and me; John raising his glass in salute; and me...

I stand right in the middle, the same place I have been forced to be for weeks.

Me, the substitute.

Me, the used.

Me, the discarded.

Fuck you, Jase. Fuck you and your dishonesty. Fuck you and your cold heart. Fuck. You.

I stand just a little taller then and raise my glass. "A toast!" My voice carries over the crowd who seems to hush as all eyes fall on us.

"Talia, stop," Jase mutters between clinched teeth. I raise an eyebrow, my gaze defiant.

"Now, why would I?" I ask softly. "You certainly didn't know when to stop, did you?"

His face turns a slight shade of pink at my questions, and I can't suppress the smirk that crosses my lips.

"A toast!" I hear someone in the background urging me to continue, and my smirk becomes a sly smile.

"To Kate and Jason!" I continue, using the names they've chosen for their banner. I will my voice steady and pray for strength to keep the tears away. "For finding their way, everyone else be damned. And for those of us left behind, here's to hoping they've actually made up their minds and quit stringing anyone else along. "

The crowd erupts in a chorus of laughter and cheers, several shouts of "Salut!" ring out. I feel gleefully satisfied as I see a tear fall down Kaitlyn's face, but Jase makes no move to comfort her.

"Are you finished?" His voice is low, his knuckles white where he grips the glass in his hand.

Well, Talli? Are you finished?

But I already know the answer.

"Yes, I am," I reply, my head held high. I raise my glass again and empty it in one drink, then turn and walk away.

Mission accomplished.

Composure is my friend as I make my way out of that party, picking my clutch purse up from a front table where I had nonchalantly placed it on my way in. I keep my head up and my gaze straight forward, ignoring everyone and everything around me. I assume John is following me, as I'm sure there will be no verbal confrontation from Jase in front of his precious Kaitlyn or all of their guests. My pace is quick and steady as I walk briskly down the hallway past the late arrivals to the elevators. The doors open as I reach them, several people disembarking, probably heading to that lovely party with that perfect woman and her lying, manipulative, conniving fiancé.

More fucking power to them.

I step into the elevator after it empties and hit the button to the floor of the nightclub, my back to the doors as they close. I turn as the elevator starts moving, expecting John to be the one standing there.

Oh... god...

"Why?"

Jase stands there, directly before me, so close if I move a fraction of an inch, I can touch him. His eyes are dark, haunting as he searches my unwavering gaze. The scent of him, of his cologne envelops me, and my body reacts immediately to his presence.

No… no he isn't supposed to be here.

He… he is supposed to be back there, with his precious Kaitlyn, explaining himself to her, having to answer to her for his dishonesty.

He isn't supposed to be here.

"I could ask you the same fucking question," I say as I finally find my voice. He hits the emergency stop button and the elevator shudders as it comes to a halt.

"I told you I needed to talk to you,"

"And you should have before last night, don't you think?" I can't keep my temper in check any longer, and my voice is rising. "Or is this customary for you, to keep someone hanging on a string, waiting for you while you bounce back and forth?"

"Damn it Talia, all I did…"

"…was kiss me, yes I fucking know," I say between clenched teeth. "And now you have what you always wanted, what you wanted weeks ago when you were sitting in my house, in my living room, when you were in bed with me." I hit the button that starts the elevator moving again, but Jase quickly hits the stop button and I jerk forward, instinctively grabbing his arms for support, then pushing him away.

I can't… I can't touch him.

I will break.

I know I will.

He is visibly attempting to control his emotions before he speaks, but I just can't listen to it anymore. I've had enough… enough of the games, enough of his lies, enough of his hypocrisy. "John told me…he couldn't fucking *wait* to tell me how even when you called the first time, you were trying to contact him to find Kate."

"John…that's just…fucking great," I hear him mutter as he runs a shaking hand through his hair.

"That's all you can say?" I nearly scream those words at him.

Of course, that's all he could say. He was busted, so busted, and… and all he could do was be pissed off that someone else told me the truth?

"So I've been this… what, a substitute? A stand-in?" I ask, hating the slight waver in my voice.

Don't… Talli, don't let him know how much he's hurt you…

"Stop." His voice is soft, his hands shaking.

"What, you can't take the fucking truth? I thought that's what you wanted from me, Jase. God, I can't believe you actually had me thinking you came out here for me!"

"I did."

"You don't have to lie to me anymore," I remind him, hitting the button that starts the elevator moving once more, grabbing his hand as he moves to stop the elevator again. He takes advantage of this and pulls me up against him. Damn it…damn it…

Please… please don't touch me… I just… I can't take it…

And don't… don't look at me that way…

What fucking right does he have to look so hurt?

"Talia, listen to me please." My breath catches in my throat at the tone of his voice, his hands on me… "You've got it all wrong…"

"Do I?" I ask, snapping back to the present, regaining my composure in spite of my body's reaction to him. "I think it was pretty fucking clear." I feel the elevator shudder to a stop as he hits the button again.

I… I need to get out of here…

"You took it upon yourself to think the worst of me," he says, a mixture of anger and pain in his eyes.

*Think the worst? Is he fucking serious? I **know**. I've seen, I've heard… I fucking **know**.*

"You're a fucking hypocrite," I hiss at him, pushing him away from me. "Why weren't you honest with me? And don't feed me that line of horseshit that you were going to tell me because you had every opportunity on this planet."

"I was avoiding your reaction." Like his explanation is going to make things better.

"Because you thought I couldn't fucking handle it. Don't!" I stop him from interrupting me as he opens his mouth. "Don't you fucking dare turn this around on me! If you had been honest with me to begin with, this never would have happened."

"So you sleep with John to get even?" he yells at me.

"I'm not like you, Jase!" My voice is even louder as I move forward, the flash of surprise, of... hurt in his eyes at my outburst giving me a sense of vindication, clouding my senses, malfunctioning that little filter between my mouth and my brain. "How's that for thinking the fucking worst of someone? I can't sleep with John...not when I'm in love with you."

Fuck... fuck...

No, Talli, why?

Why did you tell him that?

Damn it! Now... now he knows and I can't... I can't deal with...

The silence is every bit as deafening as the words shouted between us, his eyes a little wider as I hit the button and the elevator begins to move again. By then we have reached the floor I need, and I turn as the elevator doors open. He reaches out and touches my arm, pulling back when I jerk it away.

"Talia,"

"Don't," I warn, my voice low as I turn to him. "Just...stop, please, don't do this to me anymore."

I can't take it. I... I have to get away...

"Listen to me..." His voice trails off as he stands in front of me, not giving a damn that there are several people gathering around, watching.

"Just stop, please, I can't..." I step back as he reaches out to touch me. "You have somewhere you're supposed to be right now."

"Christine, please..."

No... no, no, no... you... you are supposed to be up there, with your precious Kaitlyn, celebrating your love for her... Don't... don't do this...

"Just let me get over you," I plead, unable to stop the tears any longer. I step around him as someone walks up for an autograph, knowing he'd never refuse a fan. Making my escape, I walk quickly towards the club. At the entrance I stop to glance back and see if he is still there.

I love him.

Holy hell, I love him.

I love him with everything in me, and I can't... I can't believe it's come to this...

Knowing he has someone waiting for him upstairs doesn't stop me from wanting to call out to him to follow me. I stand there for just a brief moment, our eyes locked, his seem to be pleading me to stay.

And I want to.

More than anything, I want to.

I... I need to.

"Jase!" I hear Kaitlyn's voice as she steps off the elevator.

But I can't.

His eyes slide shut briefly as I turn and enter the club, praying somewhere that someone is listening and will give me the strength I need.

Somehow, some way, I have to get over him.

CHAPTER 32

What was it Jaden had said to me on the airplane? Oh, right. She'd said my life was about to change.

I didn't see this coming, though.

I didn't see my hopes, my dreams going down in flames.

I didn't see being blindsided by people I've mistakenly put my trust in.

I didn't see the man I love engaged to someone else.

Until tonight.

And now, it is time for my escape.

The wait in line for Body English would have been long, but Jaden and I have been given special VIP passes by Pete, presumably due to Jase reserving a booth there for the evening. Is this irony? I have no idea since my definition of the word has been forever tainted. In my slightly tipsy state of mind I make a mental note to look it up, tattoo it on my memory.

I can't wait in line. See, if I wait in line, then he can catch up with me, if he can pry himself away from *her*. And no... no, I've been hurt enough tonight.

I've been hurt enough for a lifetime.

I need reinforcements. No, scratch that—I need more alcohol. Lucky for me they happen to be together, as I see Jaden standing by the entirely too large bar that I instantly decide I need a replica of in my own home. Minus the fact that it is probably bigger than my entire living room, of course.

I am wiping a stray tear from my face as I descend the stairs, my dress attracting attention from males and females alike. Well, isn't this just my night? The music is loud, pulsing, calling me to the dance floor once my thirst is quenched.

The bar is crowded, loud, and full of the beautiful ones as far as the eye can see. All it takes is one tap on a tall blonde man's shoulder by me, and the sea of people part for me to walk through, commanding the attention of all as I waltz straight up to Jaden. "Alcohol. And lots of it."

She turns to me with a smile that quickly fades once she sees my face. "What happened?" she asks loudly, and I shake my head as if to say I'll tell her later. I'm not about to get into it now, especially not knowing exactly how much information *she* has been given.

"Long Island," I order, placing my money on the bar.

"The booth isn't too far from here, you can put your purse there," Jaden says into my ear so I can hear her. "Pete should be back soon."

"What, the engagement party not enough excitement for him?" I ask bitingly, and Jaden's eyes widen with surprise. "You've got to be fucking *kidding* me," I mutter, taking my drink and turning towards the booths.

Seriously? My best friend knew. And she said... nothing? Hell, maybe that's why she'd tried so desperately to find me the night before; maybe she and John had thought Jase might try for one last hoorah before he told me the truth. Wow... tonight is just getting better and better, isn't it?

I see Dr. Craig and Pete talking beside one of the booths and walk towards them, Jaden in tow.

Not her, too. Please not her too. I... I need someone to talk to... but apparently, she knew. And that leaves me with who? No one, that's who.

Interrupting John and Pete's heated discussion, I drop my purse on the table, down the drink in my hand, and grab John's arm. "Dance with me," I whisper in his ear, dragging him onto the floor. Jaden follows behind us as I lose myself in the sea of pulsating bodies and music.

Glancing up as the obligatory fog machines let go, I am caught up in the moment, the gleaming chandelier adding to the ambience, hands all over me as I am surrounded by people I don't even know. Hell, I lose sight of John some time shortly after we hit that floor. I don't even see Jaden; perhaps she is staying out of view on purpose. I don't care. I am beyond caring. The only thing I want to feel is Talia Christine Emerson going down in flames— tonight is the night. Out with the old, in with the new.

Everyone else be damned.

I have a thin sheen of sweat forming a good five songs later— they all seem to blend together—when I feel Jaden's hand on my arm, pulling me out of my circle, off of the dance floor, towards the booth. "Wait!" I yell. "I need another drink."

She shakes her head. "You need water. To ward off hangover, Talli," she adds when I start to protest. Apparently that excuse is good enough for me as she leads me to the large leather booth where three other people sit, attempting to engage in conversation. I am sat next to a female that I don't know who is fanning herself and drinking what appears to be water. I reach for my purse to check my phone for messages—Did I seriously think that maybe he'd called me? —when my eyes settle on the other two people in the booth.

John is sitting, having a drink, but I can tell there is agitation in his face. He glances over at me and settles back into the couch, a satisfied look on his face and gestures over towards me.

The other man, the one who had been leaning in giving Dr. Craig a total earful of something the rest of us couldn't hear, looks over in my direction, and when I see those stormy dark eyes settle on me, I feel my heart drop to my feet. He is half-standing, one knee resting on the couch, his arm using the back of the couch to hold him steady as he had been going off on whatever tirade he'd decided to unleash, perhaps to assuage his own guilt and place the blame elsewhere.

Jase is angry.

And Jase only has himself to blame.

I stand to go back to the dance floor, but Jaden is in front of me, handing me some water. "You need to sit down, Talli."

"What is this, an intervention?" I snap. "I don't fucking need it. Any of it." I had already grabbed some money from my purse, so I set the water down and try to step around her, only to have Jase come up beside me.

Please… please no.

Jase places his hand on my arm and I brush him off. *No way, asshole.* I am far too angry, far too hurt to have any kind of a conversation with him, especially in the middle of the club that he'd just insisted I come to.

"Leave her alone," I hear John say, and when Jase's head snaps around to look at him again I brush past everyone, back towards the bar. I happen to brush up against one of the men I had danced with and he gladly assists me up to the bar to make my order.

Ah yes. Another Long Island.

I hold up my drink in thanks and Mr. Blonde Jock takes that as an invitation to place one of his beefy arms possessively around me and lead me towards his pack of frat boys. Yippee, just what I need, but who the hell cares as I make quick work of my drink while listening to them try to out-testosterone each other with their tales of exactly which one of them is man enough for the likes of me. I motion that I am going back to the bar, but Mr. Blonde Jock offers to go for me, and I shrug. Fuck it, the less work I have to do the better, so I turn for the dance floor with two of the five following me.

I close my eyes, feeling the music run through me as much as the alcohol. Jaden is suddenly beside me, and dress and heels be damned, we are dancing our asses off. I can feel the occasional touch of the frat boys as they try circling in, but Jaden pulls on my arm as the song ends. I follow, breathless and laughing, and collapse into the booth. "Ah, Jaden…I'm free.

"No, Talli, you're drunk." She hands me the water I'd left on the table. The booth is conspicuously empty minus the two of us and she pushes me further in, blocking my immediate way out. "I don't know what happened, I'm not going to pry…"

"Oh bullshit, you don't know what happened," I spit out. "You knew he was with Kaitlyn." She opens her mouth to say something, then closes it again, signaling to me she is admitting defeat. I roll my eyes as I take another drink of water and stand to walk around the other side of the booth.

"Talia, wait!" I hear her call after me, but I ignore her as I walk back over to the frat boys.

Fuck you, Jaden. Fuck you Ms. Best Friend, the one who should have been looking after me. But has she been? No. No, it is more convenient of her to stab me in the back to get in good with the asshole's baby brother.

Yeah… fuck all of you.

"Where's my drink?" I ask Mr. Blonde Jock seductively.

"Well you disappeared, so I drank it," he says with a shrug. "I was all like…dudes, where'd she go? You know? So…yeah, I drank it."

Oh yay. This one is real articulate.

Fuck it.

"So, go get me another," I command, pointing towards the bar, and Mr. Blonde Jock is all too happy to oblige. I stand with the other boys, holding court if you will as they all seem mesmerized by anything I say. Either that or they are staring at my boobs, but either way I have their full attention, and that is what matters. I notice Jase heading back to the booth, and completely ignoring every screaming fiber of my being, I turn away from him.

I have to. See, if I don't…

If I don't, I will have run straight to his arms, demand answers, beg him to give me, give *us* half the shot that we deserve instead of running to his past.

Drinking—sometimes not a good idea.

Drinking sometimes magnifies the hurt, clouds the judgment every bit as much as the senses.

"The hour is late, Cinderella," Mr. Blonde Jock says as he holds my drink out. I have to refrain from rolling my eyes as he makes some stupid fucking joke about my coach turning into a pumpkin, bla bla bla, as I do my obligatory quick inspection of my drink. I almost laugh at myself, noting some of my obsessive-compulsive quirks that follow me no matter how inebriated. Seeing no signs of anything out of the ordinary, I take a small sip, and noting that it tastes the same, I resolve myself to this drink being safe.

"So, what do you do for a living?" one of the boys over to my left asks. I turn to him so he can hear me, and he leans down a little.

"I'm a nurse," I reply. Okay, so that's kind of a lie. Technically I'm only a nursing student, but hey… it isn't like I'm going to ever see these boys again.

"Really? Like at a hospital?" he asks, keeping my attention.

No, dumbass, at a morgue.

"Yes," is all I say.

"Awesome," he comments, smiling as he stands back up. I turn again and see Mr. Blonde Jock touching my straw.

"It was falling out," he says, loud enough for me to hear him, and I nod. He is asking me another question that I pretend to listen to while I begin to quickly down my Long Island. I know I'll need a hell of a lot of alcohol to deal not only with him but with Jaden when the night is through.

Without warning, I feel a strong hand on my waist as another reaches around me, yanking the drink out of my hand roughly.

"What the fuck?" I demand as I turn around to see Jase yelling at security to get Mr. Blonde Jock, who has mysteriously disappeared from my side, and his friends the hell out of the nightclub.

Oh…

He… he is so pissed, and…

Wait one fucking minute, so am I.

"What the fuck are you doing?" I reach for my drink, but he holds it away from me, his other arm securely around my waist.

"Are you okay?" he asks, his voice and eyes full of concern.

Please don't be nice to me...not now...not when I can't take it...

"Give me back my drink and I'll be just fucking fine!" I push his chest and grab the glass but stop suddenly.

There's a film of white powder around the side.

Oh fuck...

"You drank so much of that," Jase is saying as he takes the glass from me and hands it to Pete, who has somehow ended up beside us. Jase's hands caress the sides of my face bringing tears to my eyes. He... he has to stop touching me. "We need to get you out of here."

I can't, doesn't he understand that? "No...no..."

"Talli, listen to me...this wasn't a big glass, you drank most of it, we have to go."

"Please don't touch me." I know he can't hear me, I've said it so softly, my eyes closed against the tears, but I feel his hands move away. A sudden coldness, emptiness fills me once his hands have left.

"Talia, open your eyes." Pete's voice in my ear snaps me back into reality. "Listen, you go with Jase, we got a better look at them than he did. Trust me...trust him. Go." I am beginning to shake, possibly from fear, but I nod, reaching out blindly until I find Jase's hand. "Take my room."

"Less chance of being seen, I know," I hear Jase mutter as he squeezes my hand, motioning me to follow him.

"Don't you need...distance?" My words are starting to slur, and he pulls me closer, his arm around me as we walk as fast as we can. Now why would he do that? He is supposed to not be seen... with anyone...

"Stay with me," he says as we step out of the club, the noise level dropping incredibly as my steps falter. "Come on, Talli, just a little bit further." His voice in my ear causes the goose bumps on my arms to rise and he laughs softly. "Oh, sure...now," he says, winking at me. I start to laugh then quickly stop as I remember I am pissed at him. "You know it's funny, you know you wanna laugh." We step into the elevator, me giving him the evil eye. As the doors shut and we are alone once more, he reaches over and tucks a curl behind my ear.

"Please don't," I beg, tears threatening almost immediately. He steps in front of me, helping to prop me up on the wall, his hands so gentle as he caresses my arms. I close my eyes, grief consuming me as I feel the first sob escape me. "How could you?" is all I can ask, unable to fight as he pulls me into his arms as I cry. "Why...did you..."

He says nothing, no soothing words, no protests of innocence as he holds me, breathing me in as I cry helplessly in his arms. I hear the doors open and am startled as he steps back, helping me out of the elevator.

"We're almost there," he says, his voice shaky. Why does he sound so emotional? Isn't... isn't he happy? "Come on, Talli, please..."

"No...I need to stop," I say, putting a hand to my head as the alcohol and other chemicals consume me.

"Stay with me." His voice is stern, his hands on my face and I open my eyes to argue with him. "Damn it, Talia, you know better...you don't turn your back, you don't leave your drink unguarded,"

He wants to play big brother now? With me?

"Save your bartender's lecture," I snap at him, my anger bringing me back around as I push his hands away. "What, no Kate here?"

"This door, right here Talli," he says, ignoring my question which pisses me off even more.

"You can't answer me now?" I ask, giving him a slight shove that doesn't even faze him as he opens the door and pulls me into the room. "Come on, Jase...where is she? Does she know where you're at? Is this... is this how you're going to treat her all the time?" He drags me by my arm back to the bedroom area of the suite. "Fuck you, get your hands off me!" I try to fight him, but instead I end up imbalanced. He places his arms around me and gently lays me on the bed.

"You'll be okay, Talli, I promise." Why does he have to sound that way, like I've hurt him? And why the hell is he taking my shoes off?

"Jase, stop…"

"I have to call John. He'll know what to do." His hand is still on my leg, caressing me sweetly, gently. His eyes… oh, his eyes… he's … he's… so perfect. Why does he have to be so perfect?

Why can't he love me?

"I'm just so tired," I say, my eyelids heavy as he leans in and kisses me on my forehead. "Please don't leave."

"I'll be right here," he whispers against my skin. With that promise, I sigh and allow the chemicals to overtake me.

CHAPTER 33

Drunk dreams can be a number of things-- strange, insightful, incredibly hot. Sometimes they're all of the above, rolled up into one. Take last night's dream, for instance.

It is so hazy, so fuzzy... but I remember being hot in my dream, so very... *hot*. And incredibly turned on. And Jase... he'd been there.

And I'd made him moan.

And I'd made him squirm.

I'd had my hands down his pants, my fingers enclosed around him, making him harder still as I stroked him. And... and I'd been sucking on his neck, kissing the most sensitive spots, telling him... oh, what was it I'd been telling him?

"God, Jase... I want you inside of me..."

"Fuck... Talli, baby, don't...don't do that."

"Mmm... fuck... that's... that's what we should do."

"Baby, stop."

"You don't want me to." I was kissing up the outer edge of his ear, *the movements of my hand quickening as he bit back another moan*

"Not like this."

Not... like... this?

Like ... like what?

The room is still dark when I am startled awake by a strong hand on my wrist. I jerk back with a screech and scramble to the opposite side of the bed, the light from the living area of the suite casting a shadow on the face of the man sitting on the bed beside me.

"Who the hell are you?" I ask, panicked, pulling the covers around me.

"Relax, Talia," he says, and his voice sounds vaguely familiar. "I'm Dr. Brooks, I spoke at the seminar yesterday. I'm checking to see how you are, and it seems you are definitely becoming more lucid."

"More lucid?" Now I'm completely confused. I look down and notice I've somehow managed to change from that little black dress into my silky camisole and my favorite pair of jammie bottoms. What the hell?

"From what I've been told, you've been in and out of it most of the night," Dr. Brooks explains. "Not to worry, Dr. Craig signed you into the seminar. Given the circumstances it's the least he could do. Speaking of Dr. Craig and such, why did you leave the party in such a hurry?"

Dr. Craig...the party...oh, fuck, the engagement party, the one for Kate and Jase. I hide my face in my hands and shake my head slightly, groaning at the pain there.

Wait...Jase... I had left the club with him. I lift my head as Dr. Brooks is taking my blood pressure from the arm he has pried free. "Where's Jase?"

"Right here," Dr. Brooks says with a smile, and I look around the room.

"Oh, out there?" I ask, pointing towards the door.

"I'm being facetious," he replies with a grin that I can see now with my eyes adjusting. Wow, he really does look familiar. "Well, somewhat. I know who you're looking for. He had an appointment, or prior engagement of some kind. He asked that I tell you that he will be right back."

A prior engagement. No shit.

"Okay," is all I can say, feeling a fresh wave of hurt, along with a tad bit of nausea.

"You're going to feel pretty much wiped out today," Dr. Brooks says as he stands and tousles his hair...wow, again with the...wait, he acts like Jase. That's what it is about him that strikes me as familiar. But there is something else... OH... I recognize him now. Dr. Brooks had been handing out the champagne flutes at the party. Oh, great... he knows how I'd made a complete ass of myself.

Just... perfect.

"Get rest, drink plenty of fluids, but nothing from strangers." He laughs softly to himself as if he thinks he is the funniest person in this world. "So...the infamous Talli."

"Pardon?" I ask, curling back under the covers as I prop myself up on the pillows. What could I possibly be infamous for?

"Hey..." I hear Jase say as he sticks his head in. "I made it back, thanks for checking on her."

"Looks like she made it back, too." Dr. Brooks stands and turns towards the door where Jase is. Jase takes a tentative step into the room, still holding onto the frame, his features soft as he looks at me.

"How are you?" He sounds so sweet and caring, it causes my heart to ache just a little more.

"Alive, apparently," I reply, then quickly add, "Thank you." He smiles at me, his genuine smile that sends a chill up my spine.

"Not a problem." I hold his gaze just a moment longer before Dr. Brooks interrupts us.

"Got a minute?" he asks Jase, motioning that they should move into the other room.

"Yeah," Jase replies, then turns to me. "Are you sure you're okay?" I nod, and he adds, "Jaden brought some of your stuff up last night. I didn't know if you remembered or not."

"No, but I kinda figured." I am grinning slightly as I tug at my camisole. He smiles briefly, wistfully, before turning to walk out to the living area. Dr. Brooks follows him and pulls the door to but doesn't completely shut it.

I know I have to be some kind of hot mess as I can't even remember changing clothes, so I slowly make my way off the bed, my legs just a little weak. I walk to the washroom, scowling as I turn the light on. Wow, does it ever hurt my eyes.

Okay, now to inspect the damage.

I expect to see hair up all over the place, makeup running down my face, raccoon eyes, the whole nine yards. Instead, I see the black dress folded neatly and hanging over a rack behind me, towels folded over the tub, and a washrag by the sink, rinsed and folded but clearly had been used to wash off makeup.

I look into the mirror, confusion settling over me. Had I...taken a bath or something last night? My hair is soft, free of all of the product I had put in it yesterday, and the curls while a bit on the messy side are definitely...well, clean. I touch my face gingerly, no trace of makeup left, so clean it has a little shine to it. If I can barely remember coming up to this room, how in this world could I have...

A foggy memory hits me like a brick and I hold on to the sink to steady myself.

Jase.

He'd sat me on the edge of the tub and knelt in front of me, white washcloth in hand as he'd gently wiped my face. I had been crying, apologizing, and he'd said...had he said anything? I can't remember. I know he had placed one finger lightly on my lips and had continued gently wiping my face, taking special care around my eyes...

My eyes that are now filled with tears, my heart with confusion. Why had he stayed with me? He could have easily called Jaden or left me with John.

And the dress...I remember a warm bath, hands gently massaging my temples, moving through my hair, water gently flowing down my back. His arms, wrapping a towel around me and holding me close.

Why?

And my dream... Was it a dream? Had anything happened?

I have to know. I need to have the answers, to everything.

Dr. Brooks is still in the living area talking to Jase; I can hear bits and pieces of the conversation, not that it makes much sense. I am about to open the door when the tone of Dr. Brooks's voice stopped me.

"Damn it, I thought this shit was...done, all of it. This isn't fucking high school anymore."

"No shit, Jack," I hear Jase snap back.

"And there you go. Same shit, different day, more people caught in the fucking middle."

"You think I meant for this to happen?" Jase asks. "Any of it? Kate and I talked about this; she's happy, I'm happy."

"Really? She didn't look very happy last night, especially not when you ran after your friend there." I stand frozen on the spot, my hand on the door. "And what about your friend?"

"That's not your concern." Jase's voice is low.

"Not my concern, but you call not just John, but me to check her, make sure she's okay. So now not only are you being dishonest with people, I have to skirt around the issue, act like everything's okay...do you really think I could tell Kate I was coming here?"

"She wouldn't mind, Jack, so you may as well tell her." I can hear Jase sigh. "All this time and you couldn't figure out she'd have more compassion than that?"

"Compassion or no, what happened last night has definitely changed Kate's outlook on everything. She says she wants to speak with you before we leave this afternoon."

I blink in surprise. What the hell is Kate doing leaving with Dr. Brooks?

"Like you said...we're not in high school anymore, Jack. You don't have to act so defensive."

"No, we're not in high school, and yet you still can't get my name right. Let's just forget it's the same as yours. Hell, most days they even shorten it, just like yours."

The same as?

No...no, no, no...I couldn't have been *that* wrong.

Jason Brooks.

Kate and Jason.

Another wave of nausea hits, and I'm not so sure it is residual from the previous night. I keep asking myself what have I done as I sit on the edge of the bed, tears welling up again.

Fuck...what have I done?

I wait until I am sure Dr. Brooks has left before I stand to go out to Jase. I so don't know what to say, how to say it, where to start. When I reach out for the door it swings open suddenly and I jump as Jase walks into the bedroom.

"Sorry," he says with a soft smile. "I didn't mean to startle you."

I am trembling slightly when I reach out for his hand. Just that touch sets me on fire. "I...didn't get a chance to really thank you."

"Actually, you did." His grin is mischievous, infectious. "Over and over."

Oh, hell... I... we...

He caresses my hand softly as he reaches out and tucks some curls behind my ear. "Okay, and that sounded wrong. I promise nothing happened, scouts honor."

I let out a soft sigh, hoping that I can believe him.

"Did I tell you that I was sorry?" I ask, and I bite my bottom lip as I wait for his response.

"Yep, that too." He kisses my forehead gently and I feel a tear fall. "No more tears," he whispers, cupping my face in his hands. "Time's not on our side right now, Talli, and I swear to you...please, this time listen to me...okay?"

Listen. Like I should have before. I nod, tears still hanging on my lashes.

"Trust me?" I hesitate before answering his question, and he drops his gaze. "Okay, I deserve that."

"Wait...Jase, please." I reach out, touching him softly, almost afraid he will step away. I don't want him to, I... I want him right where he is when he answers me. "It wasn't you...isn't you, it isn't you, is it?" He shakes his head 'no' and I feel the tears rise again. "She's marrying Dr. Brooks...not you."

"Yeah."

I sob again, full of shame over how I have acted, what I have done. Leave it to me to screw everything up so royally, again. First withholding my identity, then not realizing that this... this man in front of me was the boy who'd stolen a piece of my heart oh so long ago, and now... now this.

He holds me against his chest where I can hear his heart hammering in his chest, mirroring my own. "Well, damn...and here I thought you'd be happy over that one." I have to laugh, and I swat him, to which he replies, "Mmm, that was nice, hey...OW!" I hit him harder that time.

"Fucker," I mutter against his chest.

"What was that for?" he asks, pulling back and smiling down at me. "For taking care of you, for washing your hair, for behaving myself and dressing you instead of taking full advantage and ravishing you? Believe me, it takes great self-restraint."

I blush at his words, bits and pieces of the night still floating in my brain. But today... after everything, he is here, being sweet and gentle.

Why?

"I don't understand...after all I've done..."

"You wouldn't have," he stops my rant.

"After last night...fuck, I almost..."

"Don't," he says suddenly, closing his eyes. "I don't even want to think about what could have happened. And I would have been completely responsible."

"For what, my actions?" I ask, confused.

"My...dishonesty. You're right, Talia," he stops me from interrupting him. "Omission is the same. I didn't give you a reason to trust me, and I'm sorry."

"And I went and fucked everything up, just like me," I mutter through my tears.

"Christine..."

"No, I did!" I step away from him, throwing my arms up. "You kept telling me not to think the worst of you, you kept telling me you wanted to talk..."

He silences me with a kiss.

The kiss I have been mourning since those words had fallen from Kaitlyn's lips, the kiss I'd thought I would never feel again.

His lips are soft, teasing, erasing all thought from my mind.

He is here.

With me.

He pulls back slightly, and my eyelids flutter open. "What was I saying?" I ask breathlessly, and he smiles down at me.

"Exactly."

CHAPTER 34

"Did you have sex in that bed?" Pete asks, eyeballing Jase as we are collecting my things. "Dude, if you had sex in that bed, you're so keeping this room."

"No, dickhead, we didn't have sex," Jase replies, giving him a slight shove.

"Apparently I tried," I pipe up. "Or so I've been told, I think he's lying." I know better... I am remembering bits and pieces... but the teasing is far too much fun to resist.

"I'm not lying," he says as he walks past me, kissing me sweetly on the cheek. "You want me."

"I was under the influence," I deadpan, my eyebrow raised just so.

"Which is why I said no," he whispers in my ear, and I blush in spite of myself. Only remembering some of the night, I couldn't tell anyone if I'd actually slept with him. I certainly remember curling into him, teasing his neck to the point where he'd almost given in. That memory alone is enough to have me squirming in my pants, wondering what tonight may have in store. Anything past that, though, I have to rely on his memory and his word.

"Hey," Jaden says as she walks into the room. She is looking rather sheepish, avoiding eye contact with me thinking I am still angry with her. I admit I have my issues with everyone who thought it best that I was kept in the dark, but this is not the time or the place to deal with it. "How are you feeling?"

"With my hands," I answer, grinning when the comment causes a slight blush to come to Jase's cheeks.

Oh yeah.

He is thinking about it too.

"You're going up to your suite then?" Pete asks, and Jase nods. "We stayed in Jaden's room last night, you know...just in case."

"Which means I don't have to ask if you had sex in my room." Jase laughs as Pete shoots him a look. What the hell kind of look is *that*? Ugh. Brothers. They are a close family, something I'm not accustomed to, so I can only wonder about the bond between the two of them.

"What, is this musical rooms or something?" I ask a short time later as Jase and I are leaving Pete's room.

"After what happened last night, we were just...avoiding, you know..."

Does he have to look so adorable just shrugging his shoulders? Really?

Focus, Talli.

"The press? Do you think they could get up there?"

"Probably not, but,"

"You were avoiding more than the press," I cut him off. We step into the elevator, only going up one floor to get to his room.

"Yes," he finally says as the door closes.

Wow. An honest answer, just like that. I blink back my surprise before trying once again, to see if it is merely a fluke.

"Kate or John?"

"Both."

Holy shit. Two for two.

"I wanted to rip his fucking head off, you know?" His head is tilted to the side as he looks at me. "Well, minus the fact that he's built like a giant and would kill me."

"He's not, and he wouldn't." Jase raises an eyebrow at my first comment. Oh, that has to sound wrong. "I just danced with him, Jase. You saw the extent of what happened." That and he hasn't met my brother Eric. Now *that* man is a giant.

He avoids commenting as the elevator doors open and we make the short walk to his suite. Once inside, he sets my bag that he's been carrying by the door and reaches around me to help push the door closed. I stand there between him and the door, his arm still propped on it. He looks down at me, his eyes dropping to my lips setting my pulse racing before he smirks and pushes himself upright, walking across the room to the couch and sitting down. He pats the couch beside him.

Shit, shit, shit. I don't think I can survive him teasing me without pouncing. I'm just not that strong.

"If you can keep your hands to yourself, I'll let you sit beside me."

Fucker.

"Oh, whatever," I reply, keeping my cool. "You and your damn ego, like it needs any more stroking."

"That wasn't my ego you were stroking last night, sweetheart," he quips. "Or do you need to be told about that, too? Like you don't fucking remember."

Oh, I remember all right. Or, parts of it.

Fuck me running.

I sit on the far side of the couch and he laughs, grabbing a hold of my shirt and pulling me to his side. He leans back and props his feet up on the coffee table, holding me close to him as he uses the remote to turn on the TV. I can hear his heart beating through the thin fabric of his shirt, and the smell of him permeates my senses.

This is not good at all.

"I have to keep my hands to myself and you get to do this?"

"No." He draws the word out and I look up at his face to search for any clue of what he is about to do. "I get to do...this."

Without warning he has pushed me back onto the couch, pinning my arms above my head, lying on top of me. His face is mere inches from mine, his smile showing in his eyes as we breathe as one.

His weight on me is nearly my undoing.

"You, sir...are an insufferable tease," I am able to say, my stomach doing that whole flip thing when I see him lightly bite his bottom lip.

"No, I...am simply getting even..." His voice trails off as he leaves small kisses on my forehead, down to my cheek, my body reacting as he shifts slightly to gain better access to my neck. "Aren't you..." He kisses right below my earlobe... "so lucky..." he moves slightly lower, little nibbles along that sensitive line... "that I'm..." His tongue is wreaking havoc as he teases that spot, right where my pulse is... "a complete gentleman."

Please... don't do that...

"Gentleman my ass," I moan as he kisses along my jaw line to the other side of my neck.

You... you have no idea... how much I want you right now...

"Mmmm, but I am." He starts low, at the base of my neck this time. "No matter..." Oooohhhh that is gonna leave a mark... "how many times..." Again, where my pulse is hammering... "you said please..." I whimper as he makes his way up the side of my neck... "please..." I strain against his hands that hold me steady when he kisses up my ear... "Please..." My hips move against him as he breathes into my ear... "I still said..." His face hovers over mine, one slight movement and his lips will be on mine...

Finish... just... finish this, kiss me one time... let me lose control...

"No."

And with a smirk he pushes himself off me and walks across the room.

"Oh, you asshole," I mutter breathlessly as I hear him grab a drink from his refrigerator.

"*Sucks*, doesn't it?" he asks, pointing at me accusingly.

You're damn straight it sucks. My body is screaming, and you're across the fucking room, way too far away for my own good.

"I have no idea what you're talking about," I reply innocently, still lying down as I watch him down half a bottle of water.

"Sure you don't," he says, his eyebrow still raised at me. He adjusts his jeans, and I can see I've had the same effect on him that he has on me. "You are the epitome of evil, just so you fucking know."

"I am no such thing," I protest, fighting my urge to sigh at him standing there, propped against the wall, the look of pure heat in his eyes. He frowns suddenly and looks at his feet before looking back up at me.

"I hated seeing his hands on you."

I sit up slowly, watching the range of emotions play across his face. The mask he'd held in place last night is gone now. His eyebrows are pinched together, the pain in his eyes making my chest constrict. "He should have never touched you, not like..." His voice trails off and he looks away briefly. "I don't know if that's what got me, or if it was..."

"Or if it was what?" I know no matter how uncomfortable this is, we have seen the consequences of avoiding subjects.

"If it was how you were touching him."

There it is, that look from last night. But this time... this time I can read it, no questions asked.

It is hurt. Pure, unmasked, rip your heart out... hurt.

"And now you know." I keep eye contact with him, willing the tears to stay away.

"Now I know what?"

Really?

"How I felt," I reply, and I can tell it is actually registering with him. "For me to see you with Kate, not just last night, but in those pictures that were taken in my hometown. How you didn't even tell me she was going to be here and then she tells me..."

"...that she's marrying Jack...Jason," he finishes for me. "The other Jason." His face shows his regret, but I can't be sure if he truly grasps what I am saying.

"But there's a difference. I don't have a history with John, and you have yet to say whether or not you're over Kate."

"Touché," he whispers, then his voice is strong once more. "It's... it's complicated, Talli, I'm not going to lie and say that it's all cut and dry."

Of course not.

I blink back my tears as he skirts around the issue yet again.

"But she's happy, and I'm..."

Happy? Are you happy? Like you told Dr. Brooks you are?

"...not...replacing her, and I know that doesn't make sense, but..."

"What?" I cut him off, remembering his journal suddenly. He shrugs and shifts uncomfortably.

"When I left New York, I was an absolute fucking mess. And after a while I thought, what the hell...you know, my past...Kate...it was over, so I decided to move on." He takes in a deep, shuddering breath.

"How did that turn out?"

His eyes narrow slightly as he looks at me, both of us remembering our phone conversations, even though they seem a lifetime ago.

"I remember," I say softly.

"I've never lived the life of a monk, at least not since all this." His hand waves in the air, his gesture showing he is looking for the right word. "...success, if you will. But...my heart was never on the line. I wouldn't let it be." He looks over at me again, his expression softening slightly. "I don't know why I've been so reluctant to talk to you about this. I've never had to worry about putting my guard up with you, never had to... pretend...anything. Not all those years ago," he pauses again, tilting his head just slightly, "and not now. When it comes down to it, you're right up there, one of the only women I've ever been honest with, and I mean...fuck, that sounds wrong considering what we've been through, doesn't it?"

"Yes and no."

He walks over and kneels before me, taking my hands in his. His eyes are bright, shining with emotion, and when he speaks to me, my heart sings.

"Minus the lack of communication...when I'm with you, it's because I want to be with you. Not Kate. Not anyone else. You."

I should ask him about when he's not with me, but I kiss him then, still holding his hands as I tease his lips open with mine, sighing as our kiss deepens, his tongue warm and inviting. Have I mentioned how good he is at this? Because he is... the... the best.

He backs away, almost reluctantly, smiling softly as he lightly traces the side of my face with his fingertip. His eyes hold me captive, letting me know the ball is in my court now.

"I know I've told you that I'm sorry, but I feel I owe you more than that."

Jase shakes his head in return, his voice barely above a whisper. "You don't."

"I don't owe you, or you don't want to hear the explanation?"

"Both?" It sounds like a question, but he's answered truthfully. "I just don't know if..."

"I'm not Kaitlyn, Jase. You've told me there was dishonesty, betrayal. The things I said, the things I did...it was out of hurt, and out of anger, but I wouldn't...I couldn't be with anyone else. And yes, it was a really fucking stupid *game*, for lack of a better word, but I wanted you to hurt the way I did. And that was wrong, regardless of the circumstances."

He is quiet, contemplative. "I suppose..." He stops for just a moment, then continues. "Yeah, I know...I still have a problem with the whole betrayal thing, I know." He laughs softly, running his fingers through his hair. "Fuck, aren't we just a pair? What about you, do you have any demons from your past that you're running from?"

Holy fuck do I ever.

"Just myself," I answer honestly, knowing every single skeleton in that graveyard is there because I've put it there. "And that's not...Okay, it's relevant, but..."

"In time," he says, pulling me in for another kiss. Probably not the best idea, since it both eases and stirs my troubled mind. "But for now...don't kill me, you were supposed to be at that seminar, and I have to get down to the local TV station, so...you rest."

"Yes sir." I lay back on the couch as he stands, his eyes taking in the length of me. "What are you doing?"

"Contemplating whether or not to cancel."

"Go," I say, swatting at his legs. "I've caused you enough trouble this weekend."

"Don't sweat it," he says with a smile, his next words shooting me straight past cloud nine. "You're worth it."

I drift back off to sleep shortly after he leaves to the sounds of Classic TV in the background but am startled awake by persistent knocking at the door. I am unsure of who it is, so I quietly made my way over and look through the small peephole in the door.

Oh, God.

I'm not ready for this.

It is Kaitlyn.

CHAPTER 35

I open the door, bracing myself for it.

Go ahead, Kaitlyn Evans. Give it your best shot.

There she stands, Ms. Perfect, her beautiful dark hair swept up off her shoulders, her brown eyes registering...shock?

Ah, there it is.

Recognition.

In her pristine cream-colored suit, she looks ready for the runway, apparently making a conscious effort to get someone's attention. I am sure that person isn't me.

I am happy knowing I've gone against my original plan of doing nothing and had applied light makeup. I'd left my curls down free, falling past my shoulders and framing my face just the way Jase prefers them. I am wearing a pair of navy-blue yoga pants that hug my hips and a tight long-sleeved white shirt...comfortable, a far cry from the game of dress up from the night before. No, I'm not ready to hit the town; I am ready for a night in with the man who is coming back to me, ex-girlfriend be damned...

Right?

"I see he hasn't learned," she finally says, waltzing past me, the slight scent of vanilla following her.

"Hi, is Jase here? No? Fine, I'll come back later," I say as sweetly as I can, trying in vain to curb the sarcasm.

"Even better," she replies, ignoring my barbs. She sits on the couch and crosses her ankles demurely. "I see the dress worked for you. Congratulations, you got him to sleep with you. I truly hope you're not deluding yourself into thinking you're special."

Oh, she's come prepared for a fight.

But she doesn't know me.

"You think that was our first night together?" I ask, crossing the room towards her, omitting that we didn't have sex the night before. "My, you are a naïve one." For one brief moment her eyes betray her, and I know I've struck a nerve.

"Ah, well, Jason's only human. He makes mistakes once in a while."

Keep telling yourself that's all I am, sweetheart.

I make a mental note that she calls him 'Jason,' the same name that she calls her fiancé. Coincidence? With this woman I am doubting it. But... I may as well get to my point with her, right?

"What are you doing here Kaitlyn?"

"No, the question is, what are you doing here, Talli?"

Well, get ready to eat your heart out, cupcake.

"I'm here," I say, opening the refrigerator and pulling out a diet cola as if I own the place, "because Jase brought me here. I'm here because he wants me here. I'm here because he planned for me to be here. Any more questions, Kate? Or are you going to answer mine?"

Come on. Let's hear it.

"I'm here to keep him from making an even bigger mistake," she replies, unable to hide her disdain.

"So...you don't want him, but you don't want him to be with me? Charming."

"He's out of your league." She looks me up and down, not finding my lounging clothes any more appealing than the dress from the night before. "Far, far out of your league."

Is that so?

"I hardly think Mr. Rock Star agrees with you."

"And that," she says, pointing an accusing finger me, "is exactly my point. You see him as Jason the Rock Star, and you latched on to him the first chance you got."

Oh, she's so very wrong.

"Do you not remember the hospital? What you walked in on then? I can give you a refresher course if need be."

"Spare me," she cuts me off. "I know your type all too well."

I raise an eyebrow at her statement. "My *type?*"

"Unfortunately, Jason has yet to learn when he picks up trash, he needs to put it in the garbage can where it belongs."

Oh, you think you're so fucking clever.

"He's already learned that, Kaitlyn," I retort. "He got rid of you, didn't he?"

"My history with Jason can never be matched by whatever fling the two of you have. And trust me, Talli, that's just what it is. A fling."

"Is that the best you can do?" I ask, unfazed. Didn't Dr. Brooks refer to me as the infamous Talli just this morning? "Come on, Kate, don't disappoint me. You've been dying to do this for how many years now?"

"And what about you? How many years have you wanted to have this conversation with me?"

Oh, what a disappointment this is turning out to be.

"So...all this time, poor little Kaitlyn has been eating herself alive over little ol' me." I sit on the barstool, drinking my diet cola as if I haven't a care in the world, trying to ignore my racing heart.

"Don't flatter yourself." If it were humanly possible for eyes to shoot daggers, I would be dead right now. "Oh, and nice story you handed him all those years ago... dying mother, huh? Took her quite some time, didn't it? And John tells me it was a heart attack."

She shoots, she scores. Thanks for the memories, doll face...here, let me return the favor.

"And what kind of lies did you feed him so he'd fall for you, Kate? You know, all those times he and I had intimate talks in the hospital, he barely ever talked about you. What do you think that says, Kaitlyn? He barely talked about his *best friend*. He told me about his cousin, how sick he was, how he'd lost a friend to suicide, how it was affecting his entire life. He told me things that he said he never told anyone. When he had a problem, he came to *me*. Let's say that again, in case you missed it. He trusted *me*, Kaitlyn."

She opens her mouth for what I'm sure is one hell of a comeback, but I am far from done.

You want to hurt me? Try this on for size.

"So...how was your anniversary dinner, Kate? How'd it go after he had his hands on me? After he was kissing me?" I smile then, knowing no matter how sweet her memories of that night are it is time to put her in her damn place...the past. Omission, how many times have I argued with Jase that it is the same as lying? And yet there I am not saying I am the one who initiated everything...after the call telling me my father was gone, wanting to erase everything, lose myself in his eyes, those lips...and remembering how he'd pulled away...

No, that was the past. He wouldn't pull away now.

"If it meant that much to you then tell me, Talli..." The way she spits my name out is completely venomous, I have to give her that much. "Where did you disappear to? How many years were in between? And why was it...oh, and this one...come on, let's hear this answer, Talli...why was it that there you were, back in his life, and didn't even have the guts to tell him it was you? Oh, wait...did you not remember? And he didn't even put it together that it was you, did he? What, you think attempting to dress like a normal functioning member of society instead of a street walker would make you more credible?"

What am I supposed to say now? Gee, Ms. Perfect, I was spiraling out of control, I spent those days in a fog, and even though Jase had been a shining beacon then, I had marred that with my actions at the restaurant. What can I say?

Oh, right.

"Unlike you, I don't live in the past."

"You think I'm part of the past? Who's naïve now?"

"I'm sure your fiancé will be pleased to hear that," I say, finishing my drink and setting the empty can on the bar. "I saw him earlier, you know. I believe his exact words were 'this isn't high school.' Perhaps you should keep that in mind."

Her cheeks flush a slight shade of pink at the mention of him, the fiancé, the other Jason. Go me.

"Let's cut the crap, Talia. You're not good enough for him."

Cut the crap? Seriously?

"And you think you are? He's done with you, Kaitlyn. He's been done with you since he left New York. Or did you conveniently forget that?"

"Jason has been a part of my life for the last twenty years. You think that's nothing? I was his first. His first love, the first girl he's ever been with. *You* were merely a distraction. Like I said, a fling. You think if I asked him to pick between the two of us, he'd pick you? Don't fool yourself, Talli. I'm his best friend—"

Choose? She'd ask him to *choose*?

"This isn't high school anymore, Kaitlyn." I have to reiterate that fact yet again. "He and I have a history now. It won't be as easy as you think it will be."

"You're not good enough for him."

So you keep fucking telling me, sweetheart.

"And you're getting fucking married. *You're* the one who let him go. *You're* the one who made a mistake. Don't punish me for *your* mistake, Kate—"

"He doesn't love you. Don't you get that?"

How can I argue with that?

Fuck...how can I?

I have poured my heart out to him, I've told him I am in love with him, and what did I get in return? Oh right... I'm not a fucking replacement.

For her.

But she'll never know.

"You think coming into this room, batting your eyes, bringing up the past is going to make him walk away from me?" I ask, feigning boredom with the conversation.

"So says the girl who came to my engagement party in her little black dress. Are you sure Jason wanted you here? Because he certainly didn't tell you about the party, or about me. Oh, and…let's face it, it was so obvious…you thought I was marrying *Jase Warner*. Not a fling? Are you sure about that?"

"I *have* heard about you," I reply, still doing my best to keep my cool. "I know that no one else in his life has. But I have. Tell me, Kate…how much did you hear about me?" Her cheeks look slightly pink at my question…ah, the journal.

Perhaps there is more to the omission of me than I originally thought.

"What, no intimate details of what we've shared? No proclamations of him wishing that I was you?"

Her eyes narrow as she looks at me. Again, I must have struck a nerve.

"Come on, Kate…it's eating you up inside, isn't it? How many others did he fail to mention in that sweet little book he wrote out for you? Last I heard the answer to that was none. You think I haven't seen the journal, Kaitlyn? Please. He left it behind…in Ohio…when he flew out there to see me."

"In Ohio," she repeats, her eyebrow raised.

"Right, you know where you met him at the airport? Yeah, that was just a few short hours after he left my bed."

In spite of her nostrils flaring just a touch at my words, she had no trouble firing back. "You're not the first person he's screwed that he wasn't in love with, Talli. You're just…next."

I hear the click of the door as Jase uses his keycard to enter. I hold my tongue at my hateful reply as both Kaitlyn and I turn towards the door. Jase enters, smiling to himself as he probably thinks he'll be seeing just me lying there on the couch as he left me, stopping short when he notices Kaitlyn sitting there.

Kaitlyn who turns on her fucking charm and smiles so sweetly at him…a smile he returns.

Which leaves me back on the outside looking in.

CHAPTER 36

I feel my heart splinter as Jase holds out his hand to Kaitlyn, helping her up and folding her into his arms. She shoots me a triumphant look as she curls into him, smirking as he rubs her back before stepping back.

Again. He… he went to her *again*.

"Jack said you wanted to talk before the two of you left; I wasn't expecting you here, though," he says, his voice so warm, friendly, inviting. I'm struck with the memory of Jase and I lying on my bed, when I'd tried to recall the boy in the hospital. And Jack… I'd called that boy Jack.

No wonder he'd reacted that way.

The memory only stays for a moment, though, as Kate's smirk brings me back to the present.

Did you forget what you were expecting when you came back here, Jase?

"Well, it's been…entertaining," Kate replies. He frowns slightly, then looks towards his left.

Yeah, jackass. I'm still here, or did you forget you wanted me to stay?

I keep my expression neutral, as if it doesn't bother me in the least that he's just pulled his ex-girlfriend into his arms right in front of me. Even if I give him ten kinds of hell over it, she will never have the satisfaction of witnessing it.

I give him a half smile, not needing to go the girly route to get his attention.

"Ah," is all he says as he steps further away, running his hands through his hair and walking towards me. He smiles softly and kisses my cheek on his way to the refrigerator.

See that, Kaitlyn? Yeah, it is my time to smirk now.

"Kate was just leaving," I say, that smile firmly planted on my face.

"Actually, I wasn't," Kaitlyn corrects me. Of course she would. "I came here to talk to you, Jason. In private."

"Ah, yes, she's second guessing marrying Dr. Brooks now that I'm back in your life." I keep my eyes on her the entire time, but still see his head snap around to look at her.

"What?" he asks calmly, but he shows his confusion.

"Don't put words in my mouth," she snaps at me. "Perhaps Talli here wants to come clean about her dying *mother*..."

"Don't even think about bringing my mother into this," I say curtly. That is one line she does not want to cross.

"Okay...whoa..." Jase laughs nervously, interrupting us. "Wow. Um, let's not do this, okay? Not right now. Kate, I can always talk to you tomorrow."

"Jason, this is really important," she says, back to syrupy sweet. My God, does he really fall for this?

"Jase and I have plans," I remind her.

"What plans? It's not as if the two of you are...*together*, now, are you?"

"All right...oooookay, why don't we take a break here?" Jase asks. He pulls a beer out of the refrigerator, opens it, and takes a long drink. He seems torn as to where he should sit or stand; walk over to his best friend or to his current... fling?

Fuck, is she right?

"How was the interview?" I ask, keeping the subject light and completely off the unwanted visitor.

"Eye opening," he replies cryptically, then adds a reassuring smile afterwards. "I'll tell you about it in a little bit."

"Ah, so Talli's antics made the news," Kaitlyn pipes up with her sweet little smile. "Sorry you have to go through that, Jason."

He shrugs. "I'll live."

How the hell I keep the heat from creeping into my face I'm not sure. Lucky for me, Jase is acting as if it is no big deal.

"Please, this isn't like I was dancing on a bar or anything," he adds, smiling at me again, possibly trying to make me feel better. "Jackie was trying to call me before I got there but I'm a pro at this by now."

I feel so horrified, embarrassed, ashamed over Jase having to answer for my actions. And of course, it certainly doesn't help having Kate sitting there, hearing all about it.

"You still need to be more cautious of the company you keep." Kaitlyn's biting words are obviously meant about me.

"Talli isn't to blame for what happened," Jase says quickly, before I am able to spit my venomous reply.

Whoa... did he just jump to my defense?

Yes... yes, I think he did.

Wow. Wow and...

Score.

I don't know where I gather the strength from, or what inner spirit is guiding me, telling me to keep my mouth shut and my expression neutral. Regardless of the look of shock that briefly registers on Kaitlyn's face, I sit back in the stool completely calm, cool, collected—innocent.

"Of course," Kaitlyn replies with a smile. "She is, after all, your...*friend*. Look, Jason, we need to talk, as soon as possible. Can you do that?"

"I said I would. Tomorrow, okay?"

They seem to share some sort of silent communication that I try to hide my disdain for. I understand that they had been a part of each other's lives for a very long time, I understand that they share a past; I need to make him understand the past doesn't necessarily equal the future.

And I have all night to do it.

"Come here."

Jase is sitting on the couch, his shoes and socks tucked over by the door, his shirt untucked, a bowl of popcorn sitting next to his jean-clad leg. Is it necessary for that man to be so sexy? I suppose I can see the appeal there, see how he wormed his way into his fans' hearts... okay, I know I can.

I just don't get what he sees in me.

I smile anyway as I walk over to the couch and take a seat directly next to him, where he has patted the cushion. He wraps his arm securely around my shoulder, pulling me flush up against his body.

It is as if I've died and gone to heaven. Cliché, yes, but true.

"Mmmm." He leaves a soft kiss on top of my head, snuggling into me. "I've been waiting for this all day."

"Have you really?" I ask, my voice full of the wonder I am feeling.

"Nah, I'm lying to you." He laughs and kisses the top of my head again. "Room service for two, which was damn good if I say so."

"Yes, it was."

"And now..." He pushes the button on the remote, turning the television on. "The night is ours."

All ours.

It is equal parts exhilarating and terrifying. What is he going to say? That... that he just wants to be friends? No... he wouldn't hold me this way if that's what he wants.

"What the hell is this?" I ask with a laugh as he settles in on some gossip show.

"I think this is what they were showing me earlier. Oh... it is! Watch this...the look on your face." Jase points at the TV that is replaying the cell phone video that someone had taken. It is when we were at the elevator, when Jase had made his 'oh sure now' joke, and he is laughing softly beside me. "That look is priceless. You know you wanted to laugh." His fingers are playing with my curls, driving me to distraction.

"But they also saw pieces of the argument before we ever went into the club," I remind him.

"You say that like it's a bad thing." He kisses the top of my head again, and somehow this one feels more personal. Wow does that ever give me butterflies. "See? That proves we knew each other, and you weren't—"

"Some cheap skank you picked up in a bar," I cut him off, and he nudges me.

"Stop talking like that."

"Many things have been said about the dress, and not just last night."

"That dress is hot." His tone makes me warm in all the right places. "Especially all folded up sitting beside that bathtub."

"Perv." I laugh when he reaches over and pokes my side.

"You don't mind staying in?"

I shoot him an incredulous look. "You're kidding, right?"

His smile is sweet, warm. "Just checking."

"And what about you? You don't mind?" I glance up at him, falling even harder as he places a gentle kiss on my lips.

"This is what I came here for. So…other things got in the way." He shrugs, that half-smirk on his face that he is famous for. "I came out here to see you, spend time with you…like this."

"Minus five tons of salt on the popcorn," I joke, then accept the few kernels he places in my mouth, licking his fingers in the process. From my position I hear his heart slightly speed up.

"And the beer on the couch," he adds. "Then again…nah, I'm already in trouble for the last hotel room we shared."

"When did…oh." I blush, remembering tables we had overturned as we had christened nearly every part of that room. His eyebrows are raised at me, as if he is offended that it had slipped my mind. "Well, that room fared better than my headboard did." He laughs then, and for some unfathomable reason my body is reacting just by the slight movement.

"I'd say sorry," he begins as he tangles his fingers in my hair, "but I'm not."

He's... he's not sorry?

"Are you sure about that?" I wouldn't ask, but I remember how he'd said we shouldn't have slept together that first night.

It's as if he's reading my mind. "Technically, I'm not sorry about either time. I'm only sorry about the...complications? And I'm not even sure if that's the word I'm looking for."

"Complications," I repeat, studying his face, my heart still racing.

He's not sorry. He's... he's really not sorry!

"This whole miscommunication thing." His fingers continue twirling my curls, making it increasingly difficult to remain focused. "You know, the one I'm out here to fix, fine job I did in the beginning as I failed miserably."

I can't stop the tear that falls down my cheek; he did this, rearranged his schedule, went through hell and back to make it to Las Vegas, to "fix" this.

With *me.*

He wouldn't do that for just a fling, would he?

"If it was working, you wouldn't be crying." His voice is as gentle as his touch when he reaches over with his free hand and catches the tear with his fingertip. "I don't want you to be sad, Christine."

And again, with the middle name... oh, he knows what that does to me, what it has done to me since our days on the phone.

And... sad? No...

"Right now, right at this moment...I'm about the furthest from sad I could be." I know my words contradict the tears, but he understands my meaning and welcomes me into his arms as I turn, straddling him to freely kiss him the way I've been wanting to all day.

His arms close around me, his hands wide, protective as he holds me to him, our kiss full of feeling...emotion, rather than simply passion. My hands are cradling his face as our tongues glided together, taking our time, feeling each other. This kiss... this one reminded me of that boy, the one who wouldn't kiss me first without a dare, the one who touched me with reverence.

Just as he's doing now.

He pulls back slightly and buries his face in the crook of my neck and just...holds me. He holds me as if I am precious, cherished, treasured, and my heart soars. I am still straddling him, stroking his hair as he breathes me in. When he finally sits back, his eyes are shining, a light greenish gray as he studies my face.

"I've kept telling myself I was going to behave," he says, his hands still lightly caressing my back. "Not that I trusted myself to...but I have the best of intentions."

I tilted my head as I hold his gaze, feeling exactly how difficult it is for him to control himself from my position. "Mind if I ask why?"

"This...isn't why I came here..." He moans softly as I shift my position. "Christine, don't move like that please..." His eyes slide shut as I settle in, my position partially more comfortable, definitely more arousing, for the both of us. I am pressed up against him, and had we not been clothed, one slight movement and he would be... inside me... yeah... he is right, probably not the best idea. He opens his eyes partially, the sheer heat of his gaze making my pulse quicken. His voice is hoarse, raspy, when he asks, "What have you done to me?"

I caress the side of his face with my fingertips, tracing along the edge of his jaw where just a hint of stubble is beginning to grow. Our eyes never lose contact as I answer him in the most honest way I can.

"All I've done is love you."

His hands still and his breath quickens ever so slightly at my words. His lips part as if he is going to say something to me, but we both remain silent, breathing in unison, my words hanging in the air between us. It isn't as if I haven't told him before, but that had occurred in the midst of a heated argument. Right now, with his arms around me, our bodies touching so intimately, the words take on a completely different meaning.

This time, it isn't while we're hurt, or angry.

This time, there are no interruptions, no other people to consider, just the two of us.

This time, I'm not walking away.

I watch the different emotions flood through Jase's eyes, his silence unnerving but understood. He's never said it before, not to me; he has admitted to being 'confused' about me. But what will he say, what will he do now with this being laid so prominently on the table?

My questions are answered as he sits up straighter, pulling me to him, his lips teasing mine with soft, sweet kisses. There is no rush in his actions as he takes his time exploring me, his hands cupping my face as his kisses grow longer, his tongue caressing mine in a way that warms me from head to toe. My heart is pounding against my ribcage, my body humming with a newfound energy, knowing that this... *this* is different. It is perfect. One of his hands trails down, grasping my hip as his other hand moves around, his fingers tangling in my hair, holding me even closer as he deepens our kiss.

There it is.

No matter how much he controls his actions, there is no mistaking the fire that burns between us, how our bodies are so in tune with each other, how they fit so perfectly.

My breath is coming in short gasps as he holds me to him, exploring me with his lips and tongue, lightly nipping at my neck as he pulls my head back gently by my hair. I can't hold back the soft whimpers and moans and he eats it all up, knowing just where to touch to get me closer to the edge. I try pulling back, try gaining access to those sensitive spots on his neck, but he won't let go.

This just... oh, it isn't fair.

He leans back into the cushions, pulling me with him, his hand on my hip guiding me as our bodies begin to move, clothing and all. I want closer contact, skin to skin, but I am a slave to Jase's every whim as he holds me to him, shrugging off my advances to take things further. I swear he is trying to torture me on purpose, make me burn for him, give me just a taste of what I know could come if he will just let it happen.

He drops his hand from my hair, letting it trail down to cup my breast in his hand...did he just laugh as I whimpered? It is getting to be too much, I don't know if I can take it any more as his hips surge forward just a little harder...

"Please," I whisper against his lips, and he responds by doing it again. "God, Jase, please," I breathe as he latches onto my neck, lightly biting as he moves against me. I try reaching in between us to remove the barriers between his skin and mine, but he catches my wrist and pins it behind me, his lips finding mine once more. I am helpless to his sensual assault as he turns us together, gently laying me back on the couch.

"Ssssh," he whispers in my ear, and I tremble beneath him. "It's okay, baby. I'll take care of you."

He is lying half on top of me, his hand free to roam as it wishes, but with his body pressed so closely to mine I can't get to that part of him I want to touch so badly. "Please..." I try begging once more as his hand reaches between my legs, moving against me even with my pants in the way. "Jase...don't make me wait...please..."

He is kissing the outer edges of my ear as his hand slowly makes its way down the front of my pants, slipping beneath the silk panties, stopping just shy of where I want his fingers to be. I can feel him pressed up against me...he wants this every bit as much as I do.

I grasp his wrist, trying everything I can, every way I can possibly move, but he holds his hand in place as he leaves another wet trail of kisses down my neck. I moan in frustration, feeling him smile against my skin as he finally acquiesces my pleas, his fingers moving expertly against me.

He slides a finger between my folds, gliding up and down, the warmth and dampness spreading as he does so. "Do you remember the first time I did this?" he asks, smiling against my skin as I moan my response. "Think way back... to the orderly room."

Oh... orderly room... yes, yes he had done... this...

"And remember, when I first touched you..." He applies pressure, and I cry out against his lips.

"Right there... you... right there, oh God, Jase..."

He inhales sharply before leaving another wet trail of kisses to my neck, latching on to that most sensitive spot as he increases his rhythm. I am moving my hips along with his hand, trying to push it lower.

"What's the matter?" he asks, his voice a ragged whisper against my skin.

"I... I want..." I moan as his hand shifts slightly, his thumb rubbing circles in that most sensitive spot.

"This?" he asks, pushing two fingers inside of me at once, gliding them in and out.

Oh... oh, that is... yes, that is it...

My body seems to go into a complete state of shock at the sensation, wanting it so badly, having it feel so good that I never want him to stop. "Breathe, Christine," I hear him whisper in my ear, and I take a deep breath in, a small moan escaping me as his fingers are building me up to a fever pitch.

"Jase, please...please..." I want him right now, no more waiting...I want him with every fiber of my being, skin to skin, inside of me...

"It's okay," he says, his voice low. He places light kisses by my ear, and I whimper, pleading with him again. "Just let go, Christine...let go..." I shake my head slightly, my breathing becoming more and more labored, his fingers drawing a moan from me that he captures with a kiss. I grab onto his hand, holding him closer as he brings me to that brink that I don't want to cross without him. He kisses a trail back to my neck, his lips on my skin as he says, "Let me see you fly...it's okay, Christine...I'm here to catch you..."

I cry out, arching my back as wave after wave of ecstasy overtakes me, my body tense and trembling while Jase lays beside me drinking it all in. He places soft kisses on my face, my lips, my neck as his fingers continue playing me until I am finally still, panting and sighing in his arms. When I finally open my eyes, he is hovering over me, his eyes bright, his expression mirroring one I'd seen on him before, in the hotel room in Cleveland... back in my room in Ohio.

I just can't pinpoint what it is.

But I don't have the time to.

"Beautiful," is the only word he says before he kisses me, deep and slow, pulling me up against him.

I don't know how he manages to do it; I don't know if there is some book he has studied or if this is simply a natural talent for him... I am completely at his mercy. Even as we lay here, completely clothed, he has me whimpering, shivering, begging him to make love to me, he is in complete control. It isn't as if it doesn't cost him, I can tell by the sheen of sweat on his forehead, the moisture on his skin when I finally pry his shirt off of him a good hour later. He lets out a low growl when I kiss his neck, the taste of his skin driving my desire even more.

Two can play, right?

I kiss down his chest to his tattoos, his breath catching as I trace along the edges with my tongue. As I move further down, following the trail of soft hair, I cup his erection through his jeans, rubbing my hand along the outline of him as I leave open mouthed kisses along his waistline.

He has one hand tangled in my hair, caressing the back of my head as I continue teasing him. "Christine... you... shouldn't... mmmmm *fuck*." I have the side of his jeans pulled slightly down and am sucking lightly on his hipbone. "No... no, no, no... come here." He pulls me up, moving us both to a sitting position, but still has me straddling his lap.

"What, I can't play?"

"This isn't a game, Christine."

His eyes hold me captive as he says this, even as he is pulling my shirt up.

"This... this is real."

It's real? Is it... No... no, don't read into this, Talli. Don't...

He pulls my shirt over my head, his eyes trailing down momentarily before once more meeting with mine.

"Are you..." He licks his lips as he expertly unfastens my bra. "Are you playing a game with me?"

My eyes widen with shock. "No." And he... he should know this.

I love him.

I just... love him.

His breath catches in his throat as he slides the straps down my arms, my breasts nearly eye level with him. As he drops my bra to the floor, he begins leaving light kisses across the swell of my breasts, before growing bolder, taking one of the peaks in his mouth, sucking greedily.

Fuck. Me.

I cry out, grinding my hips against his in response, losing myself in the sensations that he is causing. The pressure is building again, my body again screaming for release as I cling to him, my hands in his sweat dampened hair, his mouth exploring my body.

"Jase please..." I moan as he switches to the other breast, his tongue flicking at the tip before he closes in. "I want you inside of me."

He moans against me as our hips moved together, the heat, the friction almost too much to handle. He pulls back then, his arms circling my waist as he looks up at me. "Hold on to me."

Oh... oh the sound of his voice shoots straight through me. I can only nod as he stands, his arms securely around my waist, lifting me. I wrap my legs around him, my arms around his neck, holding his gaze for a long moment before I lean down and gently leave one soft kiss on his lips. I lean in, burying my face in his neck as he walks towards his destination.

The smell of his skin only heightens my already raw senses, pushing me closer to the edge as I feel him gently laying me back. It is soft... so... soft...

I open my eyes to see him hovering above me, knowing he's just laid me back on the bed. I slowly move my hands, one of them caressing the side of his face, my fingertips tracing his lips. His eyes slide shut at my touch, his breathing even more labored. When his eyes open, a smile touches his lips as he lowers them to mine.

The room is filled with the sounds of our breathing, the soft moans, my whimpers as we continue exploring every inch of each other. His hands are shaking ever so slightly as he pulls my pants down, leaving my panties on, his lips kissing up my thighs. "Baby… please…"

He places a kiss right there, where my thong is wet, before moaning, pushing himself up the bed, his mouth ravaging mine. He abandons his attempts to stop me from undoing his jeans, moving with me as I push them down, and he kicks them off as he holds me to him. I wrap my legs back around him then, our hips grinding together.

"Jase…"

"I know, baby," he whispers up against my lips. "Fuck, I know."

I grasp at his hips, gasping as he pushes into me as he would if he were inside of me. Oh, he is being so unfair… he's teased me to the point of no return, moaning as I cry out, the friction, the pressure, the movement sending me over the edge, gasping, clinging to him as he continues to move.

He… he is too much…

"I didn't bring you…here to do this…"

Two hours into our friendly platonic night, we are finally skin to skin lying in the middle of his queen-sized bed, pillows tossed about, comforter in disarray. He pushes my damp curls off my forehead, placing sweet, soft kisses where they had been. I move my hips against him, wanting him inside of me, whimpering when he shakes his head 'no'. His breathing is heavy, labored and in spite of his words he continues kissing me, pressing up against me without entering.

"If this...isn't what...you intended," I manage to say, "then why..."

"Because I want to," he moans, pulling me closer...so close that one slight movement of his hips and he'd be entering me...

I take advantage of his admission, rolling us over as one, gasping as he fills me completely. He arches his neck and back, grabbing onto my hips as I begin to move. This... this is ecstasy, being filled completely, my walls caressing him, grasping him as I move my hips, taking him in deeper and deeper with each stroke. This is what we'd been building to, this is what I've craved from the first touch.

This.

Him.

Us.

"Talia...Christine..."

"Do you want me to stop?" I breathe into his ear, sure I won't be able to if he says yes. He rolls me over onto my back, pushing further and further into me in response, and I cling to him as I am lost again.

"I...missed you...Talli, I missed you," he moans, kissing me, that one sweet declaration sending me soaring once more. My body constricts around him, holding him in, protesting as he continues thrusting, his strokes hard, uneven. My eyes are closed so tightly I swear I see stars, his name being torn from my throat as the Earth-shattering orgasm shakes me to my core. This time, he is with me, his hands grasping me so tight I know there will be bruises, and we soar together, trembling in each other's arms.

Finally.

As we slowly become aware of our surroundings, our breathing returning to normal, he props himself up on one elbow and smiles down at me.

I know I'll never forget that smile.

It isn't cocky, it isn't triumphant. It is full of emotion, one that he hasn't stated, one I can't be completely sure of.

As he gently pushes my curls back again, his fingers lingering on my skin, I think to myself he has to care about me. There's no way I can be just a fling...not when he touches me as if I am the most precious gift in this world.

I return his smile, kissing his fingertips as they passed by my lips, praying whatever Kaitlyn has to say won't change his mind.

CHAPTER 37

"Wake up, sleepy head."

I open one eye and scowl briefly before a smile touches my lips. "What happened to you not being a morning person?"

"I lied." He sits down on the bed beside me and I feel his hand pushing my hair back out of my face. "Actually, I didn't. I just have a lot to do today before I leave, and speaking of leaving…"

"Do I have to?" I am enjoying his light touch on my skin, the way it is soothing me, lulling me…

"I wish I could keep you here all day," he whispers against my cheek before he leaves a soft kiss there.

Me, too.

"But you need to be up, showered, dressed, and ready for Jaden."

"How long do I have?"

"Oh, about a half hour."

"What?!" I sit up quickly, my eyes wide as I look at him.

"Um… sorry?" He looks so damn adorable, that sheepish grin on his face. "I have everything in there for you."

"Oh gee, thanks." I push back the covers, for once not shy even in my state of complete undress. I note the blush to his cheeks as I make my way towards the washroom. "You said my stuff is laid out?"

"Yeah, I... um... I've already showered."

"Are you sure?" I look over my shoulder, grinning as I can visibly see him swallow.

"Yeah, yeah... I just... you were tired, and... ah, fuck, Talli. Go, take your shower."

I laugh as he turns towards the living area, walking away from me while muttering under his breath.

Good Monday morning to me.

"I think I have everything," I say as I step out of the washroom, freshly showered, blissfully happy. Jase is sitting on the couch, slight scruff growing in, T-shirt and jeans filled out quite nicely. "Jaden normally double checks me, but since someone didn't wake me up in time..." My voice trails off as I raise my eyebrow at him.

He stands up and walks towards me. "You were tired."

"How very presumptuous of you, sir." I already know there was no way I could possibly deny it; I am blissfully exhausted. He flashes that damn cocky smirk at me right before we are rudely interrupted by a knock on the door.

"Told you time wasn't on our side," he says softly, just a brush of his lips across mine before he walks over and answers the door. Jaden rushes in, giving Jase a quick one-armed hug before walking quickly to me.

"We have got to hurry, we're going to miss our plane." She says this so quickly that if I didn't know better, it would have sounded like one long word.

My smile is a lazy one. "Relax, Jaden, it's all good. We'll make it."

"Oh...crap. Jase, who the hell is she and what did you do with Talli?" She shakes her head. "Scratch that, I don't want to hear it."

"Chicken," Jase mutters, and laughs when Jaden flips him off.

"Oh, you're one to talk," I tease her, and her pink cheeks tell me I am right. "Uh huh, you just shut the hell up. I got my things together."

"A...hem..."

I smile sheepishly as Jase. *"Jase*...got my things together, and now we're ready to go."

"And you have everything?" Jaden asks. Jase hands my return ticket to me and smiles at his brother's non-girlfriend.

"Now she does."

"Okay...then...we have to go!" She picks up my bag and places it on my shoulder. Damn, it's heavy.

I inhale deeply and let it out with a sigh as I turn to Jase. "Guess it's time."

He leaned in for one last lingering kiss. "Until later," he whispers against my lips.

And I fall a little more.

"Of course."

Jaden and I are rushing out the door when I remember that Jase is going to be speaking with Kaitlyn. I turn back and am stopped before I even say a word.

"I'll tell you all about it," he says, his eyes almost sad as he leans up against his doorframe.

I can only smile in response.

"Are you still angry with me?" Jaden is asking as we fly over the country.

Hmmm, how do I answer that?

With honesty, of course. "Not...exactly? I would say I was more hurt than angry, to be completely honest with you." I shrug it off... *wow*, that is so unlike me. "I'll get over it, though. Best of intentions, right?"

"Right." She draws the word out, still looking at me as if I am an alien. "You...realize that's a window seat, right?"

I am staring dreamily out at the scenery. "Mmm hmm."

"Earth to Ms. Emerson."

That isn't Jaden's voice.

I turn to see Dr. John Craig standing by our seats, leaning over slightly. "If you don't mind, I would like to speak with you."

I feel the heat creep into my face as I look up at him. My, but he is a hot one. If my heart wasn't so invested I would do more than take a second look, without a doubt. And now...Now, he probably would like to throw me off this damn plane.

"You could take my seat in first class, if you wish," he says to Jaden, whose eyebrows seem to disappear into her hairline.

"Go ahead," I whisper to her, giggling as she kisses my cheek and walks quickly towards the front of the plane, her little carry-on bag with her. John settles into her seat, his broad shoulders nearly touching mine. He looks over at me, flashing an easy-going smile, the dimples not quite making me feel better. "Okay, tell me how much you hate me now."

"I don't." His deep voice is soft and inviting, although his words have me a bit confused. He doesn't hate me? Really? "Ms. Emerson, I would like to show you something." He hands me his driver's license, causing me to raise an eyebrow. "See that?" He points to his birth date. "Well before yesterday. Don't think for one second that I didn't know what you were up to."

Of course he did. How could I have been so stupid? My face feels even more on fire as I hand his license back to him, unsure of what to say next. "I'm...Dr. Craig, I'm so sorry, and embarrassed, and—"

"I have to admit it was pretty damn hot seeing you like that." His eyes tell me he's seeing the image replay in his mind. "Not just the dress either. But I digress...I only had your best interests at heart. Yours and Jase's, no matter how misguided his intentions were. Or mine, for that matter."

I cross my arms, in a bit of a defensive mode. "You could have at least told me he wasn't the one engaged to Kaitlyn."

"Yes, I could have. However... hear me out, Talia." I close my mouth as he uses my first name, his dark chocolate eyes sincere.

"He needed to see what he was doing to you. And...honestly, if you had known Kate was engaged to someone else would you have had the same reaction?"

"That's a hypothetical question, of course." I ponder his question for a moment, remembering how happy, how perfect they had looked in each other's arms. "If I had walked in and seen...what I did...no, I probably would have had a similar reaction, perhaps not the same...but similar."

"And therein lies the problem," he said, his voice still as soft. "I've known both of them for what seems like forever, ever since I'd become friends with Michael." Michael, Jase's brother, the one who'd been in the hospital all those years ago. Bits and pieces of the past were coming back to me even as I focused on John's words. "Can you honestly deal with their relationship, as it is? I know dealing with all of the success and the issues with that, such as the paparazzi as you well know now...*that* has to be difficult enough. But you..." He is silent for a moment, seeming to choose his words carefully before continuing. "You don't strike me as the kind of person that lets their guard down too easily. My perception of you is one who simply doesn't give their heart away, but when you do it's given completely."

I look away briefly, wondering how he could know that much about me. When he touches my arm, I look back into his eyes, his words reaching into my soul.

"Can you live with loving someone whose heart may never be completely yours?"

"I'm not sure," I answer honestly, proud of myself for keeping the tears at bay.

"You deserve nothing less," he says, his hand still resting on my arm. "Remember that."

One good thing about that damn black dress is not a soul who had seen the video had any clue that it was me, especially not with me dressed in traveling clothes with my hair down, light makeup, and no entourage. The girls, however, are another story entirely. Once we touch down and are in the cab to go back to my house, Jaden's phone is ringing.

"What's up?" I ask as she is barely able to get a word in edgewise.

"Well, Ms. Talia… guess it's a good thing you don't work tomorrow." She's holding the phone away from her ear. "Tish and Cass are meeting us at your place."

"What ever happened to 'What happens in Vegas?'" I ask, my voice higher than usual.

"Don't whine; it's unbecoming." Jaden's words make me blush as I remember Jase saying the exact thing to me on the phone in what seems like an entire lifetime ago.

My, how things have changed since then. No, not just *things*. Me. How I have changed since then.

Once back in my apartment, I have my bags discarded along with my shoes and have grabbed a diet cola for myself, milk for Tish, and wine for Cass and Jaden. Girls' night has most definitely changed as well.

"Why are you not drinking?" Tish is pointing an accusatory finger at me.

I shake my head. "No…not like your sitch. I don't need to drink, one." *Wow, did I just say that?* "And honest, I'm just not quite up to par yet, not after that night at the club."

Cass's hands are wide, gesturing. "We haven't heard from either one of you all weekend! And then the video, and all the hoopla since…"

"Hoop..la?" I ask, my eyebrow raised, looking between Cass and Tish, who merely shrug.

At least Cass tries to explain. "Everyone's trying to speculate who you are and what your relationship is."

"And why you're pissed at him, don't forget that one," Tish adds, and Cass agrees. I have to laugh.

Okay, laugh is an understatement.

I am wiping the tears from my eyes before I can even speak. "Where the hell do I start?"

Jaden pipes up. "Okay, even I have to admit he was being a bit of a dumbass there."

I swear Tish growls in frustration. "Would you just *spill* already?"

"Oh...all right, did you two know what this freak was planning?" I gesture towards Jaden.

Cass looks almost too innocent. "Naaaah."

"Oh, fuck that, I'm not in trouble for this on my own!" Jaden interrupts. "They both knew! Not everything I did, but they knew."

"Bitches," I mutter, then take a drink. "Just for that I'm not telling you anything."

"At least tell us who the fuck Kaitlyn Evans is," Cass pleads. "And why they believe there's this big war over him."

And all at once my mood shifts.

"Excuse me?" I look over at Jaden, who shrugs and shakes her head. Of course she wouldn't know; she'd been on the plane with me today.

Cass tries to explain, and each word cuts through me. "There's some big to-do about him taking you upstairs one night, and then today being seen with her."

He... he'd said they were going to talk.

I know that. I know they were going to talk.

But why do I get the sinking feeling that I am about to be hurt? Again?

"I mean, one report is she's marrying someone else, another report says she's left her fiancé for him, another report says that they were all over each other..."

I feel the blood drain from my face with every word. There's no way... no way in hell he would be all over Kaitlyn fucking Evans just hours after being with me. Wait, he *had* done that before, hadn't he? No...they were just talking, he told me he would give me all the details when he called me.

I stand and walk over to my laptop, Jaden behind me saying, "Talli, don't... don't do it, you know how the fucking paparazzi is. He said he'd tell you, talk to him first."

"I'll talk to him," I say softly, remembering John's words also. "I would just like to not be blindsided first."

"Jaden's right, they like to spin these things," Tish adds her input. It doesn't take long to power up, and I am quickly on the web typing in the dreaded gossip site address.

"Maybe it was really nothing, right?" Cass asks, her voice small as the pictures are splashed all over the front page. "Oh...that's new."

Kaitlyn and Jase, arms around each other... kissing.

Fuck.

Oh... oh, god...

Why?

"That's such a blurry picture...maybe it's misconstrued, maybe they were just saying goodbye..." Cass, the overly optimistic one is saying. "I mean, is he all touchy-feely?"

My jaw is set as I look over all five pictures they have on their front page, in various stages of hugs, hand-holding, the kiss. Is he touchy-feely? Do I need to tell any of them just how touchy-feely he'd been with me the night before?

"I'm sure this is blown out of proportion," Jaden is saying as I hear my phone ring.

"Excuse me." I turn to get the receiver, knowing damn good and well who it is. The girls are murmuring their respective excuses as they look at the damning evidence, and I wonder briefly what Jase's excuse will be. Or will he even have one?

"Ello, Not Telling." His tone is forcibly light; I know him well enough to pick up on that.

"I've already seen the pictures."

"Fuck." He pauses, maybe to keep more curses from slipping through. "Talli, I just... I was saying goodbye to her."

"Is that all?"

Silence.

I don't have to ask if he is still there, as I can still hear his breathing. His pause tells me volumes. "You've got to be fucking kidding me."

"I said I was going to tell you everything, and I'm going to. I just want you to know, to understand…I didn't know. I thought you were…"

"I was what?"

"I thought you were just being cheeky…or catty, if you will."

"What the hell are you talking about?" I demand.

"When you said she had…"

"…changed her fucking mind," I finish for him through clinched teeth. Son of a fucking bitch.

"And not that she has, but…"

"She doesn't want you to be with me."

"She didn't say that, Talli…she said she's…confused, and you know I have been too, and I don't… Damn it." He inhales sharply, as my mind races, spirals, condemns my heart.

He's confused? Still?

"After last night you don't know what you should fucking do? Just…perfect."

"No, not after last night, after the last… hell, *how* many years now? You don't get it, you *still* don't get it even after I tried to tell you."

"And apparently you think I don't deserve any better than to be strung along… *again*." I feel the tears threaten, but my anger keeps them in check.

"You're wrong." His voice is so even, so controlled, I wonder how long he's rehearsed what he is saying to me.

"No…no, I've been right this whole fucking time."

"Christine…"

"Stop it!" I am yelling, not giving a damn that the girls are now paying attention to me. "My name is *Talia*. Just like with Jack, you need to get it right."

"Okay, I'm sorry."

"No, that's the problem with you," I continue, my venom renewed. "You're *not* sorry; you're so used to things being handed to you, women throwing themselves at you, people bending to your every whim."

"You know better."

"No, what I know is you've expected me to understand that you'd rather be with Kaitlyn…"

"I didn't say that."

"You don't have to." I wipe a tear away, so tired of the drama, so foolish for believing one night could fix anything. How could I be so fucking stupid?

"Talia, everything I have said to you has been the truth."

"It's what you're *not* saying that tells the whole story."

He sighs quietly. "I have some time off soon…"

"Don't." I can't stop the tears this time. "I can't go through this again."

"Talia…"

"What is it going to take for you to see?" I push Jaden's hand off as she walks up behind me. "You are just setting yourself up, Jase. And when I'm not there anymore, how soon before Kaitlyn changes her mind? Again."

"Not there…" The words are so quiet I barely hear them.

"You have to choose. Yeah, I'm being *that* girl, Jase, and before you say I have no right, you need to put yourself in my shoes."

"Talli, I'm sorry."

I take a deep breath, not even letting it register that he has the nerve to try and apologize, remembering Kaitlyn's words. "I'm not kidding myself, though. I know all about your history, I know I can't compete."

"Stop."

"No…no, I can't," I say, walking up the stairs, away from everyone. "I can't stop because you…damn it, you made me believe, and right now part of me really hates you for it."

"I never made any promises to you."

"Touché," I reply, wiping the tears away. "I just can't keep doing this, I can't stay on your fucking string." The same string that I had been sure he'd pulled tight to his chest just that morning, the way he'd looked at me.

How could I have been so wrong? So blind?

"I don't know what you want from me." His voice is small, and I can almost see him with his head bowed, massaging his temple.

What *do* I want?

"I want… I want to be good enough. I want what I felt last night bottled up at my disposal whenever I need to feel happy." I know it probably made no sense to anyone but me. "I want to dance in the rain and not give a damn what anyone thinks. I want… I want to be sure, not just of myself but of all the choices I make. And I want that freedom…to love like it's never going to hurt."

"But it does."

I am silent, wondering his meaning, sure he is talking about Kaitlyn.

"Jase, I have to go."

I'm not lying; I can't rehash the same conversation with him over and over again.

"Don't say it," he cuts me off.

"Those pictures said it for me."

"No…no, they didn't."

"Jase, I…"

"Damn it, give me…time. Just give me time, okay? I'm being honest with you, Talia. I need…time. Please."

I am silent, unsure of whether I should agree. Can I do that, keep my heart on the line?

"You know…the optimist in me, it's gonna take that as a yes, okay?" he continues, and I swear I hear him sniffle just a little bit. "So, I wanted you to know…that I'm *happy* that you were here, and…I'm sorry that everything got so fucked up…and…that thing? That thing you want so badly? Yeah, I want it, too. So, until later…okay? *Until later.*"

He doesn't wait for my reply before he hangs up the phone.

I sat in stunned silence before I turn off the receiver. What the hell was that? And how… how am I still breathing now? How can I sit here on this bed, this same bed I'd shared with him? How the hell is life going to continue, now that I've lost so much?

"Are you okay?" Jaden is in my doorway... when had she come up the stairs? I peered up at her through my tears.

"I'm...not sure. I...don't know...I..."

"Ice cream?" she asks, holding out the pint she's retrieved from my freezer. I smile, reaching out for my best friend for one last night.

I know me.

I know what is coming.

"Yeah," I agree. "That sounds perfect."

CHAPTER 38

I wake alone in my bed every morning; it is something I am used to. The days that I haven't are actually the exception to the rule. I have never been in a live-in relationship with a guy, I haven't even felt comfortable spending nights away or having guys over even though I am all grown up in my own place. Hell, even when Jase and I had spent the night together, normally he'd be up and about before I even opened my eyes, so again with the waking up alone.

Can someone…*anyone*…please explain to me, then, why all of a sudden after Vegas I feel so damn lonely?

Tish is more family-focused, not to mention rather sickly, in these weeks that have followed. I see less and less of her, and only speak to her on the rare occasion that she feels up to it. This isn't anything new, either; she had been the same way when pregnant with both Moira and Kiera. I do make a mental note to do my best to get over to her house to see her, although I am all about the avoidance.

I always am when I am low.

Cass and her boy toy are actually on the verge of a full-fledged relationship, the first I can remember her having. Cass plus settling down equals something amiss in this reality, but I am truly happy for her. She's promised she'll break away from him for a girls' night; I'm not holding my breath, no matter how much I can use her bubbly enthusiasm. Or can I? Because I'm sure that somehow I could talk her into at least a movie, if my heart is actually into it.

Jaden.

I guess it's sad to say that Jaden and I have drifted the furthest apart, mostly of my doing. It's easier to avoid her now that the stupid class with the stupid assignment about fate is over, of course. I know that she feels torn since she is still in her non-relationship with Pete. Regardless of the fact that we are friends, and I'd believed to be very close, I still don't want to put her on the spot. And I can't answer questions, or deal with the inquisitive looks, or have her tell me that I am being unreasonable because in all honesty, I don't think I am. He hurt me. Sure... I let him, but... somehow this hurt is different. And I don't want to hear about how fabulous Jase is doing in his quest to capture some long-lost part of his youth, which can accidentally slip while she is telling me about her fabulous non-relationship. Okay, I am also afraid that if I am in her presence, I may just ask how he is, and I certainly don't want to feel as if I am prying.

Prying...yeah, speaking of prying, I miss my mom more and more every passing day. The prying would grate my nerves beyond all rhyme and reason. But mom... she would ask how I was, and she would give her motherly advice whether I want it or not. I want to speak to her, pour out my heart to her, cry on her shoulder the way I used to. I want that unconditional love that I've only known from her, that I've always had no matter how many times I pushed her away. I often wonder what she would think of my situation, whether or not she would approve of my handling of it.

No...I know better. She would call me out every time I pushed people away. She would tell me that I was being...oh, what was her word for it? Right, she'd tell me I was being a fool, acting foolish. I hate that word, mostly because when she would say it to me, she was right which would absolutely piss me right off.

Thing was…I'm not so sure I am being foolish this time.

Nearly a month has passed since I have seen Jase. It isn't as if we don't speak to one another, we just simply didn't *talk* anymore. I can't bear to hear about Kaitlyn, and there are still simply so many raw emotions attached with nearly everything having to do with him. I avoid many, many subjects.

Feelings? Forget it. He knows I love him; he is confused about me.

Dancing? And bring up the club? No thank you.

His brother Pete? He is dating, or not dating, Jaden, and I can't listen to how happy they are, and how all of them spend time together.

My work? Dr. John Craig has talked me into pursuing cardiology, and apparently that is a sore subject for Jase.

So that leaves us…what?

Useless trivia and occasional picking apart of movies. After everything… *that* is what we have become.

It is a gray, misty, melancholy Saturday morning of my actual full weekend off. I find the weather typical, but fitting, as I set about on my day's quest. Stopping off at the store, I pick up my provisions including my gas station cappuccino since even caramel macchiatos bring bad memories for me.

How much more pathetic can I get?

At least the press about me has died down. Ah, yes, a couple of those sweet nurses couldn't wait to give my name out, and after much warning about how it better not interfere with patient care, all of us—including me since I had unceremoniously given them a piece of my mind—had been relegated to normal day to day activity. College students haven't paid me any mind, since most of them don't even know I'd gone to Vegas to begin with. I was handed a couple of phone numbers, which went straight to the trash can because no thanks. Celebrity gossip keeps up on their daily Kate watch, though, and there is no shortage of it much to my chagrin.

Kate back in her hometown.

Kate going shopping.

Kate on the phone... is it with Jason? If so, which one?

Just. Fucking. Shoot me.

I pull into the nearest parking space, knowing it is still a little walk to my destination. I have my book, my coffee, my keys, and my cell phone; all the essentials of a single, lonely girl, I suppose, but if that is my destiny then so be it.

Ugh, I really dislike feeling sorry for myself; it's even more unbecoming than whining.

I walk over the hill, smiling at the familiar site before me up by the large oak tree. The path is familiar to me and becoming more worn as the days turn into weeks. I stop just short of my usual perch and placed a kiss on the headstone.

"Hi, Mom. Hi, Dad." I sit cross legged beside their grave with my book and coffee. "The weather absolutely sucks today; you mind sending some sun?" I look upwards at the clouds, the gray sky completely matching my mood. "Nah, on second thought, this is perfect. You know...I'm not much into this book today, though. Today...well, today I want to tell you about a boy."

I have been thinking back a lot lately, of that hospital in Illinois. I can see now how I'd missed putting two and two together. Jase has changed greatly, maturity adding even more to his looks. His voice has even matured, not that he had ever sung to me back then, but his speaking voice has a much richer tone to it. But it is the eyes...the eyes that I can't believe I had missed.

Chalk it up to one more thing that slipped past me.

"I know that you two already know...well, *everything* now, but I'd kinda like to share this with you, if you don't mind," I continue, leaning against the stone as if it will comfort me. "See, this boy was...well, he was my comfort in a very dark time for me. I was so angry, so upset all the time. Daddy, you may not have been aware, but Mom...I know you saw it, I know you saw how angry I was, especially with Dad suffering the way he was. I just wanted to run away, completely away, and never come back..." My eyes slide shut at the memory, the pain as real as if it had been just yesterday. "But...one night, in the waiting room, there was this...this boy, and he had the most beautiful eyes. He was just...wow. You know? Wow..." I laugh, remembering how much Mom hated it when I would say that, she'd always chide me to elaborate.

"He was hurting, too," I continue. "And we just connected, through everything we were both going through." I pause for a moment, remembering what I had, and hadn't, told him. "No, I wasn't completely honest with him, though, but I could talk to him, and he...helped me, so very much, just knowing he was there, listening. Is...this irony? Talking to the two of you about wanting someone to listen?" The leaves rustle in the light breeze and I laugh softly. "Okay, so you're listening, point made." I take a drink of my cappuccino, missing my usual coffee choice but refusing to be reminded of Kaitlyn any further. "Hey...I didn't get to tell you, did I? Mom...that boy...that was Not John. He'd said once..."

Oh...god... he'd said something about it to me... something about reaffirming the theory about being right where you're supposed to be...and what had I said in return? Oh, right, it had completely slipped by me in my tirade over Kaitlyn.

I brush back a tear before I continue. "He'd said...that..." My voice falters once more. "Nah, forget it. It's inconsequential anyhow. So...yeah, I guess that's what I miss about him the most. Talking to him, because I...could. Does that make sense?" I sit in silence for a moment, taking sips of my cappuccino and looking out at the gardens. "Daddy picked the perfect spot for the two of you..." I am interrupted by my phone buzzing in my pocket and I sit up straighter to retrieve it. I glance at the number, then over at their headstone. "Showoffs," I whisper before I answer.

"I'm glad you called," is the first thing I say.

"Really?" Jase sounds pleasantly surprised, although a bit tired. "So...then you don't mind that I have?"

"No...I was just thinking about you." I wonder if he can tell that I have been crying, but then I decide I really don't care.

I am glad that he has called. There are a few things that I have to say, have to get off my chest.

"I'd be flattered if you didn't sound so sad."

"I was...reminiscing."

"Ah."

"About the hospital, in Illinois."

"Oh." He sounds slightly surprised, as we never really discussed it.

"Yeah, I'm just sitting here in the Gardens and...I wanted to apologize to you, explain a little of what was going on."

"I was going to say you don't owe me an explanation, but I'm afraid if I do that then you will go back to not talking to me."

"I'd be flattered if you didn't sound so sad," I try to joke, knowing this is no laughing matter. I can hear his light breathing in the background, so I know he is still on the line regardless of the fact that he has said nothing in return. "I suppose it would be pointless to tell you how messed up I was; that was pretty evident...but...I wasn't honest with you when I told you why I was there."

"I...kinda gathered that, yeah."

"My Dad..." I choke back a sob at the memory of him lying there, gasping for every breath he took. "My Dad had been sick for a very, very long time, as long as I could remember. He'd said so many times he was ready to go, and as much as that selfish part of me wanted him around, seeing him like that...it hurt, it hurt beyond...well, beyond the telling of it. Others in my family, they kept pushing these treatments, even when he wasn't able to speak for himself any...more." I take a deep shuddering breath to try to steady myself.

"Talli, you don't have to..."

"No, it's okay, I want to," I cut him off. "I do, because it's been eating me up inside. I... I wanted to tell you, and I never took that chance. I was so...so very angry, I kept saying to myself that it shouldn't be Dad in that bed it should be *her*, for keeping him alive when it hurt so much for him. So, see...when I told you...I said it was my mom, and it was mean and spiteful and wrong and..."

My voice trails off, instead of going on forever about how wrong my actions had been. I could, though. I really could.

"You were a Daddy's girl then?" It is actually more a statement then a question, and the memories it brings back were so very warm.

"Oh god, yes, he spoiled me fucking rotten," I say with a laugh. "He was always so kind, so loving. He knew...he knew he didn't have forever, and he tried to cram forever in the few short years we had." We are both silent, each knowing exactly what that feels like. "And... then, I was dishonest with you, not that it's exactly something new considering what else I've done..."

"Talli, don't...it's so...inconsequential now...what?" he asks as I start laughing.

"Get out of my head," I giggle through my tears. "And it does matter, it matters to me, and the guilt has been eating away at me for longer than you could possibly know, whenever I let myself think about it."

"Not to sound philosophical, or like some damn shrink, but I understand...I think if I were in your shoes, I could have easily done the same thing. And don't think I'm just saying that to you."

"No, you wouldn't," I admit, then take a deep breath. "But that night...at the restaurant..." I stop, closing my eyes to the myriad of emotions trying to consume me. "That night in New York that I interrupted your anniversary dinner with..." It is so hard to even say her name. "...with Kate, the phone call? The one I wouldn't tell you about?"

"Yeah, I remember that."

"That was Lisa, my sister. Dad had... um, he... he was... gone. And for the first time in a week, they'd realized that I wasn't there."

"Talli, I'm so sorry...God, I was there, I was right there and..."

"What was I supposed to say? Gee, Jase, thank you so much for being there for me, but I lied out my ass to you? Oh, and yeah...I got the lecture from Lisa about how I was out whoring around instead of at the hospital, where I should have been. I just didn't want to feel anymore, I didn't want to hurt anymore. And...there you were." I almost add 'with Kaitlyn,' but I refrain from doing so.

"The timing sucked," he states honestly.

"So did my behavior," I add. "And I'm sorry."

"There were two of us there, you and me. You don't have to apologize to me, Talia, not over that."

"Yes, I do, over that and so much more."

"If anyone should be apologizing here, it's me." His voice is soft, a slight waver to it. As per the usual, I hear a bustling in the background.

"Ah, duty calls," I say, and he sighs.

"Yeah, I just got back."

"Did you enjoy your time off?" I ask, praying I won't hear about all the time he spent with her.

"No."

I wasn't expecting that.

"I'm sorry to hear that," I say, my brow furrowed. Lately he's learned to enjoy his time off, catch up with people he's missed, spend time with his family.

"There was somewhere I wanted to be but was told emphatically no."

Where did he….oh…right.

He'd initially said he wanted to spend his time off with me.

"Say you did," I speak up suddenly. "What then, Jase? What…then?"

"I don't know," he replies, just as I know he will.

"Then we're at an impasse."

"Again," he adds with a sad laugh. I hear Jackie in the background barking orders at someone, and Jase sighs again, swearing slightly under his breath. "Hold on," he says to me before I hear him cover the mouthpiece and ask for just another minute, which is denied.

"It's okay," I say to him.

"No, it's not," he replies, frustrated. "I haven't talked to you in…fuck, in forever…"

"We spoke a couple days ago."

"But we didn't *talk*."

"We'll talk later," I say quickly, knowing in my heart it is true.

"Will we really? Or will it be niceties and formalities all over again?"

"What do you want from me, Jase?"

"I just...miss you....I miss you."

We both fall silent, remembering the last time words similar to that had been spoken between us, an ache in my chest at the bittersweet memory.

"I just miss you," he repeats, and I choke back a tiny sob. "Talli?"

What can I say? What should I say? How can I be any clearer than what I've already said?

A small ray of sunshine peaks around the clouds, settling in by the tree, removing any doubt from my mind as I finally answer him.

"I miss you, too."

CHAPTER 39

Two thirty-five rolls around and I'll be damned if my phone isn't ringing. Okay, so I realize he said he'd call—I'd even told him I wanted him to—but are we *really* reverting back to the old ways? I grumble for only a moment before answering the phone, enjoying with all of my soul giving him just a little bit of hell.

"Listen, Not John…if you're gonna be calling me at this ungodly hour all over again, it would be nice for a liiiiitle bit of warning, 'kay?"

"Well, alrighty then," he quips back. "Hey, Not Telling…remember when you said I could call whenever I pleased? Well…I…um, please. There's your damn warning."

I can feel the smile before it ever crosses my face. "All right, smart ass, what are you up to?"

"I dunno, I haven't measured myself in a while. Oh, and Jackie says hello."

"Hello to Jackie," I reply after the obligatory roll of my eyes at his attempt at humor. I can't believe how much I've missed it.

"Hey…Jackie! Not Telling Christine says hello!"

I blink a couple of times, shock keeping me silent. What…he isn't alone? And he is calling me?

"It's about damned time," I hear Jackie's voice in the background, and Jase laughs softly.

And Jackie said that... about *me*? I might cry if I wasn't so stunned.

"Apparently I've been getting on everyone's last nerve," Jase explains to me, and I suddenly find my voice.

"You just got back! How could you be on everyone's nerves already?"

"Nah, this has been going on for a while. Close to... a month, actually."

My mind immediately shoots straight into overdrive, a gazillion questions jumbled together.

A month? Ever since... Vegas? But...what about Kaitlyn, isn't he trying to work things out with her? Isn't that what all the tabloids are talking about?

But I can't ask him.

Not yet.

"You're pretty much biting the hands that are feeding, clothing, and driving you, so my suggestion would be to chill the fuck out." Having missed our conversations so much I'll do whatever it takes to keep this one going. "And if I hear about you giving Alfred...er, Jackie a hard time after he took such good care of me, you're going to answer to me, and it won't be pretty."

"Hey, Jackie...bite my lily-white ass!" he calls out with a genuine laugh.

That little fucker.

"You're just testing my patience tonight, aren't you?"

"Whatever it takes," he says softly, and my heart does a nosedive to my feet.

Settle down, heart.

"Sooooo..." He draws the word out, a playful lift in his voice. "What's my punishment?"

Hmmm, good question. Got it.

"I'm gonna drag your ass back here,"

"Uh huh, okay."

"Up to my bedroom,"

"Iiiinteresting, interesting. Go on."

"Tie you up,"

"Really, now?"

"And make you…"

"What?"

Hmmm… "Listen to Starship's 'We Built This City' until your ears bleed."

"Aaaahhh, bullshit, cause you'd have to hear it too."

Damn. Didn't think that through good enough. "With headphones on."

"I'll just sing it at the top of my lungs."

Hmph. "Fine, I'll make it the Spice Girls then."

"What, *'If You Wanna Be My Lover'*? I can sing that one too, sweetheart. Try again."

And that would be all kinds of torture too. Ah. HA! *Now* I've got it. "Hanson's *'MmmBop'*, over and over and over…"

"Well, now there's a snappy, catchy little tune. You'd get to hear my falsetto for hours, and it would drive…you…crazy."

Good point. "Well, fine!" I finally cave, laughing more than I have in weeks. "Then I'll just…stop speaking to you altogether. There, that will be your punishment."

"That's not funny." His voice is soft and low now, the sudden change almost tangible.

Oh, that… that hurt. "It wasn't meant to be, hence the whole punishment thing." I am trying to re-lighten the mood.

"Talli…" His tone is serious when he speaks now. "I didn't mean to hurt you…I never, ever set out to intentionally hurt you. You know that, right?"

Damn it… damn it, damn it…

No, I need to know. I want to know.

"I never thought it to be intentional," I admit, my heart hammering in my chest. "You don't strike me as the type, and if you had I wouldn't be in this predicament."

"What predicament is that?" he asks, and I sigh.

Now or never, Talli.

"This...holding pattern," I say, hardly believing I am confessing this to him. "This going through hell every time I hear your voice because I can't say what I want to."

"Who says you can't?"

"I do. My heart can only take so much."

Am I really saying this to him? No alcohol, no prodding, no argument even?

"I hear ya, I hear ya."

And what is this, he is agreeing with me?

"I don't know..." he continues, "it's like...once you've been hurt, and I'm saying you as in a collective being...yeah, once you've been hurt, it's just an automatic response to kinda just shut down."

"Defense mechanism, I suppose."

"Yeah...um...you know, I didn't mean to wait so long to call you and apologize. After Cleveland, I mean."

Of course my heart constricts in my chest. Damn it. But do I let him know? No. Not yet. "Oh, bullshit, you didn't call until after Pete told you that I really didn't get my messages."

"True, true...but...well, it's that defense thing." I can almost see him shrug. "Which is in its own merit a bit hypocritical I suppose, because I could have handled the situation much differently...I should have handled it differently. There, let me put it that way. Hell, I may have still gotten lucky, who knows?"

I can't help but laugh at his comment, which is a welcome reprieve to the damage he is inflicting on my heart.

"What? A guy can dream, right?"

"That ball was in your court the whole time. I was already a goner."

Talli! Seriously?! You just said that to him?

"So was I, if you recall my message your absentminded ass couldn't get to."

Oh... oh, he...

He was?

Yeah, he *was*.

How could I forget that?

343

"Hey, did you ever figure out your code?" he asks, and I laugh again in spite of the tears coming to the surface.

This is why I didn't want to talk to him about feelings, our past...any of it...*this* is why.

"No, and no more teasing me about it, you've put me through enough hell over that damn code as it is."

He laughs with me then, and the nostalgia over the ease of our conversation is hitting me straight in my heart. I wonder if it is having the same effect on him.

"Well, all right...Not Telling Christine Talia, I won't tease you at all. Ever again. Scouts honor."

"At least you got all my names right."

"You have to give me credit on that one. Brownie points of some sort?"

"Depends."

"On what?"

"On what you plan to cash them in on," I answer, my cheeks starting to ache from smiling. Has it really been that long since I've smiled so much?

"Well...give me time and I can get real creative."

"Listen to you! All you ask for is time, you fucker!"

"Tsk tsk, such a potty mouth Ms. Emerson."

Even with his words, we are back to reality. This kind of pain is so new to me, such unchartered territory. I've known the pain of losing a parent, I've known the pain of being cast aside in the family, but this? This is so foreign, and I don't know how to stop it.

But I don't want this conversation to end.

I want to hold on, just a little bit longer.

"And what's my punishment?" I ask, biting my lip as I wait for his reply.

"I'd say I'd never talk to you again, but I'd be lying. I can't do it, I honestly can't. And not just because everyone was giving me hell about my mood either."

I can't do it either. "So you called for your fix?"

There is no double meaning intended with my words, but it leaves us both speechless for just a moment, remembering how he had initially planned his trip to Vegas to "fix things" with me. This also brings back my reaction to his confession, my admission that I love him...the night we shared afterwards...

"Jase?"

"That really is why I went to Vegas," he says, as if he is reading my mind. "No, not for sex...you know, when I told you I went out there to fix things, I meant it."

"What happened?" I curse myself as soon as the words leave me. I don't want to hear it, I can't stand hearing it, hasn't my heart suffered enough?

He sighs then, deep and long, and I hear him crack open what sounds like a bottle of beer. "Jack...Jason, Jason Brooks...he was speaking at that seminar that you were going to. I'd said in passing I was going to be in that weekend, and he got this wild hair up his ass to plan a huge engagement party."

I am silent as I listen to him finally tell me everything he should have said weeks ago.

"Kate wanted me there, and I didn't want to say no. It wasn't...Talli, I didn't go there to pull any shit, I wasn't there to try to stop her from marrying him, that wasn't my intention. I mean, when she met me in Ohio, and she was so...so happy...okay, *that* bothered me. Or it did at first, but she was happy, and I told her that would make me happy for her. You know...she could tell something was different with me too. And I told her." He pauses, takes a drink and sighs again.

What? What did you tell her?

"I told her...about you," he continues, and then laughs softly. "She was so...pissed at me, Talli, so fucking pissed. She couldn't believe I was with you...I mean, not *with*...fuck, I'm going to end up putting my damn foot back in my mouth, damn it."

I am trembling, biting my thumbnail as he continues his explanation, my stomach in knots as the anticipation threatened to overwhelm me nearly as much as the anxiety.

"I know I was wrong to not tell you," he says after taking another drink. "And I've paid for it every fucking day."

He has?

"But...I don't know, Talia, it's like being between a rock and a hard place, my past and...and...you."

His breathing isn't as steady as before, and I'm sure mine isn't either. I can't find my voice, even having everything I've already put together being validated by his words.

"But I'm not answering the question, am I? Because you sort of already knew this part, or bits of it." His voice is beginning to waver and I hear him clear his throat.

Here it comes.

"I told you that I was going to talk to her, because she'd asked me to. I didn't go in there thinking for one second that I was going to get blindsided like that..."

For someone who has spent a good deal of time reminiscing and longing for his first true love, 'blindsided' isn't a word that seems to fit. "What do you mean?" I ask, confused.

"John told you I was looking for her, and I *had* been. I had been, and I'm not going to lie to you about it, but...I found you. And please don't think... you're not a replacement...not a fucking replacement... I'm just...again, putting my foot in my mouth, so let me get back to what I was saying, okay?"

I bury my face in my hands waiting to hear all about Kate's undying love for him and how he feels the same, cursing myself for allowing this distance between us by being dishonest with him back in Cleveland. I am shaking, curled up in a ball, wishing even though he is breaking my heart that he will be here to help pick up the pieces.

"She said..." he pauses, taking a deep breath, "she said that seeing you, knowing it was you...hurt her, because she couldn't stand to think of...*us*. And she said she couldn't... couldn't move on until she knew why."

"And that's all it took," I can't help but snap.

"No," he admits quietly.

Oh...oh, here's where he's going to tell me...

"We talked, Talli. About... things, about our breakup, about all the time we hadn't seen each other, about...what we'd meant to each other..."

"Stop...please, just stop," I beg through my tears. "This is why I couldn't... why I didn't want to really talk with you."

It hurts so much... *too* much. It hurts too much.

"I just need you to understand,"

"What, that you called me to tell me you're still so in love with your ex? To tell me how your perfect past...let's face it, Jase, it couldn't have been that perfect or it wouldn't be a *past*."

"Easy with the temper, Christine. And please don't put words in my mouth. It's not cut and dry, it's not easy, it's not..." He stops for a moment, and I can hear his breathing on the other line. "Talli," I hear him say, almost in a pleading voice, "I swear with everything in me I never meant to hurt you."

I can't hold back the sob that breaks through, not just from his words but from the tone he speaks them with.

"Ah, don't sweat it, Warner," I say with a harsh laugh, trying to cover. "You only hurt the one you love."

"Is that so?" It is more of a statement.

Yes, that's fucking so.

"What exactly is it that's not so cut and dry, huh Jase?"

"You."

Oh...OH.

Me.

"I'm fine, don't worry about me." It is an automatic response, not bitter or angry in any way. I'm just trying to keep my heart from leaping straight out of my chest.

Don't... don't do it, Talli, don't read too much into that, no matter what you wish.

"Talli...what about... John?"

I took in a deep breath. "Revenge? Spite? A means to get into that party and see for myself what you wouldn't tell me. Was it right? No. I'm not proud of it either."

"No...not then, you'd already told me about that..." His voice trails off. "Talia, is there... are you...seeing him?"

What?

"Is that why you called?" I ask without thinking. "Wait, I'm sorry...that was just... No. The answer is no."

Did I just hear him exhale?

"It's not...why I called, no. I just...I couldn't help but think maybe he was the reason you wouldn't talk to me, and it...hurt."

My heart constricts in my chest and I wince at the sudden pain. Hurting him is the last thing I want to do. Yet, I can't help but find the... irony? Is it irony? "Aren't you just a mess of contradictions?" I finally ask.

"At the very least."

"I can't wait forever, Jase."

As much as my heart shatters at that confession, I know it is the truth.

"I know."

Again with the melancholy. Why have we even strayed into this territory, knowing the outcome will put a damper on our moods?

"I don't have the right to ask you to wait, Talli, I know I don't."

I wipe away a tear. "You're right, you don't."

"Is this why you don't want to see me?"

"No...I think it's best that we don't..."

"Why?"

Does he really have to sound so close to tears?

"Because..." I take in a deep breath before finishing. "Because I love you, that's why. And I couldn't be in the same room without reducing myself to some sobbing, babbling idiot telling you that you shouldn't walk away from your future for your past. Because...I'd look into those eyes and I'd beg you to stay, and when you didn't, I'd be broken. Even more so than I am now."

"Talli, I don't know what to..."

God, he is crying. No, no, no...I can't deal with it right now.

"You'd say all that, huh?"

"Yes, damn it, and I could just...kick your ass over doing this to me." We both laugh then, breaking just a little of the tension.

"You're not going to hang up on me, are you?" he asks, sniffling slightly.

"Not yet," I reply, one corner of my mouth up in a smile. It almost feels as if a ton of bricks have been lifted off my shoulders with my admission to him, and I wonder if his confessions helped him as well.

"You'll stay on the phone then, until it's time for you to go?"

Now my smile is full. "Just like I used to."

"Good."

And I do.

CHAPTER 40

Exhaustion, you are my friend. I know that at times I'm dragging a bit behind the curve ball (is that the expression?) but it's worth it.

So, so worth it.

I could talk to Jase forever, and while we aren't quite on the subject of everything, we are close. I have my friend back, I have my confidante back. I'm… not *just* happy.

I'm over the moon.

But back to exhaustion.

My school this semester is rather easy, since it is mostly review and checking in for my rotations. I am so afraid that my work is going to suffer because of it, though. This is it, the final stretch. Once I get through this and pass my boards, I have already been told I will be bumped up into the nursing pool. So, here I am… at work. Cardiac clinic, to be precise.

Thursday in the hospital is rather quiet, and I take it as a good sign, catching up on paperwork and studying, like the good little (distracted) nursing student that I am. I am sitting at the table behind the front desk double checking my work when I feel a strong arm on my shoulder. I glance to my left where a tanned, strong hand sits, then back behind me to my right as Dr. John Craig kneels down beside me.

"Ms. Emerson," he says smoothly, "I have a request of you."

"Do you now." I raise an eyebrow at him until he removes his hand.

Still, he's smiling even as he pulls his hand away. "Sorry."

That's what I thought.

"Lunch is in precisely half an hour, and I'd like for you to join me.

"Yes?" I ask, half tempted to tell him we shouldn't go to lunch but deciding I should be completely open and honest with him. Maybe lunch will be the place we can do that, out in public.

"Good. Meet me in the car port in a half hour."

"Aren't we going to the cafeteria?" I ask, and he shakes his head 'no.' "You'll have me back to work in an hour?"

"Scout's honor," he says softly, and I think he actually winks before he turns and walks away.

I decide that it is a good thing for me to go to lunch with John, get a few things off my chest. One, I'm still not interested, especially with the way he seems to be making his way through the nurse pool. Two, I don't appreciate the digs he will take at Jase in front of me, for a reason.

Approximately forty minutes later, John and I are seated in a semi-private room at an exclusive club waiting for our drinks to be served when this conversation comes back to me. "John?" I say sweetly, batting my eyelashes.

That should be his first clue.

"Yes, Ms. Emerson?"

"Is this your payback? For Vegas, I mean?" I motion around the room that I so do not fit in.

"What's wrong with this? It's one of my favorite places for lunch."

"I'm hardly dressed for something like this," I explain. "And don't even try to play like you didn't talk them into letting me in."

"Well, I didn't have much warning, or I would have asked you before and made sure you had more appropriate attire." His dark eyes are sparkling with unsaid mischief.

"Much warning about what?" I ask, but my answer is staring straight at me as Jaden and Pete enter the restaurant. Jase hadn't mentioned to me about Pete being in town, but then again he may not have known. I am expecting perhaps a scowl or indifference from Pete, so I am unprepared at the smile he sends my way. Jaden smiles also, a little tight but it is still there, as they motion to the greeter...maître d? Hell, I don't know... whomever it is, they let him know they are coming over.

"Have a seat." John motions to them, standing in true gentleman fashion until Jaden is seated.

My heart is hammering in my chest as she sits right next to me. She is my best friend, and I have all but abandoned her, and for what? To spare my feelings? That is hardly fair to her. What if she is pissed at me? No, I'm sure she is... what if she won't forgive me?

"How have you been?" Jaden asks me softly as Pete and John are getting caught up. I smile weakly at her, thankful that she is at least going to speak to me.

"I've been better, but I've been worse, too. And I'm feeling unbelievably out of place here."

"Don't sweat it, those scrubs are cute." She smiles, playing with one of my curls, tears brimming in her eyes. "Are you sure you're okay, though? You look beat."

I am beat. Jase and I have spent the past three nights talking for hours on end, and although we are back to avoiding the subject of us it is so wonderful to have my confidante back.

Every bit as wonderful as having my best friend by my side.

"I'm fine, don't..."

"...worry about you, whatever woman," she cuts me off, then gives me a one-armed hug. I lean my head on her shoulder briefly.

Let the healing begin.

"I've missed you, Jaden. Are you still mad at me?"

"Why the hell would I be mad at you? You're the T to my J," she adds, sitting back and wiping her eyes quickly.

Is she being serious?

"I could name all the reasons, but I'm starved, and we're pressed for time."

"They'll be back for our orders soon, but you're off the rest of the day," John speaks up, and I look over at him. "I have some pull around there." I am unsure if I should thank him or be offended at his presumptuousness.

"And you couldn't at least let me change?" I decide to be graceful with others around.

"Well, I know a little black number you look smashing in," he says with a cheeky grin I nearly want to slap off his face. There is no question that he is doing this on purpose.

"That's humorous," is all I say in response and turn towards Jaden. "I probably will go back to work, though; I don't want to intrude on your time."

"It's not intruding."

It is Pete who says this to me, the look in his eyes understanding as if he knows my agitation at the offhanded comment about the dress.

"I hear they never caught up with those assholes that put that stuff in your drink," he continues, his tone just as friendly as it had been before all hell had broken loose.

"No...but I suppose it's okay that they haven't. I have had to relive that night enough."

"Or what you remember of it," John jokes, winking again at me. Does he really think that is funny?

"Hey, I never really got the chance to thank you," I say, leaning forward so that Pete can hear me better.

"Nah, don't mention it," Pete replies. "I'm just glad we got up there in time. Jase would have lost it if anything happened to you."

I blink back sudden, unexpected tears at his comment, the moment brief but poignant. Is he serious? Or... or is he just saying that to make me feel better, or to shut someone else up?

Speaking of...

"So how are Jase and Kate doing?" John asks quickly bringing me crashing into reality.

"Jase's good," Pete answers, a slight frown upon his face. "Don't know about Kate."

How can he not know about Kate? Is Jase shutting Pete out the way I have been doing with all of my friends? No...I banish that thought from my mind quickly, smiling at the waitress that brings my diet cola and takes Pete and Jaden's drink orders.

Do I ask Jase about it next time we talk? Or... or do I wait for him to tell me? And when will my mind just shut the hell up and let me be?

Lucky for me, Jaden keeps me occupied for the rest of our time at that restaurant, keeping my million questions at bay. She has been to see Tish, who is definitely not having an easy time with this pregnancy. "She's had a lot of spotting, and she's really not supposed to be on her feet much."

"Is this really something we want to discuss while eating, ladies?" John asks with a laugh and it is difficult to hide the rolling of my eyes as I ignore him.

"Why hasn't she asked for any help? Both of us live really close," I say. "I know Moira's older and Mark is there sometimes too, but that doesn't mean they can do it all."

"Yeah, we should get over there some time this weekend," Jaden agrees. "We could do a..."

I know she is going to say we could do a Jase Warner marathon, like we used to, but given the circumstances it seems a bit odd. Okay, more than a bit odd-- I don't know how I can ever watch that DVD again and drool, not knowing *everything* that I know now, not after having seen what that happy trail leads to and...

"Let's not and say we did," I joke, and we both laugh.

"Have you..." She bites her lip, perhaps wondering if she should even ask.

"Seen him? No," I answer her unspoken question. "Talked to him? Hell, he won't shut up."

"That explains…" She stops, lowering her voice so the guys can't hear us over their conversation. "Pete said he'd been in a fantastic mood this morning. Tired, but fantastic." She smiles wistfully. "I wish there was something I could do, some way I could help."

"There's nothing anyone can do," I say with a shrug. "Not even me. This is all up to him. Or, I hope it's just up to him."

"Talli…"

"No, don't," I cut her off. "I'm just not able to handle it, really. I don't want to hear about Kaitlyn, not unless he's going to tell me."

She smiles at my words. "Did that really just come from you?"

"I know…sick, isn't it?" I can't help but laugh, which Jaden quickly joins in with.

"What the hell are you two up to?" Pete asks.

"Nothing good and pure, I'm sure," John adds.

Dude don't even pretend to know.

"Listen…we've got some running to do," Pete says suddenly, and Jaden smiles at him. Mmm hmmm, running, I'm sure.

Oh, wait.

"I need to get my car; I left it at the hospital."

"Nonsense, I'll take you home," John speaks up.

"No, I don't like being without my car," I disagree, being completely honest. It is one of my many quirks. I *have* to have a mode of transportation, a way to get away. A way to escape.

Wow. I… I haven't realized that about myself before, not with the full comprehension anyhow.

"I take it you're not going back to the hospital?" I ask him.

"We can swing you that way," Jaden says.

"You don't mind?" I ask, almost relieved to be away from the sudden uncomfortable situation.

"Nah, we don't mind," Pete answers. "Besides, you two need more time to catch up. And that way…I can drive."

"He likes my car," Jaden says with a roll of her eyes.

"Talia…"

355

"Thank you for inviting me to come out here," I say quickly to John, whipping out my portion of the bill. "I've missed Jaden like crazy! So, I'll see you tomorrow at work, right?"

"Right," he says, leaning in and kissing my cheek, ignoring my raised eyebrow. "I'll call you later."

Jaden has walked ahead to get the car, leaving me and Pete by the front doors of the restaurant. I don't feel the least bit uncomfortable to be *near* him, per se, but what had transpired with John is just bugging the living shit out of me.

"That was...odd," I comment as Pete and I stand there. "Thanks for driving me back; I don't know what's up with him, he's acted so...*weird* since you two got there."

"He's wanting me to send a full report, I'm sure." Pete's voice is flat, his annoyance visible.

"There's nothing to report," I say softly, not looking up at him. When he doesn't say anything in return, I look over at him. He is standing next to me, hands in his pockets, a soft smile on his face. "What?" I ask. He doesn't answer, he just continues smiling at me, making me self-conscious. "What?" I put a hand up to my hair, checking to see if it is lopsided. "Pete...*what*?"

Without warning, he sweeps me up in a warm, friendly hug. "Thank you. Just... thank you, Talli." He steps back from me, still smiling.

Talk about being completely confused by that boy's actions. "For what?"

"For making Jase so fucking happy." I open my mouth to protest, but he stops me. "Just...trust me. I knew he was talking to you again, I just *knew*."

Wow... really?

"I didn't know that." I mean, Jaden had told me that Pete was talking to Jase, and that Jase was tired but happy. But is he really *that* happy that we are talking?

Does he really feel the same way about it that I do?

Pete reaches over and tousles my hair...he is so much like his brother when he does that. "Trust me."

"Famous last words," I joke as Jaden pulls up. He motions for her to get out so that he can drive.

"Are you sure?" she asks. "You don't exactly know your way around."

"Eh, I'll find my way. Or you can help me." He flashes his famous Warner grin that prompts a roll of her eyes.

I climb into the back of the car, propped up against the back-passenger side to face Pete. "Are you sure you don't want me or Jaden to drive? I can at least drive up to the hospital; it's not too far."

"I'm sure, damn, you two are giving me a complex!"

"Just shut up and drive," Jaden quips. He pulls away from the curb, following the directions Jaden has given him. "Oh, Talli, what do you say about Sunday going over to Tish's and helping her out?"

"Sounds fantastic. I'm not working on Sunday...I work a mid on Saturday, but Sunday is good. Let me guess, you won't be here Sunday," I say to Pete.

"Actually I will. I was probably going with you to see that shameless hussy."

I laugh at his comment right about the time Jaden is screaming for Pete to look out, and the world goes momentarily black.

CHAPTER 41

My ears are ringing as I jolt awake, sounds of shouting and crying lingering in the air. For a brief moment I have no idea where I am, as I look all around me... what the hell? I am lying haphazardly across the back seat of Jaden's car, the lower half of my body on the floorboard, covered in broken glass. My head is throbbing so badly that focusing is an issue.

"Talli...God, Talli, please help me!" I can hear Jaden shouting. "I don't know what to do!"

What the hell is she talking about? Don't know what to do about...what?

When I try to push myself back on the seat, my hands go into a pool of something wet. I lift them, seeing them stained bright red, and reality begins to sink in.

An accident. We've... we've been in an accident.

"Is everyone all right?" I heard a man's voice and looked up, vision blurred as I tried to focus on whomever was speaking.

"He's... he's bleeding, and I can't get it to stop," Jaden says.

He...he, who?

Oh...No, no... Pete.

"Pressure," I manage to say. "Put...pressure on it." Wait, is that me saying it?

"Ma'am, lie still, the ambulance is on its way," our Good Samaritan is saying. I see him pull his shirt off and wad it up, leaning in the driver's seat.

"Jaden?" Fuck, my throat feels dry. Didn't we just have lunch? Right, we are driving back to the hospital.

"I'm fine, I'm fine," she calls back to me. "Damn it, Talli, weren't you wearing your seatbelt?"

Was I?

No... no I hadn't been wearing my seatbelt, I had been leaned back against the passenger side of the car. Pete was wearing his though. I glance over at the driver's side, which is now bowed in towards us. The impact must have hit right by where he is sitting.

"Where is he bleeding from?" I ask.

"I can't tell. It was just...it's everywhere."

I push myself back onto the seat, a shooting pain in my side that I ignore as adrenaline starts kicking in.

"Sir," I say to our Good Samaritan, my voice suddenly stronger, "where is his bleeding coming from?"

"He has a head wound, but..." The look on his face that I now bring into focus shows his concern. I look slightly down where he is holding his light blue shirt, now stained red, up against Pete's neck.

"More pressure." I guide him, unable to move enough to reach over myself. I hear the sirens in what seems to be the distance. "Don't be afraid, push in."

"His phone's in pieces," I hear Jaden say. "I have to... I have to call Jase before... before this gets out, and Pete's phone..."

"Use mine," I say, leaning back into the seat as I feel tunnel vision coming on. I remember holding it out to her and closing my eyes for what seems to be a brief moment.

"Ms. Emerson," a voice is calling in the distance.

What the fuck is behind my head? And why can't I move my arms?

"Ms. Emerson, can you hear me?"

"Get that fucking light out of my eyes," I mutter, squinting. "Jaden, what the hell are you doing?"

"Ma'am, my name is Carrie, I am an EMT, and you're on your way to the hospital."

Ma'am? I'm not a fucking ma'am. On my way to a hospital… right, the accident. Where the hell is Jaden? And… Pete? Just… open your mouth, Talli. Ask.

"Where is everyone?"

"On their way to the hospital, ma'am."

"Don't fucking ma'am me." I don't mean to be belligerent; I don't seem to have any control over it. "Are they okay? Is Pete okay?"

"Ma'am, I need you to calm down."

"No! No, I'm not calming down, I want to know how they are!" Panic is setting in; I can feel the sweat breaking out all over.

"She's in shock," I hear another voice coming from a direction I can't turn my head in. "Calm down, your friends are on their way. Is there anyone, next of kin that we can reach for you?"

"My mom, please call my mom," I say, momentarily forgetting that no one can. I close my eyes again, fighting a wave of nausea that is threatening, and I welcome the darkness as it envelops me once more.

Everything is eerily quiet when I open my eyes next. Quiet and…white. No, there is blue. And beeping. And…

Lisa?

"You can't do that, Talia," she says, her voice tight and strained. "You have to be more careful, you know that, above all people."

"Hi, it's nice to see you, too." My voice is oddly scratchy.

"Oh…god." Is that a sob from her? "I mean, I know they said you were going to be okay, but that's what they said about Mom, too."

I feel her squeeze my hand, which apparently has something attached to it. I laugh to myself as the next thought that enters my mind is what my oxygen absorption rate is.

"Where are Jaden and Pete? Are they okay?"

"Jaden's okay." Lisa is squeezing my hand so hard it hurts. "I...I don't know about...Pete? Is that what you said his name was? I know he's still in surgery. Yours wasn't very long at all."

"Mine? My what?"

"Surgery," she says, as if I should already know that. How would I know if my ass was knocked out? "Ruptured spleen, no complications right now."

"Well, hello there," I hear Iris's voice before I see her. "I heard you came back to us today even with the rest of the day off."

"Are you my nurse? Please say yes," I say, holding out my hand to her.

"You're still in recovery, but once you're out of here, yes." She leans around Lisa to place a motherly kiss on my forehead. "Dr. Craig has ordered everyone to take special care of you."

"Like a cardiologist would have a say so over here," I mutter, even knowing that he is technically still *my* cardiologist.

"Dr. Craig was so sweet, so concerned," Lisa comments, almost seeming to push Iris aside as she places herself between us. "He even told that...crazy looking...*guy* that you wouldn't want him anywhere near you."

"Crazy...oh, God, Iris are the press here?"

"Yeah, baby, but that's not who she's talking about," Iris replies. "Oh, and...our patient here needs her rest, so I'm going to have to ask you to leave." I see her raise her eyebrow as Lisa opens her mouth to protest. "I'm only nice when I say it the first time."

"I've called the rest of the family," Lisa says, grabbing her purse. "We'll make sure you get no unwanted visitors."

I hear a swooshing sound, as if Lisa is leaving my recovery area, my mind going a million miles a minute.

"Iris, who was it?" I ask, gladly accepting the glass of water she hands me before starting my vitals. "That Lisa was talking about?"

"Who do you think it was, baby girl?"

Oh...

361

"He's just beside himself right now, completely inconsolable."

Jase.

He's... he's *here.*

Of course he's here... duh, Talli!

"How's Pete?" I ask, trying to sit up more.

"Careful, baby, you have a concussion, too. Pete's still in surgery."

"Iris...his *condition.*"

"Critical."

Fuck. Fuck, fuck, fuck...I'd been right there, and I couldn't help, and...

"Where's Jase?"

"Calm down...calm down. Your blood pressure and pulse will spike, and I won't be allowed to let him in."

"But you would anyways."

She smiles at me. "Of course I would. He's in a private waiting room. How are you feeling?"

"Sore," I reply, trying to adjust my position and wincing slightly.

"With that concussion I can't give you much, even with your surgery," she says, checking my chart. "You're not even due for anything for another hour."

"I'm fine, don't worry about me." I close my eyes ignoring the slight buzzing in my ears. It seems I am losing time because the next thing I remember is a soft kiss to my forehead. "Iris, please go get Jase," I whisper.

"So she wasn't lying, you really did ask for me."

With the monitors hooked up, there is no masking my heart's slight increase in speed. I open my eyes slightly to see him staring at the machine, concern etched in his features.

He's here...

He's close enough to reach out and...

No. No I can't do that.

"I'm sorry, I didn't mean to startle you." He looks so sweet as he glances back and forth between me and that damn machine that totally gives me away.

"You didn't." My voice sounds similar to our time together in Cleveland. His brow furrows slightly until I add, "That's just what you do to me."

His beautiful stormy eyes are rimmed red, slightly puffy around them where he has been crying. Even with his attempt to smile at my comment, his eyes are filling with tears again.

No... no please... please don't cry...

His hair is even more disheveled and the fingers he runs through it doesn't help matters any. He looks as if he is struggling for his words and his eyes slide shut briefly as I reach out and take his hand in mine.

Touching him is just... heaven, even under these circumstances.

"How's Pete?"

"In recovery." He squeezes my hand softly. "Critical but stable...they said the next 24 hours...um...they said..."

"I'm sorry I wasn't any help."

"What are you talking about, Talli?" His voice is so soft I could barely hear it. "I mean...you were hurt, and you still were telling people what to do. That's what Jaden said...when she called." He covers his face and steps away, trying to control himself.

Seeing him like this... oh, it brings back so many memories.

"Jase..."

"Fuck, I was so excited, here it was the middle of the day and *you*...were calling...*me*." He sniffs back his tears, wiping his eyes with his sleeve. "And then, when she said... it felt like my whole fucking world was being taken away from me. And I still... it still... Talli, I can't lose him, too."

I know exactly what he is talking about, and it has nothing to do with me. I have to comfort him somehow, and I wish with everything in me that I could pull him close, hold him, tell him everything is going to be just fine.

But I can't do that.

Not when I don't know.

"This is one of the best trauma hospitals in the country, and I'm not just saying that because I work here," I try to console him.

"And the ambulance, I remember hearing them...they were quick, they had to be."

"Yeah, they had him stabilized and here in a matter of minutes, that's what they said." Jase is pacing back and forth, a habit he seems to have whenever something is bothering him. "Did he say anything, Talli?"

"No. I was in the back seat; I couldn't even tell if he was awake."

"I guess they hit...right where he was sitting, and...and... there was debris from the truck that hit you guys..."

"Was it his carotid?" I ask, and he looks over at me, his eyes conveying how frightened he really is.

"They said there was a lot of glass, and it nicked the...yeah, that...what you said. But, they said the surgery was a success, and I just have to wait..." He runs another shaky hand through his hair. "This isn't like Michael, this isn't him being sick, there's no... no warning, no nothing, you know?"

"It's okay if you go back there," I say, and he stops pacing for a moment to look over at me, his eyes so pained I could cry for him.

"Do you want me to go?"

"Don't read anything into that, please. He's your brother, that's what I mean." I reach for his hand again and he timidly approaches and places his hand in mine.

"My mom, she should be here any time," he continues, caressing my hand repeatedly as if he can draw some kind of strength from me. "And... and..."

"Kaitlyn," I say for him.

"I think John called her, yeah," Jase says, trembling now. I squeeze his hand, my heart breaking, but my mind telling me it is the best thing to do.

"Jase, you should go."

His eyes darted back to my face, the pain evident. "Go? I...I thought that you..." His breathing is shallow, uneven when Iris walks in the room.

"Jase, honey... you can go see your brother now."

364

He looks back at me...is he looking for reassurance? I can't tell. I motion for the door, and his shoulders slump slightly as he lets go of my hand and walks towards it.

"Let me know how he's doing? Please?" I ask, groggy once more. Why am I so sleepy so soon? He looks back over his shoulder towards me and smiles through his tears. I wish I could go with him, hold his hand like I did all those years ago when it was Michael and my dad.

"It's okay," he says, convincing me he can read my mind. He covers his heart with his hand. "I carry you right here...you'll be with me."

I feel my entire body relax at his words. With another soft smile, he walks out the door.

CHAPTER 42

"I'm bored."

It is Sunday afternoon and I am convinced the powers that be are keeping me here to torture me. Jaden has stopped by to keep me company, so I take the opportunity to attempt to sweet talk her into sneaking me out.

It isn't working so well.

"You know," she begins, "you probably would have been treated and released if you had worn your *seatbelt*." She stresses that last word, glancing at me sideways.

"Yeah, yeah...whatever. You could have at least brought me some Starbucks. Watching you drink that is cruel and unusual punishment." She takes a long drink of her caramel macchiato and licks her lips. "You...bitch."

She smiles. "But you still love me. Pete says hello...or, he writes hello. He still won't speak; he claims he sounds like E.T. on crack."

I hold the pillow to my stomach as I laugh, still feeling rather sore. "But he knows the other guy ran the red light, right? He knows the accident wasn't his fault?"

"As soon as he was able to comprehend what was going on, I told him."

Good. That is good. Tiny baby steps for recovery, and he knows it wasn't his fault. This makes me happy.

"Have the press died off any?" Jaden shrugs at my question. "What does that mean?"

"It means they're trying to decipher what's going on in here, making up all kinds of stories about Kate coming to your room and making your condition worse."

Oh, whatever.

I roll my eyes at the audacity. "I haven't seen her. What, is it a slow news week?"

"Obviously. But you and Jase?" She leaves the question hanging out there, and it is my turn to shrug.

"We're...well... I see him; he comes by when he gets the chance."

"Which is pretty much when he's not sleeping or with Pete. Talli..."

"Please?" I cut her off. "Please don't tell me; I have to hear it from him."

Which is the truth.

Things are going well for us... so well, perhaps a little too well. He is attentive, sweet, kind. And he *talks* with me, answers any question I have for him, never shies away from any subject, just like we used to be. Well, except the fact that there are some things I am still afraid to ask.

Jaden smiles at me as she curls up in her chair. "Suit yourself."

Suit myself?

Oh, she probably knows things that I don't. Of course she does. Look at that shit eating grin on her face. The bitch.

She's lucky I love her.

"Oh...ohoh, look, they're playing *'So I Married an Axe Murderer'!*" she exclaims, and I giggle with delight turning the small TV up. I am sipping on my water while she continues teasing me with her Starbucks and junk food that my mean ass nurse Iris won't let me have. We are a good half an hour into the movie, my side hurting from laughter, when a small knock comes on the door.

"Hey." Jase sticks his head inside. "Is this a bad time?"

He's kidding, right? "Nah, not at all." The usual butterflies whenever I see him come out to play in the pit of my stomach. "Come on in, pull up a seat."

He walks in slowly, his leather jacket in his arms, his hands hidden, and glances at Jaden. "Pete was asking for you."

She perks up at the mention of her non-boyfriend's name. "Asking or writing for me?"

"No, he's actually talking, his voice is starting to come around." Jase can't suppress his grin. "He still sounds like shit, though."

"I'll be sure to tell him you said so." Jaden gathers her provisions and then turns to me. "You don't mind?"

"Hell no. Tell him I said hello."

"Will do." She gives both of us a quick hug before scurrying out of the room. It is so damn cute I can't help but grin at her.

But now...

"What are you hiding?" I ask Jase, who has turned towards me with a devilish grin. He pulls one arm out from under his jacket revealing the Holy Grail...a caramel macchiato with whipped cream, double shot, just calling my name. "Thank you!" I exclaim, reaching for it. He pulls it back out of my reach, his grin widening.

"Nah, it's not that easy for you."

"What do you mean, not that easy? I've suffered enough, haven't I?"

He leans in, his eyes a brilliant green, his grin sweet as he lightly bites his bottom lip. "Say it." It is a bit of a command, and I feel a blush creep across my cheeks.

"Over a cup of coffee?"

"Not just...a cup of coffee." He holds it further away from me, never losing eye contact. "This will put you in absolute..." he kisses my forehead... "Complete..." He kisses the tip of my nose... "Ecstasy." He wiggles is eyebrows up and down before planting a soft kiss on my lips. "Say it."

"But it will sound so..."

"Not when you say it," he whispers, his eyes full of so much joy my heart feels like it will burst. "Never when you say it."

"Jase..."

"Okay." He shrugs and grins, stepping away from me and sitting in the chair Jaden had occupied. "Suit yourself."

"Jase!"

"Don't whine; it's unbecoming," he says like he always does, leaning back in the chair and crossing his legs. "You gotta say it."

What a fucker.

"Why?"

"Because..." He uncrosses his legs and leans forward, his elbows on his knees, that cup in his right hand beckoning me, his eyes piercing into my soul, every word from him making my heart sing. "Because I want to hear you say it. Because it does all kinds of things to me...things I can't even begin to describe, nor would I in these settings. Because... you mean it."

"Yes, I do."

"Say it."

"I love you."

His smile could light up the entire hospital.

"Of course you do," he replies, holding the coffee out to me. I hesitate a moment before taking it, lost in his gaze. "Christine, don't you want it?"

"Huh? Oh, yeah." I take the cup from him, our fingers brushing against each other briefly.

Damn it, there go those butterflies again.

He sits back watching my face intently as I take my first sip of my favorite beverage in what seems to be ages. "Mmmm, heaven," I murmur, settling into my bed.

"Agreed."

We smile in unison, enjoying each other's company for the rest of the afternoon, movie forgotten.

Monday morning comes with the good and bad news. First the good: I am getting released. Second, the bad: I have to go stay with my sister Lisa.

"Oh, come on!" I don't care if I sound like a child. "You've got to be kidding me!"

"She has agreed to look after you for another couple of weeks before I feel okay with you maneuvering any stairs." Dr. Roberts, the resident who is caring for me, is looking over my chart.

"I think I can handle a few stairs; besides it's been what...four days already?"

"If you disagree, I will keep you here."

"You're doing this on purpose."

"I'm not going to argue with you about this, Ms. Emerson."

"But..."

"If Dr. Craig had his say so, you'd be here until he could escort you home personally," Dr. Roberts cuts me off. "Is that what you'd like?"

"No." I cross my arms in front of me. That fucker has no say so anyhow.

"It's only two weeks," Jase's voice startles me. "Sorry; I was eavesdropping."

"But...it's...Lisa."

"She's family," he points out.

"But...*Lisa*."

"Talli." He sits on the bed beside me. "She's family."

"But..."

"I'll rescue you as soon as I can, I promise."

I blink a couple of times, momentarily stunned. "You will?"

"Depending." His fingertips lightly trace the side of my face. "This time if I tell you there's somewhere I want to be... will you say no?"

He...

He wants to be...

With me?

"Talli?"

"No. I mean... I won't say that. No... you know."

He leans in, placing the sweetest kiss on my lips. "Then it's settled."

"So, I'll have your release papers drawn up, and your nurse will come by with instructions." I glance back at Dr. Roberts who has to feel like a third wheel by this point.

"It's Iris's day off, isn't it?" I ask him, and he nods. "I bet you anything she was behind me having to stay so long."

Jase gently nudges me. "I think you know better."

"Aren't you supposed to be on my side?"

"Always, but you should have had your damn..."

"...seatbelt on. Whatever. So, how soon am I sprung? Or do I have to wait for Lisa to get here?"

"I could drive you," Jase suggests.

"You would?" I asked, and his smile makes me momentarily forget I'm about to stay with someone who up until this accident had deemed me unworthy of being in their presence.

"Your nurse should be by shortly," Dr. Roberts says just before he leaves the room. I am still looking at Jase, questions forming in my mind that I am all too afraid to ask.

"Let's get all your stuff together," he says with that easygoing grin. I smile and grab my clothes that Jaden has brought to me.

"First things first." I walk over to the washroom, provisions in hand, ready to make my escape from this place ASAP.

"You really don't have much here," Jase says, looking around. "About how long before your nurse comes?"

"Don't remember," I mutter, flipping through and making sure I have everything I need. "Sometimes it takes them awhile."

"I need to tell Mom where I'm going." He stops and places a sweet kiss on my cheek. "I'll be right back, okay?"

I'm blushing just from his touch. "Of course. I'll be waiting."

After he leaves, I go into the washroom and change into a very loose pair of yoga pants and a large sweatshirt, praising all that is holy for real clothes. Hell, I would sing the Hallelujah Chorus out loud at this point, aside from the fact that I shouldn't. It is a bit of a struggle to get my socks on, but I grit my teeth and deal with it, not allowing them any more reason to keep me in this hospital.

My hair is already pinned up loosely and my makeup, although light, keeps me from looking like the walking dead. I have refused to lie around looking my absolute worst; I have always been that way. Perhaps it is some sort of sickness, but then so be it. It is just the way of...me.

I step out of the washroom, my hospital gown on my arm as I look for a place to set it. Hearing someone behind me clearing their throat makes me pause and turn around.

The last thing I expect to see is Kaitlyn Evans sitting in the chair beside my unoccupied bed. She is in a nice fitting pair of jeans, her hair in a messy bun, a light jacket folded around her to ward off the chill in the room. She looks...well, she looks approachable, which was also one of the last things I expect.

"Jase isn't in here," I say, breaking the uneasy silence.

"I know; I saw him just a little bit ago." Her voice is soft, no bitterness present. "He said he was going to get his rental car, something about you being released."

"Okay." I am confused but I don't want to be rude. "Is there something I can help you with?"

"I'm not sure," she admits, and I look at her hands, folded demurely on her lap. No ring is present.

Oh...hell. No ring.

So it is true; her engagement has been called off.

"Talia," she begins, tilting her head just to the side, "I believe you and I should talk."

CHAPTER 43

"Hate is such a strong word." This is how Kate decides to start our little conversation. "I think I'll stick with dislike then, since I honestly don't know you."

Okay, so I have to give her points for honesty. Doesn't make me like her any more, though. "Fair enough. And just for the record, it is mutual."

"And that's fair as well." She sighs softly, glancing over her shoulder at the door.

"I'm not concerned with Jase hearing what I have to say," I tell her, just in case that's who she is looking for, and I mean it.

I have nothing to hide from him anymore.

"Good, I like hearing that." She pauses again, as if searching for words. "Talli... this... *dislike* I have for you, it stems from many, many years ago. Some of it was warranted..."

"Like when I interrupted your anniversary dinner," I finish for her as her words trail off. She squares her shoulders then and looks me in the eye.

"Yes. However...back in the hospital... you know, Jase never really spoke about you. Ever. I found out you existed because I walked in on the two of you."

I'd almost come to that conclusion but hearing it from her shines an even brighter spotlight on it, but there is still one thing I need to make clear. "You weren't an item at the time."

"No, we weren't. But I loved him even then. He was my best friend, and all of a sudden, he had *you*. He talked to you. He poured his heart out...to *you*. And I really hate...*disliked* you for that."

Is that so? Interesting.

I shrug. "That wasn't in my control. And I didn't really know about you until after I saw you. Afterwards he told me you were his closest friend, but not much more."

"And all he would tell me about you was he was completely honest with you." Kate's head is held high. If she is in any way upset now, she is a master at hiding it. "And I didn't find that out until I made him tell me why you weren't in the journal."

I open my mouth to say something in return but stop as her words register. "I'm sorry... what did you say?"

"Jase's a very proud man, Talli," Kate continues, her voice even stronger. "He owns up to mistakes and stands his ground when he feels he's right. And he's quite adamant that he has been right...*always* been right... about you."

That can be taken in more than one way. I have made my fair share of mistakes from day one, and I paid the price many times over. I can't exactly sit here and ask what all Jase has said to Kaitlyn about me; that would be admitting that he isn't exactly telling me, which may or may not be because I fail to ask. I feel the anxiety burning in me.

But there is something that I need to say to her.

"Talli,"

"I feel," I cut her off, "that your reasoning for wanting Jase back wasn't necessarily because you wanted him to be with you; you just didn't want him to be with me. You were happy and content to marry someone else until you saw me, recognized me."

"Had the past thrown in my face?"

"I'd be lying if I said that wasn't the point I was trying to make." See that, Kate? I can hold my head high as well.

"And you made your point well." She pauses to take a deep breath again. "Jase explained to me...many things, actually. I do want to apologize for bringing your mother into our last argument, Talia. That was completely unfair for me to do." Her eyes are earnest, perhaps a bit of pain behind them as if she knows the heartache of losing someone.

I don't have it in me to hold what she'd said in anger against her. "Apology accepted."

"I understand it was your...father? He was the one in the hospital in Chicago?"

"Please, I really...don't want to talk about it." I'm unsure if I can handle the emotional toll it will place on me to discuss this with someone I don't even know.

"Okay." She is still regarding me with suspicion, which I understand; it's the same thing I'm doing with her. "Jase told me that my perception of you was completely distorted. He told me that the girl in the hospital...and the girl in the restaurant... that what I saw wasn't an accurate depiction of the real you." She shrugs slightly as my mind races...why is Jase saying these things to her? And why is it that he talked so freely with her about me, and has yet to really talk to me about what is going on with the two of them? "Please try to understand when I tell you that I... well, I still have my doubts."

"Why would it possibly matter, Kaitlyn?"

"Because...because ever since I saw him with you, that night in the hospital... I have had this intense... *dislike*...okay? For once, for the first time, he didn't need me."

I have to laugh at that one. "Didn't need you, right. His first love, his first *everything*, the one person that no one else could compete with."

"No one except the perfect girl with the perfect body and the perfect dress that made him completely forget about me."

"Who the hell was that?"

"Very funny."

Well...what do you know?

"That couldn't have been directed at me," I say softly. "Not...from you."

The silence is profound as we sit there for a moment, sizing each other up, all of our insecurities about one another laid out for the world to see. She has yet to deny, if she is going to at all, the accusation I have thrown at her, but I am so afraid of her answer... I just know if she says she wants Jase back, he will go in a heartbeat, no questions asked.

"I was wrong about one thing, though," she finally says. "You're obviously no fling."

I can barely suppress a smile. "Is that so?"

"I'm happy that all of you are okay," she says without commenting further. "I don't think he would have handled it at all well if any of you...hadn't...made it." I am reminded then that she has known his family for years, her concern for Pete nearly tangible. "So..." Her voice trails off as my nurse comes in.

"I'm here for your discharge instructions, and I'm told that I am to make you be quiet and listen."

"Good luck with that."

"I should go," Kate says. "I imagine this won't be our last opportunity to talk, Talia."

"It was much more cordial," I admit, and she almost smiles. Her face is suddenly serious when she looks back at me.

"I still don't think you're good enough." Her eyes are unwavering as she steps closer to me. "Just do me a favor, would you?"

"What's that?"

"Prove me wrong."

I am still confused as Jase drives me in near silence to my sister's. I'm not aware of whether or not he even knows Kaitlyn had come to see me. I am staring out the window softly murmuring the directions as we near the streets we have to turn on, my stomach in knots.

Is this how I am going to feel every time he leaves? Like… like he is running off somewhere to be with someone else?

No, not just someone else.

Her.

In spite of everything, to me I still haven't gotten his answer. He hasn't told me what I've let him know I need to hear. I can't be on his string, no matter how much it hurts to let him go.

It is all or nothing.

And yet, I can't help but feel that somehow, he's already let me know what his answer is.

"This isn't very far from John's place," Jase comments as he pulls up in front of Lisa's one-story brick ranch.

"I wouldn't know."

"Hey…" He reaches out and stops me with just a light touch on my arm. "Talli… what's wrong?"

I sit back in the seat and sigh as I look into those beautiful eyes. "I…don't know. And it's not that anything's wrong per se, it's that…"

I am silenced by his lips and I let out a trembling sigh against him. He instantly takes advantage and deepens our kiss, teasing me with his teeth and tongue until I am whimpering, my hands buried in his tousled hair. He pulls back and smiles. "It's that…what?"

"Huh? Um…oh, hell, I don't know." I shake my head, regaining my composure as he opens his car door. "You don't fight fair."

"All's fair in…" He stops suddenly, his eyes narrowing with his lopsided smile. "Let's get you inside."

Being hot, bothered, and ever so slightly confused is not really the way I want to enter my sister's home, but that's exactly what happens. Lisa has the guest room all ready for me, equipped with a Bible and a magazine or two on Christian living, no small hint there. Her husband Jack—again with that name, maybe this is where I got it from—takes my bags and welcomes Jase into their humble home. I almost have to roll my eyes, remembering all those years ago that Jack, Lisa, and I had spent our time numbing our senses.

"You should be nice and comfortable in here; this is your old bed, remember?" Lisa is asking.

"Yes, I do. Not the same mattress, though, I'm sure." I had cut that mattress to ribbons after Dad's funeral.

"And I'm sure your doctor won't mind you going to church with us," she continues, ignoring my comment. "And you understand that Jase will not be staying with you while you're here…"

"No, we're saving the sex until after I'm cleared," I cut her off, giggling when she glares at me. "Oh, come on, Lisa… like I never walked in on you and Jack."

"Jack and I are married."

"You weren't married then."

"But I knew we would be," she counters. "Can you say the same about your rock star?"

It is my turn for silence as my face turns an uncomfortable shade of crimson.

"Dr. Craig promised us he'd stop in to check on you," Jack is saying to me when Lisa and I walk out to the living room. Jase hesitates while bringing his drink to his lips for just a moment but recovers before my sister or her husband notice.

"That isn't necessary," I reply with a smile.

"But of course it is!" Lisa insists. "He's genuinely concerned, and I just want some reassurance that you're doing fine."

"You realize he's just trying to get in my pants, right?"

Jase chokes back a laugh, covering with a cough, and Jack's brow furrows at my statement. I have to smile. That will pretty much put the kibosh on Dr. Craig being left alone with me under this roof.

"Oh, pish posh," Lisa says with a wave of her hand. I stifle a giggle of my own as Jase mouths the words "pish posh" to me, one eyebrow raised.

"Just the same, I think we should ensure your sister's well-being while in our home," Jack added.

Jack and Lisa are discussing back and forth the importance of Dr. Craig's physical examination, or lack thereof, of me while Jase and I walk out to the back yard that I've told him about only roughly a million times. I have always loved their back yard; it seems to roll on forever, and back when I'd allowed myself romantic dreams, I'd always pictured this to be the perfect place for a reception. They have a small gazebo and a bench swing, a couple of beautiful flowering trees that kill my allergies in the spring. A large privacy fence that seems disproportionate with the size of the house, but fits the lawn perfectly surrounding it. I am standing, staring up at the blue sky when I feel Jase's hands circle my waist. He pulls me close and buries his face in my hair, inhaling deeply before leaving a soft kiss and resting his chin on top of my head.

"Are you okay?" he asks.

Well, that was a loaded question. "I think I'm going to have to remind myself over and over that they're family. But other than that, I'm wonderful. How about you?"

I can feel his smile. "Peaceful." He leaves another kiss in my hair. "Like all is...almost right in the world."

"Just almost?"

"Almost," he repeats, snuggling in. I wince as I feel a sharp pain that quickly dissipates. "I'm sorry." He steps back and turns me around by my shoulders.

"I'm okay," I reassure him. "I'm just not a hundred percent yet."

"Hence the almost," he explains, lightly tucking a curl behind my ear. "And Pete's still in the hospital for now, and... I have to play some shows to make up for the cancellations, thank you contractual obligations."

"Now?"

"Don't whine; it's unbecoming."

Somehow, I am comforted by his constant answer.

He smiles, placing a light kiss on my lips. "I won't be gone long, I promise. Now that Pete's out of the woods and now that you're okay, I need to do this."

"Will you call me?"

His laugh calms the edges of my nerves. "Do you really need to ask that question, Not Telling?" His kiss helps even more. "You'll keep me sane..." He kisses a trail to my neck. "...and in a decent mood..."

"Which Jackie should appreciate," I half-moan as he nips at my neck.

"Mmm hmmm." His hands are holding me to him as he kisses my lips once more. He is careful with me, holding me as if I am fragile, ignoring my protests when he won't hold me closer.

"I'm not... interrupting, am I?" John's voice causes us both to jump. Lisa is escorting him out to the back yard.

"Of course you are," Jase says to him, and Lisa laughs as if he's made the funniest joke in the world.

"Dr. Craig is here to examine Talia," Lisa explains.

"Talia was examined before she left the hospital." Jase's tone is guarded, his glare icy.

"I'm sure he..."

"Lisa, could you excuse us, please?" I interrupt her, giving her my sweetest smile.

"Of course," she says begrudgingly. "I'll be inside if anyone needs anything." There is an awkward silence while the three of us wait for Lisa to go back inside and shut the door.

"I wanted to see for myself that you were okay," John says, ignoring Jase's glare. "And I wanted to let you know if you need anything, call me."

"I think she's just..." Jase stops as I squeeze his hand.

"How's Kate?" John asks when he finally looks at Jase.

"Kate is fine," I speak up. "I talked to her before I was discharged from the hospital." I feel Jase's eyes on me, but I hold John's gaze as I try to get the message through to him. "I appreciate your concern, John... but the drama's over."

"Is it?"

Two simple words that I don't honestly have the answer to, and I feel awkward having made such a bold statement without talking things over with Jase first. I open my mouth to say something but have no witty reply. Hell, who am I kidding? I have no reply at all.

"It doesn't concern you," Jase says simply.

Oh, wow. I must have spoken too soon.

"As a friend, it does," John corrects him. "Talli, you can call me whenever you need anything, and it doesn't have to strictly be medical either. I'm here if you need me."

"Thank you," I say politely.

He smiles at me. "Anytime. I'll see you around." As he walks back into the house, I feel Jase still tense up beside me.

"I don't like this…"

"Don't worry about any of this," I cut him off. "Just promise me when the tour dates are done…"

"I'll be right back here," he says with a smile. "So long as you want me to."

"Talia?" I hear Lisa calling out to me just as I am getting ready to answer him. "It's nearly time for supper and our daily reading."

"Reading?"

"Today's from the book of Job," she replies.

"Ah, suffering… nice," I say softly. Jase is grinning sheepishly at me. "Oh, they're *family*," I mock him. "You should be with them… *family*."

"I will rescue you the first chance I get." He pauses for a moment, shifting, looking almost nervous before he continues. "You didn't tell me you spoke with Kate."

"I didn't know what to say. I still don't."

"Is that why you were upset?"

"I can't really say that I'm upset," I try to explain. "It's just… Jase, I don't understand."

"What don't you understand, Christine?" His voice is as soothing as his hands. I shrug slightly, uncomfortable with asking. "Just say it."

"Why are you here?"

"Ah."

"Ah? That's it? Ah?"

"No that's not it...damn, woman, give me a chance to answer." He is smiling at me. Fucker.

"Jase..."

"I'm here because I want to be," his words silence me once more. "Because I *chose* to be."

He holds my gaze as I wrap my head around his words, taking in the full meaning of them. I am unable to say anything in return as one small tear slips down my cheek.

He... chose to be.

He wants to be with... with...

Me.

Ignoring the discomforting tug at my side, I wrap my arms around his neck and kiss him...full, lingering, deep, leaving us both gasping slightly for air. I want nothing more than to show him how much I love him, more than any words could ever convey.

"Oh, come on, Talia... not in my back yard either."

We jump slightly as Lisa walks out, but his arms stay securely around me, supporting me, holding me to him.

Damn, I love this man.

"Sorry," I mutter with a cheeky grin as Jase and I step apart and walk hand-in-hand to the back door. I stop and grin at my oldest sister. "You know...except I'm not."

At least this time I see her try to stifle a smile as she ushers us back into her house.

CHAPTER 44

"T minus five days and counting."

This is the greeting I receive at 2:35 in the morning, reminding me just how long I have until Jase is coming to rescue me from my sister's house.

"That's still too much time." I know I'm complaining, and I wait for his usual retort to my whining.

"Fuck, I know," is what I hear instead. "I miss you."

I shiver as a chill goes straight down my spine, my heart fluttering in my chest. Will he ever know what he does to me?

"I miss you, too." *I won't cry, I won't cry, I won't cry.*

"Did she torture you too much today?" he asks, trying to lighten the tone. "Are you still reading from the book of Job?"

"They're pushing any kind of scripture on me that tells me I'm going to hell if I don't change my ways."

"I like your ways."

Even without him being in front of me, I know I am blushing.

"She's not convincing you to dump me and head off to some… convent or something, is she?"

"And live out eternity without ever ravishing you again? Not a chance."

"Not Telling Christine, you insufferable tease, whatever am I going to do with you?"

"Is that a rhetorical question, or do you really want an answer?" I ask as I always do.

He inhales sharply. "Have I mentioned that I miss you?" His voice sends another chill through me.

"How much?" I ask, testing just a tiny bit to see if he'll tell.

"I can't sleep." He sighs at his confession before continuing. "I can't sleep, I'm not eating well, I can't concentrate, I can't write, I... just... miss you."

I try masking the tears his words have brought to me, but he hears anyway.

"Talli, please...please don't cry."

"I'm...okay, I am, but I know... Fuck, I know exactly what you mean."

"What a pair we make," he says in reply. "Well...yeah, we do. What a pair."

Really? I can feel myself sigh and melt at his words. "Think I can just stay on the phone with you until the five days are up?"

"I wish. I'm actually on my way to the airport, catching the redeye to the next city."

"Is Alfred driving you?"

"Nope, he's sitting right beside me, rolling his eyes and making those faces like he's getting ready to gag."

I have to laugh at that, along with my slight shock at the fact that he's having *this* conversation in front of anyone.

"Jeez, Talli, does this mean we're like... one of... *those* couples?"

"Yes," I hear Jackie say, and I laugh even harder.

"Are we?" I ask, closing my eyes and waiting for his reply.

"Yes... Emphatically yes."

And my heart soars once more.

"Do you make it a habit to spend your nocturnal hours on the phone?" Lisa asks me the next day. I am curled up in the den sipping on a diet cola with one of the many movie channels on waiting for my fifty millionth run of *So I Married an Axe Murderer*.

"I have for a few months now, yes," I say as I place my can in its obligatory coaster. Hell, there is no point in lying, regardless that she is already convinced that I am going to hell. "Does it disturb you?"

"There are... several things that disturb me to be quite honest with you, Talia."

Oh, whatever. "Lisa, please..."

"I watched you head down that path of self-destruction when we were losing Daddy and I said nothing," she cuts me off.

Thanks for the reminder, sweetheart, not that I don't remind myself every chance I get.

"I watched you go through men like water."

Translation: Lisa thinks I'm a slut.

"I watched you ingest any chemical you could get your hands on..."

"If I recall correctly, for most of my teenage years the majority of those chemicals I acquired from you."

She pauses and lowers her head briefly. "I have had to live with that every single day, Talia. I had to look Mom in the eye and tell her that you were fine when you were so stoned you couldn't see. I had to cover for you when you went chasing after men, after numbness... god, after *death*, because let's face it, that's where you were headed. And I'm the one that introduced this to you."

"Lisa, I'm...not some druggie or some degenerate. I turned out okay for all the shit that happened, and just for the record if I hadn't gotten the alcohol or the drugs from you, I would have gotten them from somewhere else."

"I know that you've pulled your life around, somewhat." Lisa is quick to add that 'somewhat.'

"What do you mean, somewhat?"

"I know you're almost done with nursing school and you're self-sufficient, which is more than we can say for some of the other members of our family."

"Nice way to not gossip, Lisa."

"Damn it, Talia, you're going to listen to me!"

Her stern tone causes the hairs on the back of my neck to bristle. Oh, she is damn lucky at this point that I am recovering from surgery.

"You still run around the bars, you still get into more trouble than you can handle or I wouldn't see it in the tabloids, and you've become some... some... groupie..."

"Ex*cuse* me?"

"You think he's faithful to you when he's on the road? You think that because he's calling you at some ungodly hour that it must mean that he's not screwing around on you?"

I narrow my eyes at her accusations. Wow, does she ever have nerve. She has *no* idea; she doesn't even know *me* anymore.

"I'm just looking out for you. I've seen what happens when your life spirals out of control, Talia."

"You want to know...if I think he's faithful?" I ask, choosing my words cautiously.

"Yes, I want to know," she reiterates.

I consider my answer carefully, feeling my facial features relax as I think of him, of our last conversation.

"Absolutely," I reply, a goofy smile threatening to break forward.

Oh...hell.

We are one of *those* couples.

"Okay," she says softly. "Well... if I find out differently... if he hurts you... I swear to you... I'm going to chop his balls off."

"Lisa!" I swat at her. "You shameless hussy you, go wash your mouth out with soap!"

"Screw you," she mutters, reaching over me and taking a handful of popcorn. "And what are you doing watching this movie? This was my favorite movie first, you damn pipsqueak."

"Go," I point at the door teasingly.

"Just remember whose house you're at, Brat."

"Shesh, whatever."

"Jase," I am saying in the middle of the night when he has called again, "I think my sister has a split personality."

He laughs, one of those endearing laughs that I can listen to for hours, making me miss him all the more.

"No... no, seriously, like one minute she's all... 'You're going to hell for hanging out in bars', and the next she's saying that if you hurt me, she's going to chop your balls off."

"Hey...hey... no joking about the nether regions there." His tone of voice has changed drastically.

"Who's joking? I think Sybil was serious."

"Oh, great; one fuck up by me and it's Castration City. How would I sound as a mezzo-soprano? Hmmmm."

"You said you could do the Spice Girls," I reminded him. "Oh, and Hanson, let's not forget Hanson."

"And is it...spayed, or neutered? Which one of that is done to the male?"

"Do you really want to find out?"

"I think the question here is... do you?" I swear I can hear his smile.

"Nah, I haven't had my fill of you yet," I reply breathlessly as I flop back on the bed.

"Damn it, woman, stop it!"

"T minus?"

"Four days and fucking counting," he replies through gritted teeth.

"Mmmmm, I love it when you do that."

"Talia... Christine... I swear to you I'll hang up this phone."

"Liar."

"Okay, you called me on that one." I hear him exhale slowly.

"You sound so tired," I comment.

"I am."

"Still can't sleep?"

"I'm trying, Talli, I really am."

"It doesn't sound like you're trying hard enough," I say. "So I'm making you hang up, whether you want to or not, and close your eyes. Rest."

"When I close my eyes, I see you."

"Oh, that's good Jase. That's... that's clever."

"That's serious." I can tell he isn't joking.

He just needs to come back right *now*.

"Well, what the hell good are you gonna be to me if you're so damn tired that all you do is fall right to sleep when you get here?"

"But...it's different."

Really, now? "How so?"

"Because," he begins, "this time... we'll have all the time in the world."

Now, how the hell am I supposed to sleep after hearing that?

"Jack, you don't honestly believe your constant bitching is going to make me, say... snap my fingers and become Mary freakin Poppins, do you?" I ask this on my final night here. I do believe I've finally made it to my breaking point. "Enough about how I'm going to hell already!"

"Now, Talia..."

"Say, do you remember when we threw that big fuck off party and I walked in on you and Lisa totally screwing in my Mom and Dad's bed?" I don't want to tell him that Lisa and I had been laughing our asses off about it while Jack was at work; something suddenly seems amiss to me in their perfect life.

"We don't talk about such things."

I know he is continuing his speech, but luckily my phone is ringing, and I excuse myself by merely holding up one finger and walking away to answer.

"T minus how many hours before you get your ass here and fucking rescue me already?" I ask with a smile through gritted teeth, ignoring Jack's protests about my 'colorful' language. *Fuck you, buddy.*

"Aww...did I interrupt Bible hour?"

"Jase... you don't sound like you're in an airport."

"That's because...I'm not."

Oh, this isn't good.

You're not?" I feel my heart sink. "What do you mean you're not? They're not keeping you back there, are they? Please tell me they're not..."

"Talli..."

"I mean, I'd survive, but damn it, I miss you! I love you and I miss you..."

"Talia..."

"...and you need to be here now! Like right now, so I can hold you and kiss you and..."

"*Christine...*"

I sigh when he says my middle name, feeling that familiar tightening in my stomach. "What?" I ask, finally ending my rambling.

"Get your ass out here, now."

"What?" My head snaps around to the front of the house. Looking through the sheer curtains that cover the large picture window, I see a familiar silhouette, shadows of the setting sun catching the subtle highlights in his dark hair as he stands, one hand holding his phone, the other raising slightly to wave hello when he knows I see him.

"Christine, I'm not going to stand here..."

I don't hear the rest of what he is saying as the phone slips from my fingers landing with a soft thud on the carpet where my feet had stood before I'd taken off in a sprint, throwing the front door open and bounding across the lawn. Neither of us gives a damn about discretion as he scoops me up into his arms, burying his face in the side of my neck and inhaling deeply as we hold each other.

"I missed you," he breathes, and I sigh as my body responds instantly to his touch and his voice. As if he can tell, he moans softly in my ear, "Mmm, baby, I know…I know…"

My eyes slide shut as he kisses my neck.

"It's been too long," he whispers up against my skin.

A slight gasp leaves my lips, and he captures it with a kiss and a sigh as we stand there, the cool breeze not fazing us. My palms are cupping his face as he kisses me deeply, fully, sighing, "It drives me crazy when you do that," against my lips.

Is that so?

"I thought I made myself clear," Jack's voice resonates from somewhere in the vicinity of the front porch.

Jase's words are punctuated with kisses and sighs as he refuses to let go of me. "We… are not… in… your house…Jack."

Damn straight we're not.

"The least you could do is get a room," Lisa whispers as she brings my bags out to the lawn. I finally stop kissing Jase long enough to smile at her.

"I didn't get a room," Jase says quietly. "I hope that wasn't too presumptuous of me."

"Not at all." I place a sweet kiss on his lips before turning my head to look at Lisa. "Thank you, Leesie," I use my pet name I'd called her as a child, trying to not sway as Jase nuzzles my neck once more. Holy hell, we are going to have to hurry or this neighborhood is *really* going to get a show. "If you need anything, call me."

"Thank you, Talia." She shakes her head as she looks at Jase and me. "Jeezus, Jase, come up for air and let me say hello, goodbye, and all that stuff."

"Show your hands so I can see that no butcher knives are present," he says with a raised eyebrow, and Lisa…laughs.

A genuine heartfelt laugh.

She gives him a quick hug, whispering, "Take care of my baby sister. She's very precious to me."

"To me, too," Jase replies softly back to her. He steps back from her, still keeping me in his arms. "Hey, this won't be the last I see of you, will it?"

"I'll drag her out to play, kicking and screaming if I have to," I speak up.

"Talli…"

"Even if playing consists of dinner and a movie," I cut her off, knowing she still has a problem with the bar scene. I suppose I can give if it means she will take.

She is, after all, *family.*

"Throw in popcorn and it's a deal."

"Just to let you know," Jase starts, "the words 'throw' and 'popcorn' should never be used together around her. Hey, ow!" he adds as I swat him.

"I was going to say that since you're here instead of on the road, perhaps she'll get some sleep. Somehow now I'm doubting that."

I smile at Lisa who is ignoring the dirty looks Jack is shooting her. "I'll be fine, don't worry about me. But…no offense… I wanna go home."

From my position, my head nestled up against Jase's chest, I could swear I hear his heart skip a tiny beat and I smile as he places a kiss on top of my head.

All of my nerve endings are tingling the entire twenty-minute ride through traffic to my apartment across town. I sit in that passenger seat of his rental car, seatbelt buckled, my head resting against the back of the seat as I keep my eyes on Jase.

"You're making this ride a little uncomfortable, looking at me that way." His voice is low and raspy… sexy. Just sexy. My eyes glance down to his jeans and I smile, knowing the full meaning of his words.

"I could always…you know…unbuckle my seatbelt and…"

"Don't you fucking dare," he says quickly, his hands gripping the steering wheel a little tighter. I am about to laugh and make a lewd comment about how he can't handle my mouth on him and driving at the same time when I realize what he is saying.

"I was just joking."

"It's not funny...it's not...fucking...funny." He takes one hand off the wheel to give mine a squeeze before returning to his original position.

"Jase..."

"I could have lost you, Talli, don't you get that?" He doesn't take his eyes off the road for good reason, but I wonder if we weren't in the car whether or not he could keep eye contact with me then. Somehow judging by the tone of his voice, I doubt it.

"We weren't exactly a ..."

"Then you don't get it," he cuts me off before I can remind him that we weren't together.

Don't get *what*? Okay, so I know he is upset over the accident, but I am okay. His brother is the one who'd been severely injured and is still in the hospital at this point. Besides, it is just a joke. It shouldn't make him all broody like this... right?

He remains silent the rest of the way, pulling into the apartment complex, his hands shaking ever so slightly as he shuts off the engine.

"Do you need help with your things?" He shakes his head, still not looking at me. I sigh as I exit the car and reach in to get my bag.

"Leave it, Talli. Let me get it for you." He is still sitting there behind the wheel looking forward.

Please not tonight, Jase...

"Are you going to sit there all night, or are you going to come in and let me throw popcorn at you?" I ask, finally getting a soft grin from him.

"How can I resist that?" is his reply as he quickly exits the car. He grabs my things and follows behind me, pausing as I unlock the door.

I haven't been home since the accident, and I wonder for a brief moment how bad the place must look and possibly even... smell, oh fuck I haven't been here to take out the garbage, or anything, and...

He has his hand on the door pushing it open from behind me as if he senses my hesitation. My mouth was open to protest, but my eyes catch a glimpse of something rather... colorful...

My floor lamp in the living room is set on low, giving off a soft glow in the downstairs. The stereo is playing my collection of classical music that I love to unwind to, there is a bottle of wine chilling in a bucket on my dining room table, and everywhere... nearly everywhere I can see, there are lilies.

Lilies.

My favorite.

I remember that conversation we'd had oh so long ago on the phone, when I had caught a glimpse of some lilies in some late-night TV show that was playing in the background. I never in a million years thought something so small would be tucked away in the recesses of that incredible mind of his. A tear escapes and runs down my cheek as I slowly walk through to my living room, stopping briefly here and there. My apartment is spotless...absolutely spotless, and the floral scent is breathtakingly beautiful.

"How...how could you..."

"I have to admit, I didn't actually... *do* it." Jase is standing directly behind me, his arms wrapped securely around my waist, his words breathed into my ear. "I asked Jaden if she could help, told her what I wanted and when the flowers would be here. Apparently, someone's a little absentminded and makes sure one or more of her friends has a key to her apartment." I laugh softly at his words. "Perhaps if you gave them..."

"One more word about that damn code and I'm cutting you off."

He kisses my neck, his teeth and tongue drawing a soft whimper from me. "Liar," he says, his hands finding their way under my shirt, hot against my skin.

Now that is more like it.

"What makes...you...so...sure?" I feel my body's betrayal, knowing even without an intimate touch that I am ready for him.

His hands work quickly, one unclasping my bra as the other slips beneath the silky fabric. "Oh...that..."

"Oh that?" he interrupts his teasing nips at my neck to ask. "Just... oh...that?"

I turn to him then, my hands twisting in his shirt and roughly pulling him to me. Our kisses on my sister's front lawn look like child's play as we frantically make short work of our shirts, Jase tossing my bra to the side just before his kisses leave me breathless once more. Just the feel of skin on skin has me helpless, trembling, begging for more.

"Oh, this... I've missed this.," I moan between kisses, his tongue teasing mine.

"So have I." His head falls back as I leave open mouthed kisses on his neck, down his chest.

"I want you."

"You've got me."

"You know what I want, Jase," I say, standing on my toes, kissing his lips once more.

"I...don't know..." His breath is coming in ragged gasps even as I am unbuttoning his jeans, cupping him with one hand while sliding the zipper down with the other.

"The hell you don't." I slip my hand inside, and a low moan sounds in his throat as my fingers close around him. *This* is what I want.

"Talli, I don't want to hurt you." He says this even as he is laying me back on the couch, my hands pulling his jeans and boxer briefs down past his hip bones.

"I'm injured, Jase, not dead." I pull him down beside me, gasping as his hand reaches between my legs. He is right, he is so right...it has been far too long. His fingers stroke between my folds, sending shivers straight through my body.

"God, you're ready for me..."

"Yes," I whimper against his lips as his fingers continue teasing me. "Please, Jase."

"I don't want to hurt you," he repeats, hushing my moan with a kiss. "I...*won't* hurt you." My eyes fly open as he pulls his hand back just in time to watch him move quickly, roughly pulling the rest of my clothes off in one fluid motion and crawling back up my body, his kisses on my inner thighs nearly my undoing. There is no hesitation as he moves upward, his tongue delving in, making me cry out in absolute bliss. Holy hell, he is far too good at that... and I am so far gone by merely being in his presence that I know I won't last long. When he pushes two fingers roughly inside of me, I am lost...utterly, completely, lost, crying out at the sudden ecstasy that is flooding through my body. My back arches, heightening the pleasure even more, and I find myself tangling my fingers in his hair, holding him as he draws every last shudder and sigh from me, only kissing his way up my body after the tension has finally left my limbs. "Beautiful," he moans. "Always, always beautiful."

Even as breathless as I am, my hands are tugging at the waistband of his jeans, my thumbs hooked inside the boxers as well. "No...no, baby, it's too soon after the accident," he is saying as he is placing soft kisses on my neck and face. I can feel him pressed up against my hip, knowing he wants this no matter his protests.

"I said..." I surprise him with my strength as I roll to my side, pushing him on his back. "...I'm not fucking dead."

"Talli..."

His protest dies in his throat as I make my intentions clear, kissing down that happy trail as I work his jeans and boxer briefs down, and finally off his body. It is his turn to moan as my tongue runs up the length of him, his turn to bury his hands in my hair as he nears his own release. I stroke him with my hand as my mouth moves up and down, applying pressure, my tongue swirling around the tip. I can feel the tension in his limbs, his hands guiding me just a little faster, and I know... oh, I know what is coming. I hold him to me as he goes over the edge, tasting him the way he has me, glowing in the fact that I have just as much power over him. He is still breathing heavily, a thin sheen of perspiration across him as I return the favor, kissing my way up his body to his neck as his breathing is slowly returning to normal. He wraps his arms around me, holding me to him in the warmest embrace, his heart hammering against his ribcage.

"Welcome home, Talli," he is finally able to whisper.

"Right back atcha." I am still a bit breathless myself. "I love you, Jase."

I have no idea whether or not he answers as we both drift into a well-deserved sleep

CHAPTER 45

"You know," Jase is saying to me, "this may sound... *odd*... but I'm really glad that we didn't figure out we'd known each other before. You know, not until later."

"Why's that?" I ask, sorting through the laundry I have finished.

"Because," he continues, helping me by putting his clothes into a separate pile, "then there would have been all these..." He pauses, making grand gestures with his hands. "Expectations."

I ponder his statement for a moment. "Do you really think so?"

"Yeah, I do." He stops and takes a drink. "We both would have expected the other to be if not the same, then at least remotely similar to how we'd been as teenagers."

"And that's one thing neither one of us is," I add for him, and he smiles at me.

"Exactly."

He is right... absolutely one hundred percent right. If I'd had any inkling that Jase Warner was J (whom I'd thought was a Jack for the longest time... okay, not long. He was simply 'J'), things would have been *very* different. I would have acted differently, if I would have gone near him at all. Hell, with my perception of how that night at the restaurant had gone, I would have steered clear. About a million miles clear.

Only after bragging to the girls that I'd made out with him as a teenager, of course.

My, has he changed, though.

"You certainly have more confidence than you did back then," I comment.

"Yes and no?"

I look at him inquisitively, wondering what he means by that.

"I can fake it better? No, just kidding… sort of. You're right, I'm more confident in several aspects, like my music."

"You doubted yourself musically? You're kidding, right?"

"Sometimes, sure." He shrugs. "Not with the kidding but doubting… yeah. And there are times now when I still do, but with the success I've been blessed with, I feel vindicated, like all those hours, all those years I busted my ass trying to prove I could actually do this was all worth it."

"You've earned your success, Jase."

He places a kiss on my forehead. "Along with this time off."

"Three weeks holed up with me and you're telling me you're not the least bit antsy?"

"I've enjoyed every single second of it," he whispers in my ear, leaving another soft kiss on my temple. "However," he adds, standing back and swatting my behind. "You had no business carrying that basket of laundry."

"The hell I didn't, I'm fine," I argue, flipping him with a shirt before I fold it.

"We'll see how fine you are at your appointment today." He has a grin on his face when he says it, and I feel my stomach tighten.

"You're right… that is today."

And it's about fucking time. Being with him for the past three weeks without actually taking that final step is about to *kill* me. Anyone who thinks differently should try sleeping in the same bed, all curled up next to him, the scent of his skin enough to…

Oh, hell. Distracted again.

"You never know, the doc may tell you that you still have to take it easy." He pulls me into his arms, throwing the sweatshirt that I've had in my hands aside. He leans down, leaving light, wet kisses on my neck as he continues, "I don't know about you...but I've had fun being creative these past few weeks."

"Of course I have." I moan softly, my hands holding him to me, and I gasp as my body instantly responds. "Jase, please, you don't know...what that does... to me."

He laughs lightly in my ear. "Yes I do." One more kiss, one more touch of temptation. "God, Talli," he breathes, pulling back slightly, his hands shaking.

"We already know the doctor will say it's okay." I'm trying to reason with him, and he's just standing there staring at me with absolute hunger in his eyes... and shakes his head 'no'. "No?!" I ask, raising an eyebrow as he goes back to folding clothes. "Are you serious... *no?*"

"We have to get going soon." His voice is tight, his pants even tighter.

"I don't think—"

"I get you up in that bed, Christine, and you're not going anywhere the rest of the day." His head is down, eyes looking up at me, and I feel my knees start to go weak.

"Is that so?"

"Go...get ready." He points up the stairs.

"Help me?" I ask, smiling innocently. I feel my pulse quicken as he reaches for me, expertly pulling my shirt over my head. He tosses it to the side, still holding me under his intense gaze.

"Go," he repeats, his voice lower. I step closer to him instead.

"Is that all?"

He reaches around with one hand, unclasps my bra, and pulls it forward and off my arms, adding it to the shirt on the floor. I don't cover myself and instead take another step closer.

"Go." He still holds my gaze, refusing to move even when I pull his shirt up slightly, pressing myself to him.

"Come with me."

"Fuck, Talli," he mutters through clenched teeth, his eyes sliding shut.

"Exactly," I whisper, kissing his chest.

"No." The word is shaky, but his hands are on me, one of them tangling in my hair, pulling my head back slightly to give him perfect access as he kisses me, leaving me breathless. "I don't want...to fuck you, Talli," his words are hot in my ear. "I want... to make..." He growls as the phone began to ring, interrupting us.

Stupid thing is always interrupting us.

"Ignore it." I pull him into another passionate kiss to keep him from walking away.

"You know we shouldn't," he says, stepping back. He clears his throat, before giving me one last warning look. "Go...get ready."

I stick out my bottom lip as he answers the phone, attempting to not sound hot and bothered. "Wait, you're... answering my phone now?"

"Quit your bitching, woman, and go get ready," he says to me, pointing at the stairs again. I stick my tongue out at him and start walking up the stairs slowly, listening to his side of the conversation. "Over at Tish's? Tonight? Um..."

"What's over at Tish's?" I asked, turning towards him.

"Pete," he replies. "And Jaden. Oh, and Cass and... Derrick?" I smile warmly in response to his words. "Well, judging by her face the answer is yes."

"You shouldn't have rejected me," I tease, continuing up the stairs.

"Hey! I so did not..." he calls out after me, then quickly adds into the phone, "Dude, sorry, I didn't mean to yell in your ear. What time, then?"

I had already showered this morning so getting ready merely consists of changing clothes and touching up the hair and makeup. In no time I am going back down the stairs deftly, as if the accident had never happened at all. Jase has also changed clothes, looking casual but oh so comfortable. He smiles at me, grabbing a baseball hat and his sunglasses as I walk up to him.

"Hello, beautiful." Another kiss to my forehead. I'll never tire of them. "I told them we'd be by shortly after your appointment."

"But...but..."

"I know, we have somewhere else to go first. Do you have everything?"

I check my tote bag, making sure all of my provisions are present. "Yes, I do."

"Are you sure?" he asks, and I bite my bottom lip as I try to think of what he is implying I am missing.

"I...think?"

He holds up my keys that have been sitting on the back of the couch and I grin at him sheepishly.

I guess some things never do change.

"Come on," he says, putting his arm around me and urging me forward. "Let's go hear some good news."

"I've had three weeks of good news," I comment, feeling him smile against my temple as he leaves a soft kiss there.

"Hows come you never let me drive?" I am asking as we leave my doctor's office.

"Hows come? Hows...come? Don't you have a 4.0?" Jase peers over at me as he cranks the ignition. "As in... your bachelors, all that medical jargon, and..."

"Quit avoiding the question," I cut him off.

"Ask properly and maybe I'll answer," he replies with a smile, pulling out of the parking spot with ease after glancing at the directions I have written down.

"Never mind," I say dreamily. "This way I can watch you."

This could easily become one of my favorite past times. He looks so at ease behind the wheel and watching his face as he concentrates on the road is pure heaven. There is just something about it, just like there is just something about the way his hands rest on the steering wheel, or the way his legs are slightly apart, his right thigh flexing just so when he steps on the brake. And of course, he always catches me staring at him and either makes goofy faces or starts giving me that come-fuck-me stare.

He's far too good at that.

Today he is smiling devilishly, reaching over and cranking the stereo as my most loathed song comes over the airwaves. "Hey!" I swat at his hand and change the station, laughing along with him.

"No hitting the driver."

"Says who?"

"Says me, and it's according to the rules...that I just made up. So there." He sticks his tongue out, never taking his eyes off the road.

"So there?" I roll my eyes at him. "How old are you again?"

"Old enough to behave myself until I get you home."

Hellooooo come-fuck-me stare. This man is going to torture me today. I feel my cheeks flushing with color, my pulse quickening slightly.

"Told you they'd clear me today." I feel vindicated somehow.

"No, he said he doesn't want you going back to work for a couple more weeks."

Oh picky, picky. "We didn't discuss anything about work."

"You said you'd be cleared, they said you couldn't go back to work yet, so..." He shrugs.

Whatever, Warner. "You just don't want to admit I was right."

"Don't put words in my mouth," he says, still grinning.

"I could put more than words in your mouth."

Again with vindication as his cheeks start turning pink.

"Talia Christine, I told you..." His hands are gripping the steering wheel a little tighter now. "If I'd gotten you up in that bedroom..." He steals a sideways glance at me. "We'd still be there."

Oh fucking hell. Okay, composure Talli. And two can play that game.

"Promises, promises," I murmur, reaching over and lightly tracing the outline of his ear.

"*Christine...*"

"You're right, you're right." I smile and face forward in my seat. Score one for me. "Besides, we have a couple places left to go first. Then..." It is my turn to glance sideways at him. "You're all mine."

"Eh, promises, promises." He laughs when I swat his arm again as we continue on to our first destination.

He pulls into the lot, his choice of parking spot available. "It isn't very busy during the week... unless..." My voice trails off as I looked out. "Nope, looks like it's fairly quiet here."

"It's beautiful." Jase steps out of the car and stretches just a little.

"Isn't it?" I pull the tote bag out, placing it on my shoulder. "You ready?"

"As ready as I'll ever be."

We walk hand in hand down the small path that has started growing over. I haven't been able to make the trek since the accident, but today...well, this day is special.

I still can't believe Jase has agreed to it.

It means more to me than he will ever know.

I kneel down and kiss the headstone as I always do. "Hi Mom, hi Dad." I sit down and pat the ground beside me. Jase sits down, places an arm around me, and kisses my temple softly. I lean against him, breathing in the scent of the fresh flowers that are placed on the grave.

"Looks like Lisa's been here, too," he remarks, and I smile.

"Or one of the others...but yeah, I'd like to think it was her." I reach out and gently touched them. "There's even a couple lilies in there."

"I think they'd be happy the two of you are getting along so well."

"Oh, I know they are." I turn to smile at him. "This is it, right where I was sitting that day...when I told you I was so happy that you called me. You know, when we finally started..."

"…talking again," he finishes for me when my voice trails off, wiping a stray tear that has escaped and ran down my face.

"I would just bring a book, my coffee, and sit up here every chance I got. Or, I'd just…think, you know…about my mistakes, and what I needed to do to fix them. Sometimes," I smile as he kisses my cheek. "Sometimes I would talk to them, and I swear they were listening."

"What were you doing that day?"

"Talking," I admit with a soft smile. "I was talking to them about you."

"About me?" He blinks a couple times before I continue.

"Yes, about you. About how I missed you, how I missed talking to you. How I missed… everything about you."

"You don't have to miss that anymore." His voice is barely above a whisper when he says it.

I lean towards him, cupping his face in my hands just before I kiss him. I can't find any other way to show him how much I love him, at least not at this exact moment.

"Young lady, not where your parents can see us," he teases after I pull back.

"Yeah, yeah, whatever." I can't stop the smile as I reach into the tote bag and pull out a large photo album.

"What's this?"

"This…" I open to the front page, an older picture of my entire family smiling up at us. "…is my dad, James."

"Is that you on his lap?" Jase asks, and I nod through my tears. "God, you look just like him."

"Thank you," I say, glowing with pride. "And this is my mom."

"Elizabeth," he says with a smile. "Now I have good memories of that name…oh, wait… her eyes! They're the same color as yours. She's beautiful, Talli."

"She would have eaten you up with a spoon." Jase laughs at my comment before I continue. "And you know Lisa. She's the oldest."

"She had a sour puss look on her face then, too."

"She was probably mad at Shelly. That's..." I point at her. "Her. She isn't much younger than Lisa. And there's Jeff, and Eric...that's one's Eric."

"That pipsqueak?"

"That pipsqueak is about 6' 5" now." Jase's eyebrows disappear under his bangs. "Don't worry, he's a bug wuss."

"That's nice to know."

"And this is Anna. She's only about a year or so older than me...yeah, just over a year older."

"Damn, your parents were busy."

"I don't think they watched much television," I agree. My eyes linger over that family photo another moment, the nostalgia more comforting than painful, before turning the page.

"So you don't really speak to any of them?" Jase asks. "I mean, aside from Lisa now?"

"No," I reply, my voice wistful as I look at the old photographs. "Lisa had kinda taken me in as I got older. She and Shelly always argued, just like I always argued with Anna. So it was Shelly and Anna, and me and Lisa. Oh, and Jeff and Eric, when they weren't trying to kill each other."

"Looks like your dad was a big Rocky fan," Jase comments, looking at another page of Dad with the boys. Just before his diagnosis we had gone on a trip to Philadelphia, and there they were, all three of them on the top of the steps with their Rocky pose.

"Oh, yeah. From what I was told, I was named after the actress who played Adrian. You know, since Mom wouldn't let him actually name me Adrian."

"Talia Shire," Jase says with a grin. "So, he almost got his wish."

"I have hated my name from day one."

"Who doesn't?"

"True, true... but Anna couldn't say it, so she called me Talli. And it stuck." I crinkle up my nose. "You have no idea the teasing it got me in elementary school. Of course, no one would have called me that if she hadn't."

"The bitch."

"Absolutely."

"I was kidding," Jase says, nudging me softly.

"So was I, so was I." I turn the page again, unable to stifle a giggle at the pictures of me getting into Lisa's makeup.

"I bet she was pissed."

"Actually... no." I sigh... not a burdened sigh, but one full of memories. "I was only eight or so...I think? She was a senior in high school."

"Damn, they did have you all close."

"Told you so. Lisa stayed while she was in college. I was thirteen when she gave me my first beer."

"Thirteen?"

"Yeah." Back then it had seemed so cool, but now... now as an adult, now that I see these kids running around trying to be an age they'll reach all too quickly, I wish I'd cherished my childhood instead of squandering it. "I had grown up way too fast...I think we all did. We had to." My voice trails off again as I am lost in the memories.

Jase laughs and asks questions, and I answer them the best I can, alternating between laughter and tears. Little by little I introduce him to my absent family, telling the stories that have shaped my life. I don't know which means more to me, the fact that he is listening and seems truly interested, or that he is holding me, comforting me when I need it so badly.

Towards the back of the album, we start getting into pictures from *that* era... the one where my time was spent split between Ohio and Indiana, when Dad was near the end.

"Wow." Jase actually seems rendered speechless. "Wow, I remember..." His fingers trace the page, looking at the pictures of me then. I seemed to always dress provocatively, always have that same pout on my face.

"My mom called that 'The Look.' I guess I can see why now."

"You never glared at me like that," he says. "Not directly at me, anyway. But I remember that look. God, Talli... I... I *really* remember you now."

"You were…" I take a deep breath before continuing. "Jase, you were the only person I could talk to, and I mean *honestly* talk to. No, I know I wasn't honest…the whole saying it was Mom thing… but…" I smile at him through my tears. "The boy with the beautiful eyes," I say softly, noticing the tears there.

"It was the same for me." He tucks a stray curl behind my ear, the sweet gesture tugging at my heart. "That's what was so different…is what's so different, even now."

How in this world did I get so lucky? I must have some guardian angel up there that sent him to me.

Or… perhaps… two of them.

But I'm not quite done with the photo album.

"One last one," I say, my voice soft as I turn the page. "Lisa gave this to me when I was staying with her."

I watch his face as he glances down at the photograph, one edge bent even in its protective cover. I can feel his body tense as he recognizes the scene, that old hospital waiting room we'd both spent hours on end in. There, in the far corner, huddled together are two kids in their teens—one a thin boy with wild hair, the other a young girl with far too much makeup and clothes that fit like a glove. They are facing each other, holding hands slightly between them, and smiling…glowing as if one had said something insanely funny and they both got it.

"Talli…that's…that's *us*." His eyes are wide with wonder.

"Lisa just happened to have a camera that night," I continue, my lower lip trembling as I watch a tear fall down his face. That time had been difficult for the both of us, but seeing this, now… I understand exactly what he's feeling. "She said it was…" I take in a shaky breath. "She said it was the only time she remembered me smiling back then, and she was so surprised she wanted…a memory."

"I don't remember smiling much then," he says softly. "Except with you." Our eyes meet then, and we sit in silence, the memories in the air between us. "This…" He points at the picture without looking down. "*This* is what I'm talking about. And I meant what I said when I told you I'm happy we didn't know at first. This proves it, Talli. This proves that something…something bigger than us knew what to do when our paths crossed, then and now. That without even trying, without expecting anything, we…connected." He shrugs again, even through his tears. "We're right where we're supposed to be."

All of this coming from a man who swears up and down he doesn't believe in fate.

And he says it to a girl who doesn't believe in it, either.

Until now.

I am where I am supposed to be. I am with who I am supposed to be with.

"I love you, Jase," I whisper as he pulls me in for a kiss, the breeze slightly blowing over us. "And I'm going to throw your phone in a fucking lake if it keeps interrupting us."

"Hey, hey, watch your language around your parents," he teases, pulling his ringing phone out of his pocket.

"What are they gonna do?" I ask, the rumble of thunder in the distance answering me. "Crap, sorry," I whisper, patting the headstone, making Jase laugh as he answers his phone.

"Hey, what's up?" He pulls me close with his free arm, holding me to him as he talks with his brother. "Yeah, yeah, her appointment's done. Talli's…" He pauses, pulling back slightly to look at me. "Pete, she's perfect."

Perfect?

I lean in and kiss him, teasing his lips as his brother continues talking. Jase pulls back, shooting a warning look at me before saying, "We'll be there in just a little bit. We had something to do first."

I am still grinning when he hangs up his phone. "What?" I ask innocently.

"Get your things together, woman," he says, his half-smile getting to me as it always does. I giggle like a fucking schoolgirl, damn him, as I close the photo album and lift it to place in my tote bag. A tiny slip of paper slides out and falls to the ground as I do so. Jase picks it up, eyeing it suspiciously while I continue to zip up the bag.

"What?" I ask as he looks between the paper and me.

"Talia...um...your answering machine code..."

"Oh, shut up about the code already! I told you I made it something easy so I wouldn't forget it, and I forgot it! I'll just have to check all messages from home, and...what are you doing?" He is dialing a number on his phone, grinning from ear to ear.

"Testing a theory," he replies, that tiny slip of paper still in his hand. He waits for just a moment, punches in four numbers, and waits just a moment more before roaring with laughter.

"What?" I ask, confused. He is doubled over, holding his side when he hands his phone to me. I hear a message that is left on my home answering machine just barely over his laughter. "How did you..." My question is cut short when he hands the piece of paper to me, wiping the tears from his eyes as I read my writing.

EASY- 3279

3-2-7-9.

My code.

Easy.

"Oh, for fuck's sake," I mutter as I stand up, hanging up his phone and holding it out for him. "Are you gonna spend the rest of the day laughing at me, or are you gonna come with me to Tish's?"

"Oh come *on*, it's funny!" he exclaims, standing quickly and scooping me up into his arms. I am giggling—again with the giggling—as he swings me around. The breeze has picked up considerably at this point, and we both notice the approaching dark clouds.

"Come on, giddy boy, let's get going before we're caught in the rain."

"Would you mind being caught in the rain?" he asks, his eyes still full of laughter as we begin the walk back to my car.

"With you? Wouldn't mind it at all. Why?"

"Just checking." He places my tote bag in the back seat and opens my car door, bowing slightly as I got in.

"Oh, it's getting deep here," I tease. He smiles then, closing my door and walking around to the driver's side. Once secure in his seat, both of our seatbelts fastened, he starts the car and pulls out of the lot.

"Hey," he begins as he drives towards Tish's house, "hows come I have to drive all the time?"

"Hows come?" I asked, raising my eyebrow. "Hows...come? Hellooooo, what kind of vocabulary is that?"

"I'm just sayin," he replies with a wink and a smile, and our back-and-forth continues all the way to our next destination.

CHAPTER 46

The atmosphere at Tish and Mark's house is full of energy. There are pizza boxes open on the table, paper plates beside them, and everywhere I look there is someone else to say hello to, give a hug to, share the latest story with. It is almost like old times, minus Tish's expanding waistline and Cass having an actual boyfriend. Oh, and me.

I am most definitely different.

That feeling of being disconnected? Yeah, it doesn't exist anymore. I'm not living my life from a bubble, staying on the outside and looking in. I've learned to enjoy my life, learned to accept my differences and instead of using them to hold myself aloof, I embrace them, the same way my friends had embraced me to begin with. It's just that now…

Now I let them.

"Easy? Seriously?" Pete is asking Jase as I pass by.

Really? "Oh, come on, you're so not talking about that now."

"But…it's funny!" Jase replies since Pete can't due to being doubled over with laughter.

"It's not that funny." Of course my smile gives my lighthearted mood away. Pete catches me with one arm as I try walking away from them and gives me a quick hug and a kiss on the cheek.

"Easy there, little man," Jase says, pulling me close. "Go grab Jaden for some action, Talli's off limits."

And Jase has changed too. Mr. Arms-Length is getting possessive? Who would have thought?

"Okay, get me out of the middle of this testosterone field here," I say with a laugh, kissing Jase before stepping back. "Did you see where Tish went to?"

"Basement, I think," Pete replies.

"Are you doing okay?" I ask him, and he smiles.

"Yeah, I'm good."

"Aunt Talli," Moira says, poking her head through the door that leads to the basement. "We're watching the DVD."

"The DVD? What...oh, the DVD?" I ask, grinning as I follow her down.

"What tape is this you speak of?" Jase's voice is soon filling the finished basement as he takes the steps two at a time. "Oh...fuck, no, turn this off." We laugh as he realizes we are watching the compilation DVD that Moira had made of Jase's televised performances and interviews.

"See this?" I point at the screen, during his infamous 'Emphatically yes' answer. "That's how I knew it was you on the phone."

"Oh, is that why you dumped your purse?" Cass asks with a giggle, and I nod.

"She didn't even tell us it was you." Tish is sitting in her big black recliner rubbing her slightly bulging tummy.

"Why the hell not?" he asks, turning towards me.

"To keep you all to myself, duh," I quip, one tap on his butt as I pass him. He grabs my arms and pulls me to him, and as he presses himself up against my back I can feel my body start to sway.

"As soon as we're home," he whispers just as Tish is saying something else that I completely miss.

"Promise?" I whisper back, feeling him smile against my neck.

"Helloooooo, are you two still with us?" Tish asks.

"Hmmm?"

"Mom was talking about all I had to hear was, like, two seconds of him talking to know who it was," Moira catches us up.

"Oh, that." I smile at the memory. "Yeah, that's another one they won't let me live down."

"And yet you're standing there with a smile on your face." It is Jaden who makes the comment from her place on the couch that Pete is walking towards, and I shrug.

"I'm... happy."

Wow, what an admission.

What a lift off my shoulders that I so didn't know was there.

I am absolutely, unequivocally happy.

Although I miss my parents sometimes more than words can explain, the rest of my life has piece-by-piece fallen into place. I am mending fences with at least Lisa so my family ties are no longer severed; my friends are healthy, happy, thriving; the man I have dreamed of, longed for, cried over, has his arms around me, and I am full of love for him.

Life is officially good.

Jase and I stay longer there than either of us had intended on, or even anticipated. Night has settled in, along with the steady rain that taps against the windows, its sound hypnotizing as we all gather in the living room. At this point I can't tell you why we are all up there rather than in the basement, but here we all are. Jase and I are sitting next to each other on the floor, positioned so that I am in his arms, his back leaning up against one of the speakers. He reaches over with one hand, his long fingers entwining with mine, his eyes watching our hands, a smile softening his features. He glances over and catches me watching him, my whole body reacting as his eyes drop to my lips just before he kisses me.

"I love you," I whisper as he kisses the tip of my nose.

"Are you ready?" he whispers back.

"I'm always ready for you." His eyes slide shut at my admission, and when he opens them again the sheer heat from his gaze is nearly tangible. "Are you ready?" I ask.

I can't quite comprehend where this sweet smile comes from that crosses his face right at this moment. "Yes," he says. "Yes... I'm ready. Let's get the hell out of here."

I hug each of my friends just a little tighter that night as we say goodbye; my appreciation for life, and those precious to me, has grown in leaps and bounds over the past few months. "Tish, are you sure you're okay?" I ask her. She is the last one I am saying goodbye to, and we're standing by the front door.

"I'm wonderful," she replies. "And it looks like you are, too."

"Pretty damn close." I hug her tightly.

"No matter what, you better promise you'll be here when this baby's born."

I pull back, confused. "Why would you say that?"

"Just call it a... hunch."

"You and your damn hunches." Her eyebrow raises slightly, and I recall how each of her hunches have come true. "Hunch about what, anyhow?"

"Pete said he'll give us a shout tomorrow, we'll 'do lunch' or whatever before he goes back," Jase says as he walks up to us. "And you, gorgeous." He gives Tish a kiss on the cheek. "If you need anything you let us know."

"Absolutely," she agrees, smiling at him. "Right now, I need you to take care of her."

"Consider it done." He puts his arm around me and pulls me close as he opens the door.

"Oh, and Jase?"

"Yeah?"

"Turn into a royal douchebag like you were before, you will be missing your nether region's hardware."

Jase smiles but doesn't answer.

"We'll see each other soon," she says to me.

"Yeah, we'll... 'do lunch', or whatever," I say with a smile, walking out into the soft drizzle listening to Tish's laughter as she shuts the door behind us. Jase steps slightly ahead of me, taking me by the hand and guiding me around the parked cars and puddles of water to where we had parked on the street. "Do you want me to drive?"

"Nah, I got this." He opens my door for me, waiting until I am comfortably seated before shutting it.

"You're spoiling me, you know," I say as he settles into the driver's seat. "What am I going to do when you go back?" He silently glances over at me, his face serious. Instead of answering, he drives us back to my apartment complex with only the soft music playing. I keep my eyes on him, my body reacting to every slight movement he makes. What *is* it that is so damn sexy about how he drives? His hands, those long fingers lightly pressed against the leather, relaxing occasionally, his wrists visible from under his leather jacket. Oh... my, what those hands do to me, literally as well as figuratively. I shiver in anticipation, watching his silhouette as he drives.

He pulls into the parking lot of my apartment, easing the car into my spot by the stone steps that lead up to my front door. As if on cue, the skies open up and the rain cascades down the windshield. "Well... you afraid of melting?" he asks me, a smirk on his handsome face.

"Not in the least." One look from him and my breath catches in my throat. His eyes are skimming over my face, focusing on my lips, down further to the dip of my shirt before they return to my eyes. "Shall we?" One slight nod, one I almost miss, and I turn from him with a smile.

We open our doors and stepped out into the downpour, my clothes and hair instantly sticking to my skin. I can't remember a time I've felt more alive as I stretch my arms out and lay my head back, the rain washing down my face.

"What are you doing, woman?" he asks, walking around to my side of the car, his hair clinging to his face, already soaked from the rain.

"Dance with me!"

I hold my hand out to him and he takes it willingly, gathering me in his arms and twirling me around in the rain. I am laughing, carefree, blissful as we sway there, oblivious to the cold, the heat from our bodies more intensified with the wet clothing between us. We dance our way across the parking lot until we are under the light, laughing and spinning, his hand holding mine as he twirls me around.

And then he stops.

I open my eyes, blinking through the raindrops to see what is wrong, and the look on his face nearly makes my heart stop.

You know those moments? You know what I'm talking about; one of those moments, good or bad, that you know will stay with you throughout eternity, where you know your life is forever changed. This...this is one of those moments.

I know it.

He stands there in front of me, his face sobering, rain-streaked, his hair dripping with the rain that is still pouring down all around us. His breathing is becoming more labored, his hands shaky. He opens his mouth and shuts it quickly, closing his eyes tight for a brief moment before opening them again.

"Jase...what's..."

"I love you."

Oh... god...

"I love you, Talli," he says, gently cupping my face with his hands. "I love...everything about you...your eyes, those curls, fuck...those lips..."

I feel them start to tremble as he continues.

"I love how...unpredictable you are, I love how you call me on all my bullshit, I love that... I love that you understood me, that you waited for me..."

"Jase..."

"I love that I can talk to you, and that you... that you listen. I love that pout when you don't get your way, I love your smile, the one that lights up your whole face... and your laugh. I love your laugh, and... and what it does to me, what you do to me..."

"Jase, I..."

"Talia, I love you...above all others."

I feel my tears mix with the rain.

"I love you as if there was no tomorrow. Talia...Christine... I love you...like it's never..." He takes a deep breath, his fingers caressing my face. "I love you like it's never going to hurt."

He seals his confession with the sweetest kiss I've ever known, our lips parting, the softness, the emotion unmatched to anything I can recollect. My fingers are buried in his soaking wet hair, the kiss tastes of rain, mint gum, and promise. He steps back slightly, his breathing ragged, his eyes searing into me.

"I want to make love with you," he whispers against my lips as he kisses me again softly, then begins kissing down my throat.

"Yes..."

"Now."

"Yes..." I moan, holding him to me as he latches onto that spot where my pulse is hammering. He steps back then, steadying me slightly before he takes my hand and leads me up the steps to my front door. His hands are shaking as he uses the key, unlocking the door and pushing it forward roughly, dragging me in and pushing me against the wall as he kicks it closed behind us, his mouth on mine before that door clicks shut.

"Fuck, Talli," he moans between kisses as we move, peeling each other's clothes off as we go. "I...love you..."

"I love you," my reply is half-whimpered as I am making my way backwards up the stairs, his hands all over my near naked body.

"Even with..." He kisses my neck as we approach the bed, "...every time... these past three weeks... that I've watched you fly..." He moans as I push him on the bed, yanking his soaking jeans off, then reaches for me, pulling me down beside him on the bed. "All the times... I tasted you..." It is my turn to moan. He has all of my clothes off and is crawling up the bed, between my legs that he has parted easily. "Talli, I just wanted... to make love...with you..." He is pressed up against me then and we lay there for a moment, both of us knowing our lives will never be the same.

Silently he moves, our eyes and fingers locked as he presses himself into me slowly, my body adjusting to him, our labored breathing in unison. He lets out a soft sigh when he has filled me completely, his smile bright enough to light the darkened room. He leans down and captures my lips in a kiss as he begins to move, slowly at first as we savor each moment, his pace quickening as we lose ourselves in each other.

It is... different.

It is so very different.

He holds me to him as we move, each stroke hard, measured, binding us heart and soul. The kisses we share hold so much promise, so much emotion. His caresses on my skin are long, lush, the words whispered against my skin full of love. As I feel my release closing in on me, I arch my back, crying out against his lips. My legs circle around him, holding him to me as he continues to move, drawing it out, heightening the pleasure.

"Open...your eyes."

I hear his words and struggle to do so. Oh, it is so...so hard to...

"Talli... baby, please."

I open my eyes just as he reaches his own release, the ecstasy etched in his features just before he buries his face in the side of my neck... the moans that tear from his throat as he pushes hard, holding me to him as he stays there... it is the most intense experience I have ever been a part of. He trembles in my arms, his voice a whispered plea in the night, the way my name falls from his lips making me feel precious. Adored.

Loved.

And as he whispers in my ear how much he loves me, over and over while we drift to blissful slumber, I know I'll never have to wonder, never have to go a day without hearing those words again.

CHAPTER 47

The large manila envelope sits on my dining room table, opened, contents spread out for inspection. I have received said envelope two months after that wonderful night, the same day that Jase returns for a short visit while he takes a break from recording. We've spent just under four weeks apart... four sleepless, miserable, lonely, longing weeks... and don't even make it up the stairs when he walks through that door.

No words are exchanged between us as piece by piece our clothing is discarded on the floor, the apartment fills with moans and sighs as our hands seek and find the most sensitive places. When he lays me down on the couch, covering my body with his, I know the wait is finally over, but damn it has been so long it actually hurts when he thrusts hard and fast inside of me.

It hurts... so... damn... good...

I move my hips with his, matching him, moaning and whimpering at the sheer intensity of it all. And then... oh... then... he pulls one of my legs up, hooking it on his arm, his other hand braces on the arm of the couch using it for leverage as he pushes harder... and harder...

I cry out as wave after wave of the most exquisite pleasure I've ever known passes over me, I'm sure a few choice words leave my lips as I claw at his back, completely lost even as I feel his orgasm rip through him, filling me as he lays against my chest, trembling slightly in my arms.

Hot. Fucking. Damn.

That boy needs to come home like this more often.

Home? Oh... wait...

He pushes himself up, grinning down at me, his hair damp with sweat. "Hi, baby. I missed you."

He's too fucking cute for words.

I pull an oversized t-shirt and a thong on, deciding lying around naked is probably not too prudent at this point, and I pick up the discarded clothes to place them in the laundry. We've already discussed ordering in for dinner, and I can just see me lying there on that couch butt ass naked. Nope, isn't going to happen.

Jase is standing at my dining room table wearing his boxer briefs and pulling on a white button up shirt when he sees the papers.

"What's...this, Talli?" he asks, giving them a once-over before turning to me, looking so damn sexy buttoning his shirt that I completely miss his question. He waves his hand to pull me out of my daze.

"Hmm?"

"This...these papers." He picks one up, then places it back down, a frown crossing his face.

Oh, those. "It's a copy of the new lease."

"Yeah, I see that now."

Jase and I had many long talks when he'd stayed with me, about how wonderful it had been for us to have all that time together. He'd even stayed after I went back to work, helping out around the house...well, in his own way. As much as I love him, he's definitely not a neat freak. He would listen to my rants and raves about work, I'd listen to the beautiful music he was creating. When that dreaded call came and it was time for him to go, it was devastating. By the time he was walking out the door I was an absolute mess, and he wasn't much better. I was still taking intermittent gasps for air from crying so hard when he slammed the door and had begged me to go with him.

I couldn't.

I have obligations. I have my job, they are short-staffed as it is; my mother's estate is coming out of probate and many of her belongings have been left to me; Lisa and her husband have separated, and even with Jase here I've done everything I can for her and don't want to leave her at Shelly and Anna's mercy; Tish is still having a difficult pregnancy, and I have promised I'll be there for her at the drop of a hat if she needs me.

I just... couldn't.

The timing sucked.

We promised each other that when he came back on this break that we would talk about it, and I'm not breaking my promise to him. The fact still remains that my lease is up for renewal, and crunch time is coming fast. So, the papers sit on my dining room table, places highlighted that I need to pay closer attention to, and a short note beside them with Jase's arrival information.

"Jase..."

"We were ordering in, right?" he asks, turning away from the table, tousling his hair.

"Yes... did you want Chinese or pizza? Or, if you want, I could cook something." He shrugs in response, walking back into the living room and sitting on the far end of the couch. I watch as he silently, sullenly picks up the remote and turns on the TV, only a trace of a smile when he realizes the channel was still on Classic TV before he is frowning again. "Are you all right?"

"I'm fine."

Have I mentioned that no one on this Earth sulks or seethes with anger the way this man does? The fucker even has the audacity to look sexy when he does either one of them.

"All right, but this means you're at my mercy."

No response from him as I order the pizza, possibly because I am being nice and get the kind he likes, without even having to ask what it is. I pull a couple of beers out of the fridge, open them up and walk out to the living room. I hand him his and he takes it without a thank you or even a glance, drinking a good third of it in one gulp.

"Are you angry with me?"

He sighs. Well, at least that is somewhat of a response.

"Jase, I asked…"

"No, I'm not…" His hands gesture as he continues, "…angry. I'm not angry."

"Then what's wrong?"

He looks over at me, aggravation clearly showing in his features. "Talli, what the hell have we been talking about every chance we get?"

Ah. "About us… about me moving out there."

"Right. To be with me." He pointed at the table. "So what the hell is that?"

Shit… "It's an unsigned lease."

"For here, this…" There his hands go again. "This apartment, across the entire fucking country…don't give me that look! Almost then, okay? Almost across the entire fucking country."

"We never came to any decisions."

"No, *you* never came to any decisions. *You* couldn't decide, Talli. *You.*"

Really? "So on a whim, because all of a sudden you decide it's what we should do, I should drop everything?" I ask, my temper rising to the surface. "We don't even know if…"

"What the hell do you think we were doing before?" he asks, his voice rising. "What, because I didn't put in a change of address, we weren't cohabitating? That's nice to know, Talli, because I felt…"

He stops suddenly, as he always does before saying something he thinks he will regret. Beer still in hand he stands up and starts pacing, rubbing the bridge of his nose with his free hand. "It's funny," he continues. "I remember this one conversation we had, when you told me that when it was time for me to leave, you'd beg me to stay."

"I don't have the right to," I say softly. He stops and looks at me then; no tears, but the hurt is displayed all over his face.

"So...I don't... have the right to ask you to come with me, then? Is that what you're saying?"

Damn it! "No, that's not what I'm saying."

"Then what is it?" he asks. "You've already graduated. Is it... Lisa, or...or Tish? Talli, last time I checked they were adults, and they would be okay if you weren't here. I mean...shit, how many brothers and sisters do you have? And what about Jaden, or... or Cass? Can't Tish call on them?"

"Jase, that's not fair."

"Or is it the hospital? You're still working in the cardiac wing, aren't you?"

"Yes I am, you know I am."

"So what did they do all that time that you were out due to the accident?" Since I have no reply for that one, he continues, this time kneeling right in front of me. "Your parents are right here," he places his hand over my beating heart. "Everyone else is just a phone call, or a plane ride, away."

"Jase..."

"How have you been these last few weeks?" he asks suddenly, taking my hands in his, those eyes a deep green as his gaze holds me captive.

He's got me there. "Miserable." His features soften slightly at my admission, but he has to already know that's how I've been. How many times have I told him?

"I love you, Talia," he says, for about the thousandth time since he walked through my door an hour before. He smiles softly as his fingertips trace the outline of my lips. "So, you can tell me I'm absolutely crazy," he continues, mirroring his words from that long-ago message on my machine, "and I can say no...I'm just crazy about you."

"You don't fight fair."

His smile widens. "Good," he says, standing up and finishing his beer. "Geez, woman, I realize you're pretty much a nurse now and all, but the beer? Come on."

I know he isn't in near as good of a mood as he is pretending, perhaps for my sake, to be. He pulls on a pair of pants as the pizza delivery person knocks on our door, and since I am still only in a t-shirt and thong, Jase is nice enough to answer and pay...and throw in an autograph, of course. "Babe, your cover's blown. I didn't tell him not to say anything." Jase smiles at me as he brings in our dinner.

"My cover? What about yours?"

He shrugs. "I'm used to it. Scoot over, gimme the remote."

"Scoot...over...give you the remote? What the hell? I haven't said yes yet."

"Yet?" he asks, nudging me gently as he sits down, reaching over and prying the remote from my hand.

"Convince me," I say half-jokingly.

He sits there looking at me, his eyebrows doing that furrowing together that just drives me to the brink of insanity.

"Okay."

The word is soft but spoken in a way that causes a knot in my stomach. He sets his plate and the remote on the table and walks over to his bag.

"What are you doing?" I ask with a half-laugh, almost expecting him to have some sort of gag gift in there, something that I will find insanely funny to help laugh away all the tears I've cried the entire time he's been gone. Imagine my surprise when he pulls out a small wire bound notebook. Just as I am about to ask him what the hell he is doing bringing it back into my house, I realized this one is... different. Newer. Still beat up, but... but this one isn't the same notebook I had flipped through looking for even the slightest mention of my name.

He sits beside me, staring at that book for a long while. "I took this with me, out on the road," he says softly, still staring at it. "It was where I kept... everything; my thoughts, some lyrics... anything that caught my attention that I thought I should store for later. That's what it was supposed to be for, anyhow, and it's not that..."

He sighs, glancing over at me, and when our eyes meet, he doesn't look away. "I had one of these before, one that I wrote in during those lovely teenage angst-filled years." He flashes his half smile. "You knew that, though." One brief pause before he adds, "Kate told me you knew what was in it." For once my face doesn't flair at the mention of her name. "I never did tell you why you weren't mentioned, did I?"

"No, you didn't."

"It would have been...awkward at best." He watches his fingers trace the outline of the notebook in his hand. "I was writing that whole notebook for her, to show her how everything I did, everything I said was about her." His fingers stop and he looks at me. "But this... us... it wasn't about her. At all." He reaches over pushing a stray curl out of my eyes.

"I was honest with you, Talli. Completely honest with you. No, don't... don't feel guilty about all that shit, I understand," he stops me from interrupting him. "Just... I'm just trying to, I don't know... *explain*. For the first time that I could remember, it... god, Talli, it had nothing to do with Kate. It had to do with *you*. I wasn't with her at the time and..." He pauses, biting his bottom lip slightly before continuing. "And when I was with you, I didn't want to be... with her." The corner of his mouth turns up in a smile and he shrugs. "That's it. Pretty simple, no big drama, no conspiracy."

"I never said there was, dork," I reply, nudging him softly. "But what's... what's that?" I point at the notebook in his hand.

"This is mine," he says, still smiling. "So it wasn't written... *to* you." He gently places it on my lap. "If you would like."

I curl up next to him on that couch and spend the next two hours asking him to hand me yet another tissue as I read. I have my head on his chest listening to the soothing rhythm of his heart when I reach the day after we had come face-to-face, the day after we had destroyed that hotel room. The first line rips my fucking heart out.

'What have I done?'

Instead of an entry where he wished he'd never laid eyes or hands on me, here he was pouring his heart out to a sheet of paper. He wished he'd made me stay. He wanted to believe that I didn't get the messages. He had been so afraid of rejection... *rejection?*... that he didn't want to repeat what his messages had said. His heart... his heart was breaking, and he didn't know how to fix it. He wanted to call but was afraid to. Fuck... Everything... everything I had been feeling, the days of just going through the motions...

I read about how he'd move heaven and earth to be there after my mother died... and he had.

I read about... fuck, I read about how Kate had finally gotten in touch with him.

I read about his struggles to get to Vegas, actually laughing at his list of people that needed to die, the number one being some Chris Webber person.

I read about...after...

How one day, shortly before we started talking again, he'd had lunch with Kate. How it was so hard for him to explain, how he didn't think she'd understand that he couldn't go back, he couldn't be with her...

Not when his heart belongs to me.

I can't finish, I can't read another line I am so emotionally drained. Jase hasn't said a word while I read; I'm not even sure he is paying attention since he's found a rerun of James Slade's reality show... how could the name of it escape me right now? Jase is softly playing with my curls and staring at the television when I put the journal down.

"Jase..."

"You're right, Talli, it is completely selfish of me to just expect you to walk away from your life."

I wasn't expecting that.

With me stunned silent, he is able to continue without interruption. "This is your home, your life, your friends, your family. You wouldn't ask that of me and... it was presumptuous of me to think you'd be okay with just..." His voice fades away, his sentence unfinished as he stares at the TV screen.

"I'm sorry I made you angry," I say softly, my voice sounding odd due to my persistent crying.

"I wasn't angry, Talli," he disagrees and kisses the top of my head.

"Then what were you?" I asked. He waits a moment before answering.

"Hurt."

I sit up slightly, reaching over and turning his face towards mine. "Hurt?"

"I thought you were running, or pushing me away, or..."

"I'm not, I swear I'm not."

"It's okay, Talli." His smile is sad, and it breaks my heart a little more. "As long as you tell me we'll still have... this... it's okay."

"Why would you think that?" My tears start again, and he gathers me up to him, my head once again resting against his chest.

"No more tears, please," he whispers, rocking me gently. "You're breaking my heart."

"No...no, it's not like that."

"Let's...we'll... talk about it tomorrow, okay?" he asks. "Different day, different perspective. Deal?"

"Deal." I say, wiping my tears away. "Jase?"

"Yeah?"

"I love you."

"I love you, too."

We sit there curled up together in silence, flipping through different channels after that show was done, both of us deep in thought. Is he right? Am I running? Am I pushing him away? And... what about all the things he has said? Are they just excuses I am making up to keep this distance?

Can I stand another four... possibly even more... weeks without... this? Without his arms around me? Will I be content with his voice on the telephone?

The clock on the wall reads a resounding 12:01 am when I glance at it.

It is officially tomorrow.

"Jase?" I feel him jump slightly at the sound of my voice; we have been silent for so long.

"Yeah?"

"Could you make sure we're here when Tish's baby's born?"

His arms tighten slightly around me as he takes in a shaky breath. "Of course."

"I'll still get the right side of the bed?"

"Unless you're on top of me."

"Will you start putting that damn cap back on the toothpaste?"

"I don't know about that, woman," he draws out his words. "I am the king of my castle, you know."

"Oh, whatever."

"Whatever?" He pulls back, looking down into my eyes. "Whatever? I won't tolerate such insolence from you."

"You and your fucking ten-dollar words," I say with a roll of my eyes as I stand up. "Is that supposed to impress me?"

"It does impress you," he says matter-of-factly, following me as I head towards the stairs. "You love a man who uses his brain. You find it..." He bounds quickly up the stairs behind me, his breath hot in my ear, "...sexy."

I shiver in spite of myself and he laughs before hooking one arm around me and carrying me up the rest of the stairs to the bedroom. "You... are taking entirely too long, woman," he says as he places me on the floor by the bed. "Take your damn clothes off."

"Take my... listen here, Warner,"

"Mmmm, I love it when you talk to me that way," he teases, his hands under my shirt rubbing against my bare skin.

"Jase! Oh..." The last word is a breathless sigh as he begins teasing my neck with his teeth and tongue.

"Damn it, Talia, you've got to stop doing that to me," he breathes in my ear.

"Not on your fucking life."
He cradles my face in his hands, his eyes serious once more.
"I love you," he says, and my heart melts just a little more.
I know, beyond a shadow of any doubt, this is all I need.

THE EPIC-LOGUE

"Jeez, Moira, you act like you've never seen a baby before." Tish is teasing her, and it makes me smile.

"I can't help it, she's so cute!"

"Did you see those little toes?" Cass asks.

"What do you mean little? This child has monkey toes!" Jaden exclaims, leaning down and kissing the baby's head. I can't help but laugh.

"Hey...guys?" Jase's voice fills the room, and he is immediately verbally assaulted, the loud voices causing the baby to start fussing.

"Dude, out!" Tish has moved to where she can see him, he is still around the corner from me.

"What the hell! You know better!" Jaden yells, and I can see her put her arms out as if she is pushing someone.

"My eyes are covered! I see no nakedness!" Jase defends himself.

"No one's naked in here, dork," I call out to him.

"Damn."

"That doesn't mean you can come in here!" Cass squeaks.

"Well, quit hogging my daughter then!"

Our tiny four-month-old daughter is fussing in Moira's arms, her little hands balled into fists as she waves her arms above her. Jaden takes her out of Moira's arms, who pouts, "I'm not hogging her."

"More people arrived?" I ask, still around the corner, unseen by Jase.

"Yeah, Mom just got here…hi, baby girl…" I hear his voice soften as Jaden must have handed our daughter to him, and my heart swells. That baby has him wrapped every bit as much as he has me wrapped. It is a beautiful thing.

"Don't be gone too long, she'll need to eat before I get poured into this dress."

"And no bringing her back in here yourself!" I hear Lisa snap at him as she walks in. "Just have your mother bring her in."

"Quit yer bitchin'," Jase is muttering as his voice fades away. Lisa is still smiling when she walks around the corner.

"Jeff and Eric's boutonnieres are in place, and they're both ready," she says, then stops short as she looks at me. Tish is still working on my curls, but my makeup is already done, which means absolutely no crying for me.

"So they're still willing to do this?" I ask.

"Well, Eric's already a blubbering mess."

"He's such a wuss," I hear Tish say as she is finishing my hair.

"But they're both all for this," Lisa continues. "One on each side of you."

I can't help but smile. Everything is falling into place. Almost all of my family is here, and none of them have openly admitted to backing out of anything… yet.

Don't think that way, Talli. Everything will work out. Today is your day… yours and Jase's.

"Everything's ready," Jaden says as she walks up to me. "Anna and Shelly are here. Don't worry, as soon as they saw the baby, they made a beeline for her."

Anna and Shelly, too? Hot damn.

All of my brothers and sisters are here.

"With all those rock stars out there, I think they'll be more interested in flirting than traumatizing you. Oh, and thanks, all of you... you know, for warning me how drool-worthy James Slade is," Lisa said, raising her eyebrow. "It's a good thing he has a girlfriend."

"James made it?" I ask, and Jaden nods. Good... Jase had told me how difficult it was to see his friends, and with James being the most successful of all of them, their time together is short and fleeting at best. His friends Brody and Max had also arrived with their girlfriends, and he'd been having the time of his life.

"And," she adds, "security is working double time today."

"Man," Cass speaks up, "you know it's love when he agreed to have the wedding here."

We are back in Ohio, not far from where I lived, where I'd spent most of my childhood. This is the same church my parents had married in. The pastor officiating is the son of the man who had performed my parents' wedding, and the members of the church had unanimously agreed to allow us to hold it there.

Today is just...

Perfect.

"Knock knock," Jase's Nan's soft voice fills the room, followed quickly by the baby's cry. "I think my great-granddaughter's hungry, and last I checked no one out there can feed her."

"Okay, lady, other than your dress, you're ready," Tish's words barely register as Nan gently places the baby in my arms. She is squirming, her mouth seeking out nourishment, my heart melting as she peers up at me with her beautiful blue eyes.

"Can you give us a moment?" I ask everyone, and they all know what I mean. I'd asked for this—to be ready, minus the dress, a little early so I could have a moment's peace with my little girl.

I sit on the couch in that dressing room cradling her as she eats, staring in wonder at the miracle in my arms. Her hair is a soft blonde—Nan said Jase's hair had been blonde also, only for a brief time—and the light fuzz is sticking up around her headband. I laugh softly, recalling Jase and Pete's discussion about 'brain squeezers' as they call them. As I laugh, she opens those beautiful eyes. They are the shape of Jase's and the color of mine. Every time she lays those eyes on her Daddy, her face will fill with joy, and her lips—those perfect lips, the carbon copy of Jase's—will curl up in a smile.

"Well, this is it, baby girl," I say softly. "We made it; we're doing it. Today...today, your Mommy and Daddy are getting married." I blink back the tears that threaten. "And Mommy can't cry because Tish will kill me for ruining my makeup." I pause, looking at that precious face. "I still can't believe this is happening, like it's some kind of... dream. Married. Not to say we haven't tried getting married before, but that's another story for some other time."

I continue talking to her in hushed soothing tones as she eats, stopping as she needs to, having her switch sides midway through. She is dozing intermittently towards the end, and when she is finally finished, I lay her down beside me as I fix my nursing bra.

A soft knock sounds at the door just before Kaitlyn Evans enters. "Hi!" she says with her warm smile. "Is she about ready?"

"She's done," I reply, smiling down at my daughter's sleeping form.

"She's getting so big!" Kate gently scoops the baby into her arms, carefully so not to wake her.

"Thanks for doing this," I say as I glance at the clock.

"For what, holding her during the ceremony? Yeah, that's such a chore."

"I'm just still so... you know, I don't want her passed around, or people getting annoyed with her, and I don't think..." I pause as I unzip the bag containing my dress, "...that it would be prudent for me to be holding her while I'm up there."

"Talli, it's an honor," she says, still smiling down at the baby. "I'll let the girls know you're ready for the dress."

"The dress," I mutter. "What the hell, I hate long dresses! And now I have one that requires...help to get in."

"I could always go pick you up some little black number."

"Ha ha, very funny."

Kate is laughing as she gives me a one-armed hug. "Thank you, Talli," she whispers in my ear.

"For what?" I ask, watching her walk towards the door. She turns around and flashes her brilliant smile.

"For proving me wrong."

One thirty in the afternoon—to start on the upswing—I step out into the hallway to greet my brothers. There they both stand in black tuxes; Jeff, the mean cuss that is barely taller than me next to Eric, the giant teddy bear. I step between them, hooking arms, holding onto each of them for support.

"If you start skipping and singing about some damn wizard, I'm kicking your ass," I hear Jeff mumble, and I laugh, grateful for the ease in tension.

I spy Jackie checking the hallways before he re-enters the auditorium, and when his eyes meet mine, the big burly man breaks into a fatherly smile.

"It's about damn time," he whispers as my brothers and I approach the doorway.

I know exactly what he means.

My eyes close as I hear the wedding march start, and I pray I have the strength to do this without falling apart. Since walking actually requires having my eyes open to do so without falling on my face, I slowly open my lids, drinking in the sight of what has to be a dream.

The room has been transformed into a sea of white, candles and lilies everywhere. The soft smells calm my fraying nerves as my eyes scan over the crowd. For merely close friends and family, the church is absolutely packed. I saw all three of my sisters sitting together with their spouses, including Jack who is still trying to reconcile with Lisa. Iris and her husband are there, sitting right behind the newly-engaged Cass and her soon-to-be husband Craig. Speaking of Craig...Dr. John Craig is there also with his very young, very pregnant wife. I smile at Tish, who is trying to see if I've cried my makeup off. Kiera is on Mark's lap with Moira beside him holding her two-year-old brother, Aiden.

Across the way, James Slade is holding his girlfriend's hand, and they sit in the same aisle with Brody Harris, photographer extraordinaire, Max, my caterer, and their girlfriends. Behind them are other assorted musicians, authors... Derek Gentry? Entertainment mogul Derek Gentry is at our wedding... this is unreal. Kaitlyn holds my daughter safe in her arms, Jason Brooks beside her. Jason Brooks...now that's a man who knows a thing or twelve about persistence...

All of my Jase's immediate family is there, including both of his parents, their spouses, and all of his siblings, half and step. I know for Jase that having them in his life helps ease the loss of his brother. Speaking of brothers, Pete is standing beside Jase, winking sideways at Jaden, my maid of honor, who is blushing ever so slightly.

Not on my wedding day, babies.

And Jase... heaven help me, my knees get weak when I see him. He is dressed all in white, his hair perfectly disheveled, just a hint of stubble on his face, and his eyes...the most beautiful eyes, the same eyes that haunted me for years, are calling me home.

At the exact moment that I wish my parents were here, a small stream of sunlight peers through the single window near the ceiling, shining down next to Jase where I will soon stand. "Showoffs," I whisper to the sky just as I begin my journey down that aisle.

Lisa's backyard looks like a scene straight out a storybook, just as I'd always imagined it would. White twinkling lights cascade around, the warm glowing light illuminating all of our guests. The soft breeze carries the scent of the dozens of lilies that are placed on every table, and a collective "awwww" had gone through the crowd when Jase picked one and placed it in my hair, tucking the shortened stem behind my ear just before our first dance as husband and wife. Much champagne is flowing, although I don't touch a bit of it, so I am handed a glass of sparkling cider as Pete stands.

"A toast!" he exclaims, raising his glass. "Not to worry; I'm not as hateful during these as *some* people," he added, a smirk on his face as he looks at me.

"At least you know who's gotten married!" Jason Brooks pipes up, and all of us that know the story share a good laugh. That fucker just has to get his digs in, doesn't he?

"But seriously," Pete continues, "even though meeting Talia also meant meeting Jaden, which put me in this town where my ass was nearly annihilated..." Again with the laughs as Jaden cozies up to him, softly kissing the scar on his neck. "Oh, hell, what was I saying?"

"Annihilation!" someone calls out.

"Annihilation, right... um... well, shi...er, crap, sorry Mom." He grins sheepishly at his mother, who merely smiles and shakes her head. After the laughter has died down a bit, Pete continues.

"Jase, my brother... I've known you since I was born. You have tormented me, tortured me, taught me all of your bad habits... blackmailed me into doing your chores when you caught me getting into your stash of alcohol, which was technically Nan's."

"I knew he'd throw that in," Jase whispers.

"You became Mr. Moody Rock Star, calling me at all hours of the night, guilting me if I couldn't stay on the phone..."

"He's the king of the guilt trip!" Brody calls out, and Jase raises his hand as if to accept his crown.

"And then, nothing. No calls. It's like I..." Pete mock-wipes his eyes. "It's like I didn't exist anymore. No, seriously, he started phone-stalking some chick he didn't even know, and the next thing he takes my ass out and gets me in trouble for dancing on a bar...I cussed, didn't I? Fuck..shit... sorry Mom." My cheeks hurt from smiling already, but I can't stop the laugh that comes from me.

"And now... um... ah... Cleveland. Cleveland, the city that rocks, the city where my brother lost his heart... to you." Pete holds his glass out to me. "And I had to hear about it for fucking *ever* until he had the nads to tell you... shit!"

"Sorry, Mom, yeah yeah I know," his mother quips above all the laughter. Pete hides his face as he tries to retain control over his obvious case of the man-giggles, then he crooks his neck and straightens his tie.

"So, for real..." Pete wipes a stray tear. "A toast! To Jase and Talia..."

"And to Body English!" another heckler calls.

"That little black dress!" Oh, that sounds like James Slade.

"Tops Migraine and diet cola!" Iris adds.

"Hell, ibuprofen and sports drinks! Woo hoo girls' night!" Cass exclaims, to which there is scattered applause from the women, myself included.

"To Classic TV!" Who was that? Was that Derek Gentry? Shit, doesn't he *own* that station? Those who know Jase and I well—which is everyone here—share a laugh over our obsession with that channel.

"To Not John and Not Telling!" Moira chimes in.

Indeed.

"To wrong numbers!" Dr. John Craig shouts from the back, his glass of champagne raised, causing the crowd to erupt in laughter and applause.

"Amen to that," Jase whispers softly in my ear. I couldn't agree more.

"Hell yeah! To ... to wrong numbers!" Pete finishes at last, "and how they've blessed us all." He holds out his glass towards us. "Salut!"

After taking a drink from our glasses, Jase takes mine from my hand and places it on the nearest table. He cradles my face in his hands, his eyes changing to the most beautiful shade of green, full of promise. "I love you, Talia Warner," he whispers just before he covers my lips with his, giving the crowd what they are cheering for, leaving me absolutely breathless.

The reception is still in full swing as I change into dark clothing. I have just fed the baby and she is laid back on the bed of the room I had once stayed in, her legs kicking, her eyes wide. I hear the door open, the noise filtering in as Jase enters the room. "What are you doing?" he asks, eyeing me warily.

"Trust me?" I ask, placing a soft kiss on his lips. "I just have to do this one thing."

"Do you think you can actually get out of here?" he asks, knowing the paparazzi has most of the neighborhood staked out.

"Yeah, I think so." I slip my dark shoes on.

Jase is smiling softly down at our beautiful little girl, who lets out a tiny squeak when he comes into view. "Hello, baby girl," he croons to her as he always does. The contrast of such a tiny child being held in his big strong hands always fascinates me. "I'm so happy you're here," he continues talking to her as he cradles her close to him. "I'm happy...and I'm grateful that you're okay... that everything..." he continues, looking up at me, "is okay."

"I think someone was looking out," I say softly, closing the small distance between us, putting my arms around Jase.

"And you have her all dressed in black, too?"

"She'd glow in white," I pointed out.

"Dun dun dunnnnn... stealth baby." I have to laugh as he bounces her, a small squeak coming from her as he does his faces and voices that always keeps her amused. "So you're taking her?"

"Of course. We'll be back."

He helps us make our escape to the neighbor's house, out their back door, through their yard across to the next street over where Cass's vehicle sits, a car seat strapped in and ready. Once the baby and I are secure, we are on our way, winding through the streets to the open road I know so well.

I have to park further away than usual but walking onto the grounds isn't difficult at all. I hold my daughter close to me, wishing I'd brought a blanket as the night air is starting to get cool. As I walk up the hill and follow the path, I can almost feel them with me, watching me.

"Hi Mom, hi Dad," I say, kissing their headstone as I sit in the grass that is moist with dew. "I'm sorry it's been so long... but guess what! Since you cannot guess I will tell you. Today was my wedding. Yep, we did it... Jase and I were married today. Same church as you. Oh, and I brought you a surprise visitor." I kiss my daughter on the cheek, and she nestles into me.

"This is your granddaughter," I continue. "Elizabeth Christine Warner. Jase named her even... it's a long story, but... it's for you, Mom. It's for you." I smile at their headstone, tears touching my eyes when it hits me just how much I wish they could be there. Elizabeth fusses slightly when one of my tears falls on her. "I'm sorry, baby girl," I whisper as I hold her closer. My phone begins buzzing in my pocket and seeing the number I answer.

"What's wrong?"

How can he tell, just like that?

"I'm... just..." I shrug even though he can't see it.

"I know, I know. Hey... do me a favor."

"What's that?"

"Cross your arms."

I snuggle our daughter into me, crossing my arms just as he asked, my heart overflowing. "Done."

"Now squeeze... not too tight, baby girl needs to breathe."

I almost laugh at his last statement, but I do as he asks.

"Did you do it?"

"Yes," I breathe, my heart hammering in my chest.

"That's a hug—for my girls, from me."

"Jase..."

"But that's not enough anymore."

"What?" I ask, confused.

"Turn around."

I turn slightly and see that familiar figure coming towards us, all dressed in black now and putting his phone away. The only light-colored object besides his skin is the soft fuzzy blanket he carries on his arm. "I couldn't leave my girls all alone like this tonight," he says as I silently watch him through my tears. He sits down beside me taking Elizabeth from my arms and holding her up against him, her favorite blanket draped over her.

"Thank you," I whisper. "For... everything."

He kisses me in response, soft and sweet. "I could say the same to you." He smiles down at me, gently wiping my tears away with his free hand. "So, did you tell your Dad I finally made an honest woman out of ya?"

"Of course."

"Guess that means you can't lie to me any damn more," he says with a wink, stretching out and laying his head on my lap, our daughter lying on top of him, pushing herself up with her arms.

"Funny, Warner, real funny. No more... *omissions* from you, then."

"Whatever, woman. I'm the king of the castle, lest you forget."

"You, sir, officially made me your queen," I remind him.

"Oh, hell, what have I got myself into? Huh, baby girl? What did Daddy get himself into?" She smiles and kicks, her drool making a puddle on his shirt. "Great, my wedding night and the only puddle is from baby drool."

"The night's not over yet, sir," I say, running my fingers through his hair. I love it when he has his head in my lap, like this.

"Really?" he asks in response. "Cause last time I checked we were sitting at your parents' grave and... who the hell is calling you?" I pull my phone out of my pocket and answer it.

"Hello?"

"Hi, Chrissie?" the male voice on the other end of the phone asks.

"No, I'm sorry, you have the wrong number," I say, and after polite goodbyes I hang up. "Anyhow... where were we?"

"Um..." He points at the gravestone. "Parents. Grave. Drooling baby. Wedding night." He scowls. "And your phone...again."

"Sorry," I whisper, answering it again.

"Chrissie?" It is the same man.

"No, this isn't. You dialed the same number."

"Well then...who are you?"

I feel Jase's fingers, warm against my hand as he gently takes the phone from me and puts the receiver up to his ear. "Dude...dude, you got the wrong number. Nope...nope, just... rip it to shreds, don't call it again, 'kay? Sure thing."

I stifle a giggle as he hangs up my phone, handing it back to me. "Jase..."

"Nah, that's *my* gig. No more wrong numbers for you, Not Telling."

"Same goes for you, Not John."

He smiles up at me, and I feel the butterflies in my stomach start up all over.

"And... where were we again?"

"Shesh, woman, pay attention! Parents, grave, drooling baby, wedding night."

"Got it."

"Hey, Talli?"

"Hmmm?"

I watched Jase as he slowly sits up, still hugging Elizabeth against his chest. He pulls her close to him and I can't help but smile as our daughter snuggles in with a sigh, her way of saying she's had enough and is going to sleep. Jase looks back at me, his lips breaking into a smile, that same smile I am so in love with. Gently he reaches out, his warm hand cradling my face, and my eyes flutter closed, the wind blowing through the silence. His smile, those eyes, his hands securely around our baby girl—I know then that all of it in this moment will forever be engraved in my mind, tucked away for me to pull out on those days when tempers are short and sleep even shorter. I feel the touch of his lips on mine that brings a shiver all the way to my toes, and I inch closer with eyes closed, returning his kiss.

After a moment—or was it much longer? —he pulls back slightly, his absence sending a shiver through me.

"Talli..."

"Hmm?"

"Open your eyes," he murmurs against my lips, and I do.

I meet his intense gaze, staring into the same beautiful eyes that first drew me to him when we met years ago, losing myself as they pull me towards him now.

Who knew we'd end up here?

"What is it, Jase?"

He looks for a moment as if he is going to say something really profound, then he smiles at me. "I'm really glad I called you," he whispers before pulling me in for another kiss. For a moment we stay like this, until Elizabeth suddenly stirs in his arms, and we draw back, laughing softly.

"She's absolutely beautiful, isn't she?" Jase whispers, glancing down as our baby girl wraps her little hand around one of his fingers and settles back to sleep.

He is going to be a great father.

I nod, my heart swelling as I look at him. He gives me another one of those beautiful smiles, moving closer towards me...

"Okay," he mutters against my lips, "who the hell is calling you again?"

I can't help but laugh at his annoyance, and I grab the phone once more, pulling it open. Lisa's voice is on the line, her tone angry, loud... annoying.

"Where the hell are you? This is *your* reception, young lady. You're supposed to be here. You better not be back inside my house, engaging in inappropriate behavior reserved for a hotel suite, Talli, because I swear, even if it's your wedding night—"

I bite my lip, repressing the urge to smile. Jase raises his eyebrow in question, and after a minute, Lisa muttered a quick goodbye, saying how James Slade is heading her way and his girlfriend isn't with him. I hang up my phone without another word.

"Who was it?"

Jase pulls me to his side with one arm while still cradling our daughter on his left and places a kiss in my hair. I look up at him, our faces inches away.

"Nothing, just a wrong number." I whisper softly against his lips.

This... this is what I had longed for, for so long.

Security.

Passion.

Love.

I draw him for one long sweet kiss that makes my heart sing, makes me believe.

And I know I will always have this—this love, this serenity— for the rest of my life.

I guess I could even call it... fate.

Authors (especially indie!) rely on your reviews. Please take a moment to review this novel on the platform that it was purchased from. It is appreciated more than you will ever know!

ABOUT THE AUTHOR

Carlie Yates (That One Writer Chick) has been writing stories since she was in the fifth grade, convinced that if she didn't get her thoughts and characters down on paper, her head would 'plode; it could be ex- or im-, but either way, it wouldn't be pretty. Inspired by S.E. Hinton, she always said when she grew up that she would be a published author. She is currently renouncing her pledge to grow up. This Midwest mom of boys has addictions to reading, road trips, hair dye, and the Oxford comma, and is thoroughly convinced at any given time the theme track to *My Three Sons* will start playing in the background of her home.

STALK ME (really just follow, but stalk me was catchy)

https://www.thatonewriterchick.com
https://www.facebook.com/thatonewriterchickakacarlie
https://www.instagram.com/thatonewriterchickakacarlie
https://www.goodreads.com/thatonewriterchickakacarlie

ADDITIONAL BOOKS BY CARLIE YATES

<u>The Entangled Series</u>

Entitled (Entangled Book 1)

Entrapped (Entangled Book 2)

Enlightened (Entangled Book 3)

COMING SPRING OF 2021

Right Reasons (Time Stands Still Book 2)

THANK YOUS AND LOVE BOMBS

Zachary, Marcus, and Jacob My whole heart, I love you beyond the telling of it!

Rose I'm beyond blessed to have you in my life, thank you for everything.

Tami The T to my J, and now people will understand.

My Visions loves For all of the original alpha readers, thank you from the bottom of my heart for sticking by me as I learned and grew as an author.

My beta readers For letting me know I got it right.

Christa for encouraging me to be my best self.

Stephanie my editor, and most of all, my friend, thank you for EVERYTHING.

My BDC family for putting up with me while I was writing the original all those years ago.

Crissy Conner my website and teaser graphics goddess!

Cody Bailey for always finding exactly what I'm looking for and turning my words into covers to die for.

Amber for being one of the most amazing humans on the face of this planet.

Nellie for pushing me past what I thought my limits were.

Marianne and all at New & Olde Pages Book Shoppe for giving this indie girl a chance and for providing the best place in all of Englewood, OH to be.

My family for helping to shape the person I've become.

My tribe because I'd be lost without all of you.

My readers for EVERYTHING! I keep going for all of YOU!

And to typos for any making it through years of writes, rewrites, edits, proofreading, alphas, betas, more edits... kudos, you're the MVP.

www.ingramcontent.com/pod-product-compliance
Lightning Source LLC
Chambersburg PA
CBHW021213260626
47172CB00002B/403